Death C

This edition first published 2016 by Fahrenheit Press

www.Fahrenheit-Press.com

Copyright © Derek Farrell 2016

The right of Derek Farrell to be identified as the author of this work has been asserted by him in accordance with the Copyright, Designs and Patents Act 1988.

All rights reserved. No part of this publication may be reproduced, stored in a retrieval system, or transmitted in any form, or by any means, electronic, mechanical, photocopying, recording or otherwise, without permission in writing from the publisher.

F 4 E

Death Of A Nobody

By

Derek Farrell

Fahrenheit Press

This book is for;

David Gray, my very own honourable man, who saw something I wouldn't, and didn't let it lie. I Love You, Mr G, and always will.

And for Elizabeth Farrell (6th Sep 1943 to 26th Jun 2015) who gave me the strength to be a man, and the confidence to look in the face of bullshit and laugh; and who loved me unconditionally. Thanks, mam. Sleep well.

And – as always – for my father, Paul Farrell.
You've never doubted for a second, and you've always been proud of me even when I wasn't. And, above all, you took me to books and stories dad, and I hope this one makes you smile.

*"Remember, it's true:
Dignity is valuable,
But our lives are valuable too."*

David Bowie 'Fantastic Voyage'

CHAPTER ONE

The cider was opaque, flat, and a dirty yellow colour reminiscent of old man's piss.
I held it up to the light, turned to Caz, and frowned. My nephews, Ray and Dash stared hopefully at me, their fingers already, I was sure, itching for the cash that would come their way if I agreed to purchase the booze in bulk.
"It's a bit cloudy," said Caz.
"Well it's unfiltered, innit," Dash shrugged. "That's sodomy."
"I think," said Caz, "You mean sediment. It goes straight to the bottom."
"Whatevs," Dash shrugged.
"Forget cloudy, boys," I said. "This looks like fucking soup." I sipped it. It tasted of apples, hay, and acid. It was like sucking a dandelion soaked in caramel.
I looked at Ali. Ali Carter was the Bar manager of the Marquess of Queensbury Public House, the crew-cut keeper of the bar and bottles, and, ultimately, it would be her choice whether we stocked this cider – which, in keeping with anything my nephews ever had a hand in – was of dubious provenance.
"You've tried this already?" I asked, knowing that she had. Ali was the worlds dourest bar manager, but she was rigorous in her duties, and I suspected this tasting was a formality to allow me to think I still had some say in running the place.

"Nah," she smirked, "It looks rank, so I thought I'd let you get the shits first. Course I've tried it," her smirk widened into a smile. "It's good, innit?"

I shrugged, sipped again from the glass, and held it out to Caz. "It's spectacular. How many bottles can you get?"

The tension in the air dissipated instantly as the twins exhaled, high fived each other, and smiled triumphantly at Ali, who – if I wasn't mistaken – returned what could be considered a conspiratorial wink.

"Wait: When you said West Country, you didn't mean Fulham, did you?"

"Geez!" Ray Mc Carthy, Dash's identical twin, sighed in mock frustration. "What d'you take us for, Danny? This stuff is Kosher. It's as West Country as anything."

"So where's it come from, then?" I demanded, noticing as I did so that Caz had drained the recently proffered glass and was now refilling it up with what was left in the bottle.

"Yog Stopidorous has a cousin right out in the fucking sticks," Dash responded. "Proper yokel. Runs a Kebab shop in Glastonbury. So: d'you want it or not?"

"Only, if not," Ray noted, "That geezer what runs the Magpie 'n' Merkin on Commercial Road said he'd have twenty gallons."

"Twenty Gallons? Where's this coming from? The local swimming pool?"

"Tha's a artisan cider," Dash answered in mock umbrage. "Handmade in the West."

"By Romanian immigrants on their day off from working illegally in a Kebab shop," I finished. "You sure this aint gonna get us in trouble with the Revenue?" I asked Ali.

"Says the man who keeps two sets of books," she snorted humourlessly. "Look, we've tested it, it's not poisonous, it looks, tastes, and smells the business, and you can get it for less than twenty pence a pint. Why are we still talking?"

I glanced at Caz. Caroline Holloway – or, to give her her full name, Lady Caroline Victoria Genevieve Jane De Montfort, only daughter of the thirteenth Earl of Holloway –

drained the second glass, smiled glassily back at me, and belched genteelly.

My best friend existed, like me, in a permanent state of near penury, but unlike me, she had had the best education that money could buy. Private education to a certain age, then three years in a Swiss finishing school where, even if they had failed to teach her how to balance a cheque book or purchase a tube ticket (useless skills for the children of the gentry), they had taught her how to expel gas with discretion and style.

"Go for it," she responded, managing to slur an entirely guttural sentence. "And put me down for a case."

The deal sealed, Ray and Dash scarpered back to the bar, one to continue stocking up, the other to make some phone calls to my new suppliers, and Ali, glancing around the vast kitchen of the pub shook her head.

"You gonna be OK here?" she asked, "Only, it's like a bloody oven. I don't want you getting' heatstroke or nothing."

Oh, Ali, I almost replied, any sort of stroke would be appreciated right now. But I didn't: I might not always manage it, but I always strive for professionalism.

Instead, I wiped my arm across my forehead. "It is hot," I admitted.

"An' it's gonna get hotter once them ovens get going," Ali reminded me. "'Less, of course, you're doin' a cold buffet."

"If only," I sighed. "They're getting the full works."

"Right then, Fanny," She smirked, shrugging her t shirt onto her shoulder, "I'll let you and Johnny," here she nodded at Caz, "Get on with it. Don't expire or nothing, cos I don't think I could do them much more than a plate of ham an' cheese sarnies."

London had been lying under the oppression of a heatwave of record – almost biblical – proportions for the past two months. This was unheard of; usually, a London summer was a week – two at most – of warm-to-hot weather, bookended by rain and, in some years, arctic temperatures. But since mid-May, no rain had fallen, the temperatures had been slowly rising, and for the past two weeks, the mercury had rarely dropped below twenty five degrees.

Not exactly Death Valley, but the inhabitants of this oldest, most ill-prepared city had spent most of the past ten days crawling around like Bedouins who'd lost their camels. The usual hustle and bustle had been replaced by a slow almost agonised approach to movement. Work – where it had to take place away from air conditioning – had almost entirely ceased as the number of casualties had slowly risen and the TV news had fixated on the story of a plumber in Greenford who, in the midst of installing a new water tank in someone's attic, had suffered a heart attack and died.

The Marq was as far away from air conditioning as it was possible to be. The building had been erected in the mid 1800s, and – with the exception of electric light – most of the cons were original rather than mod.

I'd have liked to revamp the place. I'd already put what little money I could afford into turning the upstairs rooms into a flat that I could live in, thus making it, I'd reasoned at the time, easier to save money in rent.

The savings, I'd reasoned, could be ploughed back into the business, and in no time at all, we'd be refurbishing the entire place.

That plan had been borne in the early days of February, during which I'd been in receipt of a small financial windfall, in the throes of a new love affair, and in the press every day for my part in unmasking the killer of a certain Disco Diva who'd been discovered dead in my very own pub.

Now, it was July, and the windfall was gone, the media attention had passed, and I wasn't even sure if the romance was a going concern.

Lately, my boyfriend – Nick Fisher, he of the almond shaped hazel-green eyes and the smile that made my knees go weak – had become a little more distant. Nothing dramatic, just small things like long silences broken by "There's something

I need to tell you," only for that something to turn out to be a detailed breakdown of his shift patterns.

Never, my grandmother used to say, trust a man who gives you too much detail. They're trying to cover something up. I would have said she got that from a fortune cookie, only I know she wouldn't be seen dead eating Chinese food. "Nah, love; give me a nice sausage and mash. I can't be doing wiv all that foreign stuff. I mean, I'm sure it's perfectly lovely – them Chinese do well on it, I'm sure. But I think food should be brown or beige. Or green, maybe. But if the sauce on yer plate is brighter than the paint on yer walls, it's not for me…"

So there we were: Nick was (by my gran's standards) hiding something, and avoiding me to boot. He'd shared his shift patterns with me some weeks previously, so I knew that he was supposed to be off today, and working tonight.

Last week, we'd agreed that he'd come over to help Caz and I out. We had a function today – a big function. A possibly very lucrative function, if some of the wealthy people booked in today liked what they saw and tasted. But Caz and I, with the three ovens in the Marq's ancient kitchens were going to be hard pressed to get everything out on time, so I'd asked Nick to come round and help with prep, plating and garnishing – all stuff I could direct, but which would leave me free to actually cook.

And he'd happily agreed. He'd be here at eight thirty, he'd said.

Then, this morning, at seven thirty, he'd emailed. SORRY. SOMETHINGS COME UP. YOU FREE TOMORROW?"

Tomorrow? I'd thought as I slammed the phone down on the kitchen table.

I had a small army of customers due this afternoon for a private function.

OK, so it was a wake, and I'd much rather have been hosting a party for the launch of some celebrity bedlinen, scent or ghost-written memoir, but beggars – and I wasn't far off that point – can not be choosers.

Besides, this wasn't some local post-internment knees up – a half of lager and a scotch egg per head. Oh no, the deceased, in this case, was a local girl made good.

Very good.

And the terms of her will had demanded that her wake be held back in the old neighbourhood, which, nowadays, featured a handful of grim chain pubs, a couple of burger joints, and The Marq, which had been gaining a bit of a reputation for decent pub food, so we'd been pretty much a shoo-in for the job of hosting Lady Margaret Wright's Wake.

Oh, the neighbourhood was on the way up – there were rumours of a certain TV chef looking to put another one of his ubiquitous chain Italians into the opposite end of the high street. But if we pulled this off, the word of mouth from the people attending might just give us the security we needed to see off any incomers.

So I'd scoured my cook books, put together a menu that was doable but impressive, rounded Caz up to help with, if not prep at least keeping my panic under control, and hired – at not inconsiderable expense – a troupe of professional cater waiters.

Then, the dead woman's granddaughter, one Olivia Wright, had been in touch to discuss the menu and it had somewhat spiralled.

"No nuts, no carbs, I'm basically a raw vegan fruitarian with an aversion to Kale," she'd said, giving herself the worst Tindr profile I had ever heard.

Caz, when I'd stopped sobbing and related the conversation, had pulled my discarded plans from the bin, reinstated the home made sausage rolls, pork pies and chicken Caesar canapes, and stood shaking her head – more in sorrow than anger – at me.

"Livvy Wright," she'd announced, "Is a loon, with the social skills of a slug. She'll be drunk within ten minutes and demanding pasties and chips twenty minutes later. Besides, she's not the only attendee whose tastes you need to impress."

"But she is," I said, "Footing the bill."

"Stop whining," Caz replied. "It's horribly middle class like Livvy Bloody Wright. Do her your Babaghanoush, make her Quinoa with a lemon dressing," she said, visibly resisting the urge to gag on the word Quinoa, "And – if she asks – tell her you haven't had nuts near you since 1975. You can do this."

Today, looking around the room at the Herculean task, and with sweat beads gathering on her brow, even my unflappable friend seemed a little uncertain.

"Maybe we should open the back door," she suggested. "It'll let a bit of air in…"

"It'll also get every riff raff in the neighbourhood walking in and pilfering the stock," Ali sniffed.

"I'm in here," I said, "And the waiters are in and out all the time. Anyone not supposed to be here'll soon get kicked out. Don't worry."

"Worry?" Ali snorted, as she bustled back to the bar, "I'm the most laid back person in this place."

CHAPTER TWO

"Daniel, I think you're meant to flatten, not pulverise it."

I paused in my exertions, the hammer held above my head. "Paillards," I said.

"Yes, dear; same to you. But really: You're hammering that chicken with a degree of passion that suggests Lizzie Borden at that time of the month."

"He's blown me out," I said, recommencing hammering the chicken breasts with the heavy, spiked meat mallet.

"Literally or euphemistically?" Caz was poking around in the kitchen cupboards, clearly only half listening to me, and dragging out every bottle of booze she could find.

"You expecting a drought?" I asked, pausing once again in my exertions.

"Punch," Caz explained. "For that hideous bowl."

That was another of the requirements of Maggie Wright's Will: At the wake, punch was to be served in the punchbowl that she had personally served guests from during her wedding (in, judging by the state of the cut glass monstrosity, 1875).

I doubted that the punch in question had contained the half a bottle of Ouzo, third of a bottle of Jose Cuervo and splash of Angostura bitters that Caz was now dumping into the Baccarat nightmare.

"So this," Caz said, pausing in her own exertions just long enough to pry the top off the bottle of bitters with her teeth and dump the remaining contents into the bowl, "Was a wedding present from her new in-laws, apparently."

"It's not so much a wedding present." I opined, slopping the now wafer thin chicken breast through some beaten eggs and dousing it in flour, "More a hate crime. I mean: apart from serving delicious fruity beverages from it, what do you reckon Mrs Wright used it for?"

"Drowning kittens, from what I've heard of her."

Caz is landed gentry. This means she knows everyone (or has at least heard bad things about them). I'm not, which means I know my immediate social group (who all know the bad things about me).

"She was one of those ones who likes to appear all charitable and caring, but I heard a couple of stories that'd straighten your perm," she said, opening another bottle with her teeth, and making to dump its contents into the bowl.

"Caz, I'm not sure Balsamic vinegar goes in a punch," I called, stopping her just in time.

She paused, raised an eyebrow, sniffed at the bottle, shrugged, said "Daniel, nobody has actually drunk punch in this country since Queen Mary popped it. It's. basically, the alcoholic equivalent of a garnish. You look at it, smile, then hit the hard stuff. We invented binge drinking to avoid having to drink anything in a teacup served out of a bloody basin."

And, so saying, she sploshed a glug of the black liquid into the bowl.

"Oi, Robert Carrier," Ali called from the hallway outside, "Yer waiters are here."

A moment later, what I can only describe as a Greek Chorus Line shuffled into the room.

The first one to enter was a tall, thin man in his 40s. His face was gaunt, pockmarked, and bore the sort of jowls that would have allowed him to go to a fancy dress party as droopy dawg with minimal expenditure on costuming.

"David Walker. Dave," he said, shrugging his cuffs and holding his hand out formally. I reached for it, then realised I still had the meat mallet in my hand. Putting down the implement and wiping my hands on my apron, I shook hands, and half expected him to click his heels.

"Nice to meet you," I muttered, my eyes already roving over his shoulder to where far more attractive – if diminutive - propositions were waiting.

"These," he gestured behind him in a way that suggested that 'these' were of little relevance or use, "Are the rest of the team: Filip."

"With an "F" said a short, heavily tanned himbo, his eyes raking me up and down, and his bitter little smile dismissing me instantly.

"With an F," Walker repeated, in the same tone he might have used for, say, the phrase With Genital Warts.

Filip ('with an F') held out a hand to me, and – having exchanged the pleasantry with Dave Walker – I now felt obliged to shake his hand. I needn't have bothered; it was limp, softer than kid gloves, and it almost immediately dropped from my grip.

"Troy," another diminutive server pushed himself forward. This one had the sort of eyebrows that suggest someone has drunk a bottle of gin without first locking up the tweezers. If Joan Crawford had been around (and I can almost imagine every Queen's favourite (alleged) child abuser knocking back a few of Ali's Absinthe Frappees at the bar) even she would have gone Too Much!

The barely-extant eyebrows were either side of a nose that should have had a tattoo reading "Test Your Breaks" at the top of it. It jutted out from his suspiciously smooth skin before deciding, after a couple of centimetres to change direction downwards, lending it the air of the most treacherous black run in Switzerland.

Troy was wearing a t-shirt stretched tight over heavily muscled shoulders and a chest that had to be at least a 36DD with the words "The Best Actor is..." emblazoned on it. There had, I figured, to be at least one...

Mind you, at least Troy – for all his close-to-Vulcan eyebrows – had a handshake. It was firm and controlled, and accompanied by eye contact which, by the time he'd pumped my hand for the third time and stared in to my eyes, had progressed from reassuring to ever-so-slightly creepy.

"Yes, thank you, dear," Walker intoned, separating our hands and shooting a look at Troy, "We'll call you." He gestured at a specimen who, had he been any taller than five foot one, would have been described as Godlike. "The last one," he said.

"Can speak for himself." This one stepped round Walker, made eye contact with me (which required him to tilt his head backwards, despite my being not exactly gigantic in stature). "Darryl O' Carrol," he said, in an accent that sang of Guinness, peat bogs and the lyricism of W.B. Yeats., the effect of which was somewhat ruined by the immediate creation, in my mind, of a mental picture of this bald, muscle bound midget dragged up as a comedy leprechaun.

"I'm not really a waiter," he confided, "I model. Mostly."

"When he's not oversharing," Walker muttered darkly.

Darryl shot him the sort of look I imagine Darby O'Gill received every time he knocked over a pot of gold. "But it's lovely to be here today," he finished in a sing-song voice before (in my dream) leaping into the air and waving his shillelagh overhead.

"Well," I said, wondering how on earth I'd ended up with this mismatched set of waiters, "It's, um, lovely to have you all here."

Darryl held up the garment bag at his side. "Anywhere we can change?"

I directed them back to the bar and the gents loo, and, as they trooped out of the room, turned to Caz, who had taken the opportunity to fill two glasses with Gin and tonic.

"Don't worry, Mr Bird," Walker paused in the door, "I run a tight ship. I'll keep these three in line." And with that, he was gone, leaving a sense of dourness mingling with the whiff of magnolia scented moisturiser that Filip had left on my hand.

"Lord," Caz dumped the gin in front of me and swallowed half of hers in one gulp. "Where the hell did you find those three?"

"They were cheap, have their own penguin suits, and so long as they hand out the canapés on time and in silence, we're going to be fine."

"Oh you sweet, deluded boy." Caz smiled, ducking down to retrieve her ever-present litre of Tanqueray from her ever present Gladstone handbag before topping up her drink. "Those four hate each other. Or, to be more precise, three of those four hate the fourth, who seems to have decided he's in charge. This is going to make Who's afraid of Virginia Woolf look like Mary Poppins. You better just make sure the guests are half cut before the staff start offing each other with the fish knives."

"I'm not serving fish," I said, as she slid the booze back into the bag, "And since when do you get topped up without topping me?"

"Since you, my love, became chef in an all-in-wrestling themed Wake. You're going to need sobriety – or as much as you're likely to get while I'm around."

I recommenced hammering chicken breasts. "And that's another thing," I mused, "You're in a pub. Why on earth do you persist in bringing your own booze?"

"Because," Caz answered, looking for a lemon to slice into her gin, failing to find it, and making do with a slice of cucumber pinched from one of my garnished platters, "At the prices you now charge, either I'd be bankrupt in a month if I was paying, or you'd be bankrupt if I wasn't. Besides which, I'm not drinking anything that Oilcan Ali's sourced. I'd be blind inside a week."

And with that proclamation, she toasted me. "Tempus fugit, sweetheart. Time you stopped banging your chicken and got on with the vol au vents."

CHAPTER THREE

Temperatures had – according to the radio in the corner – hit 30 degrees at lunchtime. In the kitchen, where trays of puff pastry vol-au-vents had been going in and out of the oven since mid-morning, the temperature had to be ten degrees higher.

The pub regulars had been told we had an event on, and would be closed till the evening, so the bar itself was empty, which meant that most of the team migrated, at one point or another, to the kitchen, where they stood, sweating, complaining about the heat, and watching me cook.

Dash was slumped in one of the kitchen chairs. On the opposite side of the table, a petite blonde, her hair a cloud of curls, was leaning half in and half out of a leather armchair that had been repurposed from an upstairs room. Held in her hand was a phone, and she stabbed spastically at the screen, attempting to crush an army of electronic cockroaches.

"Dream on, loser," she muttered, her sapphire blue eyes never leaving the screen before her.

"You talkin' to me?" Dash asked.

"Well I don't see no other losers in here," she responded, tearing her eyes from the phone just long enough to cast a dismissive glance across the table. "An' if you don't stop staring at my tits, I'll 'ave my grandad on to you. Loser."

Dash blushed to his roots, and the blonde sniggered nastily. "Frightened?"

"I wasn't staring at them," Dash muttered, desperately trying to find something believable in the room to focus on. "Anyways, I've seen better."

"I bet you 'ave. On the internet. But this," she stood up, arms spread wide in a display that made her already tight white t-shirt stretch further across her bosom, "Is real, loser. And you aint never getting' near it. So, unless you want your bollocks hacked off with a fucking spoon, I'd avert your eyes."

"Avert?" Ali, a bottle of vodka in her hand, entered the room, stood just inside the door, and scowled at the blonde. "Such a posh word, for such a ropey little tart. She giving you any gyp?" This last addressed to me.

I shook my head, and began piping guacamole into a tray of flaky pastry nibbles. "Not me," I said, glancing at Dash, who remained embarrassed.

"Listen, Elaine" Ali advanced on the blonde, who stared back defiantly. "Let's get one thing straight,"

Elaine snorted "Straight?"

"Yeah," Ali continued her progress until she was almost nose to nose with the girl. "Despite what you might think, you're not wanted here. Danny doesn't want you, Dash and Ray don't want you, and Christ knows I don't want you here."

"Feeling's mutual."

"Yeah, I think we'd all gathered your feelings on the situation. But here's the thing: You are here. Mainly cos your dear old psycho of a grandad wants you babysat and we're the perfect mugs, cos this one," (this, again, addressed to me, and accompanied by a gesture with the vodka bottle, though her eyes never left Elaine's face) "Is too soft to tell the old bastard that we're a pub not a crèche for lazy self-obsessed nasty little slags who think threatening kids is fun."

Elaine Falzone's eyes blazed. "Did you just call my Nannu an Old Bastard?" she hissed?

Ali brought the bottle up so that it rested under the perfect chin, and her nostrils flared. "Oh, love, I've called Chopper

Falzone worse than that in my time. And I'll call it him to his face if he ever shows it round me again. Yep," she nodded as the sapphire blue eyes flickered in their certainty, "I know how it is. Round here, the threat of a visit from Chopper's usually enough to get grown men wetting themselves. But guess what? I aint scared of him, and I aint scared of you, little girl. Now, unless you want me calling the old bastard an' telling him, first, that you're refusing to do the job you're here to do, and second, what you've just threatened to do to this nice young man, you will shift your arse and get that bar stocked. Pronto."

Elaine's face set into a mask of fury, and the standoff was maintained for several seconds before Ali stepped to one side, and, eyes never leaving Elaine's, gestured towards the doorway.

Elaine, head held high as though she were a duchess and Ali a nasty smell, wafted from the room, muttering, as she went, "Fuckin' dyke!"

I put the piping bag down, and began using a tweezers to place tiny, almost translucent slivers of pickled apricot on top of each guac-filled vol-au-vent.

"And you," Ali shook her head at Dash, "Need to stay away from that one. Keep your eyes in your head, your tongue in your mouth, and your cock in your pants. Or there will be trouble. Now," before Dash could protest innocence, she gestured him, too, off, "You need to get changed, and help your brother stock up.

Dash fled the room, and Ali turned to me. "You doin' all that on your own?"

I shrugged, reminding myself that I was, at least nominally, the boss here, and making a mental note to tell Ali – when she'd calmed down – not to call me a mug in front of the juniors.

"Where's that posh bint?"

"The Posh Bint," Caz announced, entering the kitchen, "Is behind you, sweetness. Daniel, dear heart: Allow me to help you."

Caz, her Armani ensemble completely encased in the sort of voluminous kitchen whites last seen in the nineteen hundreds, tottered over to the table, plonked her handbag on the floor, and commenced piping cream cheese into the recently hollowed out shells of what had been described as heritage dwarf tomatoes, but which Ali had described as "Under ripe cherries. They'll all get the shits if they eat them."

Ali, her face suddenly transformed into a battle between composure and hysterical laughter, raised an eyebrow. "Well, if it isn't the Michelin Woman. Nice of you to join us. Oh- " her eyes strayed downwards, "You can not be serious."

"What?" Caz innocently enquired, as her own gaze travelled down to her feet, where the most exquisite pair of Louboutins shone like peacock feathers in a midden heap. "Too much?" She raised an eyebrow that said she knew exactly how fabulous the shoes were.

"You're gonna wear them in a kitchen? Have you ever heard of Health and Safety?"

"Oh, let me think. Fortnum and Mason. Dolce and Gabanna. Shampoo and Conditioner. I've heard of those. Is Elf an Soifety a grime band?"

"You can't wear them in the kitchen," Ali stalked over to her. "They're a trip hazard. Sides: they're gonna get destroyed if you get any grease on the suede."

Caz, recognising a fellow stilletophile, nodded approvingly. "You're right," she agreed.

"I'll get you some Crocs," Ali said, eliciting a gasp of horror from Caz.

"I'd rather die," she said, slipping the shoes from her feet, and placing them on the table as she bent down to grab a pair of flats from the ostrich skin black hole that was her handbag.

Now, it was Ali's turn to shriek, as she leapt forward and snatched the shoes off the table. "New shoes. Table," she gasped in horror.

"Is this more health and safety?" Caz asked as she slipped the flats on.

"I'll put these somewhere safe," Ali said, shaking her head in despair at Caz, who had already recommenced filling the tomatoes.

"You know, Danny," Caz murmured as Ali, still shaking her head, placed the shoes next to the dresser on the opposite side of the room, and left to supervise the bar staff, "I think she's warming to me. I appear to have been promoted from a Posh Tart to a Bint. Progress, wouldn't you say?"

"She wants your shoes," I said.

"No, dear, they're Louboutins; she wants my soles. But as anyone who knows me will tell her, that went long ago. Any sign of Dave, Dozy, Beaky and Titch?"

"They're prepping the buffet tables," I answered.

"So," she said, putting the piping bag down, "And, en passant, life really is too short to stuff a tomato, dear heart; what are you going to do about young Mister Fisher?"

"Do?"

"You know: Don't give me that innocent look. I've seen you looking at him like you'd quite happily jump him in the middle of the high street. Yet here we are, with you and he appearing – to these trained eyes, at least – to be drifting somewhat."

I was saved from having to respond by the arrival, at that moment, of one of the twins, resplendent now in a crisp white shirt, thin black tie, black trousers and the shiniest midnight black brogues ever seen.

"'Ere, your ladyship," he said, twirling slowly, "This is a proper bit of gear. I've never had couture before."

Caz sighed. "Couture should only ever be worn by the young and the beautiful," she noted. "Sadly, it's only normally purchased by the old and the toad-like." She nodded appreciatively. "It looks wonderful, Dash. Just don't spill anything on it. Domenico wants it back in time for

Milan, and a crotch smeared in cream cheese is not the look he's going for this year."

"I'm Ray," Ray smiled, and Caz blushed.

"And I'm mortified, dear boy," she apologised. "But in those outfits you both look so alike."

"We look alike out of them, Caz" the boy laughed, "We're identical twins."

"Identical in every way?" Caz flirted, and Ray, flirting back, twitched his eyebrows.

"That's for us to know. Right: what needs doing?"

"Here," Caz gestured at the tray of tomatoes, "You could get them inside."

Ray hefted the tray, nodded his head at Caz, clicked his heels "Bien sur, m'lady," he said, and was gone.

"Did he just speak French?" I was flabbergasted.

"Juste un petit mot," Caz – who, in preparation for an upcoming vacation to Nice, had taken to playing Berlitz French language and Edith Piaf CDs at every opportunity – shrugged.

At that point, the waiters trouped into the room, and the temperature dropped to almost freezing.

Clearly, something had happened in the bar, as the three younger members of what I was still mentally referring to as "The team" were clustered together shooting daggers looks at the sombre figure of Dave Walker.

Troy, in a voice that was clearly intended to carry, offered his opinion to the other two: "Course, you can't really call yourself an actor when you haven't acted since Thatcher was in power. I mean: what you are then is less an actor, more a has-been."

This was all said whilst staring directly at Walker, who displayed no emotion as he crossed to me. "Mr Bird. We await your orders," he intoned in the voice I imagine Lurch from the Addams family would use to advise that dinner was served.

"Oh," I was flustered, as the phrase "Mr Bird" usually referred to my father, and, on those occasions when it referred to me, had been said by coppers or bailiffs. "This lot," I gestured at the huge wooden kitchen table, now covered in platters of food, "Need arranging. Caz, can you go with the guys and let them know what goes where?"

Caz raised an eyebrow at me as if to say I'm supervising staff?

Walker lifted the first platter up, held it high overhead, and, as he passed Troy, said "I'm assuming your theatrical experience is limited to Panto." He paused, running his eyes over the diminutive trio, "You know: along with your six mates."

"Fuck you, granddad," Troy snarled back. "I'm Shakespearean. I toured in Midsummers Dream," he announced, managing to mangle the name of the play he'd presumably performed eight times a week. "They loved my Bottom in Blackpool."

"I stand corrected," Walker murmured, as he left the room.

CHAPTER FOUR

Left alone momentarily, the rest of the waiters having grabbed trays and minced off to arrange them in the bar, I had time to think about the situation between Ali and Elaine, and I was worried.

Here's the scoop: Once upon a time, I had (I had thought) it all: I was a correspondence co-ordination executive (alright: mailroom boy) for a popular fashion magazine, happily (I thought) partnered with Robert, a lawyer in the city whose annual income was the same as mine, only with two more zeroes added to it, and I was living the dream (though not, as it had turned out my dream).

Then, one day, I had lost it all: the job "Downsized," (a bullshit phrase, meaning "Fired all the little people so the big people could be seen to be doing something to justify their obscene salaries, whilst saving – in the grand scheme of things – a pittance") and, on arriving home, I'd discovered the love of my life in bed with the window cleaner (which was apt, as there was definitely some polishing going on when I'd walked in).

And so, with no home, no job, and no money, I'd ended up living at my parents, sleeping in the bunk bed I'd slept in as a kid, surrounded by my vintage Kylie posters and wondering what the fuck I was gonna do.

Till I walked in to The Marquess of Queensbury public house, noted that they were looking for a new manager, overlooked the fact that the place was not so much a Gin Palace as a Hooch Hovel, and applied for the job.

Which I'd promptly got.

At which point, several facts became obvious: The full extent of my experience in the licenced victual trade had been standing on the other side of the bar ordering drinks. I had no idea what I was doing. And I was actually working for one of South London's most notorious gangsters, one Martin "Chopper" Falzone.

Falzone owned pubs, shebeens, chop shops knocking shops, and one fully functioning Pound shop rumoured to be the site of several 'disappearances' over the years, which was believable as there was so much tat in the place you could have leaned Jack Hat McVitie in amongst the discount brooms and nobody would ever have found him.

And Falzone had a deal for me: I could run the pub any way I wanted, so long as he got 50% of the take, all the slot machine money and a guaranteed place to entertain his cronies if they ever got tired of The American Bar at The Ritz.

I had little option, so I'd taken the job.

And that was how I'd met "Lainey," as Chopper referred to his granddaughter.

If her Nannu was attempting to clean his act up somewhat, he was doing so at the same time as his granddaughter came of age and decided to position herself somewhere between Bonnie Langford and Bonnie Parker.

Cue Chopper – in his guise as concerned Grandfather – lumbering me with the job of keeping an eye on the nascent juvenile delinquent for the term of the summer holidays.

"She'll be alright once she gets back to school. They keep 'em under control at Saint Ethel's," he said, making me wonder if Saint Ethel's was a school or an institution for crazed delinquents, "But till then, I'm worried, Daniel. This city's not a place for a young girl like Lainey. Full of scumbags, it is; an' it's getting worse every day. Paedos, perverts and ponces all over the fuckin' place. No offence."

Uncertain which of the trinity I'd been lumped in with, I had simply nodded, and awaited the dreadful request I'd already sensed coming (though request was something of a misnomer. Chopper didn't do requests. He did instructions, which were to be obeyed without question, hesitation consideration, deviation or repetition. Sort of like an episode of Just a Minute, only with added menace.)

"Make sure she works," he'd ordered. "I want her to get a sense of the value of a good days work."

Since – rumour had it – a good days work for Chopper consisted of having at his enemies with a meat cleaver, before handing the remains over to his goons for distribution to the dodgy burger kebab and pizza places he owned, I was somewhat unsure what skills, exactly, he was hoping I would pass on to the younger generation.

Still, we were here, Elaine was – in her own words – "Trapped in this Fucking Dump for the whole Fucking Summer," and Ali, who had taken an immediate dislike to the young lady and her attitude, had made it clear that no shirking would be allowed.

I was, to be honest, a little worried that she'd push the apprentice superbitch too far. Elaine was the classic teenager – all resentment, frustration, selfishness and hormones. Add to that recipe a good dash of the sort of family life she must lead, the constant knowledge of just how some of her family were viewed, and it was little wonder she was turning into what my mum would refer to as a proper little madam.

I made a mental note to tell Ali to ease off a little, and got back to cooking.

Next up was endive cups with bacon and Roquefort, so I put a heavy pan on to the hob, turned the gas on underneath it, lifted a couple of pounds of bacon out of the fridge and started to dice the meat.

Dave Walker, a tray of canapes held at arm's length, stormed into the kitchen. "Unbelievable!" he exclaimed, crossing to the bin and dumping the entire contents of the tray into the bin.

I paused. "Something wrong with the guacamole puffs?"

He turned to me, his face running through a range of emotions from fury to despair. At one point, I was sure he was about to burst into tears.

"Mr Bird,"

"Danny. Please," I said.

He took a deep breath, obviously struggling with the concept of allowing himself to slide into informality, "I've worked many of this city's great restaurants, including the Michelin Starred Duomo," he announced, and I nodded as though I had a clue what the Michelin Starred Duomo was, "And I'm used to dealing with difficult colleagues, but never in my life have I come across such outright nastiness."

Oh God, I thought, what have the three evil queens done now?

"Look, I know the others are a bit bitchy," I began, before he waved my comment aside.

"Those three? Oh," he laughed dismissively, "They're amateurs. In every way."

"Then who," I asked, but got no further.

"That little blonde..." he struggled for the words "Saboteur. She flicked fag ash over the whole tray."

"Elaine?" I put the knife down, wiping my hands on my apron.

"The very same. I put the plate down, was just heading back here to get the next one, and I saw her, out of the corner of my eye, take a handful of something from an ashtray on the bar and throw it over the food. How can someone be so... so... disrespectful?"

I sighed. "She's a special one, alright," I admitted.

Ali came into the kitchen, the other waiters trailing behind her. "What's going on here?" She asked, spotting Dave, empty plate in hand, standing over the bin.

Walker, with the same degree of emotion, told her.

I'd already filled a replacement platter, and was about to head into the bar. Ali gently, but firmly removed the platter from my hands, and nodded at the pan on the hob.

"Lots to do," she said, "I suggest you get on and do it, and leave our problem to me."

The Himbos watched Ali , her face set in a mask of determination, leave the kitchen, and turned to each other, their mouths open in shock.

"Well," Darryl sighed, "there's drama."

Walker, regaining his composure, crossed to the table as I turned my back on the foursome, and slid the diced bacon into the pan.

The sizzle when the meat hit the heat drowned out the next few words, but as the spitting died down, I heard Fillip mutter something about "Professionalism. You deal with it amongst the team, don't you?"

This last seemed to have been aimed at Dave Walker, who shot back, almost immediately, with "Professionalism? You three wouldn't know professionalism if it smacked you in the face and introduced itself."

"Still," the voice of Troy noted, "You could have just told her off and got rid of the damage."

"And what? Leave our employer in the dark as to her character?"

"Character? When did you become a Grand Duchess?" Fillip snarked. "She's alright, Elaine is."

I wondered how on earth she had managed to ingratiate herself with him in the short period of time he'd been here.

"Listen," Walker spat back, and it was at that point I realised that they'd all clearly forgotten I was even present, "I don't know what shambolic little lives you three live, but in my day,"

"Oh Gawd," Troy moaned," 'ere we go again."

"What?" Fillip enquired "Penny farthings and top hat times?"

"Sneer all you want, but in my day we had a thing called Standards. A thing called Pride."

"I've been to Pride," Darryl piped up archly. "Off me face, I was."

"What?" Fillip goaded, "Pride in snitchin' on a little girl who was having a laugh?"

"Pride in a job well done, you moron," Dave fired back. "I've done Michelin service, and let me tell you: You three wouldn't even get across the threshold."

"Yea?" Filip snorted, "Well, I've done him off Corrie in the back of a taxi, but I hope to Christ I'm not still going on about it when I'm ninety."

The trio tittered evilly, and at that moment, the air was rent by the sound of an airhorn going off as a set of tribal drums hammered away in the background.

I dropped my ladle, turning to see where the sound had come from, and was in time to see Dave Walker – all composure gone – drop a platter back on to the table, his face blushing furiously, and fumble desperately in his jacket pocket.

"Hello," he called, pulling a mobile phone from his pocket and holding it to his ear.

The three queens tittered, nudging each other. The source of their continued amusement soon became obvious when the phone continued to ring, the next blast of Techno Rave blaring itself right into Dave Walker's eardrum.

"Jesus Christ," he winced, pulling the device away from his ear and stabbing at the screen with his forefinger.

The phone continued to ring, and his frustration levels built with every blast of the bloody airhorn.

Fillip, Darryl and Troy were, by now, in hysterics.

"New phone, dear?" Fillip asked.

"Maybe you should've kept the old one," Darryl added. "Size of a house brick, but at least you could answer it."

At that moment, the phone stopped ringing, and Dave looked around the room, his gaze resting finally on me. "My apologies for that," he said, before excusing himself and leaving the room.

CHAPTER FIVE

Ali eventually returned, advised me that she had "Dealt with the issue," and asked, pointedly, when the waiters were likely to finish laying out the buffet spread.

"Only the funeral party'll be here soon," she finished, checking her watch and staring from the platter covered table to me in a way that made it clear she was also questioning my ability to be ready in time.

Fillip, Darryl and Troy busied themselves, Dave Walker returned to the kitchen, silently hefted a couple of platters, and was gone.

Left alone, I began to assemble the endive cups, and had almost finished, when I heard a man's voice.

"Hello," it said, with a trace of a northern accent, "Sorry to bother you."

I turned, and staggered slightly.

Standing in the doorway, as though awaiting an invitation to enter, was the most handsome man I'd ever seen. He was tall – about six foot three, I'd say – and had dark hair, shaved to a zero grade around the back and sides, but spiked on top in a way that suggested he might be a bit punky, but liked to take care of himself.

The vision's shoulders were broad, his hips slim, and his skin tone the sort of golden brown smoothness that I'd only ever seen in magazines.

I steadied myself against the table, and smiled, thinking, as I did so, that I probably looked a bit simple – this silent salad savant leaning against a table and grinning like a loon.

"Hello," I finally blurted, and he seemed to accept that as an invitation to enter the room.

"I'm Mike," he said, holding his hand out, as he advanced on me. "Mike Green. From number fifty-three?"

Number fifty-three? I mentally walked down the street. Two doors away was a derelict shop. Most of the market around here was empty or – like the Marq – had seen better years.

I introduced myself. "You're reopening one of the shops?" I asked, as we shook hands (he had, I noted, a firm grip, and a tendency to maintain eye contact, but unlike Troy, none of this appeared, at any point, to approach creepy. At least, not from my perspective).

He nodded, extricating his hand from mine, and smiled dazzlingly. "Well, that's the plan. Just in the process of refitting it." His eyes strayed over my shoulder. "God, are those endive cups?"

I smiled, pleased that he'd recognised my work. "We have a large party this afternoon, so I'm pulling out the stops, to be honest. If this succeeds, we might get some more buzz and more buzz means more business."

"But you're the local pub, right?"

"Well," I felt oddly irritated that we were being dismissed as the local pub. "We've been building a bit of a reputation for our food. Nothing fancy – pies and stews and stuff like that. Good, honest food, but all cooked here, and all by mine own fair hands."

Oh God, I thought, why do you always do fake Chaucer when you're trying not to flirt? It's worse than the actual flirting…

Aloud, I said, "So what sort of shop are you opening?"

Mike Green smiled, tearing his eyes away from the remains of the spread on the table behind me. "It all looks delicious. I'll have to pop in here for lunch someday."

"Daniel!" Caz entered, her tone the one she only ever uses when she's either about to announce momentous news, or tell me off horribly, and stopped dead. "Well hello," she purred, spotting Green.

"Hi," he smiled again, turning away from me, thus allowing me free range to rake my gaze across those shoulders, down that back – so straight, so firm looking – and on to those buttocks. And I knew, at that moment, that God not only exists, but that he's a bum man.

"Caroline," Caz announced, stalking across the room, her arm held straight in front of her, the hand hanging loosely on the end, as though she were attending a Viennese waltz party and just naturally knew that Mike Green would wish to press his lips to the back of her hand. "Lady Caroline De Montfort."

Green took her hand, hesitated a moment, and – perfectly on cue – pressed his lips to it.

"Charmed," Caroline murmured, in tones that would have made it impossible for Mike – or anyone else, for that matter – to know that only last week she'd been forced to hock the last of her grandmothers jewels to pay the electric bill.

"Really?" Green stared, awestruck, from Caz to me and back. "You're a real lady?"

"Sometimes," I muttered, gaining, for my trouble, a flicker of annoyance from the female in question.

"Minor aristocracy, Mister Green. We have the title, the contacts, some lands, and none of the money any more."

"Wow." Green seemed a little too impressed to be true, if I'm being honest. I mean: the only people who are ever that impressed are the Americans, for whom anyone with a family tree that goes back beyond the eighteenth century is a wonder equivalent to a unicorn.

"I mean... Wow. You don't really expect to meet royalty in a place like this."

That got my hackles up. "Aristocracy," I corrected, "Not royalty."

"Potato, potahto," Caz responded, bestowing the smile that once got her either a grin or a grimace from the Queen mother ("I still can't tell which it was," Caz had once confided to me. "She was either fond of me, or had gas. And now, we'll never know...")

"Speaking of which," I said, gesturing to the bowl of warm potato salad on the table, "This needs shifting."

Caz smiled beatifically at me, and there was no question as to the meaning behind this one: Back off, buster, or I'll brain you with the spuds.

"And how did you come to be in this bar, Mr Green?" she simpered.

"Oh," Green was pulled back to now. "I'm reopening the store at number fifty-three. And I've got the builders in right now, remodelling the shop. Only problem is we've run out of milk, and you know how it is if you've no milk for builders tea: They seriously consider demolishing the whole place. I noticed your back door was open, so I thought I'd pop in here and see if you had any I could borrow."

"Caz," I prompted, "You had something you were going to tell me?"

"Hmmm?" Caz tore her gaze away from the deliciousness that was Mike Green, and seemed completely disorientated for a moment. "Oh, yes. "That was The Guardian. I think they might be coming in next week to review the place. Angie Lang – you know, the one I met at that Feminist Marxist thing – said she might pop over and do a bit on the food."

"Well," Green smiled at me, "It sounds like you're getting that Buzz."

I forgave Caz for all her recent attempts to appropriate young Mr Green for herself, reminded myself that I still had a boyfriend – even if he had recently been largely absent– and that I should let Caz have full reign with the neighbours.

"Yes," I said, bestowing a huge smile on Caz and popping over to the fridge to grab a carton of milk from it.

"What sort of shop are you going to open?" Caz asked.

"Menswear," Green responded, gratefully accepting the carton of milk. "Somewhere funky and cool, selling classics and the latest looks. I haven't thought up a name yet."

"Where is he?" Elaine stormed into the room, her eyes blazing. "Where's that fucking lying old poof?"

"Problem, Elaine?" I asked, jerking my head at Mike Green as if to say don't embarrass us in front of the cute guest, but to no avail.

"That lanky bastard. He's lying about me, Danny. I never touched them vol au vents."

Dave Walker stepped into the kitchen behind Elaine, a look of concern on his face.

"I'm told," he said to Elaine's back, "That you're looking for me."

Elaine spun on him. "I never touched them vol au vents, and you fucking know it!" she stormed.

"I know no such thing. In fact, I saw you with my own eyes sprinkling something all over them."

"It was fucking parsley!"

"And since when did herbs smell like Lambert and Butler?" Dave asked.

"You're a liar; he's a liar!" she protested to me.

"I don't really care either way," I slid another tray over to her. "Take these in, put them on the bar, and keep away from them. Understood?"

"If he tells another lie about me, he'll be sorry!" She snarled.

"Elaine!" I barked, shoving the tray into her hands. "Go! Now!"

She left, still grumbling, leaving Mike Green, his jaw hanging in amazement at her fury, Caz simpering still at Green's beauty, and me shaking my head.

"Why is nothing ever easy?" I asked nobody in particular.

Dave Walker coughed discretely. "If I may, Mr Bird: The funeral party is arriving. Mizz Carter asked me to come let you know."

"Right!" I turned back to the table. "Action stations, please. And, Dave: Please. No more drama."

"Drama?" Walker stared into the middle distance as though trying to translate a term he was unfamiliar with, nodded his head, and left the kitchen.

CHAPTER SIX

I dropped my whites on a kitchen chair, and, leaving the bemused looking Mike Green standing in the kitchen, followed Caz and Dave Walker out to the public bar, where a small group of people had just arrived and were helping themselves to glasses of Champagne and Pimms held aloft on serving trays by the trio of Filip Darryl and Troy.

Standing in the middle of the room were the couple who were paying for the event. I came out from behind the bar, my hand extended, a look (I hoped) of sorrow and consolation on my face.

"Smile," Caz whispered through gritted teeth.

"It's a funeral," I hissed back through my frown.

"So smile sadly. You look like you've got stomach cramps."

"You must be Miss Wright," I held a hand out to a petite blonde in her early twenties. Olivia Wright had her hair styled in a short page-boy bob, was wearing a diaphanous black silk tea-dress with what looked like peacock feather trim, and a pair of high heels with straps that wound around her slim ankles and looked entirely unsuitable for trekking around graveyards.

In fact, the whole ensemble had the look of "Downton does Mourning," which was apt as Miss Wright (I'd been reliably informed by the oracle that was Lady Caroline blah blah blah De Montfort) had just inherited an enormous country pile and enough money to pay the gas bill for the greater London region for the next decade.

"Livvy, please," she smiled at me (not sadly, I noted; though if I'd just come into more money than God, I, too, might find it hard to summon up some tragedy) and shook my hand. "Thanks for this," she gestured around her, "It looks... lovely," she finished, in tones that suggested if it had been left to her, the wake would have been somewhere that had been decorated since the turn of the twentieth century.

"You're very welcome," I gushed. "I think we've covered everything, but if there's anything you need, please don't hesitate to ask."

"Well, you can tell the Chinese to go fuck themselves," the man at her side said, and it was a few moments before I realised he was talking to his mobile phone. "The deal was for two hundred thousand units. They start fucking me 'round with the pricing, I will go to India. Listen, Malcolm, I Gotta go. We're at my fiancées grandma's funeral. Yeah, tonight. Thanks." He ended the call, slipped the phone into his pocket, pecked Olivia Wright on the cheek, and turned to me.

I introduced myself, and repeated my bit about them not hesitating to ask for anything they wanted.

"A beer would be a good start," he said, in a broad American accent, as he, seemingly seeing the place for the first time, cast a shocked glance around the joint. "Christ, Livvy. Maggie came from this?".

At that point, Caz appeared at my side, designated herself as 'Mr Bird's event coordinator,' and shook hands all around

Olivia Wright introduced the man "This is my fiancé Kent Benson."

"Mr Benson is American," I offered, hearing myself stating the blindingly obvious, and willing myself to shut up.

"The accent give me away?" he asked with a twinkle.

I shrugged, allowing – since the grieving relatives were clearly loosening up – a smile to cross my own face. "It's sort of unmistakeable," I answered, realising that the permatan, fashionably cut salt and pepper haircut and the fact that he was wearing what looked like the Ralph Lauren

Mourning in The Hamptons collection all provided strong clues of their own. The fact that there appeared to be at least a twenty year age gap between his fiancée and him left me unfazed. Chac'un a son gout, as they say.

I gestured to Ali, and a bottle of beer was duly removed from an ice bucket, opened, and delivered on a platter alongside a tall, chilled glass.

Benson ignored the glass, lifting the bottle and slugging straight from the long neck. "You OK, honey?" He asked, laconically putting an arm around Olivia Wright, and pulling her closer to him.

She nestled into him, and sighed. "I'm going to miss her."

"I'm so sorry," I said, "For your loss."

"This, "Caz oozed sincerity, "Must be very hard for you."

Olivia Wright shrugged, "Maggie had been ill for some time, but I suppose you're never really prepared, no matter how much advance notice you get."

"That's true," Kent murmured, rubbing his hand up and down the small of her back, "Very true."

"Livvy," another mourner, dressed, like Kent in a black suit and white shirt, approached, threw his arms around Olivia Wright, and hugged her. "So very sorry, old thing; so very sorry." He snagged a glass of Champagne from one of the passing Himbos, then went back to hugging Olivia, who, after a moment of confusion, patted him sympathetically but firmly on the shoulder.

"Thanks Desmond," she said, as the man, finally getting the hint, released her and turned to Kent.

Olivia, noting that Caz and I were still there, introduced this new comer to us as Desmond Everett, an old family friend, and I got a look at his face for the first time.

Where Kent Benson spoke of the virility and frontier spirit of America, this one spoke very quietly, and, I expected, with a great deal of apology, of the English public school system at its worst. He had a chin, but it was so recessive as to be virtually an Adams apple. His eyes – red rimmed and watery – blinked from behind a pair of round horn rim frames, and his hair was a floppy dark rag that had been simply dumped onto his head. All told, unless his family owned huge chunks of the Home Counties, the honourable Desmond Everett was not exactly what you'd call a catch.

He was accompanied by a vision in purple. Where Everett had exuded a doughy weakness, this woman – stooped and bulky as she was – exuded all the solidity and unyielding bulk of a garden shed.

The shed was clad in a floor length skirt and matching knee length jacket in a dark purple velvet. When she moved, the jacket wafted, displaying the inner lining of silk in the same purple colour.

If Prince had had a scary arthritic white auntie, I could imagine her looking like this one.

Her hair was a crazed birds nest of various browns, dumped on top of a face which appeared to be a stranger to foundation, let alone to lipstick, and a single caterpillar unibrow hulked menacingly over two beady little eyes that surveyed me quickly and then turned to Olivia Wright.

"Olivia," her voice was deep, quiet, in keeping with the body language that made her seem as though she just wanted to curl into herself, "how are you holding up?"

"Oh Jane," Olivia opened her arms, and the shed shuffled forward into the hug. Olivia Wright's arms barely made it round the shoulders. "I'm going to miss her."

"Well everything has a time," Jane – who was quickly introduced to us as Jane Barton, a great friend of mine, stepped away, holding both Olivia's hands in hers. "And this shall pass too."

Mention of the word pass reminded me that Caz and I should be back in the kitchen. As I made to excuse myself, Caz suddenly gasped, grasped my arm, and nodded at a couple who had just entered the bar.

The man was tall, thin, had a shock of well-groomed hair and a surgically trimmed goatee beard, both the beard and the hair being snow white. He, too, wore the regulation black suit, white shirt and black tie, though he'd accompanied the ensemble with a pair of black hornrimmed glasses, which gave him the air of a somewhat morose Colonel Sanders on a day out to the local crem.

At his side was a younger woman, who had chosen, for the day, a more tailored version of the obviously expensive suit and trousers that her companion had worn. Her hair – cut short and boyish – was slicked back so that she looked for all the world like she'd just stepped out of an amateur production of Victor Victoria.

"Do you know who that is?" Caz hissed excitedly in my ear.

I shrugged "Is he finger lickin' good?" I asked.

"Not him, you fool," she whispered, gripping my arm so as to keep me where I was. "Her. That's Monica Vale."

"The artist?" I asked, my heart rate picking up, as thoughts of what would happen if London's favourite conceptual artist were to big up The Marq.

"The very same. I told you this would be worth doing."

At this point, Colonel Sanders approached, offered his condolences, had his hand shook, snagged a couple of glasses of champagne, offered one to his companion, and both of them retired to the bar without so much as a glance our way.

"What do we do?" I asked, desperately wanting to be introduced to, and have the opportunity of impressing, Monica Vale.

"Well you," said Caz, patting me on the rump, "Get back to the kitchen to churn out some more fabulous canapes and I," she added as I shook myself out of my reverie, and, nodding at Olivia Wright, made to head back to the kitchen, "Shall hang out there to open the conversation with her, and to make sure that none of the staff have a knock down punch up in her presence."

CHAPTER SEVEN

"Well? How did it go?" I slid another wafer thin slice of panko crusted chicken into the pan and looked up as Caz wafted back into the room.

She smiled as she spotted Mike Green, pint of milk in hand, still hovering around. "No dice right now," Caz answered, "I'm sure we'll get some time later. But right now, Monica Vale and her granddad are ensconced at the bar and do not appear to be welcoming intrusions."

"Monica Vale?" Mike asked. "The Monica Vale?"

"The very same," Caz answered, almost glowing with pride. "If we can get her to spread the word, we'll have the art set queuing up to get in here." She lifted a ladle, dunked it into the punch bowl, scooped out a measure of the dingy looking liquid and sipped it.

"Hmm," she paused, considering, then held the ladle towards Green "It needs something. What do you think?"

Green sipped, gasped, gagged, and, eyes bulging, commenced a coughing fit. "Less alcohol would be a start. Isn't a punch supposed to be mostly fruit juice."

"Nonsense," Caz corrected him. "It's all about the alcohol and the garnishes.

So saying, she dumped half a bag of ice into the bowl, lobbed a handful of raspberries, one of sliced peaches and a small jar of pickled lemon slices into the mix, retasted, sighed happily, and placed a tea towel over the bowl. "Perfect!" She opined, as she wheeled the bowl into the hallway out of the hot kitchen.

"Now, Mr Green," she turned to Mike with the look that a lion might give to a particularly tasty looking antelope, "You have your milk. Is there," and at this point, I swear, her cleavage actually shifted itself upwards and outwards, "Anything else we can get for you?"

"Oh," Green, giving her the look that I expect the tasty antelope might give to the stalking lioness, snapped himself into the present, "No, No, thanks, really. I actually just," he walked over to me, leaning in so that no doubt was left that his words were meant only for my ears.

"Listen," he said, "I can see you are up to your ears right now, but would be good to see you some time if you're free. You know: get a feel for the neighbourhood."

I stopped what I was doing. There'd been an odd stress on the word feel. Was he chatting me up? It felt like it, but maybe I was mistaken. He was, after all, genuinely new to the neighbourhood, and maybe he was just looking for a friend.

Mind you, if that were the case, why wouldn't he have taken Caz up on her obvious offer of friendship-and-a-bit-more?

My jaw dropped as the penny did likewise. He liked me.

But I already had a boyfriend.

Then I remembered the texts. Something's come up. You free tomorrow? I'd been here before – put my life on hold for a man who wasn't that bothered. And it had left me with next to nothing.

I smiled at Mike. "Well I'm here," I said, "most of the time."

"Good." He smiled. "Then I'll know where to find you," and, patting me – fraternally? Hopefully? – on the shoulder, he left, nodding his farewells to Caz, who stood, mouth open, in a look that could only be described as the lioness after a plumber from Wisconsin smacks her with a .45 right between the eyes.

As Mike left, Ali barrelled into the kitchen. "We have a problem," she announced with – I was sure – a hint of joy in her voice.

"We usually do. Does it involve a corpse?"

"No."

"Good, then we're ahead of our batting average." I turned the chicken. "So, spill: What's up?"

"Someone's bunged up the loos. Ladies Gents and the Disabled. All three of 'em look like they've had a bag of cement dropped down them."

"Shit."

"Or not," said Caz, "As the case may be. Did that," she nodded at the doorway through which Mike Green had exited "Really just happen."

"Looks like it," I grinned back, turning to Ali "Put an out of order sign up," I said.

"And where do that lot go?" She jerked a thumb behind her in the general direction of the public bar.

"They'll have to be allowed to come through the bar and use the one back here," I said.

Ali stiffened. "Punters do not use the staff loos," she intoned in exactly the voice that Jeeves might have used if he'd been a South London bar keep with a crew cut.

"Well they do tonight, Ali, unless you want them weeing in the street outside."

CHAPTER EIGHT

"Wonderful canapes," Monica Vale snatched another mini roast beef and horseradish stuffed Yorkshire pudding from Filip's tray, stuffed it into her mouth, and – I swear – swallowed without chewing. It was – not that I was counting – the fifth she'd swallowed whole since we'd started chatting.

"But tell me more about the murder. Was it as grizzly as it sounded in the papers?"

"Worse," Caz jumped in. "So much was never reported, and was then excluded when the thing got to court. It's a miracle Daniel is still here, let alone quickly becoming South London's hottest gourmet brasserie chef."

I shot her a look. We'd discussed this; cook I could tolerate. Gastropub cook was pushing it, but we could go with it. But Gourmet Brasserie?

I looked around the Public Bar. How many Gourmet Brasseries had customer loos that looked like a set from "Junior Jack: The Ripper's early years," a barmaid that looked like she might have trained in Backstreet School with Vera Drake, and a carpet that – despite several cleans – still kicked back the distinct odour of nicotine gin and regret that, if we'd been able to bottle it, would have been on sale behind the bar as Eau du Marq?

I doubted that Les Deux Magots had ever retailed snide cider from behind it's hallowed bar. I didn't want Caz going hyper on the place. I wanted it to be seen for the up and coming local boozer that it was – or at least that I saw it as; because even I had to admit that 'Filthy backstreet hovel with dodgy cider and some nice canapes' wasn't a particularly viable sales pitch.

But Caz was already in full flow, and there was no way to stop her.

In fact – thanks to the champagne she'd been knocking back – she became even more voluble in her description of the murder that had occurred shortly after I'd become the pub's manager.

As a result. a number of the other guests ambled over, drawn by her description of a scenario that read like a cross between The Silence of The Lambs, Psycho, and My Fair Lady as directed by Guy Ritchie and featuring myself, my loyal and brave best friend, and a psychotic serial killer.

The truth, I wanted to say, had been far more prosaic, and far less cinematic. But I couldn't get the chance to.

"Of course," Olivia Wright, clearly, herself, a couple of bottles in, cried out. "The Lyra day killings! They were here? Oh how fascinating. And you," here, she beamed at me, stroking my shirt sleeve in a somewhat proprietorial way, "figured it all out. I followed it avidly. How clever of you."

I made some noises about how it had all been more through luck than judgement, but Caz shushed me with a wave of her hand "He's too modest, but between the sleuthing and the food – which I'm sure you'll agree is delicious – well, I wonder sometimes if there's anything our little Danny can't turn his hand to."

"Pouring a pint, according to Ali," Dash whispered in my ear as he appeared behind me. "D'you want that punch brought out now? Only I think it's beginning to burn through the crystal…"

I jumped. "Yes, of course. Can you get Dave to wheel it out?" I turned to Olivia Wright, murmuring "Miss Wright: do you want the punch brought out now?"

"God, yes," she gasped, "I'd almost forgotten about it. Everyone," she raised her voice, "Grandmamma loved a party, and she was never happier than when she was surrounded by her loved ones, all drinking her famous punch recipe."

Her famous punch recipe? I looked at Caz, who stared back. To the casual observer, she might have appeared calm and relaxed, but I saw the clenching of the jaw, the slow, controlled blink, as the same thought that was going through my head went through hers:

There was a recipe? I racked my brains back, and remembered a six inch thick pile of papers covered in post-it notes, which I'd flicked through. From it, I'd gathered the requirements for a buffet, the timings, the preference for silver service, the whole Punch must be served from the antique monstrosity that will be delivered by white van the day before the funeral.

At no point had I seen the words Grandmamma's special punch recipe.

And so, instead of Maggie's special punch recipe – made, as her surviving relative was informing the gathering – with pineapple juice, rum, a scraping of nutmeg, some cranberry juice, a splash of brandy, a pinch of cinnamon and a good old glug of champagne, and which had been consumed since the fucking Restoration, for all I knew, as her guests danced the Gay Gordon around it, I had just watched Caz constructing something that might have been served on a blasted heath as three toothless hags danced the Time Warp around it.

We're Fucked, I telepathically messaged Caz, who, jaw still locked tight, stared, with horror, over my shoulder, as Dave Walker appeared, straight backed and pushing the trolley as though it were a pram containing Rosemary's baby.

To make matters worse, Walker had found – God knows where – an enormous silver cloche, which covered the entire bowl, making it look as though he were about to theatrically expose a concoction of delights rather than the monstrous melange that Caz had manically dumped into the Baccarat.

Nobody drinks the punch, I recalled her saying, as Walker, having shrugged his cuffs, reached forward, slowly, dramatically, reached for the hook on the top of the cloche, and, at that moment, behind me, the pub door opened, and everything got very interesting.

"She used to say I'd be late for my own funeral, you know," said a man's voice, "but Maggie was wrong: I was late for hers. Hello Olivia. You're looking well."

There came – from some of the guests – a communal gasp, someone – I couldn't tell who - let loose a half strangled squeak that might have been a shriek, and a glass was dropped and smashed.

Standing in the doorway was a tall, slim, rather dishy proposition. His hair was dark, curly on top, cropped tightly on the back and sides, and his tan was deep. By his side stood a small Louis Vuitton suitcase.

Olivia stood frozen for a moment, as her face flickered from horror to happiness, on to confusion, back to horror, and then settled on something that looked like gastric problems.

"Anthony. What. The hell. Are you doing here?" She asked, through a smile that didn't look forced, so much as superimposed.

"Me?" He arrived at her side, leaned forward to plant an air kiss on each of her cheeks, and she visibly recoiled for a second, before leaning in to the greeting. "I wanted to say goodbye to the old girl. She was almost the only good thing that ever happened to me here, you know. Almost."

He straightened up, looked around the room, and I noticed that the smile on his lips didn't quite reach his eyes, then turned back to Olivia.

"I would have been here sooner, except I had a stopover in Bangkok, and the bloody plane broke down, so, well, you know how it is: when in Bangkok…"

Olivia pulled back from him. "Same old Anthony," she muttered.

"Same," he acknowledged, "but even older. So: what have I missed?" His coy gossipy manner failed – nor did I think it was ever intended - to mask his disdain.

"Mr Bird," Dave Walker appeared at my side. "We have a problem."

I turned, and followed his eyes to the punchbowl. In the drama that was unfolding, all eyes seemed to be fixed on the central tableau, which was a good thing, as it meant that nobody had looked at, or – thank Christ – attempted to drink from the Punch Bowl.

Because, even from where I was standing, I could clearly see half a dozen fag butts floating on top of the punch, and a thick layer of fag ash collecting at the bottom of the bowl.

CHAPTER NINE

"I never touched it." Elaine spat the words out, her face a little pinched mask of fury.

"Look, I get it: You didn't want to be here; you don't want to be spending your summer holidays working here. Well get this, Elaine: We didn't want you here either, but your dear old Nannu wants this to happen, so unless you want me to call him right now and tell him why I won't have you round here anymore…"

I didn't get to finish the sentence. Elaine's eyes blazed furiously. "Listen, you fucking loser," she said, "I don't give enough of a fuck about this fucking place to sabotage your fucking Poofy Punch. Yeah, you're right: I don't wanna be here. But I am. And if I wanted out, I'd torch the fucking place and go off shopping. But I haven't."

I looked around the kitchen, which appeared scarily huge, and oddly empty. I'd dragged Elaine straight back here, while Dave Walker had quietly removed the punch bowl, and Ali had – with much grumbling over the cost of the diversion – started opening and serving more champagne.

"It's not in the budget," she'd muttered darkly.

"Well neither was having our own fucking barroom Jihadist," I'd snapped back.

"It's fagash, mate; not fucking decapitations," she answered, before instructing the ASBO twins to get pouring.

And so here I was, alone with Elaine, whilst – from the sounds of it – the wake matured into a full on party.

Alone.

With Elaine.

Who was now giving me such evils that I wouldn't have been surprised if she'd lunged at me and attempted to throttle the life out of me.

"No," I admitted, "you've not torched the place. Cos that would hit Chopper in the pocket, and you wouldn't want that. But you've done everything to fuck up my chances."

"Your chances?" She stage laughed. "Don't make me fucking laugh. You're running this fucking pub for my Granddad. You aint got no fucking chances. Cos as soon as he wants you out and some other nonce in here, you'll be gone.

"If I wanted to fuck up your chances, I'd make a call, sweet talk the old man, and you'd be out of here and straight into casualty at Saint Thomas'."

I had to admit that – chilling as her words were – she had a point. But Elaine, since arriving here with a snarl and an introductory announcement that "This place mings to Fucking Heaven," which was not entirely untrue, but which, nonetheless, set a tone of anger, disdain and barely supressed menace, hadn't exactly entranced me with her natural sweetness.

"Listen," she said, her pinched little face going a rather alarming pink, "you want to know who fucked up the punch? Check out that long streak of piss you got pushing it round like a fucking nanny. He had the stuff all to himself for ages. He could have dumped the fag ash in there himself."

I shook my head. "Why would he do that?"

"Cos he's already tried to make me look bad today and failed, so he decided to have another go."

Motive and opportunity. "Why would he do that?"

Elaine threw herself back in her chair, exasperation making her throw her hands up, "'Cos he's fucking mental, you twat! You all are. You got Dikearella stomping round behind the bar out there like it's Stalag Fucking Southwark, the Queen of Sheba slumming it like she's Princess Margaret, and them two numpties behind the bar."

"Danny," I looked up. One of the numpties in question was standing in the doorway. "She's right," Dash said. "She couldn't have sabotaged the punch. Elaine's been behind the bar for the past hour. I've been watching her. She didn't get back here."

Elaine turned her face towards him, a look of confusion softening the anger for a moment, before she turned back to me.

"See?" she spat, and, kicking back the chair, she flounced out of the room, stopping only long enough to say, "You fucking watch me again, you nonce, and I'll cut you," to Dash, who blushed to his roots and, turning on his heels, followed her like a lap dog.

I sat in silence, wondering what the fuck I was going to do with Elaine, whose dear old Nannu had – whenever he got angry – a tendency to make people – or at least various parts of them – disappear.

He'd been running his empire with an iron fist for several decades now, and clearly some of his character had rubbed off on the third generation.

But I was still fed up babysitting the grim granddaughter, and I determined to call him the next day and tell him she'd have to go; I'd had enough of her tantrums and her sabotage.

Because what had just happened had to have been her. Hadn't it? I mean: why on earth would Dave Walker have wanted to get her in trouble? What could she have possibly done to a middle aged waiter to piss him off enough to set her up?

No, it didn't make sense.

I was so engrossed in my thoughts that I didn't even realise someone had entered the kitchen and was advancing towards me until I looked up and started.

Which, of course, since I'd been so still, caused Monica Vale to shriek and jump backwards.

"I'm so sorry," I rushed to my feet, arms held out to steady her.

"You scared the living daylights out of me!" She stammered, still gasping for breath. "What the hell are you doing sitting alone in here."

"It's," I glowered, wondering why on earth I was about to justify my presence in my own kitchen, "My kitchen. I was thinking."

"Thinking?" She said in a tone that suggested she considered it an unsanitary and possibly unhealthy pastime. "Don't think," she shook her head, as though trying to clear the clouds that a trayfull of cocktails had placed there, "Do. That's what I believe. Thinking is overrated. Action; that's what counts."

"Okayyy," I moved slowly towards her, as though attempting to snare a skittish dove, all the time wondering whether it was the heat that was making everyone a little weird today.

"And why are you here?" I asked.

"Oh," she focussed on me, as though something had just registered, as though she was seeing me for the first time, and smiled a weary gap-toothed smile. "I'm looking for the loo. They said the ladies is closed. Out of order, or something."

"Ah," I nodded, and, guiding her gently from the kitchen, directed her towards the loo at the end of the corridor.

Monica glanced back over my shoulder at the chaos on the kitchen table. "Are they," she asked "Chicken fingers?"

"Thins," I answered, thinking just fucking say yes, and get rid of her before she hurls all over the floor, "Chicken thins."

She nodded absently. "Thin's good. They say. Make sure you keep me some," and, smiling that gap-toothed smile again, she tottered off towards the loo.

I went back into the kitchen, placed a tray of olives into the oven to warm while I piled the chicken fingers (goujons, thins, whatever) on two platters with bowls of home-made mayonnaise and Caesar dressing, and was just removing the olives from the oven when Dave Walker came in.

"I know it's not my place to say," he said, deciding to say it anyhow, "But there's an atmosphere in there you could cut with a knife. The way half of 'em are looking at each other, I wouldn't be surprised if there wasn't a punch up before the night is out. And as for them three useless kids you've hired…"

I handed him the first of the platters, nodded wordlessly in the direction of the bar, and hoisted a tray with the bowls of warmed olives on it, following him out of the room.

As we left, I heard the loo door slam shut, and, just as we reached the door to the bar, it opened, and the floppy-haired, chinless wonder that was Desmond Everett stood blocking my way.

"Oh," he blinked from behind his round horn rimmed glasses, looking, for all the world, like Harry Potter the Later Years, and said, in a tone that suggested he expected to be snarled at, "The Loo?"

"Back there," I jerked my head down the corridor, "But be prepared for a wait; I think there's a queue."

"A wait," he sighed as he stood aside and we passed into the bar. "Oh I can wait. I've been waiting most of my life."

CHAPTER TEN

In the bar, the heat had built. Most of the male guests had taken their jackets off. The juke box had been switched on, albeit that the volume had been turned down so that the dulcet tones of late 80s Kylie Minogue were almost unheard under the rumble and chatter.

Caz sidled up to me as I placed the last of the bowls of olives on the bar, and pulled me to one side.

"It's all going terribly well, but you really need to spend a bit more time out here with this lot. They've all been asking about you."

"Odd that, since you've painted me as something between Julia Childs and Taggart."

"Oh, dear heart," she chuckled, tickling me under the chin, "You're not that butch. Julia would have drunk you under the table. Now get out there," she patted my behind, "And socialise."

"Where are you going?" I asked.

Caz paused, as though uncertain of where, exactly, she was going. "The loo," she finally announced, smiling nervously. "Now, go," she shooed me away, "Schmooze."

Lifting a glass of champagne from a passing tray, I strolled into the throng, desperately looking for someone I could stand and talk to. Everyone seemed to be in groups already, except for the latest arrival, who, curly hair glistening with pomade, stood, back to the bar, a glass of clear liquid in his hand.

I strolled over, and introduced myself. "Nice place you've got here," he said, looking sardonically around.

"You think?" I was, quite frankly surprised. He didn't seem the spit and sawdust type. Not, of course, that The Marq was a spit and sawdust pub. We were several notches below that.

"Honest," he smiled, turning his attention to me. "I'm Anthony Taylor. Maggie – the dearly deceased – was my aunt."

"So that would make you," I guessed, gesturing at the figure of Olivia Wright, "Miss Wright's cousin?"

"Second cousin," he clarified. "Maggie had a penchant for waifs and strays, and when my parents died, she adopted me. Livvy and her brother were always around the place, so we sort of grew up together. Then, when Olivia's family was killed, Maggie sort of added her to the fold, so we were even closer for a bit." He stared sadly into the middle distance.

"Killed?" I found the choice of word odd.

"Well, how else would you describe it? They were in a car – Livvy, her brother Damien, and her parents. It went over a cliff near Cap D'Antibes. Livvy was the sole survivor. She spent years in and out of hospitals having the scars dealt with."

He glanced, almost fondly, across the room. "Looks beautiful now, but you should have seen her before the accident. She was..." he searched for the words, and finally settled on "A vision. Mine was far less dramatic: Cancer and alcoholism within the space of three years."

"And you've been away," I noted, gesturing at the suitcase by his side.

"Mmm," he said noncommittally, "And now I'm back. And not, it seems, a moment too soon. The vultures are already circling. Speaking of which..."

He switched on a thousand watt smile and gestured expansively, splashing me, as he did so, with his drink The object of his enthusiasm, a tall, thin elderly gentleman with grey hair that had been backcombed and boufannted to a shape that could only be described as meringue-like, paused in his journey to the bar, and squinted suspiciously at Taylor.

"Well, well, well," Taylor smiled at him, though there was little – if any – warmth in the smile, "If it isn't filthy Freddie. Freddie, have you met my new friend – heck, in this place, he feels like my only friend. Freddie Rosetti, this is Danny Bird. Danny runs this delightful establishment. Danny, this is Freddie. Freddie leeches off old ladies and – well, what do you do nowadays Freddie? You still talent spotting for Vogue?" Taylor tittered, and toasted silently to the elderly man, who, if looks could kill, would have been looking at a ten stretch.

"Still the same old Anthony," the older man managed to spit even though he was furiously chewing a wad of gum. "The angry angel to the end."

"Oh not angry, Freddie. I got over the anger long ago. No, nowadays, I like to think of myself as the, shall we say, avenging angel."

"Avenging?" Rosetti pulled himself up to his full height, which was considerably taller than Taylor's, and looked haughtily down his nose at the other man, "I would have thought you were due some avenging on, surely?"

"Sins of the past, Freddie," Taylor replied, sipping from his glass, "We've all got 'em. And we all need to atone for them. Isn't that true, Danny?"

I was mortified to have been dragged into what had felt like a standoff between two Tom Cats, and made various noises that said absolutely nothing, before Rosetti, still oozing sarcasm, nodded at each of us, "it's been so nice talking to you Anthony. Now, I'll let you crawl back inside your gin, while I go and spend a penny."

"Oh, I think there's a queue," I said to his back, but he was already gone.

Taylor drained his glass. "Daniel," he said conspiratorially, I don't suppose you could be a gem and ask your bar staff for another Perrier for me. Only, they seemed keen to push the booze, and, well frankly, I don't drink these days."

I called Dash over, instructed him to keep the soda water rolling for Mr Taylor, and, murmuring something about needing to check on the rest of the guests, rambled off into the crowd, only to be snagged by Olivia Wright herself.

"What does he want?" She demanded.

I was puzzled, before she nodded surreptitiously in Taylor's direction, "Anthony. You've been speaking to him. What does he want?"

Beside her, Kent Benson's phone rang, and, excusing himself, he stepped away from his fiancée to answer it. Left alone, Olivia linked her arm through mine, and pulled me into a corner. I looked, worriedly, over her shoulder towards where I had last seen Anthony Taylor, but he was no longer propping up the bar.

"So?" Olivia asked, "Why is he here?"

"Um…" I racked my brains, "He.. Well, I don't really know."

"What was he saying to you?"

"To me? Um," I prevaricated, knowing I was beginning to sound like an echo chamber, "He was talking."

"About me?"

"Yes."

"What did he say?"

Oh shit. He was discussing your family history and how you were orphaned in a car crash. I really didn't want this important customer thinking I'd been gossiping about her with her clearly estranged cousin. "He said how you and he had grown up together," I blurted, deciding to skip the whole how you ended up growing up together bit.

Olivia's face clouded. She drained her champagne flute. "I think I loved him a little, you know," she said, though I wasn't sure if she was talking to me or not.

"Anthony was the most exciting person I'd ever met. He was," she searched for the word, "wild. Maggie used to call him her angry angel."

I'd heard the phrase coming out of Rosetti's lips just a few minutes earlier. Then, the angry had been stressed.

"She'd tried so hard to help him, but Anthony as a child just seemed to have a self destructive streak. You name it, he did it. Drugs, drinking; he graduated from stealing from the tuck shop at school to stealing a Maserati from one of his school friends father's, and using it to ram raid an off licence."

"It must have been difficult for your grandmother," I mused.

Olivia Wright shook her head. "Not at all. She seemed to have an infinite capacity for forgiveness. Every time Tony did something that placed him in jeopardy, she'd take him to her study, and give him a talking to, and he'd be back on the straight and narrow for a few more weeks.

"Then, he branched out."

I waited. There was clearly more to come. I didn't wait too long.

"It was like Tony had built up scar tissue. Hurting himself, hurting Maggie didn't give him a buzz any more. So he started hurting other people. Innocent people."

She shook her head, and I was suddenly aware of raised voices from the other side of the room.

"And now he's back, and the innocent are bound to suffer again." Olivia – clearly already a little more than squiffy - went to swig from her glass, only to realise it was empty.

"Here," I took it gently from her hands, "Allow me."

She smiled sadly at me. "I like you, Mr Bird. You're a good listener. And you seem... sensible."

I accepted the compliment and turned to look for a waiter. And it was at that point that the raised voices gelled into a man's voice saying "Take that back, you bastard!"

The voice that replied, audible only because everyone else seemed to have stopped talking to observe whatever was occurring on the opposite side of the bar, was Anthony Taylor's, and it said, "If the cap fits, James..."

At which point something happened which I couldn't see, because of the throng. But suddenly, there were screams, a couple of shouts of consternation, a loud "Hey, watch it," from someone, a tray of glasses flew up in the air, crashed to the ground, and the crowd parted to display two grown men wrestling on the floor.

It wasn't exactly Die Hard levels of fisticuffs. It looked, to be honest, like a slow motion cuddle with grunts, strains and occasional profanities. If they'd been unclothed, it probably would have been classed as a Sex Show, and I would either have had my licence revoked, or Chopper asking for a cut of the proceeds.

Taylor, an odd look of almost triumphalism, was on top, attempting to pry the other man's hands from his throat, when Ali, moving like a particularly bulky gazelle, and accompanied by Ray, came from behind the bar, linked her arms round Taylor's chest and under his arms, and hoiked him as Ray yanked the other man by the shoulders so that he slid across the floor as Taylor shot upwards.

Separated, the two, gasping for air, glared at each other.

The other combatant, I could clearly see now, was the Colonel Saunders lookalike who had arrived with Monica Vale. Just what I needed: My chances of getting the Art set back into a pub where their dates were set upon by drunks was probably close to zero.

Then I remembered that Taylor hadn't been drinking, watched as the look of excitement on his face was visibly suppressed, and remembered his words about avenging angels, and a little voice in my head wondered what, exactly, was going on here.

Ali looked at me, her unspoken do I throw them out crossing the bar, and, having glanced at Olivia Wright, I gestured to her to let them be.

Dash came from behind the bar with a mop and bucket, and commenced clearing up the spillages, as the two men stalked to opposite ends of the bar and glared at each other.

I turned to Olivia again, who smiled at me. "Thank you," she said, "for that. I need to try to figure this out."

Dave Walker approached us, a tray of drinks held in one hand, and I snatched two glasses, handing one to Olivia, and swigging from the other. Olivia Wright thanked me again, and crossed the bar to where Anthony Taylor sported a look like a scientist who's just watched some bacilli do the Macarena.

"Mr Bird," Walker dropped his voice, leaned in and down to me conspiratorially, and nodded at the bar. "I've been watching our friend."

Our friend? I followed his eyes to the bar, and slumped in exhaustion. Elaine.

"Look, Dave," I began, but he grabbed my arm with his free hand.

"Watch her now," he said, "she's doing it again. Watch!"

As I watched, Elaine smiled at a customer, turned, went to the bar behind her, lifted a tumbler, filled it full of ice, and pressed it against the Vodka optic. She paused and her shoulders twitched, before she turned, smiled, lifted a bottle of mixer from the shelf under the bar, and poured the contents in on top of the spirits.

"Did you see it?" Dave asked me triumphantly.

"Um…"

"You didn't see it?" His face fell. "She's been doing it all afternoon. Customer orders a double vodka. She fills the glass with ice, pours a single, then mimes the second one. She's just given him a single and charged for a double."

"But why would she do that?"

He looked at me like I was the child who'd eaten too many lead pencils, and shook his head. "Money, Mister Bird. She's pocketing the difference."

"But it's an open bar, Dave. There's no money changing hands. I've supplied all the booze and Olivia Wright will pay me for every bottle we open, whether it's drained or not."

"What? But that's insane!"

"More money than sense, I reckon. But there's no way for Elaine to be working a scam. There's no money for her to pinch."

He deflated before my eyes. "But I saw her doing it."

"You were mistaken, Dave. Now, those drinks aren't going to serve themselves, are they?"

CHAPTER ELEVEN

"Ah, Danny," Kent clapped me on the shoulder, "D'you mind if we have a word?"

Shit, I thought, he's clocked the fag butts in the punch, but I smiled eagerly (I hoped, though my mum has noted that when I try to do my smile eagerly bit I look Less eager, and more backwards). Still, eager or simple, I followed Kent across the bar to where Olivia Wright was engaged in a hushed and somewhat tense-looking discussion with her newly returned cousin.

The Prodigal Returns was not the atmosphere I was picking up. More, to be honest, why the fuck aren't you dead?

Still, Kent leaned in, whispered something in Olivia's ear, and she straightened up, turning briefly to mutter something that didn't look like How Lovely to see you again to Anthony, before stepping away and commencing a hushed discussion with her fiancé.

I stood, feeling increasingly like staff (which, as they had paid for my time, I was, really) and awaited orders.

At last, Olivia kissed Kent on the lips, smiled, and both turned to me.

"We have a proposition to put to you," Kent announced with a smile that had me, for a moment, concerned that they were going to put something more than a proposition to me.

Cursing that eager smile, and wondering whether they'd misconstrued it as an Up for being a rich couples sex toy grin, I waited, the rictus wobbling only slightly.

"Well," Kent looked around the room filled with people, "is there somewhere we could go? Somewhere more private?"

I've got fifty mini trifles to decorate, and you want to pop upstairs for an afternoon delight? I thought. What sort of boy d'you think I am?

Aloud, I said "There's the parlour," and was relieved when both nodded happily, and Kent waved me ahead with an "After you, Mr. Bird."

We pushed through the crowd, squeezed behind the bar, down the hallway and turned into the dusty parlour, it's décor a pristine example of the Backstreet abortionist style favoured by old biddies in the 1950s.

Kent closed the door. "We need some privacy," he murmured, turning back to me and my slightly simple, slash Up for being a rich couples sex toy grin dropped like a stone.

"What's this about?" I asked nervously, as the couple settled themselves at the table.

Kent's phone buzzed. He took it from his pocked, glanced at it, shook his head, hit redial, held up a finger to me, and, after a moment, spoke to someone on the other end of the line:

"Tell them I'll go. Five million for eight percent, but not a penny more… I'm done, Franco; Five for eight, or I'm out. Ciao," and hung up before turning back to me and the still gooey-eyed fiancée, who was doing a better impersonation of eager smile than I ever could have.

"Sorry about that," he said. "Where were we?"

"Someone," I said, "Was going to tell me what this is all about."

"It's about you." Olivia said. "We need you."

"Look," I wrung my hands, realised I was about two beats away from I was only a bird in a gilded cage, stopped wringing them, put my hands on the table and looked hopefully at each of them, till I realised I looked like I was bracing for an impact from behind, and finally, exhausted at trying to make my body language say anything other than

This is mortifyingly embarrassing, dropped like a stone into a chair on the opposite side of the table from them.

"This is very flattering, but I'm not sure that I'm the right person for you."

"Oh, but I think you are, Danny. We think you are," Kent smiled seductively at me, as he put an arm around Livy Wright. He was, I had to admit, somewhat dashing. But then, in my mind's eye, I saw Nick Fisher, and knew that whatever kinkiness Kent and Olivia had in mind, I was not up for it.

"No," I shook my head, "I don't think I am."

"But you're so good at it," Olivia Wright simpered. "Everyone says so."

"You've been asking about me?" And – more worryingly – who've you been asking, and what have they been saying?

"Well, it's hard not to hear about it," Kent said "I mean, it might have been a few months since you did it, but it's still something to be proud of."

A couple of months, maybe, I thought, but we've both been busy. And Nick's been a bit odd lately. Plus, y'know, with this big gig coming up, I've been stressed and – wait! What? Proud of? I mean, I know it was good – very good – but I hardly think Nick posted an Amazon review about it.

"What" I asked, "Are you both actually talking about?"

"Well, your special skills," Olivia said, a puzzled look on her face, as though she were wondering what else we could possibly have been talking about.

"Skills?" I thought, deciding we were definitely not discussing my sexual prowess, and trying to decide between my devilled eggs vol au vents, and my mini Yorkshires. "What skills?"

"Detecting," said Kent, in the same tone someone might have taken to Nancy Drew if she'd asked which of her clearly vast range of talents were being complimented.

"Detecting?" I looked at each of them in turn, as they looked back at me eagerly.

At that point, there was a knock, and Dave Walker popped his head round the doorframe. "Oops," he said, backing out of the room, "Sorry to bother you."

"It's alright, Dave," I called after him. "D'you need anything?"

His head popped back into the room, his eyes taking in the three of us hunched around the table as though negotiating something important, like, say the Treaty of Versailles, or whether to watch Strictly or X Factor, and a hint of a smirk crossed his lips. "Nothing important," he said, and was gone.

"The thing is," Olivia Wright explained, "we've got a problem. One we've been trying to solve for some time. I wanted to go to the police, but Kent wouldn't hear of it."

"Overkill," he murmured, dismissing the problem – whatever it was – with a wave of his hand.

"But the thing is, they're not going away. And I'm sick of it. So we need someone who can figure out who's doing it, and put a stop to them."

Jesus, they really did think I was Nancy Drew. "Well, like I say, flattering as all that is…" I would have killed it there, but for the next words out of Olivia Wright's mouth:

"He didn't murder her, Danny. I know he didn't."

The Thanks, but No Thanks died on my lips. "Murder? Who mentioned anything about murder?"

Kent sighed. "I've been married before, Danny. My wife went missing. There was," he searched for the word, "a scandal, suggestions that I'd killed her. I hadn't. I didn't."

"He didn't," Olivia confirmed emphatically. "I know him, and I know that Kent is one of the gentlest, sweetest men I've ever met. He's perfect for me. But someone's been sending these letters. Horrible, horrible things."

"Wait!" I held my hand up, stopping the torrent of words. "Take a step back. Start at the beginning. What happened?"

I meant, of course, what happened with the wife that Kent didn't murder, but I hadn't counted on Olivia Wright's ego. She took my words to mean tell me your romantic love story, and kicked into what sounded like a well rehearsed spiel:

"It was Jane, really. She'd just ended a relationship. Poor girl – they never last long; she's so unlucky with men, and has such low confidence. No idea why, cos she's quite pretty really, when she makes the effort."

I mentally pictured the hunched hairy creature that I'd last seen at the bar, and wondered just how much effort would be required.

"Well, Jane was really depressed, and needed to get away, so she suggested that we take a little girlie trip to Florence to recover. And that's where I met Kent. He was at a conference."

"I'd skipped a session to take in the Uffizi," Kent explained, also missing the point that whilst their How we met tale was lovely, they had actually mentioned murder – or implied murder – then just casually put it to one side. "And I was looking at The Birth of Venus when I literally bumped into Olivia."

"Lovely," I smiled, trying to pull them back to the pertinent point. "Now, about this murdered wife."

"It was love at first sight," Olivia made puppy dog eyes at her fiancée. "We hit it off immediately – Kent loved the same paintings as me, the same food, laughed at the same jokes and read the same books. It was like he'd been made for me." She smiled fondly, and reached a hand out to stroke his face. Kent caught the hand, and kissed it gently.

"He's perfect for me," Olivia said, and Kent blushed.

"You're perfect for me," he answered, and I resisted the urge to retch.

"So," Olivia carried on, "Kent followed me back to London, and eventually had to go back to L.A. It was horrible," she said, misting up momentarily. "I missed him so much. Everyone said so. I was moody, and weepy, and I just knew I had to see him again."

"The murdered wife?" I tried, again, to no avail.

"So she followed me out to L.A." Kent filled in.

"Which was Jane's doing," Olivia admitted sheepishly. "I thought he'd gone off me, but she was all Go after him. He could be the one for you, which – when you consider her heart had just been broken – was really pretty decent of her."

"Was all a bit of a shock, I've got to admit," Kent took up the rambling, "But a very pleasant one. I'd never met anyone before who was so," he searched for the word, "Vibrant. Olivia's the most wonderful girl. But finally the time came closer for her to return to London,"

"Well, a girl can only stay on holiday for so long."

Unless, I thought, you're an heiress with shitloads of money in your future, then you can bunk off as long as you like.

"I knew that I had to do something," Kent continued. "she was going to come back here, and I was going to lose her. So, after two months in LA, we were suddenly back here in London, and engaged to be married."

"And then the letters started to arrive," Olivia said.

"Letters?"

"Yes," said Kent. "And that takes us to Sophie, which is something I told Olivia all about when we were in L.A."

"I knew, and I still wanted to marry him, Danny. Which is what makes these letters so hateful."

I waited, looking from one to the other. "Go on," I said.

"My wife," Kent began at last, "Was a complicated woman. She had mood swings, and they had been getting worse. We had a business; one that had done quite well. But, as can happen, the business was going through a difficult patch.

"The lawyers were gathering, people with – what do you say here? – an eye for the main chance?" He sighed. "The whole thing just started to get to her. Which, of course, made her," again, he paused, as if searching for the right word, "difficult to live with. But we loved each other, Danny; of that, I can assure you. I would no more have harmed Sophie than cut my own hand off.

"Then, one day, I came home, and she wasn't there. We had a boat, a little thing we used to take out to fish in, or just to escape all the shit that was going on in the business. And the boat was gone from its mooring. I assumed she'd gone out for the afternoon. She liked to do that, sometimes: Would take a book, and a bottle of wine, and anchor somewhere, and just drift till she was ready to come home.

"Except she didn't come home. Ever."

"I see." I said, and the parlour – bakingly hot a moment ago – seemed a little chillier for a moment. "What happened?"

Kent shrugged, sadly. "You can probably guess what happened. The police were eventually called, they did some sniffing around, realised that things hadn't always been great, let it be known – as they so easily can – that I was a person of interest in the case."

"Trial by media," Olivia muttered, her eyes blazing.

"Indeed," Kent shrugged. "It was like something by Kafka: They hadn't charged me with anything, but everyone knew I'd killed her, because, well, why wouldn't I? Except, of course, I hadn't and I wouldn't have. Because I loved her."

Olivia placed her hand over Kent's, and sighed sympathetically.

"Eventually, of course, the police made a move. They had Sophie declared dead, so that they could charge me with her murder."

He sighed heavily. "I spent several months in limbo before they finally had to admit that they had no real grounds for even suspecting foul play, let alone for suspecting me of murder. On top of which, I had a rock solid alibi for the whole day.

"Sophie was declared missing, presumed dead, I was shunned by the people who continued to believe I'd killed her, and everything just sort of faded away. Then, a couple of years later, I went to Florence, and met Olivia."

"And as soon as we announced our engagement," Olivia picked up, returning to what was clearly her favourite topic,

"The poison pen letters started to arrive. Vile things suggesting that Kent's a murderer."

"Wouldn't be the first time someone called me that," he said.

"Kent said to just ignore them; then whoever was sending them would just get bored and go away. But it's the outright cheek that bothers me. How anyone can be so nasty? It's just not on."

"So, we thought…"

"Well, I did. Kenty's been totally against bringing anyone in to look into it. He wouldn't even hear of having the police round, would you dear?"

"It's a poison pen letter. Probably some dried up old spinster somewhere. I figure the police have got bigger things on their plate."

"But then, today, he's had a Damascene conversion, haven't you sweetie?"

"Listening to Lady Caroline, singing your praises."

"I must remember to thank her," I murmured, unenthusiastically.

"And it just struck me that…" Kent began, before Olivia finished his sentence.

"Maybe you could hunt down whoever's been sending the horrid things, and get them to stop."

"Stop? How?"

"It's my experience," said Kent, "That the sort of people who send these things thrive on the anonymity. Their power comes from you not knowing who's saying these things, not from whether the things they're saying are true or not."

"And they're not!" Olivia interjected.

"You've had a lot of experience with poison pen letters?" I asked.

"Some," he admitted. "When Sophie vanished, I received my share of hate mail. But in every case, once the sender was identified, they – usually after some furious denials – tended to vanish back into the forest."

"So you want me to find the sender?"

"Oh, we'll pay for your help, of course," Olivia smiled.

"Umm… I'll need to get today out of the way."

"Won't we all," murmured Kent. "If that cousin of yours stirs up one more argument…"

"I'll deal with Anthony," Olivia replied, a steely look in her eyes.

"How frequently have these letters been arriving?"

"One – sometimes two - a week," Olivia said, "But the last one was about three weeks ago."

"So they've stopped," I said.

"For now," Kent murmured, "But I suspect they haven't stopped for good."

I looked from one to the other, a million reasons to say No running through my head, and at that moment, there was a knock, and Filip opened the door.

"Sorry to interrupt, Danny," he said, "But have you seen Dave?"

I looked around the parlour, at the print on the wall – some sort of mashup between The Hay Wain and the Fighting Temeraire - the standard that had a pink shade so dusty it might have come out of Tutankhamun's tomb if Tut had had a decorator with a taste for kitsch and frills, and the wallpaper that, had Wilde ever staggered in here on a night out with Bosie, would have killed him off before all the trouble could begin.

"Not lately," I answered Filip, "But he'll be around somewhere. Probably keeping an eye on Elaine. Try the bar."

Filip said he'd looked there. "Maybe he's outside on the phone again," he said, in a tone that left no doubt he was dobbing Dave in.

I really, at this stage, didn't care if he was outside shooting up, so long as the food was served, the empties cleared, and we could get through the rest of today without my staff killing each other, but instead of saying so, I just smiled, said, "Maybe," let Filip withdraw, looked, once again around my dusty dingy parlour, turned back to Olivia and Kent, and smiled.

"How much?" I said.

CHAPTER TWELVE

On our return to the bar, it was immediately clear that the atmosphere had shifted from Overheated but somewhat jovial drunken wake to Dinner with the Borgias.

Anthony Taylor, a large and spreading wet patch covering the entire left hand side of his white shirt, was dabbing at his face with a paper napkin, which was quickly decomposing and leaving clumps of white tissue all over his forehead.

"…Didn't think you had it in you, old chap," he was smiling, as though to a great friend, while Desmond Everett, a look of fury still painted on his face, stood glaring at him.

Ali, lumbering out from behind the bar, came around to stand between them, proffering a bar towel to the still dripping Taylor, whilst simultaneously fixing Everett with a withering stare. "Try that again, and you're out," she advised him, with an attitude that suggested he'd be neutered prior to ejection.

"We had quieter days when we did Shitfaced Mondays," she muttered to me as she passed en route to her place behind the bar.

"What the hell's going on here?" Olivia Wright demanded, taking Ali's place between the two men.

Taylor shrugged, grinning sheepishly at her. "I appear to have upset poor Dozy Des. Sorry Doze – I mean Desmond."

Everett seethed, "Rotter," he spat between clenched teeth. "Sorry Olivia. Tried to keep out of it. But…" he scrabbled desperately for a way to explain his actions, before putting his empty wine glass down on a passing tray, finishing with "Rotter," once again, and walking out of the bar.

"Well," Taylor waved to the closing door, "That was unexpected. I genuinely didn't think he had it in him. Was always such a completely placid little man."

Olivia, eyes blazing, turned on Anthony, and physically pushed him into the farthest corner of the bar.

This was clearly going to be a strong and private conversation, so I did what anyone else would have done: I followed them both under cover of collecting empties, so I could eavesdrop on it.

"…Entirely your own fault," Olivia was saying, each word punctuated with a jabbing finger. "He's the gentlest soul, and you're back minutes before you're laying into him."

"Oh take a break, cousin dearest. Dopy Des and his loyal puppy act may fool you, but I'm wearing the proof that he's an angry little nipper. And all I did was give him the excuse to let it out. It's not good, you know, bottling things up. Not healthy at all."

"Is everything OK?" Monica Vale's Colonel Saunders Lookalike date – the man who had already, today, been rolling round the floor with Anthony Taylor – approached the two.

Taylor turned his glance to the new arrival. "Talking of unhealthy," he muttered. "Did anyone call for an ambulance chaser?"

"Oh not again," the other groaned. "Grow up, Anthony."

"Ah James," Taylor smiled nastily. "Tell me, Mr Kane, What's the difference between a lawyer and a leech?"

"Look," James Kane placed his hand protectively on Olivia Wright's left shoulder as Kent took up his place on her right, "I don't know what your game is, Anthony, but you're wasting your time here. And you're not wanted," he added somewhat unnecessarily.

Taylor's smile widened. "After you die, a leech stops sucking your blood," he answered his own question. "And, wanted or not, I am here. And I'm staying."

Olivia shook her head in exasperation. "Why couldn't you have just stayed away?" She demanded.

Taylor shrugged, his cocky look fading momentarily, before he noticed me earwigging, looked back at Olivia, put the triumphalist Patrician mask back on, and – as though relishing the fact that, between Kent Benson, James Kane and I, he had an audience for his performance – laughed in her face. "Because everyone, cousin dearest, is entitled to a second act.

"Me, Olivia, you; even your delightful fiancée here. Not sure about James. Do Lawyers get second Acts, James? Or do they just get to go on and on till they're found out? Either way, we're none of us saints; but sometimes we change."

Olivia's stabbing finger froze. She stared at him in confusion for a moment, before her eyes refocussed, and a smirk flickered across her lips. "There'll be no money in it for you, you know. What wasn't left to me, she gave to animal shelters and drug rehabs."

"Well, that was Maggie for you: Waifs, strays and losers. She had time for them all." Taylor shrugged disinterestedly. "Let's hope she's got some money left to leave them, hey James," he smiled at the solicitor, who bristled.

"She tried to help you," Olivia said.

"And she did, Olivia. She did. Getting me away from here was the best thing she could ever have done."

"And now?"

Anthony spread his arms wide, gesturing at the throng, half of whom – it seemed – wished he would simply vanish in a puff of smoke. "Now, dear cousin, I'm back. But right now, I'm wet, and I need to dry off," and so saying, he pushed past the trio, before smiling a dazzling smile at me, and saying "Loo?"

I pointed him towards the only working loo, and watched as he passed through the room, went behind the bar, and vanished from view.

When I turned back, I realised that almost everyone else in the room had watched his exit.

CHAPTER THIRTEEN

I put the empty glasses I'd gathered on the bar, and caught Ali's eye.

"How are we doing?" I asked, and received her most withering stare in response.

"We," she said, "Are doing just fine. There's nothing I like more on a boiling hot day than a coach load of pissed up ponces going off at each other in my pub. You better be making a shitload of money out of this."

"A few quid," I muttered noncommittally, "But there's a lot of exposure to be had as well."

Ali snorted dismissively, "I had a cousin once, died of exposure."

"Was he a mountain climber?"

"Nah," she said, a puzzled look on her face "He was a flasher. Till Betty Glass belted him with her handbag and started screaming blue murder. So 'e runs away from her, and – tackle ahoy – runs right in front of a Tesco delivery van. Goes arse over tit, straight through the window. Scarred that driver for live, I heard."

Now it was my turn to be puzzled. "Surely he died by being hit by a van," I said.

"Exactly!" Ali announced triumphantly, "But he wouldn't have been hit by the fucking van if he hadn't been exposin' hisself to old ladies. So the moral is: Be careful what you wish for. Sometimes exposure aint worth the pain."

I nodded, marvelling at the weird and wonderful wisdom of my Bar manager, and wondering if this afternoon could get any weirder, before I remembered the person who had persuaded me that this affair would be good exposure for the pub.

"Have you seen Caz anywhere?" I asked.

"Her?" Ali did her bull with a crew cut snort again, and jerked a thumb over her shoulder. "She aint gonna be out here getting her hands dirty with us lot. Said she had a headache, was going upstairs for a lie down.

"I'd fetch her some tea and biscuits," Ali finished, sarcasm dripping from every word, "Only I'm a bit busy here what with running a pub and stopping your posh punters from attacking each other."

"Fair point," I admitted, as my phone vibrated in my pocket.

I took the phone out and glanced at it. It was an incoming text from Nick.

KNOW YOU STILL MAD AT ME, it said , BUT CAN I COME ROUND 2NITE? I WANT TO TALK 2 U.

I froze. Talk to me? What about? I looked around the bar, feeling a gnawing in the pit of my stomach. Some might have thought it was the result of not having eaten since the night before, but I knew it for what it was:

A sense of doom.

Nick and I had been getting on well since the start of the year. I'd begun by rebutting his approach; I'd been through a messy breakup, and I really didn't want another relationship. But he'd persevered, calling me in early January and asking me to come to dinner with him. Then we'd gone to the pictures, the theatre, and the ice skating and Somerset house, and before I knew what was happening, I was spending all the time our schedules allowed with him.

I worried that Caz, who was my best friend, would feel rejected, but she'd been fine with the whole thing: "Sweetheart," she'd said, "I may be doomed to a life of spinsterism, but there's no reason at least one of us old donkeys can't get their, if you'll pardon the expression, oats. Enjoy. Because," she'd finished, "I'm off to Miami for a few weeks with Dante."

"Dante?" I'd racked my brain, coming up, only, with the Italian who wrote Inferno. And – though she wasn't fussy when it came to who paid for her winter breaks – I figured even Caz would have been unable to screw the cost of a villa and first class flights out of a long dead poet. "Dante who?"

Caz sighed, and, as though speaking to the terminally slow, clarified herself: "Not Dante. Dom T. He's a rapper. I think. Or a DJ. Something musical. And he has a house out there, so I'm popping over to escape this vile weather."

"Do you even know this person?" I asked.

"Know him?" She'd laughed heartily down the phone at me. "Oh sweetheart, you don't have to know someone to stay in their house and use their facilities."

"Well where I come from, using the facilities of people you don't know is referred to as Breaking and Entering," I updated her, and she'd laughed again.

"I love how genuinely proletariat you are, Sweetheart. It's charming, really. But I have to go, cos Dom T is sending a car around, and I haven't even decided what bikinis to pack. Have fun with your little policeman. I'll call you when I'm back, and I shall expect all the juicy details."

And, so saying, she'd rung off.

Imagine my disappointment when, a week later, Nick had announced, excitedly, that he was being sent to Albania on what sounded, when he explained it to me, like some sort of exchange programme.

"You're going to live with an Albanian family and absorb their culture?" I 'd asked, wondering what on earth Albanian culture was, and how it would affect my not-a-boyfriend.

Nick had smiled, "I'm not twelve, you know. It's an exchange program where the Albanian's get to hear about some of our policing methods, and we get to build better links with them."

"Links? Why would you want to build links with the Albanians?" I asked, before rushing home to call Caz, who I luckily caught in the first class lounge at T5.

"Is Albania even a real country?" She asked. "I mean: isn't that only in books with endless winter, the snow queen and all that?"

I sighed deeply.

"No, Caz, you're thinking of Narnia. Albania's definitely a country; I looked it up."

"Well where is it?"

"Eastern Europe, but that's not relevant."

"Be bloody relevant if you had to walk there," she returned. "So what's the pretty policeman's rationale for going?"

I told her about the exchange of ideas, then added "Plus, there's a couple of villains the Met have been after for a while, only every time they think they have them, they vanish to Albania, where the local law and the whole extradition setup is a bit dodgy. So the hope is that, by building some bridges, it'll make it easier to nab them next time they pop up."

There was a silence at the end of the line, then: "Nope, sorry. You lost me when you started talking like a character from a Linda La Plante. I heard villains, dodgy, and nab 'em, and none of it made as much sense as an Opera in Esperanto to me."

"Whatever," I waved her objections aside, "The thing is that he's going away and I'll be all alone. So we can play."

"Oh, sweetheart," she murmured sympathetically, "I see where this is going."

"Don't go," I pleaded with her. "Stay here and we can do fun stuff."

"But I'm already checked in," she answered, "And besides, this is good: You have lots of work you need to do."

"I do?"

"Certainly: You can sort out that bloody Barmaid for a start. Put her through charm school. And you can draw up some menus for the coming months. I'll only be away for a few weeks."

"A few weeks?"

"Oh, they're calling me," she said, "for my massage."

"Massage? I thought you were in the airport?"

"I am. But I couldn't very well get on a long haul flight without having things loosened up, could I? And besides, your tale of woe has stressed me so much I need my chakra realigning or something. Toodles."

That had been then.

This was now.

I looked at my phone again. I WANT TO TALK 2 U.

What about, I wondered.

"Oi, Delia," Ali was back, "Can you have a word with her," she jerked her head towards the end of the bar, where a clearly shitfaced Monica Vale sat in front of an empty glass.

"Paralytic." Ali said, "And wants serving. If you OK it, I'll do her another, but if she turns into one of our merry band of brawlers, I'll have every last one of 'em out on the street and shut the doors on 'em."

I headed over to Monica. "Miss Vale," I smiled, "How are you doing?"

Monica Vale looked up from the spot on the bar where her eyes had been fixed, and worked hard to focus on me.

"I've had a bit of a shock," she slurred. "James throwing a punch like that – made me remember…" She shuddered, and clammed up. I'd been running a pub just long enough to know not to ask what she remembered, whilst fervently hoping she wouldn't elaborate.

She didn't. "Where is James?" She suddenly asked, turning round and squinting at the crowd. "Have you seen him?"

I hadn't, and I said so. "Perhaps he's outside having a fag."

"Doesn't smoke," she shook her head.

"He'll turn up."

"Yes." She sighed deeply, and stared vacantly at the empty glass in front of her. "Most people do, don't they. Just when you think you'll never have to see them again, there they are in front of you."

And at that point, much like the devil of whom people speak, James Kane turned up.

"Monica," he caressed the back of her neck with hand which, I noticed, trembled slightly.

"Oh," she focussed on his face, "There you are. Was worried. You met Dan?" she waved a hand as though joining us together.

"Not officially," Kane smiled at me, though the smile didn't reach his eyes. He was out of breath, I noticed, and seemed keen to end the conversation and be rid of me.

Which meant, of course, that I stuck around.

"You're a lawyer," I prompted, and he smiled another crooked little smile at me.

"Yes," he admitted, "I'm Olivia's legal specialist. As I was for her aunt before her. You run this place," he announced, leaving no room for any confusion over his thoughts on The Marq or on me.

"I try," I smarmed, wishing Caz were present. She'd know what to say; I was this close to actually apologising for the joint.

"Well, it's been lovely to meet you," his smile clicked off, and I was dismissed, as he leaned in, kissing the nape of his drunken girlfriend's neck. "What say we make a move, Monica? Old Maggie's well and truly planted, so there's no need for us to hang around any longer."

Monica Vale looked up as though just seeing he and I for the first time, and nodded emphatically, which made her wobble precariously on the bar stool. "Wanna go," she slurred. "need to escape."

Kane chuckled "Escape's a bit strong, but I agree, dear, it's definitely time to head home." And so saying, he slipped an arm around her, slid her from the stool, and half carried, half supported the wasted artist from the bar.

Ali sidled up to me. "Cheers for that, Danny." She shook her head sadly. "I'm a barmaid," she said, forgetting, for a rare moment, that she was a bar manager. "I got no problem doling out booze, but that girl looked heartbroken."

"You reckon?" I asked. "She just looked wasted to me."

"Nah," Ali shook her head. "She looked like the bottom had just fallen out of her world. Speaking of which, let's hope the rest of them head off soon. I don't think the plumbing can take the world falling out of their bottoms. Have you got the key for that loo? The queue's vast, and it looks like whoever's gone in there has passed out."

"Key?" I said. "I didn't even know you could lock it."

I headed back that way, and wondered, once again, where Caz had got to; it was unlike her to go for a nap when there was a party – and, more importantly, free booze – to be had.

Ali was right about the queue; it seemed like half the pub were stretched along the corridor, lending the whole thing – along with the 90s house music filtering in from the knackered juke box in the bar, and the almost tropical heat, scented with Pineapple, Citrus and Cheese and Onion –the air of a student house party.

"Sorry about this, folks," I said, walking along the line, and nodding at Desmond Everett and Freddie Rosetti, "Won't be a moment."

"They've been in there for ages," Olivia Wright, who'd been giggling somewhat drunkenly with her girlfriend plain Jane Barton announced. "Hope they haven't used all the paper up," and she giggled again.

I walked to the top of the line, and knocked on the door.

"Hello!" I called, when no answer came back. "Anyone in there?"

I tried the handle. It was locked from inside, but the door had one of those locks on it that left just a thin line – like a screw head – with which one could unlock the door.

I called again, and when I got no answer, I dipped into my pocket, pulled out a pound coin, tried to slide it into the slot, and, when it wouldn't work, tried again with a ten pence piece.

It fit perfectly.

"I'm going to open the door," I called to whoever was inside the loo, hoping that they'd simply passed out, and weren't in the midst of a bout of dysentery.

I turned the coin, feeling the lock slide slowly backwards. The door popped as it came unlocked.

I pushed the door open, knocking and calling "Hello" again, in a vain hope that – if it was explosive dysentery – the sufferer would at least be able to gurgle a plea for privacy.

But there was no call.

The door stuck on something, and I shoved, finally seeing into the small room. The ceiling sloped sharply down towards the far wall, where the toilet stood, the lid up and two fresh toilet rolls stacked on top of the cistern. To my right was a small hand basin and a hand dryer affixed to the wall.

And sprawled on the floor was something puzzling. It was a pair of black shoes, black trousers, a shirt that began as white and, as it reached the collar, faded to pink then almost fluorescent red. And above the collar was something that used to be human, used to be solid, and used to be recognisable as a head.

Now, it was a darkly glistening mass of hair and flesh and slivered white bone, something viscous still oozing slowly from it and pooling around the neck and shoulders to seep into the grouting between the floor tiles and creep across the floor like some sort of macabre weed.

This man – my brain was beginning to put structure to the horror before me – this man's arms were thrown forward, as though, at the last minute, he had tried to stop his fall. His jacket sleeves were pulled back, and one of his shirt cuffs had lost the cufflink, and was gaping.

The other cufflink – a small silver stud with a red stone in it – seemed to wink at me.

The back of both hands were covered in a mass of tiny scratches, vivid and pink.

From behind me someone squeaked, someone else gasped, and a short person said "What's going on? I can't see!"

I stepped back, swinging the door shut. "Call the police," I said, though it felt like I'd whispered the words, so I swallowed, took a deep breath, controlled the shaking that had started, and tried again. "Someone call the police!" I said, "Tell them someone's been murdered."

I leant against the door frame – as much to keep myself upright as to prevent the rubberneckers from pushing the door open to have a good look. I knew this was a murder – you don't stove your skull in to the extent I'd just seen by standing up suddenly in a low ceilinged room – and I knew that I was in trouble, for – just before I'd closed the door, I'd followed one of those bloody tendrils across the floor as it's journey took it closer and closer to the weapon that had been used to smash this person's skull in.

And recognised the mallet that I had been using all morning to hammer out meat. The same one that – logic said – had to have my fingerprints all over it.

CHAPTER FOURTEEN

The door flew open, slamming against the wall, and making the cheap fan on the table wobble dangerously. "Well, well, well. Here we are again. The gang. All back together. Isn't this nice?"

A vast round tub of lard slammed its way into the room, the head – like a discount block of cheese on a hundred weight of leftover blubber – wobbling sweatily from side to side in a vaguely menacing fashion, hands rubbing together almost lasciviously.

I'd met this Would-be Kong before. His name was Frank Reid, and I'd outsmarted him the last time he'd tried to fit me up for a murder at The Marq. Then, he'd been, quite frankly, a bastard: Truculent, arrogant, aggressive and desperate to prove me guilty.

Now, he was all of those things, plus, as I quickly gathered, sweaty.

"Gawd, it smells like a bear pit in here. Fisher, can we turn on the aircon?"

Behind him, his DC – the man I liked to call my boyfriend – raised an eyebrow. "There's no AC, Sarge," he announced. "cuts."

"Cuts?" Reid swept an eye over me, the wobbly Pound Land Fan, my somewhat beige legal representative, and puffed out his already well stretched poly cotton shirt.

I glanced nervously at Mrs Dorothy Frost, a short, inconspicuous little woman, who'd reminded me, on first meeting, of a somewhat focussed shrew. I'd since come to see her as something closer to a tigress than a shrew, but I was still a little... uncertain.

My fingerprints, after all, had been all over the meat mallet.

Reid smiled, almost jovially, and nodded at Dorothy Frost. "'Ow you doin', Dot?" He asked in an avuncular tone that made me worry; it felt like the equivalent of an undertaker telling dirty jokes. Reid was supposed to be nasty and mean and spiteful and here he was playing the genial host. I half expected him – at any point – to ask if we preferred lapsang souchong or oolong, and to pass around a plate of bourbon fingers.

"How am I doing? I'm wondering why I'm here," Dorothy Frost responded.

"More to the point, I'm wondering why Mr Bird is here. Surely, after the shock he had yesterday, he should be in the hospital getting checked out."

"Well, y'see, Dot," Reid said as he advanced his bulk into the available space, lowered himself into a chair, lifted his arms and manoeuvred the fan so it was pointing directly up his short sleeves, "Danny," he poked the recording machine beside him as Nick settled beside him, opened a manila folder, and focussed on the contents.

"I can call you Danny, can't I mate?"

I glanced at Dorothy Frost.

She nodded.

I nodded.

"Is that a yes? For the tape."

"Yes," I said.

"Well you see," Reid grinned at the diminutive figure of Dorothy Frost, "Danny was good enough to confess to the first officers on the scene."

Dorothy shot me a look. I opened my mouth but no words came out.

"Confess?" Dorothy Frost said.

"Oh, not to the murder. He's not that stupid; but he did have to admit that the weapon was his, and that we'd find his fingerprints all over it. So I thought it might be worthwhile getting him in here to ask how come his meat mallet ended up being used as a murder weapon."

"I'll hazard," Dorothy responded, "That it was because the murderers own meat mallet was in the cleaners. Is there a reason, Frankie, why you've called Mr Bird in to the station today?"

"To take his statement, Dorothy. You know me: thorough to a fault."

"To a fault, yes. And is there a reason why you couldn't take his statement at the pub he runs?"

"None, really," Reid answered, "'Cept I thought he'd maybe remember some more detail away from all the confusion."

"So, not an attempt to intimidate my client?"

"As if," he guffawed.

I glanced at Nick, who smiled gently (at Reid's gag, or as a way of reassuring me?) and wished I had returned his texts the day before.

"Well," Dorothy Frost turned her eyes to me, "Danny? Do you wish to make a statement at this stage?"

I did, I said so, and I proceeded to tell them all I knew, which wasn't much.

Reid sat, silently, scratching a few notes on the notepad in front of him, and waited till I'd finished.

"That it, then?" He asked.

I nodded. "I didn't know him, didn't know anything about him. If he had enemies, I don't know who they were."

"If he had enemies?" Reid snorted. "I doubt very much that a mate of his did this accidentally. His head was smashed in like an egg. This was fury. Panic. Desperation. Sort of thing that someone who's living on the edge would do. Someone, say, who's running a shitty boozer for a nasty gangster…"

He let the last sentence – along with the meaty tang of his body odour – hang in the air. Reid knew – but hadn't yet been able to prove –who the real owner of The Marq was, and it seemed at times as though it was this – his desperate desire to nail Chopper Falzone – that was at the root of his dislike of me.

"I mean," he went on, "It's understandable. You must be under an awful strain, trying to make ends meet and still give Chopper his cut. How much is he asking these days, Danny? A quarter? Half?"

"Frank," Dorothy Frost sighed, "does this train of thought have a final destination?"

"Well," Reid smiled a thin lipped smile at her, causing all the sweat that had pooled on his top lip to slide down his face, and commence dripping from the first of his several chins, "what with Danny being, you know, one of our more artistic residents, well, highly strung people have a habit of going off, you know…"

"Going off?" Dot Frost raised an eyebrow, glanced at me as though to check I hadn't fainted away at Reid's suggestion, and turned back to the Jabba The Hutt of the Met Police, "Are you seriously, Frank, and I mean seriously, suggesting that Mister Bird may have bludgeoned this," she checked the paperwork in front of her "David Walker to death because Mister Bird was having a bad day? Seriously?"

"I know… I know," Reid held up his hands in a placatory fashion, and I glanced at Nick, who could be seen to visibly grind his teeth as he stared in obvious mortification at the file in front of him, "But worse things have been done for less believable reasons. I had a woman once who knifed another woman cos she looked like Amanda Holden. Attacker was a fan of Les Dennis, you see. Heat. Does things to people, and you got to agree, Dot, that this is all a bit odd.

"And you know, Dot, the gays are a bit highly strung."

Dorothy Frost stood and placed a hand on my shoulder. "We're going," she said, and, when I looked at her in surprise, added, "You were hauled in here to give a statement. You've given it. And now, unless Torquemada here wants to charge you with something more than homosexuality – which, I remind you Mister Reid, hasn't been a crime in this country since 1967 – we're off."

"Aw, now, Dot, don't be like that," Reid smirked. "Sit down for a minute. Just one. Please. I'll play nice."

Dorothy Frost looked at me. I still hadn't moved, and so she resumed her seat. "Frank, what do you want?"

"I want to know – from Mister Bird – who he thinks killed David Walker. I know you didn't know him, Danny, but you were with him for almost the entirety of his last day on earth. And I know – from previous dealings with you – that you're shall we say, observant. You see things, and you make connections. It's a skill. And – since you were there, and I wasn't, I wanted to know if you had any thoughts on who might have wanted to cave Mr Walker's head in?"

I shook my head again. "I knew nothing about him. I mean, none of this makes any sense."

"Had he worked for you before?"

"No. I got him through an agency."

"Name of?"

"Mastercaters," I said.

Nick cough-choked. Reid shot him the evils. "I beg your pardon?" He addressed me.

"Mastercaters," I repeated. "They were recommended by a friend of a friend who regularly arranges events."

"So: No history with Walker? Anyone else seem to be less than friendly with him?"

I thought of Elaine, of her last words to him You'll be sorry, and of the colleagues he'd referred to as the Himbos. Surely none of that – banter, maybe a little irritation - could have translated into the fury that I had seen in the loo?

"It was a busy day," I said flatly. "I didn't see much, but there was nobody in the pub who had a beef with him."

"You sure? Only, you paused, like you were considering whether to say something or not."

I paused again. He put himself across as a lumbering boar of a man, but Reid wasn't that stupid after all. I'd realised some time before that would have been difficult for him to get to where he was if he'd been truly stupid.

"I got to be honest with you Danny: The guy was a middle aged waiter. No money to speak of, no obvious reason for anyone to turn the back of his head into steak tartare. To tell the truth, whoever bumped him off did us a favour. I mean, if it had been one of the guests, I'd be getting all sorts of shit from the muk muks upstairs. You had heiresses, celebrity artists, a couple of minor aristos, and a bloody lawyer," here he shot a venomous look at Dot Frost, who returned her imitation of a sphinx. "But with this one, well, we'll make a stab, but I'm not sure how far we're likely to get. He was a nobody, Danny, and people don't make a fuss about people like him, so unless you have something – no matter how small, this aint gonna go far…"

"Yes," I finally answered. "I'm sure. There was no obvious sign of anyone with a motive for that."

"Well," Dorothy Frost shuffled some papers, "If there's nothing else…"

Reid glowered resentfully. Nick pursed his lips. They glanced briefly at each other, then turned their full attention back to me.

"Danny?" Reid asked, "You sure there's nothing else?"

"No." I answered. "You have my statement."

This time, Reid paused, glanced again at Nick, then shrugged. "If you say so," he said. "Interview terminated at 11.52," he muttered, reached over, and switched off the recorder.

CHAPTER FIFTEEN

We paused in the hallway outside. Dot placed a parental hand on my arm. "You OK, Danny?"

I shrugged, "As OK as I suppose it's possible to be having found a corpse – another corpse – in my pub."

She nodded. "I understand. Lightning's not supposed to strike twice, is it? But it does, Danny; and more frequently than you'd imagine. I have to say: You don't seem alright."

"I'm just tired. I didn't sleep so well last night."

"You didn't stay in the pub?"

"No. Back to my parents again."

"Tonight?"

"Back to the pub. Life goes on."

"That it does. But Danny? If you need anything – and I don't just mean legal help – give me a call. You did great with the whole Lyra thing, but you don't need to deal with this on your own."

Behind her, the interview room door opened, and Reid oozed out, Nick behind him. Reid muttered something to Nick, and lumbered off in the opposite direction. Nick hung back, clearly wanting to speak to me.

Dot went to move away, and Nick approached me.

"You O.K?" he asked, and I wished people would stop asking that question. Every time I closed my eyes – even with them open, if I allowed it to come – I could see that image, of Dave Walkers big oblong head, a head that nobody had ever described as pretty, reduced to a bloody pulp. And if I let myself, I could replay every conversation I'd had with him, remember the way I'd begun to see him as a whiny, miserable pain in the arse.

Dot Frost paused, a look of concern registering. "Danny? Everything alright?"

I looked at Nick, glanced back at Dot, and smiled. "It's fine."

"Ah," a slight smile, some recognition, perhaps, flickered across her face, and she nodded. "Get some rest. And remember: Anything you need…"

"Thanks Dorothy."

"Are you OK?" Nick, repeated.

I was about to repeat the as well as can be expected bit when he shook his head.

"Don't bullshit me," he said softly. "Don't tell me you've told Reid all there is to tell, either. There's something bothering you."

I sighed. "He was just a waiter," I said.

"And now he's a dead waiter, and we need to find out who killed him."

"That's what's bothering me," I said. "Like Reid said: He was just a waiter. Like being a waiter wasn't something worth being. Like it would have mattered more if he'd been just a nuclear scientist, or just an Investment Banker or a Football player."

"I think the point is that we can think of more reasons why someone would want to kill any of those people than why anyone would want to murder a waiter. Unless his waiting skills were really crap. Spilled soup? Cold wontons?"

His attempt at humour left me cold. I knew he was trying to cheer me up, but I didn't want to be cheered up. "He was actually a good waiter," I sighed. "He really cared about doing a good job. Couldn't stand to see anyone being lazy or less than correct." I stopped myself before I mentioned Elaine and her half arsed attempts at sabotage.

"So who did he have a go at?" Nick asked. "Who was 'Less than correct'?"

I shrugged. "Nick… I'm tired."

"Can I come over after my shift?" He pressed. "There's something wrong. I don't know what it is, but I want to help."

I smiled at him. Nick and I had started out shakily. I hadn't known if I was ready for a romantic relationship; for any sort of relationship, truth be told. But he'd kept making his case, kept turning up, and finally I'd caved in, and, for the past six months, even though we saw each other irregularly, and – to be honest – I'd never even seen inside his flat, I'd been happier than I might have believed I'd ever be.

But this latest murder at The Marq had shaken me. I kept trying to get my life on track, and it just kept derailing.

I was stood in the hallway, listening to Nick making soothing sounds to me, whilst internally having a mini pity party for myself, thinking things couldn't really get much worse, when the universe decided to point out how naive I was.

Nick said he'd be finished at about seven, and would come round to The Marq for about seven forty-five, and I was just agreeing and thinking of maybe making a chicken salad when another copper appeared.

"Fisher," this slim destroyer of worlds said, as he passed us by, "Your wife's been on the phone. Says it's urgent, and you need to call her back ASAP."

Then he was gone.

Nick froze, his green eyes – emerald green with flecks of blue and grey through them – widened momentarily, then winced shut; his mouth – those plump red lips I'd wanted to kiss with all my might a moment before – opened into a wordless "Oh," and his shoulders slumped.

"Wait," I smiled nervously, "he..." I gestured after the already long gone copper. "Did he..?" I looked from Nick to the back of the already almost vanished copper, none of the past few seconds seeming to make any sense at all. "What did he say?"

"Listen, Danny, it's not what you think."

It was my turn now for my shoulders to slump. But just for a moment. I was becoming an expert at rescuing the shreds of my self-respect and dignity from romantic disaster; but I still wanted this to be not what I thought. I still, desperately wanted to have misheard the copper. Your life called would have been acceptable, if nonsensical. You're rife to be balled would have worked too.

I straightened up, looked him square in his green duplicitous eyes, and said "Oh? Well what is it, then?"

"Its…" his shoulders slumped again. "It's complicated."

I ran.

CHAPTER SIXTEEN

I'm not proud of it. The voices in my head were loudly exhorting me to punch his fucking lights out, but my dignity and logic pointed out that we were standing in a police station, and wondered whether – betraying, two-timing fuck or not – attacking a copper in a cop shop was really a wise move.

The voice in my head that sounded like Caz, meanwhile, said "All men are bastards. God I need a drink."

So I turned on my heels, and tried to stride purposefully and directly down the corridor and out of his life.

I got halfway down the corridor before he caught up with me, put a hand on my arm to stop me, and said "It's difficult, but you'll understand."

That was when I turned, furiously, on him. "I already understand everything," I spat.

And that, I'm afraid to say, was when I let go of my dignity and ran, down the corridor, and out of the station, and down the steps on to the pavement where what can only be described as a phone box in a black suit halted my progress.

"Mr Bird," the giant said, the peaked cap on his head shading his eyes and making his aviator sunglasses somewhat redundant, "Allow me to offer you a lift home."

I was so drowned in my own misery that I didn't even bother to try pulling my arm out of his gentle, yet firm grip.

I knew who this was – or, more precisely, who this person worked for, and so I allowed myself to be lead a few meters on from the police station – far enough away to pretend that the long sleek dark Daimler was not waiting for someone to leave the station, but close enough to make that pretence obvious.

Last time Chopper Falzone had had me picked up from the Nick, the collection had been done by one James Christie, a compact snarling ball of nasty who, shall we say, was no longer in Mr Falzone's employ, and the vehicle of choice had been a stubby clapped out little Ford. This time, the employee – his bulk, in contrast to Reid, consisting totally of muscle – was almost deferential, and the vehicle, as I say, somewhat classier.

I wasn't fooled. Falzone was, after all, the man that even The Sun had described as London's Al Capone, which I knew irked Chopper. He'd climbed to the top of a dangerous tree by being violent, ruthless and conniving. As polite as his chauffeur had been, the charm offensive, if I didn't say or do exactly what he wanted, could very quickly turn into my hanging from my thumbs in the stock room of the Pound Shop.

I had been made so deeply miserable by recent events that I no longer cared what happened to me, but was still somewhat disconcerted, when the rear passenger door of the Daimler was opened, and I was ushered inside, to find the said Martin Falzone waiting for me on the back seat.

"Hello Danny," Chopper smiled, his little brown eyes sparkling welcomingly, as he patted the seat beside him. "Want a choc ice?"

He dipped into a cooler at his feet and extracted a foil wrapped ice cream on a stick.

I gaped, slumping onto the seat, and he took my silence for rejection. "Suit yerself," he said, tearing the wrapper from the ice cream and plunging the thing into his mouth.

Outside, the street had been an inferno, but in here – thanks to the almost silent air conditioning – the car was almost chilly. Which explained why Falzone was wearing a three piece suit, and not even breaking a sweat.

"Got an awful sweet tooth," he said as the driver – hidden behind a smoked glass screen - put the car into first, and slid away from the kerb. "The wife's always telling me that I'll get diabetes. Would be about right, if I ended up getting carried off by fucking sugar, considering the number of nasty bastards who've tried to do the job so far. But who could resist a nice sweet ice cream on a day like today. Feels like the end of the fucking world out there," he gestured vaguely at the world beyond the smoked glass windows, and I wondered how often Chopper Falzone actually experienced the world "Out there."

"Thank Christ," he smiled, "For Choc Ices, and air con. So there's a few more inches on my waist, and a few less Icebergs. Who cares? Never liked Polar Bears anyway. Nasty fuckers."

I said nothing. The monologue hadn't seemed to require a response. Besides which, there were never a few inches more on Chopper's waist; he was notorious for remaining at the fighting weight he'd carried when he'd been a featherweight contender, and for dressing – at all times – as though he were in a fashion shoot.

"So," he gestured at the cooler once more, "You sure you won't join me?"

Even if I'd fancied a choc ice, to be honest, my stomach was now tied in knots, and the thought of me spewing cocoa-streaked vanilla ice cream all over his handmade brogues didn't bear thinking about, so I shook my head. "No thanks, Mr Falzone. I'm not really hungry."

He shrugged. "Fair enough. Like I was saying," he said (though he hadn't in fact been saying anything beyond eulogising frozen desserts) "I'm grateful. That you kept Elaine and I out of this during your little chat," he gestured behind us, at the now distant Police station.

How could he be so certain, I wondered, that I'd left them out of it? Did Chopper, I wondered, have the place bugged? Or did he have an inside man who'd report to him on whatever he wanted reporting on? Neither option seemed outrageous, but both still managed to be rather disconcerting.

"It's appreciated," he clarified, and I, apropos of nothing, made what I hoped were acknowledging noises.

"Not a problem," I said, wondering at that point, whether I should tell South London's most violent criminal that his dear darling granddaughter was mental.

"Unfortunately," he continued, pausing as he shoved the choc ice into his mouth, sucked noisily on it, and slowly – almost flirtatiously – withdrew it to disclose that he'd sucked off all the chocolate coating, "We still have the problem of a violent nutter on the loose in my pub, and the fucking rozzers, once again, crawling all over one of my businesses."

There was, I knew, room for only one violent nutter in Chopper's world, and no place whatsoever for what he charmingly referred to as the rozzers. "Mr Falzone," I said, "I have no idea what happened yesterday, but I'm sure it was just a passing crazy."

I wasn't of course, but suggesting otherwise – that I, via my hiring choices, or the type of customer I'd actually sought out – had brought this difficulty to his door – was not, I figured, at this stage, a wise approach.

Besides, the third option – that the homicidal loon had been one foisted on me by the old man sat at my side– was even less likely to endear me to him.

"Is she safe?" He asked, in a South London version of Laurence Olivier's famous Catchphrase.

"Safe?" I replied, feeling, despite the almost sub-zero temperature, a cold bead of sweat run down my back.

"Lainey," he clarified, using his pet name for the piranha he'd lumbered me with. "Is she safe? That's the only assurance I want from you, Dan. My little girl is a treasure to me, and if anything ever happened to her…"

The threat lay between us, as he sucked the last of the ice cream from the stick, locked eyes with me, and snapped the wood cleanly in two, throwing the broken halves back into the cooler.

"She's safe, Mr Falzone," I answered. "Elaine was working the bar all afternoon with Ali and," I almost used Ray and

Dash's joint nicknames the ASBO twins, but thought better of it at the last minute, "My nephews."

"Nephews?" Chopper raised an eyebrow. "How old these boys are?"

"Um," I searched my brains, "Seventeen."

He raised an eyebrow. "There's different types of danger, Dan."

"They're OK," I said, rushing to defend them, as I imagined the grief that would befall them if Chopper ever decided they weren't.

"They better be," he said. "I like you, Dan. You're smart; respectful. That's why I let you employ Lainey."

I boggled at this, but, channelling Caz, chose to nod like a duchess instead.

"She's young. Easily influenced. And I want her to have good influences. These boys," he changed topic, "They good boys?"

"Oh yes, yes," I stammered, wondering how quickly I'd be able to spirit them out of the country, and what I was going to tell their parents if Chopper took a dislike to them. The boys? Oh, they've decided to become missionaries in Bora Bora. No, I don't think that's anywhere near Ouagadougou. Why do you ask?

"They faggots?" he asked, before shaking his head in annoyance. "Sorry. Sorry, Dan. No offence meant."

"None taken," I responded, deciding that Choppers use of offensive pejoratives was, by and large, one of the least of his crimes.

"I meant, y'know, they like you? Cos shirt lifters I got no problems with where Lainey's concerned."

I pondered informing Chopper that I'd never lifted a shirt in my life, though several had been discarded carelessly on my bedroom floor, but decided that a smart mouth was not required.

"No," I said, definitively, "They're not," I searched for the word, then settled on "They're straight."

Chopper sighed. "Shame. Bent would've been safer. But you're keeping an eye on them, right? No monkey business?"

I recalled Elaine's threat to them yesterday, and felt that monkey business was unlikely.

"They're OK," I assured him. "She's OK."

"OK." He nodded, seemingly satisfied. "If you say so."

The car slowed, and I realised we were outside the pub.

Chopper dismissed me with a casual wave of his hand. "Tell Lainey her Nannu sends his love. And Danny," he said, as I moved to open the door, "Take care of her. This killer – or either of them boys - turns out to be anywhere near her, there'll be a price to pay."

I nodded my understanding.

And left the car.

CHAPTER SEVENTEEN

The fact that All Men Are Heartless Bastards had long been a central tenet of Caroline Holloway's world view. Bastardy, of course, wasn't just a trait amongst men. She held the same true of some females, particularly the ones who were politicians, PR agents, and certain editors she'd dealt with in her time.

And the Bastardy, she freely admitted, wasn't always a bad thing. In much the same way as suggesting that all Lions were Calculating Carnivorous hunters, the knowledge was simply factual, and the sooner one accepted the fact, the sooner one could get on with living.

But I had to admit that her reaction to my news of Nick's deception took me aback somewhat.

Expecting a purse lipped I told you so, I got, instead, a look of disbelief, and an "are you sure?"

"Sure of what?" I asked. "That he's got a wife, or that he made no attempt to deny it."

"Both. Either. Whatever." She shook her head, as though to clear it. "None of it makes any sense."

I sighed. "I think it sort of does. He's always been a bit distant on detail. I know hardly anything about his life. His family. His history. I've been seeing a bloody ghost."

"But he seemed," she searched for the words, found none, and threw her hands up in dismay. "Jesus. So what did you do?"

"Do? Why, I offered to go shopping with the wife for her fall wardrobe, of course. What d'you think I did? I ran, Caz.

I put my foot down and I got as far from the fucker as I could."

"But what I don't understand is why he never mentioned her?"

I choked. "Have you been drinking?"

"Is the Pope an old man?"

"Caz, why do you think he never mentioned her?"

"Well, what I mean is: he couldn't have thought that you'd never find out. I mean, a wife – believe me, dear heart – tends to pop up sooner or later. Without fail. So what was he playing at by not mentioning her?"

"I don't know," I shrugged. "Maybe," I brightened up, "She's got a fatal illness, and he figured she'd be dead before he had to tell me about her?"

"That's what I love about you," Caz said, pouring a large gin and waving the tonic over the top of the glass, "Your positive outlook, and love for all humanity. Oh," she slid the glass across the table to me, "There's some more bad news, I'm afraid."

"Let me guess: This heatwave really is the end of the world, and the whore of Babylon's been spotted riding a dragon down Shoreditch high street."

"Sweetheart, that sight's visible almost every night of the week. No; the Standard's been in touch."

"They're not coming round?" I guessed, and Caz sadly shook her head.

"Said something about how reviewing the Caesar salad on page ten when the latest homicide is still all over the front page might not look too good."

I sighed. Quite frankly, the no-show of a hoped-for reviewer in the midst of everything else that was going on was not that big a disappointment to me.

There was a cough, and a gentle knock on the doorframe, and we both turned to find Mike Green standing in the doorway. He was wearing a pair of cut-off jeans that showed his solidly muscular calves, the olive skin glistening slightly, and a pale blue t-shirt that stretched enticingly across his chest. "Sorry to disturb," he said consolingly, and I couldn't help wondering how long he'd been standing in the doorway.

"Just came over to check in with you both and see if there was anything I could do to help."

He gave me a hug that was somewhere between comforting and disconcertingly exciting. Did I imagine it, I wondered, or did Mike hold the squeeze a little longer than was strictly necessary?

Turning, he repeated the manoeuvre on Caz, though this time, I swear, the hug was shorter, somehow more perfunctory.

"I can think of one thing you could do to help," Caz muttered, and, catching my eye, clarified, "you could tell all your mates that the food here is still amazing, the pub is still friendly, and that as only the staff ever seem to be murdered, it's perfectly safe for them to come and have lunch here."

Green smiled. "I don't think you need my review," he said, gesturing towards the bar, "That place is rammed out there. Besides, I don't actually have many friends in London. Yet. Do the police have any idea who murdered that guy?"

I shook my head. "None. And to be honest, I'm not entirely sure that they're looking too closely."

"Daniel," Caz advised Mike, holding the gin bottle up in a silent invite, "Has a somewhat jaundiced view of her majesty's constabulary at present. You sure we can't tempt you?"

Mike shook his head, "Too early for me, thanks."

At that point, Ali barrelled into the kitchen.

"Not that I'm fussed or nothing," she intoned in a baritone worthy of Lady Bracknell, "but it's lunchtime out there, and the place is rammed. Any chance one of you two could rustle up some of the food that you've been advertising?"

"Rammed?" Caz raised an eyebrow.

"Told you," Mike said, nodding in agreement with Ali. "I suppose there really is no such thing as bad publicity.

"Tell that to Dave Walker," Ali snapped back. "I don't think he's ever had his name in the papers as much as he has today. Not exactly great publicity for him, mind…"

She turned to me. "So, Danny, you got any more of that Gaz-Parch- Eo-O handy? Only it's flying out like hot cakes, now I've twigged it's supposed to be cold."

I shuddered at the recollection of Ali two days previously, returning bowl after bowl of the soup because it had "Gone cold while you were farting about with the garnish."

Mike gestured at the bar. "So is lunchtime usually this busy?" he asked.

"A murder'll do that," Ali commented. "Danny? Gaz-Parch- Eo-O?"

"On it," I sighed rousing myself as Ali bustled back out to the bar.

"Hey," Caz commented, "Maybe we won't need The Standard to come in. If enough people like what they see and eat – whatever it is that brings them in here – the papers'll have to review us."

"Indeed," Mike murmured. "Listen, Danny, I can see you're busy, but if you need anything – anything – you know where I am."

"Thanks Mike," I said, hoping for another consoling hug. But, instead, he tapped me on the shoulder, nodded politely at Caz and Ali, and took his leave.

CHAPTER EIGHTEEN

By three o'clock, the rush had died down, and, having filled the dishwasher for the umpteenth time, I headed out to the bar, where Ray, Dash and Elaine were restocking shelves for the evening session.

Ali was watching them, while cashing up the till, and correcting, from time to time, their work.

"How'd we do?" I asked her.

She held a finger up, tapped a few more numbers into her calculator, checked the result against the screen on the till, and nodded in satisfaction.

"Not bad." She smiled, "We might eventually make a go of this place."

"Be a miracle if we do," I said. "Pubs seem to be closing left right and centre these days."

"Ah," she smiled, "But they aint got me as a landlady."

"Bar manager," I corrected her.

She shot me a look that said, regardless of what title I decided to bestow on her, we both knew that she was the landlady.

I blanked her, nodding at the calculations before her. "So, what's all this then?"

"Stock control," she replied proudly. "One of the biggest problems in most pubs is the pilfering what the staff do. You can lose a fortune, if you're not on top of it."

I glanced over her shoulder. "But our staff, Ali – except for the odd big event – consists of my nephews and Choppers granddaughter. We're hardly running Disney Land..."

Ali shook her head at me in a more-in-sorrow-than-anger fashion. "Danny, Danny, Danny. I mostly trust the boys. They're as crooked as the day is long, but they know better than to nick off me. That much, we've made clear. But the blonde is an entirely different little number. She'd have the eyes out of your head, the teeth out of your mouth, the crisps out of the back, and torch the fucking place on her way out.

"So, I'm keeping an eye out. This," she nodded at her calculations, "Starts off by telling me exactly how much of everything we have in stock. I can then match it against how much money we've taken, and confirm that what we've got left is what we should have left."

I still thought she was going slightly over the top, but figured it was her bar to run.

"Any chance I can borrow the boys?" I asked, nodding at the matching peroxided heads of the twins.

Ali glanced over at them, sniffed, "Yeah, I suppose so. Here, Elaine," she called out, "Can you get up a crate of slimline tonics and refill the mixers shelf?"

"Why can't they do it?" Elaine whined, nodding at the twins.

"'Cos I didn't ask them to," Ali growled. "I asked you. Shift it. You two," she nodded at the boys, "Danny's got a job for you."

The boys followed me down the hallway to the kitchen, where Caz had already taken a seat at the table, a huge jug of fruit-filled Pimms before her. She doled out four glasses of the drink, toasted us, then pointed to the chairs on the other side of the table.

"Pull up a seat, boys," she said.

Ray and Dash glanced at each other. "What's going on, Dan?" Ray queried.

I sipped from the Pimms, and launched into a coughing fit. There appeared to be no lemonade in it. "Jesus, Caz. What have you put in this?"

"Pimms Royale? It's Pimms and Prosecco. Yes," she held a hand up to stave off any comment, "I know I should have used champagne, but you're not made of money, Daniel. Now, boys," she turned her attention, and a beaming smile, on the twins, "Nothing to worry about. You're not in trouble or anything. Although," she squinted sourly at them, "Your initial assumption that you were leads me to believe that one – or both – of you has been up to something you shouldn't have been. What's been happening?"

"Yes, thank you Jessica Fletcher," I wiped my brow, took a second, more measured sip from the Pimms, and settled myself at the table, "we'll call you."

"They look shifty," she insisted.

"They're seventeen," I snapped back. "Every boy looks shifty at seventeen. Especially when some posh bint starts plying them with fruit flavoured jet fuel. Sorry boys."

The twins shrugged, lifted their glasses in unison, and swigged from them. I noticed that neither of them coughed.

"We're eighteen," Dash clarified, as though that made a difference.

"Wonderful," Caz snarled. "so you can be tried as adults. Just remember that, Daniel: whatever you're about to ask these fine young men to do, they are no longer minors and thus the old youthful exuberance line won't run."

"Caz," I corrected her, "Youthful exuberance only runs for the sons of the aristocracy."

Caz shrugged accedence to my point, and drained half her glass of Pimms in one slug.

"Right," I turned to the boys. "I need you to do some digging."

"Bodies or copper piping?" Ray asked.

"Only we don't do bodies. Not any more," his brother clarified.

"Neither. Wait… what? When did you bury a body?"

"Bury?" Dash looked aghast. "We aint never buried a body, Dan. What d'you think we are?"

"Nah, we dug one up, innit," Ray clarified. "That artist bloke, Jame Montessori, needed one for something he was working on."

"Well, I sighed, I'm so glad you're more Burke and Hare than Brady and Hindley, but what the fuck were you thinking?"

"It was a dog, Dan," Dash clarified. "A great Dane."

"Fucking reeked," his brother noted, his face expressing his disgust at the memory. "An' as we was getting' him up, his head started falling off…"

"Right!" that was the point at which Caroline slapped the table. "I suggest we get on with the business at hand. More Pimms anyone?" And, like the well-bred young aristo she was, she stirred the melange, and topped up our glasses.

"OK." I sipped from the glass. No coughing this time; I was clearly becoming used to the alcohol content, a fact which was confirmed by my inability to feel anything above my upper lip. "I want you to dig up some information."

The twins glanced again at each other. "Information?"

"So no dead animals, then?" Dash asked, in a tone that seemed almost disappointed. "Only in this heat…"

"…It'd cost you," Ray finished.

"Boys!" Caz slapped the table again. "Focus, please!"

"OK," Ray turned to me, "What sort of information?"

So I told them about Kent, the dead wife, the engagement to Olivia Wright, and about the poison pen letters.

"Ray, get on the internet. I want to know about the dead wife: Who was she, where did she come from, any family or friends who might want to cause trouble? Dash, Olivia's couriering over the letters. Take a look. Anything pops out to you about them – post marks, grammar, whatever – let's hear it."

The boys exchanged worried glances.

"Problem?" I asked.

"Well, it's just," Ray began.

"Grammar is hard," Dash said, his brows already knitting together at the thought of having to spot a split infitive.

"Jesus." I rolled my eyes. "But digging up deceased pets is easy? Just do your best."

"Danny," Caz put her glass down,, "Do we need to do this? I mean: you've got a lot on your plate already."

"I promised them," I answered. "And besides, Olivia Wright already paid me a sizeable retainer, with another amount when we find out who's sending the letters. She really wants them stopped. So, if we can get to the bottom of it, there's a nice little bonus for all of us."

Caz's phone beeped. She glanced at, slid it from the table into her bag, and refocused on me. "So what are you and I doing while the boys are digging into Kent's unofficial biographer?"

"We're going to visit the lovely people at Mastercaters."

"Wait a minute." Caz put her glass down. "What have they got to do with the poison pen letters?"

"Nothing," I admitted. "They employed Dave Walker. I'm hoping they'll have some idea why he's dead."

"Danny." Caz hefted the jug, stirred it again, and topped the four glasses up. She gestured at my glass, an instruction to me to swig it because what she was about to say would not be welcomed, and, having slugged hers, fixed me with her most severe glare.

"You run a pub. You're good at it – and getting better. You make food that appears to be quite good."

"Quite?" Only quite? I was insulted.

"Sweetheart, you are a competent cook; you're not Michelin level. Yet. But, with the right publicity, and the right approach to the whole thing, you might actually make a decent living from it. People like you. You're getting a good reputation, and you're no longer hovering over bankruptcy. You got lucky – alright, unlucky – last time. Lyra being killed right on your doorstep was horrible, but you managed to find the killer and get the police off your back. But you don't need to do this. Not this time."

"I do," I answered simply.

"Oh sweetheart," she reached a hand across mine. "You don't. You really don't. It's not your job; it's with Reid. He'll snout away at it till he figures it out."

"He was just a waiter, Caz. Reid said so. There'll be something else tomorrow, something that demands more attention, and this will slowly slide down the priorities list. They don't even know where to begin."

"They'll begin where you propose," she shot back. "with the employers, the friends, the family."

"But they won't get anywhere," I answered.

She shook her head sadly at me. "Oh you of little faith."

I sighed. "I don't mean they're not smart enough to figure it out. Just that they won't have time to. They'll be distracted. He wasn't a celebrity or a politician or even someone photogenic that the papers'll keep on the front page. He was a middle aged nobody, who nobody cares about. And the police will be distracted."

"And you won't?"

I didn't respond, and she finally sighed. "I see: Nick."

"Nick," I confirmed simply, and she sighed, before lifting her glass of Pimms in toast.

"Well, she said, I guess the old firm's back in business. Here's to us. God help us."

I toasted her, and slugged.

CHAPTER NINETEEN

"So, is this a thing now?" My dad asked, as he pulled his taxi up outside a suburban detached house next morning.

"A thing?" I paused before opening the door, enjoying the last moments of the air conditioned chill.

"You. Going all Columbo every time someone in the neighbourhood gets bumped off. Only, your mum's worried that, you know, you'll get into trouble."

I bristled. "I am not going all Columbo."

Caz snorted, sounding, as always, like a pedigree pony whose funny bone had been tickled. "No," she observed, "you're more Poirot on Poppers." To my Father, she added, "Don't worry, Mr B; I'm keeping an eye on him. He gets close to trouble, and I'll have him out of trouble spit spot."

"Thank you, Mary Popout," I murmured, casting a judgemental eye over Caz's ensemble. There were bags around her eyes – expertly hidden, of course, but still visible to my trained eye – and her hair seemed a little too tousled even for her. But more alarming was the peasant smock she was wearing, which managed to flare alarmingly at the hem yet be tight enough to show off the sort of cleavage you could drown a mouse, a sack of kittens and a selection of unwanted shopping trollies in.

My eyes travelled lower.

"Why," I asked, "Are you wearing jeans?"

Caz raised an eyebrow. "Because my leopard skin leggings were in the wash. Is there a dress code I'm unaware of for suburban visits?"

"You never wear jeans. Or, come to think of it, peasant smocks."

"Well you can't get the peasants these days. Shall we go?" She asked, swinging the door open and wincing as the superheated air immediately cancelled out the air con. "Mr B, it's been a pleasure as always. And thank you for the rhubarb."

"Rhubarb?" I thanked my dad, waved him goodbye, and turned to Caz.

"Yes, your dad's sending some around from his allotment. I'm making a pie."

"Right," I grabbed her by the wrist and stared into her eyes, "Bring back my friend, or there'll be trouble ."

Caz tried to pull her wrist from my grip. "Daniel, what on earth has gotten in to you?"

"Firstly, you haven't cooked at home since – well, since ever. You're the only person I know whose oven still has the guarantee sticker on it, and the instruction guide in it. And secondly – jeans and peasant smocks? Caz: what's going on?"

"It's Stella," she said gesturing at the top, "And these are Dolce. I just fancied a change. Have you brought me all the way to," she shuddered, "Woodford to play Fashion Police?"

I released her wrist. "You're up to something."

Was it my imagination, or did she blush. "Shall we?" She gestured at number 43 Bradley Drive, and, deciding that I'd gotten as much from her as I was likely to get, I led the way to the door, and pressed the doorbell.

Almost instantly, the door opened. A young man, somewhere, I'd guess, in his early twenties, his head still turned as though talking to someone in the house stood in the doorway, an iPhone held in his left hand, a backpack slung over his right shoulder.

He pressed an earphone into this ear, snapped "I'll do it when I get home, mum," turned his head, spotted us, and stopped, pulling the earbud from his ear and flicking his black fringe out of his eyes. "Hello," he smiled.

"Jonas," said a female voice if that's the bloody Jehovas again, tell 'em if we find Jesus we'll give 'em a bell."

He smiled at me. "You don't look like the Jehovah's witnesses."

"We're not," I smiled back. "Is Mrs Cambell in?"

He shrugged down the hallway, "Just," smiled again, nodded at Caz, squeezed past us, murmuring "good luck," and, shoving the earphone back in his ear, made his way up the road.

The door stood open before us. From the other end of the hallway, the female voice continued to berate the now absent Jonas, "Make sure you do get it done, Jonas; jobs don't just come knocking on the door, and if you're not working by next week, I'll 'ave your guts for garters."

I looked at Caz, who looked at me. "Shall we?" I mimicked her, gestured her forward, and we stepped into the house, closing the door behind us.

"Even better," Jonas' mum's voice added, "I'll put you to work with my lot. They can always use some help in the kitchens."

"Hello," I called, stepping around two of the largest, most fluorescent pink suitcases I had ever seen.

"I'm in here," the voice called, "Though if you're selling, I aint buying."

We walked down the hall and into the kitchen. Mrs Cambell was bent down at the moment, stuffing clothing into a washing machine in the corner of the kitchen.

"Won't be a mo," she said, slamming the door shut and standing up.

She was huge – at least six foot five in height, and quite possibly five foot six at the shoulders. She had the sort of chest that an American college line backer can only dream of achieving, and she was a shade of tan that can really only be called creosote.

Her hair – a backcombed bleached blonde creation that defied gravity via the application of so much lacquer it deserved its own Greenpeace protest cordon - towered at least another eighteen inches above her head.

If a wardrobe and an oompa loompa had met and mated, then Jonas' mum might have been the result.

Not realising he'd already gone, she continued to berate him.

"Jonas," she called after him, "Let me know how the interview goes." She turned to me, shrugging a shoulder to reinstate a bra strap the size of circus tent rope, while the torrent of words continued. "I don't think he'd even know if I died until the microwave dinners ran out; a slave to his technology he is. Sorry about the mess. I just got back from Dubai. Fabulous place. Go twice a year, switch off the blackberry and just chill. Anyway, listen to me wittering: What can I do for you? I'm Naimee, by the way, Naimee Cambell." She held a hand out.

"You're Naomi Campbell?" I asked.

"Naimee. No relation," she deadpanned.

I introduced myself and Caz, then: "I wanted to talk about Dave Walker."

"Ah," she nodded, a hard look coming in to her eyes. "Miserable, was he? He does have a bit of a dourness about him. But he's a decent grafter. Unless he shat in the vichyssoise I don't do refunds. The invoice'll be with you by the end of the week and I expect payment in full."

I realised that the Himbos had obviously not phoned their agency to announce the murder of one of their numbers; or, if they had, that the news had not yet reached Naimee. Then I remembered the switched off blackberry, the long haul flight.

"He's dead," I told her.

"Oh," she tilted her head in a way that made it look like she'd either heard the mating call of a phoenix, had a stroke, or wanted to present the impression of someone considering the brevity of mortality, the cruelty of humanity and the poetry of absence. Then she said "My pussy needs seeing to."

My jaw dropped.

What on earth does one say at a moment like this? Caz, of course, having been trained by basilisks, had the perfect rejoinder: "We'll wait."

"Oh no," Naimee cried, "You've got to have a look."

I considered methods of temporary blindness.

Naimee opened a deep drawer, displaying a carved apart cardboard box containing, she informed us, a kitten called Heinz "Like the Ketchup.".

"Hello, my little snookums," she said in baby talk that might have approached cuteness if the intonation hadn't made it sound like Boris Karloff doing baby talk. A giant, orange Boris Karloff.

We waited as she fed and fussed over the cat, who, in the style of all cats, behaved as though he wouldn't have cared if she'd spontaneously combusted and burnt to the ground in front of him. Which, based on the amount of lacquer in her barnet, was not an entirely impossible concept.

The keeping of kittens in the cutlery drawer wasn't the weirdest thing I'd ever seen, but, the feeding complete, Naimee suddenly heaved a sigh, picked the cat up, cuddled it to her monumental bosom, and began sobbing quietly.

I looked at Caz, who raised an eyebrow, as if to say "Here we go again," and, patting the weeping orange giant on the shoulder, made some soothing noises, and guided her to the kitchen table.

"Would you like a cup of tea?" I asked, kicking into standard operating mode in my family whenever someone was crying.

I filled the kettle, as the two women spoke quietly. Eventually, Naimee's quiet sobs faded, as I opened cupboards in search of cups.

"They're in the top one, over the sink," Naimee said, murmuring to Caz about how "Poor Dave. He wasn't a bad 'un, just miserable as fuck. What happened to him."

As Caz attempted to fill Naimee in on the demise of her employee, I pulled open drawers in search of teaspoons, wondering, as I did so, whether I'd uncover, perhaps a terrarium or a basket of puppies.

But apart from the usual drawers full of tea towels, one of napkins and the traditional drawer full of crap that nobody ever throws away – Christmas cracker novelties, tape measures, pens, mismatched cufflinks and a novelty dreidl – I couldn't find the tea spoons.

When Caz got to the bit about the cause of Walker's demise, Naimee renewed her crying, but this time with a little more volume and a sob that made it sound like someone was trying to start up a misfiring Motoguzzi in the kitchen.

Midway through this expression of grief, she stopped dead.

"'Ere," she said, "Why's he poking round my drawers?"

"Teaspoons," I said, all attempts to banish the new mental picture of Naimee Cambell's drawers failing, and was delivered of a sniff, a gesture towards a drawer on the opposite side of the kitchen, and, as I found the spoons and served the tea, Naimee recommenced her sobbing.

At length, it subsided, and, the kitten snoozing in her lap, Naimee sighed heavily, swallowed half a mug of tea in one go, and smiled sadly at me.

"Sorry about that," she said. "it was quite a shock."

"I can imagine," Caz opined, pulling a litre of Courvoisier from her bag, and dropping a triple shot into the teas "For the shock," she said, recapping and replacing the bottle, before gesturing to us to drink up. "I mean: you go away on holiday, and when you get back, well, this. Did you know him well?"

"Know him?" She sighed, started to tear up again, and turned into Sartre. "How well can you ever know anyone?"

Caz nodded sagely, swigged from her tea, and looked to me as if to say well, I tried.

"How long had Dave worked for you?" I asked, trying again.

She puffed out her cheeks, did some mental maths, stroked Heinz, and finally came up with "Forever. He was the first waiter I hired. He'd been working at some fancy Italian place, but it went bust, and he was out of a job. I think the owners had done a runner or something, cos he was owed money, and didn't even have that month's rent, so he was desperate. Asked for an advance, which I would never normally do.

"But I did, in this case. He seemed – I dunno – honourable." She said the word as though it were Unicorn.

"And you know what?" She went on, " He was. He was as honest as the day was long. Which was probably what made him so fucking miserable." She laughed. "I was always getting complaints from customers: Couldn't you get him to smile; He scowled all through the starters. I even had one woman reckon he made her husband cry. Turns out the old man was a right bastard to the wife, so Dave had given him a few home truths."

She gulped back a bubbling sob, smiled sadly at the cat, swigged from her mug of spiked tea, and refocussed on me. "But apart from that – the stuff you learn when you work with people – I hardly knew him."

"Did he have any family?"

She stared vacantly into space for a moment. "Not that I know of. Oh, wait, I think there might have been a sister. I remember him saying, once, that he was going to see his sister." She nodded. "But I have no idea where she lived, or what her name was."

"He didn't really make an effort to make friends. Or to talk much, to be honest," she said. "He just did his job, complained if anyone else wasn't doing theirs, and went home." She sniffed loudly, "I don't even know if there was anyone at home."

"Where did he live?" I asked, and she gave us Dave's address. While I was at it, I asked for the contact details for Darryl Filip and Troy. They might, I figured, know something. Like Pythagoras' Theorem. Unlikely, but we had to try.

CHAPTER TWENTY

The alarm woke me from a dream about Nick's wife.

In the dream, they were dancing a tango together her draped sensuously over him as he dragged her around the floor contemptuously. My view was from a balcony looking down on them, and he would periodically look my way and mouth the word "Help," at me, then, a second later, they would have turned around so that she was facing me, and she would look up, languorously, and smile a smile that was cruel and possessive and cold and final.

It was only as I was rising from the dream that I realised he'd been dancing with Veronica Lake, and wondered how the fuck a late night supper of tuna salad with capers and beans had inspired that little touch.

The air was already hot, so that moving became a chore, but I threw an arm across and slapped the alarm off, then rose to a seated position, and reached for my phone.

I'd switched it off last night after declining an incoming call from Nick for the fifth time, and, on switching it on, I could see that he'd tried to call three more times before switching to texts.

He'd left three voice mails too.

But, really, what could there be to say? I'd dreamed of his wife as a heartless femme fatale, but what did I even know about her? She hadn't existed until two days ago.

I'd been coming out of a long term relationship when I met Nick. I'd spent many years with Robert, only to discover him shagging the window cleaner, and I'd never felt so humiliated, so angry in my life.

The humiliation had been compounded by the triumphalism of the bastard window cleaner, and I'd asked myself for ages afterwards how anyone could take so much pleasure in someone else's unhappiness till I'd realised that Andy – a man so stupid he thought a homeopath was a gay serial killer – was a greedy immature shit.

So here I was: Did I want to be the window cleaner?

I'd dreamed jealously of Nick's still nameless wife, as though the fact he'd kept her hidden was her fault, but it wasn't.

I scanned the texts. The expected entreaties to me. "Please call me." "We need to talk." "This isn't what it looks like," (which made me snort. It looks like you've got a wife, Nick. One you never even mentioned to me. Am I missing any of this?) And finally "I'm going to come round to see you. Please let me explain. You mean a lot to me." (Which, I realised, was not quite I can't live without you.)

I sighed, dropped the phone on the bed, stood, and went to the bathroom.

Nick could wait; I had other fish to fry this morning.

CHAPTER TWENTY-ONE

"Right," I dropped into my chair, and looked around the table.

The ASBO twins – differentiated now by the fact that Dash was sporting a red sunburned forehead – sat facing me, and Caz to my right. Caz, this morning, looked a little more her usual model of cool sophistication, apart, that is, from the vigorous fanning of herself with a copy of Victuallers Monthly.

"Can we make this quick," she begged, "Only if I don't stick my head back in the fridge soon this maquillage will be collecting in a puddle in my décolletage."

The twins looked at each other in confusion.

"It's French," I clarified for them.

"And it means why on earth am I sitting in the superheated kitchen of a dingy pub when everyone I know has gone to Cannes to at least escape from the heat?"

"Innit hot in Cannes?" Dash asked.

"Not on Yuri Arkhipova's yacht, it's not."

The twins nodded, as though all of that made perfect sense now, and I wondered if I was the only one who had no idea who the Fuck Yuri Arkhipova was. "So," I called them back to the matter in hand, "what have you got for me?"

Ray dipped into a bag at his feet, extracted a laptop, and flipped it open . He tapped a few buttons, then looked back up at me. "You wanted to know about the wife. He blew his cheeks out. There's a lot. Wasn't sure how much you wanted, but here goes:

"Sophie Bourne. Born third July 1975 to John and Elsie Barton of 23 Havelock Grove Dagenham. Nothing of note as a kid. She won a few dancing competitions, appeared as Eliza Doolittle, Ophelia and the Virgin Mary in various school productions."

"You got all this from the internet?" I asked.

"Oh, you can find out almost anything from the web, Ray smiled. "Especially if – well, I'll get to that. She finishes school, goes to college, then moves to the US in '95."

"Any particular reason?" I asked. "Was she, for example, following a man?"

Ray shook his head. "Nothing obvious. She arrives there March '95 and there's no sign of a man until she meets Kent Benson who, at that point, is a Movie producer."

"Anything I've heard of?"

"Only the classics. Space Zombies on the Moon was one of his, as was The Caustic Avenger." Ray saw my blank look and shook his head. "Don't worry: I've never heard of them either. They were crap; straight to DVD if they were lucky. Some stuff I read suggested he made films that were designed to lose money in some sort of scam."

"So,2 I drew him back to the point: 'The wife."

"Girlfriend, at that stage. They meet on The Caustic Avenger. She's playing – according to imDb – Hooker #3. And they hit it off. By the time the film's out on DVD, she's moved in with him, and the two are engaged.

"About a year or so later, Kent transitions away from being a Movie producer, and Sophie stops being Hooker #3 and becomes a personal trainer and yoga instructor. Then a year later, they patent The Drastic Band."

"The Drastic Band?" A bell was ringing.

"The Drastic band," Ray repeated. "So called, cos it's cheaper than a gastric band but produces physical changes that are twice as drastic. It's basically an exercise gimmick that uses huge elastic bands to make Fat Yanks sweat more. They could get it online – thanks to Kent and Sophie's infomercials – for one nine nine ninety nine, or four monthly payments of fifty dollars, and to be honest, the idea of paying two hundred notes for a bloody elastic band would probably make me sweat more than the workout."

"I remember this," I said, recalling the tall, slim brunette in the fluorescent one piece swimsuit, her perfect white teeth and a cut glass British accent. "They sold them here too, didn't they?"

Ray nodded. "Within a year or so, the two of them are married, living in a mansion in La Jolla, with a yacht, his 'n' hers Porsches, and a couple of million in the bank."

"I sense there's a 'But,'" I said.

"Not so much a But, more a Uh-Oh. Turns out, Sophie pinched the idea for the Drastic Band. Back when she was a Yoga teacher, she gets friendly with another instructor, name of Julie Roth, who shows her a prototype fitness idea she's been working on: The Fit stretcher.

"It's a fluorescent pink elastic band with various what they called proprietary aspects: basically built in rubber balls that make the thing look like a ball gag, and a 'tension ratchet' that tightens the elasticity and makes the workout harder. It is, basically, the Drastic Band, only simpler. As soon as the millions start pouring in, Julie Roth's on the phone to a lawyer, and the Kent and Sophie show hits a bump.

"Gets better: the case is thrown out of court, and Julie Roth is last seen swearing revenge on the couple. Which she – sort of – gets. 'Cos the attention – the case was all over the American media – stirs up a few lawyers to look into the claims of what they're now calling "The Drastic System," and before you can say Ambulance chaser, the company's been hit with a class action for a few dozen fatties who've been left with minor spinal injuries from using the bloody thing.

"Course, by that time, the papers have had a good old rummage round in both of the proprietors' lives. Turns out Sophie – classy Brit though she appeared – may have done some research for the part of Hooker #3 by actually being one for a few months before she met Kent.

"And Kent – apart from being a movie producer and fitness guru, has been what started off being called an Entrepreneur, and ended up – in a lot of the papers I checked – being called a grifter. He had a string of failed business ventures behind him, and in most cases, he'd walked away with as much cash as he could carry days before the whole thing caved in."

"Charming."

"Then – with everything piling up on them – this happens." Ray dipped back into the bag at his feet, pulled a bunch of printouts from it, and piled them up on the table. They were reproductions of newspaper pages with headlines like Fitness Guru Overboard? Has band Babe Been ABducted ? And Sophie: Cops Are Involved.

"The couple have let the staff go. The housekeeper was the last one, and she was fired a month earlier. Kent Benson spends the evening out with his lawyer, gets home just after midnight and heads to bed. Apparently, the two had separate bedrooms. Next morning, when he gets up, there's no sign of the wife, and the couple's boat – well, the reports say 'boat,' but it looks more like a yacht to me," he held the picture up, and glanced at Caz, who – now our resident expert on the difference between a Yacht and a Boat – nodded

"Not a Superyacht, but more Yacht-ey than Boat-ey" she said using all the technical terms at her disposal.

Ray nodded his agreement with her diagnosis, and continued: "Anyways, next morning, the thing is missing.

"He assumes she's taken it out for the day, and heads off to more business meetings. Except, it subsequently turns out he lies about this, cos he cancels his morning's meetings, and ends up with the first meeting taking place at three that afternoon. What he was doing till then is still a mystery.

"What isn't a mystery is that the boat was found by the coastguard at about 8.30 that evening, by which time Kent was having dinner with an actress called Dina Horn. When he reached home, the police are at the house. The boat's been found alright, but there's nobody on it. Subsequent checks show that Kent made 4 calls that day to Ms Horn, a couple to his lawyer, two to his dentist, and not a single call to his wife, who he hasn't seen since 9am the previous morning.

"The police quickly moved from Sophie fell overboard through Sophie's faked her own disappearance – the life dinghy was missing from the boat – and end up, eventually, with Kent's done the wife in."

"Any specific reason he'd do that? I'm assuming Dinah Horn's not that pretty."

"The money's all gone. All the millions they made on The Drastic Band has pretty much been spent on law suits, lifestyle and pointless efforts to expand into a string of gyms. Old Kent is facing ruin, and Sophie has a life insurance policy worth eight million dollars."

I whistled. "What happened?"

"Nothing much. The police had no body, no signs of foul play, and only circumstantial evidence. They tried hard for a year and then – the web says – the insurance company put the boot into them. They didn't want to pay out, and they wouldn't have had to until 7 years had passed, except – in their eagerness to kick off a murder investigation – the cops got a judge to declare Sophie Benson legally dead after 2 years. Which meant – even though they'd got nothing of any note in those two years – the insurers would have to pay Kent out.

"So the case is brought against Kent, and – as you'd predict – it collapses. There's no proof he murdered the wife. The insurers pay out. And Kent settles into the role of man about town. He seems to have become a bit more respectable since – none of his business ventures have gone tits up lately."

"And here he is, about to marry a millionairess."

"Except someone's trying to put a stop to this by raking up the past."

"What do you think?"

Ray ran his fingers through his hair. "Honestly? I don't know what to think. Do I think he killed her?" He considered this further, then shrugged. "No. It just doesn't fit. He's smart. If the people who called him a conman when the shit was hitting the fan about Drastic band were right, then he's set up all the cons so that he was clearly dirty but untouchable. Why would he murder his wife, create a missing morning – and make no attempt to cover it up, or to create an alibi – and make it so obvious that something was wrong. The whole thing was so botched, I can't imagine it's anything more than what it looks like: She either fell – or jumped – overboard."

"What about the missing lifeboat?"

"He claimed – later – that they'd taken it off for repairs at the end of the previous summer, and lo and behold, it turns up in one of their outhouses, deflated and dusty."

"So if he's innocent, who's trying to stir up the past now?"

"Top of my list would be Julie Roth."

"The supposed original creator of the Drastic Band." I considered this.

"She swore revenge."

"She might have killed Sophie," Caz suggested.

"Possible," Ray agreed, "But if she did, then she's out of the frame for poison pen letters."

I nodded, "I can't see her wanting to bring the whole thing back up if she's guilty of the original murder. So, if not her, then who else? Who'd want Sophie remembered and avenged?"

"Her parents?" Dash offered.

"Dead," Ray answered. "The father died a year into the Drastic millions. Heart attack. Still: Least he got to see his girl making good. The mother died three years later. Stepped in front of a number 43 bus, and was dead before she made it to King Georges."

"Any siblings?" Caz asked.

"None I could find."

"Right, then," I said, "On the assumption that she didn't murder Sophie, start looking for Julie Roth. Is she still in America, or did she recently make a trip to London. Dash: I assume the letters are coming from the UK?"

Dash nodded. "I went round Olivia Wright's yesterday to collect the ones she hadn't already binned, then spent the day legging it all over London talking to mates in the sorting offices."

That explained the sunburn.

"They all came via Mount Pleasant sorting office, which sorts mail for the EC postcode area, the N postcode area, the W1 postcode district and the WC postcode area. Half of London, in other words. Could have come from anywhere in the city.

"There are eight letters and a package they got of printouts from the web. Various news stories of the wife's disappearance.

Dash held up one of the letters. It was the standard Ransom demand style — all blunt threats and cut-out letters from magazines. "They pretty much all say the same thing: Kent doesn't care for you; he's a gold digger who will rip you off and leave you dead."

"So, nothing complimentary then?"

"Well, one or two of them do point out that she's young, beautiful and deserves so much more than," he flicked through the pile, 'An aging wife-killer who only wants your money.'"

"Nice," I murmured. "What about the envelopes: Handwritten?"

Dash shook his head, "All printed labels."

I sighed. This hadn't really got us anywhere.

"There is one thing," Dash said uncertainly. "The spelling."

My nephews were a pair of identical twins, except when it came to their intellects. Ray was smart, but Dash — God bless him — was more, as his teachers used to say, intuitive, which was a polite way of saying not very bright.

Dash held up one of the letters. "It's this one. He doesn't love you. He only cares about the colour of your money."

I looked at the letter. And saw nothing out of the ordinary.

"Well, it's the You, innit," Dash said.

"What's the matter with You?" I asked.

"Nothing. What's the matter with you," He answered, and Caz rolled her eyes, her rate of fanning speeding up so furiously that several of the letters were wafted across the table.

"Boys," she said, "We're basically a spit take away from a Marx brothers. Get to the point before I expire."

Dash shrugged. "Not Y-O-U You." He attempted to clarify, whilst doing no such thing. "I mean the letter 'U' in the word 'Colour.'"

A light began to dawn. "I take it Julie Roth is American?" I asked Ray.

"No idea," he answered, "You didn't ask me to dig into her."

I smiled at his brother. "You should get heat stroke more often, Dash," then turned back to Ray.

"Do some digging. I need to know if Julie Roth is American. Cos whoever wrote those notes spelled Colour in the English way – an American would have dropped the 'U'. And if these letters were written by an English person, the search comes closer to home."

"And we're looking at Kent and Olivia's immediate circle," Caz said, sitting up straighter.

"Exactly," I smiled.

CHAPTER TWENTY-TWO

"Sorry." Elaine hung up the phone and looked sheepishly at me.

We were standing in the hallway, the last of the lunchtime punters were beginning to drift out of the bar, back to offices and shops, the drone of conversations slowly diminishing, and I was on my way out, having finished the lunch service.

"Alright, Elaine?" I was feeling a little brighter. The Nick situation was still hanging around me like a fog, but the developments in the poison pen case as well as my determination to press on in search of Dave Walker's killer had helped the day feel a little more positive.

"Course it's alright." Elaine snapped back. "Why wouldn't it be?"

I paused. "No reason. Listen, Elaine," I joked, I don't mind you using the phone, so long as it's not to call Australia or anything."

Her lip curled. "Mate, it's the twenty first century. I've got a mobile. I don't need to use your shitty landline. Fact, I don't need anything from this craphole."

I glanced at the phone, her hand still resting on the receiver.

"That was a wrong number," she explained.

I let it go; I'd clearly heard a mumbled conversation as I'd been coming down the hallway; something more than a I'm sorry, you have a wrong number. But, right then, I didn't care.

"Well I'm going out," I advised, sweeping past her, "Y'know" In case anyone needs me."

"I'll update fucking Interpol," she shrugged, sucking her teeth and heading off to the kitchen. "Fucking loser."

I made a mental note to dock her wages for insubordination, then realised that – on Chopper's instructions – we weren't paying her, and considered for a moment whether this fact might not be linked to her not so subtle workplace issues.

I skipped out the back door, and round to the front of the pub, then crossed the street, the heat of the pavement burning through the soles of my All Stars, and headed up to Number Fifty Three.

From inside, I could hear the high whine of a buzz saw, and a regular banging as the builders got on with refitting Mike Green's shop. The door was open, a steady stream of airborne sawdust and an oven-like heat streaming from the interior along with the tinny noise of a radio blasting pop music, and a stream of obscenities from what sounded like a plumber with issues.

"Sodding pump aint gonna fit there," he was saying. "You do that and the bastard thing'll cave in."

"Hello." I knocked on the open door, and, raising my voice, called again. "Anyone home?"

"Sorry mate, we're closed," came a voice from within.

I was just about to say that I was looking for Mike Green when he appeared through the dust. "Danny! Nice to see you. What can I do for you?"

I smiled, stepping into the store. "Just thought I'd pop over and say hello."

On the opposite side of the room, the plumber was wrestling with what looked like an enormous Espresso machine, trying to fix it to a counter on the back wall, whilst hooking up the various water supply pipes.

"That looks scary," I said.

Mike smiled at me, then gave me a hug, and put his arm around me.

"Welcome to 'Greens,' he said 'Fashion for the discerning man.' And what does a discerning man want when he's choosing next seasons' perfect suit more than a nice blast of Espresso. If Colin can ever get the bloody machine plumbed in. How are you doing? What with the," he made a gesture intended, I assumed, to suggest the bludgeoning of one of my temporary staff.

I shrugged. "Well as can be expected, I think. So it's a menswear store. The mystery is solved."

"No mystery," he smiled, "I've always wanted to run a clothes shop. Was my dream as a kid, though I could do without trying to do a refurb in the middle of a heatwave."

"When you due to open?" I asked.

Mike laughed, a full open laugh, and spread his arms wide, the movement straining his T-shirt across his chest. "Sometime in the next century, it feels like. Seriously?" He smiled, putting his arm back around my shoulders and guiding me back towards the door of the shop, "Due to be ready by the end of August so I can open in Mid-September. I'll put something aside for you." He stepped back, looked me up and down, "What are you? A 38 waist?"

I blushed, "I'm a 34," I said, deciding I was off carbs. For life.

Mike smiled, "Well, Mr 34, what are you up to this evening? Fancy a pint?"

I shook my head, gesturing up the street, "I've got a pub to run."

"You're blowing me out?" He asked. "Nobody ever blows me out."

"Sorry," I said, and I really was. "Maybe some other night."

Mike smiled, and nodded, "Some other night would be great," and, sensing that I was being dismissed, I made my excuses and left.

The abrupt ending of the conversation – the entire way, in fact, that Mike had taken me physically and steered me from the shop in such a way that I'd seen nothing of the interior suddenly struck me as a little odd.

He'd seemed so excited and proud of the shop the day before, and yet here he was, eager not to show me around, to be rid of me.

He's got a lot to be getting on with, I rationalised as I strolled back towards the Marq.

And yet, when I looked over my shoulder, rather than getting on with whatever he had to do, Mike was standing in the doorway of the shop, his arms crossed.

He waved at me.

I waved back and, puzzled, returned to the pub.

CHAPTER TWENTY-THREE

"Caz, have I put on weight?" I asked.

"Hmm?" Caz finished adjusting her boobs, spritzed them with Jo Malone Avocado and Guava mist, and eyed me up and down. "Darling, you're sylph-like. Positively emaciated," she opined, dropping the scent back into her handbag.

I spread my arms wide. "What waist size am I?"

"You're a thirty three thirty four," she said immediately, "Though if we're talking Versace, you'd be a forty three, but don't take that personally. Why do you ask?"

"You sure about the waist size?" I asked.

"Sweetheart, there isn't a woman alive who has eyed up more men in trousers. I know a thirty-three thirty-four when I see one."

"Just wanted to be sure. Oh, and Caz: The left one's dropped. Again."

"Shit!" she jiggled her boobs. "This is the last time I wear high street underwear. It couldn't support helium. So, how long are we planning on waiting here?"

Here was the The Nifty Nosh, Café and Sausage Bar (I kid you not) in a street in west London that was bordered by the Talgarth road, Olympia and various railway sidings. Earlier that day, we'd visited Fillip and Troy, the massage therapist and actor, who lived together "But not," Troy had been keen to make clear, "Together," in a flat in Archway, "It's actually Highgate borders," Fillip had stressed, as though saying the word Highgate enough would move the property, or change the geography of London itself.

As we'd sat in their tiny dim kitchen, Troy had pulled out his phone and started flicking through Grindr. "Ignore me," he said, "I'm doing research for a role."

Fillip had tittered, "Yes, dear; we know exactly what roll you're researching for," and a spot of mild bickering had ensued before we'd managed to pull them back to the point in hand.

From the two, we'd learned little other than that, as Troy put it, "Walker was a miserable old bugger at the best of times, but he didn't deserve murdering."

This was a fact we were all agreed on.

From Fillip, we'd gleaned the fact that — after Desmond Everett threw a drink over Anthony, Fil saw Anthony behaving very furtively in the hallway.

"He was supposed to be drying himself up," Fillip had disclosed, leaning in as though he were gossiping over a fence, "But he looked to me like he was looking for someone back there."

At this, Troy had looked up from his Grindr research, and said, "Well that James Kane was the same. Poking around the kitchen looking for — he said — a glass of water; having just walked out of a bar with a whole crate of the stuff," before giving us a nod and a wink, both of which were heavy with purpose, and telling us that the address we had for Darryl O'Connor was out of date. "Oh she's moved up in the world," he'd explained, scribbling out the new address. "All that modelling and," he raised an eyebrow, "Personal training, seems to be really paying off."

We'd already ascertained that Darryl wasn't at home, and I'd suggested that, rather than hang around outside his flat awaiting his return, and risking heatstroke, we'd retire to the Nifty Nosh for a milk shake and a salad.

I'd been standing at the bar, halfway through the Milk shake (Banana Peanut butter, since you ask) when waist size had popped into my head.

"Oh," I nodded through the window, and dropped a tenner on the bar for our drinks. "Looks like he's home."

O'Carroll was walking towards us, his gym bag slung casually over one shoulder, a bright red baseball cap – the peak pointing backwards – jammed onto his head. His eyes – which might have been shaded by the baseball cap if he'd been wearing it properly – were covered, instead by a pair of wayfarer sunglasses.

"OK," Caz said as we hustled out, "How d'you want to play this?"

"Well, I'll ask some questions, and you just back me up."

She stopped dead. "That's it? I mean: That's your plan?"

"Caz, he's a muscle Mary with half a brain cell. I'm not expecting much."

"Oh dear, sweetheart, you really need to get that Gaydar recalibrated," she smirked, readjusting The Girls, and making towards O'Carroll's flat.

The Himbo had already mounted the stairs to his front door, and was inserting a key into the lock by the time we'd crossed the street. Caz called from the pavement, and he turned, a frown on his face.

He looked down on us, and the scowl deepened. Then, a smile slowly spreading on his face, an eyebrow was raised above the wayfarer frames, and the glasses were removed.

It was only later, of course, that I realised his vantage point allowed him a clear and uninterrupted view of Lady Caroline De Montfort's cleavage.

"Hi Darryl," I stepped forward, and the black look returned.

"You? What d'you want?"

"A few minutes of your time," Caz answered for me, moving her shoulders in such a way that her persuasive charms were hoiked even further upwards.

"What about?" he demanded, and I thought: we'd like to talk to you about global warming, Jesus and the price of property in Kuala Lumpur. What the fuck do you think we want to talk to you about?

But instead, I smiled in what I hoped was a calming fashion, and said "We wanted to talk to you about Dave."

The shifty look crossed his face, and –thought it might have been my imagination – he glanced surreptitiously around, as though to ensure nobody had overheard my remark.

"You'd better come in, so," he said, opening the door.

The flat was on the third floor. There was no lift, and O'Carroll – heavy looking gym bag still slung casually over his shoulder – took the steps two at a time, as though he were out for a Sunday stroll across the bogs of Connemara. If there were bogs in Connemara. And if they were hilly instead of flat.

Whatever: Darryl bounded upwards, and, behind him, Caz and I trudged, every landing feeling like we'd achieved another plateau in a Himalayan ascent.

"I am not," Caz intoned at one stage, "A fan of stairs." The phrase should have been comic, but, in the airless stiflingly hot stairwell, the scent of cabbage and takeaway Chinese food seeming to leach from the 1970's papered walls, I knew exactly what she meant.

Eventually, we made the summit, and I looked around for a Union Jack to plant on the landing. Finding none, we followed – trying not to gasp for air or look in any way out of shape – O'Carroll into what felt like a middle aged college professor's apartment. The long hallway had, apart from a shoe rack filled with a mixture of brogues and trainers, a long book case filled with well-thumbed books.

I glanced at Darryl, adjusting my prejudices. He reads? Then I glanced at the titles, and my prejudices slid slightly back: Musculoskeletal development, Everything you ever wanted to know about Pecs (but were afraid to ask), Fists of Fury; Buns of Steel, Andy McNab's Operation Deton8 and Frat House Fury.

I followed O'Carroll into his living room.

The room was small, but had the highest ceilings I'd ever seen. Light streamed in from two huge windows – one of which was opened a crack to allow – I assumed – a breeze to cool the room. Instead, all it had done was allow the oppressive heat from outside to seep inside.

The space was dominated by a huge black and white portrait of Darryl himself. Naked, oiled up, and with almost every muscle he had shadowed and contrasted for the viewers' pleasure.

Since – I assumed – he lived here alone, that viewer – more often than not – would be O'Carroll himself.

Still, as Caz is always telling me. If you've got it, flaunt it.

"So," Darryl dropped the gym bag on the floor, pulled the baseball cap from his head, and chucked it on to the immaculate white sofa in the corner, and, arms crossed (all the better to display his bulging biceps) tore his gaze from Caz's cleavage, turned to face me, and said. "What's this all about, then?"

"We're looking into Dave Walker's death," Caz said, tilting her head coquettishly. "And wondered if you could help us?"

"Me?" He frowned again, and I had to admit that he had an air of intelligence when he did that – as though he were contemplating eternal mysteries, instead of trying to understand why we thought he could help us in our enquiries. "Sure, I've already told the police everything I saw that day. Why would you two be nosing around in it?"

Caz looked at me. Over to you, Sherlock, her glance said.

"We're just trying to get a feeling for how Dave was that day," I said. "He seemed a little upset – quite snappy with people."

O'Carroll snorted, turned his back on us, and headed to the kitchen.

We followed.

"That," he said, as he pulled from the freezer a zip lock bag of gunk, and dumped it into a blender, "Was his normal attitude."

"So there was nothing unusual about the day? Nothing strange about his behaviour?"

Darryl shook his head, flipped the switch on the blender, and the sound of a small aircraft taking off filled the tiny kitchen.

"Well," he said, once the concoction had been blended and he was pouring it into a glass, "There was the phone call. That was a bit odd."

"Phone call?" I prompted.

"I was outside, having a fag. I tend not to eat when I'm coming up on a modelling job. Or drink. Well, to be honest, apart from smoking and lifting, I don't do much before a shoot, cos it just bloats ye, you know? I mean, I only took the job at your place as a favour."

"I'm honoured," I murmured with, I hoped the correct level of obvious sarcasm.

"No, I mean: Naimee was short a hand. Some other fella dropped out and she was off on holidays so she didn't have time to find anyone. So, eventually, I said I'd do it. I figured I'd still have time to do some lifting that night, and I'd get some smokes in any ways. Dehydrates you, you see. Plumps out the muscle tone, and the veins."

"Lovely," Caz commented drily. "So," she pulled him back on track, "You were outside having a cigarette…"

Darryl stared at her, as though puzzled by the sudden shift away from his beauty regime, and it took a moment for him to remake the connection. Then, he nodded. "Yeah, that's right. So I slip outside, and Dave's standing round the corner on the main road. At first, I thought he was talking to himself. I mean, at his age…"

I bristled. "He was mid-forties," I said, the unspoken *it's coming to us all, mate* hanging in the air between us.

"I know," the Himbo replied. "You'd think – by that age – people shouldn't have to work like that. I mean, I think it affects their minds, sometimes."

"He was a waiter," Caz interjected. "It's hardly Sulphur mining up the Zambezi."

Darryl blinked, pulled the constipated face that told me he was deciphering Caz's latest assault on his intelligence, and, finally, sniggered. "Go on!" he replied, pointing his finger at Caz as if to say I've got your number.

I despaired. "So, he wasn't talking to himself…"

"No," he reconnected faster this time; I guess because he hadn't had to end the train of thought that was all about himself. "He was on the phone wasn't he?"

I don't know," I replied, "Was he?"

"He was."

I sighed. "And what, if you can recall, was he saying?"

"Well," Darryl slid in to us, his voice dropping to a conspiratorial whisper, "He was saying. 'It'll be alright, I promise,' then he listened, then he went 'Look, don't cry; I'll deal with it. I'll make it alright. I promise.'" Darryl paused, considered what he'd just reported, and nodded. "I couldn't be sure, but I got the feeling that the person on the other end of the line was upset."

"Your empathy astounds me," Caz murmured. Darryl acknowledged what he clearly assumed was a compliment by nodding graciously and saying that it was all down to diet.

"Well," Darryl finished, "He went on for a bit, said some stuff like 'She doesn't need to know yet,' and 'I'll make it right,' and then he hung up. When he came round the corner and found me halfway through me Marlboro he jumped like a scalded cat and got all shirty about me eavesdropping. I told him straight: I don't need to eavesdrop. I can squat with twice my own body weight and bench press a pony; but I don't think he was paying much attention. Silly bastard just called me a Cretin. I mean: Do I even look Greek?"

CHAPTER TWENTY-FOUR

And that, pretty much, was that.

We hailed a taxi, and were on our way back to The Marq when it hit me.

"Where'd the phone go?"

"The phone?" Caz, windows wound down and hands hooked behind her head to enjoy the breeze, turned her head towards me.

"Dave's phone. The Himbos took the piss out of him for not being able to answer it. Then Darryl overheard him talking on it."

Caz dropped her hands into her lap, and resumed her normal ladylike demeanour. "And your point is?"

"Well, he didn't have a mobile on him when he was found, Caz. So where did that go?"

"Are you sure the police didn't find it?"

I shook my head. "I didn't see them leave with anything more than a body."

"Perhaps Nick would know," she murmured suggestively.

"Forget it, Caz; I'm not talking to him."

"Well, I could call and..."

"Caz: He's married. With wife. And – for all I know – with child."

Caz – rooting now in her capacious handbag – looked up at me and smiled the sort of pitying smile she usually reserved for those tragic enough to try to pair McQueen with Monsoon. "Oh sweetheart, this whole married to a woman thing: it just doesn't add up." She jerked her head in the general direction of Olympia. "Your Gaydar may be perpetually out of whack, but d'you really think I wouldn't have noticed if there was a real life heterosexual within sniffing distance? I mean, I'm basically the child catcher, only for straight men of marriageable age."

"It doesn't matter. He lied."

She'd resumed her exertions within the depth of her Gladstone. This time, she didn't even look up, merely instructed me in a detached tone. "Speak to him," she repeated. "For me," looking up at last, as she handed me an expertly mixed gin & tonic, the cucumber slice carved expertly into a heart shape.

"I can't," I admitted. "Not yet."

"Well if you won't," she announced, "I'm going to call and ask if they found the phone."

I sighed. I really didn't want Caz talking to Nick. Christ alone knew what they'd cook up between them. "Ok," I said, "I'll call him later."

"Now," she pressed, slugging from her gin.

"Not now, Caz. He'll be on duty. I'll call later."

"Promise?"

"Cross my cold dark heart," I said, crunching an ice cube between my teeth and wondering how the fuck she'd kept ice cold in a handbag during this heatwave.

"Addaboy," Caz grinned the gently victorious smile she always smiled when she'd completely levelled my resistance. "Chin chin!"

"What are we doing tonight?"

"Ah," she examined her manicure. "I'm off out tonight."

"Out?"

"Yes," she bristled, "And you don't have to say it like you're Anne Franks' mother. I'm going to see Lucy. My friend Lucy Fawcett-Jones. She's in hospital."

I immediately felt guilty, and apologised.

"Oh it's nothing serious. She's just having her lips redone. They went wrong last time and she ended up looking like some sort of deranged clown, so the surgeons are redoing them gratis. But I should at least pop in and say hello."

She was up to something, I knew. There was way too much detail for that story to have been true. But I didn't care: If Caz went out, I'd have some time this evening to call Nick. Much as I dreaded the conversation – and much as I hated admitting that Caz was right – I needed to know what was going on.

CHAPTER TWENTY-FIVE

"Whatever you're looking for is not going to be in there."

Elaine Falzone leapt a good half inch in the air and shot me a look of pure venom. "I was just tidying up," she said, though it would have been slightly more believable if this angelic looking monster had said she was just looking for the resting place of the Holy Grail.

"Yeah," I said. "Thanks for the tidying, but I need to make a call." I waved my mobile in her general direction.

"Well don't let me stop you," she said, cracking open another cupboard door and attempting to peek surreptitiously inside it, "I'll keep quiet and just get on with this."

"Elaine, I've no idea what this is, but I want some privacy. So hop it."

She rolled her eyes. "God, you are so fucking Gay," she whined, as she stropped out of the room, slamming the door behind her.

"And don't you forget it," I hollered after her, whilst still wondering what on earth she had – clearly – been looking for.

I sat at the table, laid my phone flat before me, and stared at it.

Nick and I had seemed so happy. Yes, I knew that that was the usual mantra of the romantically abandoned. Lord knows I knew it: I'd already sung that song a little over a year previously, when I'd arrived home to find my partner of many years playing hide the squeegee with the window cleaner. The sense of betrayal had fought with the horror that I'd been paying full price for the windows for ages, when Robert should, by rights, have been able to negotiate me a discount, at the very least.

And I'd sworn that I wouldn't ever get that close to anyone. That I'd keep Nick at arm's length, not ever give him the ability to hurt me.

Yet here I was. Not heartbroken; I'd been heart broken, and I knew how it felt: I knew the feeling of having all the oxygen in the world sucked out so you couldn't breathe, and weren't even sure if you wanted to. Of feeling – literally – a lump in your chest, as though the very heart had split into two pieces, and each were shifting independently around the cavity.

What I felt now was heart sick.

Because, despite what I'd told myself, I had trusted Nick. I had let myself imagine a future with him. I'd dreamed I knew him, and could do these things safe in the knowledge that he and I understood each other.

I didn't want to call him.

I didn't want to open the door and be hurt again. I didn't want him to persuade me there was a rational explanation to all of this, that I was being silly, that we could carry on as before, and yet – at the same time – that was exactly what I wanted him to do.

But I'd promised Caz I'd call him, and I wanted to know what was happening with the Dave Walker case.

So I picked up the phone, and hit dial.

The ring tone sounded once, twice, and then he answered.

"Danny." No 'Hi,' or "Hey Danny.' No cheery bright tone, just a rather flat stressed sounding voice on the end of the line.

My heart sank. "Hey Nick," I said, injecting – without meaning to – a bright and breezy tone.

"I need to talk to you," he said. "I'm sorry you had to hear… what you heard the other day. I wanted to tell you myself."

"But you didn't."

"No." There was a pause, as though he were searching for the right words, and then I heard it: a woman's voice. Clearly, distinctly, his wife's voice.

"Nicholas!" It called, seeming, almost, to be in the same room as he.

"Just a minute," he said, and I wasn't sure if he was saying it to me or to her. Then I heard the sound of his hand covering the mouthpiece on the phone, and the muffled sound of his voice – too compressed for me to make out the words, but clearly talking to her.

There was another silence, and then a higher pitched voice spoke.

"Listen," he said as soon as his hand was removed from the mouthpiece, "None of this is what you think. But I can't explain it right now."

"Explain it?" I wanted to reach through the phone and slap him solidly. "It doesn't need explaining, Nicholas. I'm not so stupid that I need this explained to me. I understand."

"No," he butted in, "You don't. You couldn't. It's complicated," he said, reverting to the relationship status of the very simple. Things, in my experience, are really rarely complicated. Unless they start to get duplicitous. Then, the act of remembering which lie you told last tends to complicate things.

"Listen," I said, "I don't want to argue. And I don't want your explanations."

He was silent. Waiting. "Then what," he finally said, "Do you want?"

"I want an update. On the Dave Walker investigation."

"You want... what?" He asked, sounding both confused and upset.

"I want to know if you have any leads, any suggested approaches. I want to know, first off, if you found a mobile phone on the victim?"

"A phone? You..? Listen, Danny, I need to explain this to you. But I need to do it to your face. This isn't the way to do it."

"Oh, Jesus," I moaned. "Listen, Nick, I get it: It's complicated. You're married, but you're still fond of me."

"No!" he called, "That's not it. Well, I mean, it is it, but there's more to it."

"There always is." I took a deep breath, resisted the urge to beg him to explain it to me, and said, instead: "So, did you find a phone?"

"No," he was still exasperated, but I no longer cared. I was heartsick, and the last thing I needed was to give him the chance to twist the knife even further.

"Listen, Danny: Why are you asking me questions about this investigation? We're all over it."

"Got any suspects?" I asked.

"Nothing yet, but I really don't want you getting involved. Whoever did this is a sick puppy, and I don't want you in danger."

"So nothing, then?" I said.

"Danny, whoever killed Walker is clearly dangerous. Please don't poke around in this. Even if you don't care about us any more, I still care deeply about you, and I don't want you hurt."

But he had hurt me. And he hadn't said Love. He'd said Care Deeply, but what did that mean? That was the sort of language that bet-hedging politicians use.

"I'm not Poking around," I said, "I'm just taking a look. I'm good at that, remember. Though clearly not that good, I mean: I failed to spot you were married."

I hadn't meant to say it; it had slipped out. But there it was.

"I'm so sorry," he said, again. "I promise it's not like it looks. When can I see you? I have to explain this to you properly."

I sighed. I wanted this explained. I wanted this to be all the way it had been – even if how it had been was little more than the slow waltz of two people who seemed unwilling or (it now seemed) unable to commit to anything more than a tentative arrangement.

And then, in the instant it took me to make my mind up, the spell was broken by a laugh. Her laugh. Ringing in the room, as though she'd never left, and was finding the scene too funny for words.

And my mind was made up.

"Thanks for the update, Nick," I said, and ended the call.

In seconds, he was calling me back. I let the call go to voice mail, then deleted – unheard – the message he'd left.

Then I called Mike Green. "Hey Mike," I said, forcing brightness back into my voice, "Did you still want to go for that drink you mentioned?"

I paused, listened to his voice brighten, and – my depression already lifting – smiled. "Want to meet me here about seven?"

CHAPTER TWENTY-SIX

"This would have been empty, when I was a kid," I said, gesturing over my pint at the mass of drinkers thronging the riverbank.

The Founders Arms was a round, sixties construct dumped – like a badly designed spaceship – on the south bank between a squat block of flats and the Thames. When I was younger, the area – slowly rising from decades of seemingly terminal decline – was still a far from desirable hangout, and yet, tonight, it was heaving with city workers, builders, tourists, locals, all milling around, all smiling, a mass of people enjoying the summer evening, shimmering, golden in the setting sun.

"Well, that's enough to get anyone across the river," Mike said, gesturing at the view across the wide low Thames.

The City of London – from the dome of Saint Pauls to the Ultra-modern SwissRe Gherkin building was slowly fading – almost as we watched - from smoky purple to sepia to flaming gold.

"Amazing that all the people who want to live over there get no view, and end up coming over here to see the beauty they ignore all day," he said, sipping from his pint. "Thank God for gentrification," he said.

"You say that like it's a good thing," I replied.

"Well isn't it? You said yourself: this used to be a wasteland, and now it's moving from being a no-go area to being one that decent people actually want to be in."

"But what about the people who already lived here? They were – are – decent too. Just," I shrugged, "Poorer. It wasn't a no-go area for them; it was their home."

Mike shrugged, "Yeah, but they sat there and let it crumble. Everything ends, and out of the ashes of the ruins, something better rises."

Heavy, I thought, but aloud I said, "So what ashes did you rise from?"

Mike stared into the distance, his pint halfway between the table and his lips. "I rose," he said after a pause, "From the ashes of Doctor Simon Doherty." He caught my puzzled look, and smiled. "I was with Simon for five years, and at the end of it, we were both burned out, in every way."

"I know that story," I murmured, and swigged from my pint as a way of encouraging Mike to go on with his story.

"The first couple of years were fine, but then things changed. Simon became emotionally cold, but I was so in love with him that I didn't want to see it.

"By the time he became physically violent, I was too far gone to be able to do anything about it. I figured I'd got what I deserved."

"Jesus."

Mike sighed, smiled, and sipped from his drink. "It ended well," he said, winking at me. "Eventually, I realised I was worth more. So I cashed in my pension and made the move from Manchester."

He drained his pint, and waved at the crowd, – "Though, if I'd known it'd be like this, I might have thought twice."

"Like what?"

"This crowded. I know: now, I sound like I'm doing a Northern Yokel impersonation. I've been to cities before, but it's different here. It's all so big, so impersonal. Nobody knows you. Most people don't want to know you."

I do, I wanted to say. I want to know you. Then I remembered that the wheel – the place Nick had taken me for our first date – was just a little further along the river, and I was no longer sure what I wanted.

"I mean, look at that lot," Mike continued. "A sea – no, an ocean – of interchangeable nobodies. Line em up, and half of 'em you'd never tell from the other half. All the builders in their overalls, all seem interchangeable, the city boys in their shirts and slacks: each looking, from here, exactly like the others. They make you feel like leaving, before you're as dead as them."

"Dead?" The word came out a little too sharply. Mike looked at me and made an apologetic face.

"Sorry. Forgot."

I waved his apology aside, "What do you mean by 'dead'?"

"Well, only that, back home, I was someone; not anyone that everyone knew, but there were faces and people and things you knew, and there were different levels, and you could have a good life, and – when Simon wasn't being punchy - feel good about yourself being in one of those levels. But here the place feels like you're either a Somebody, or you're a Nobody. And if you're no one, you might as well be dead."

I looked out at the smiling mass of people enjoying the summer, shimmering, golden in the setting sun, and I didn't feel like a nobody. "I don't see that," I said. "And I hope you'll learn to see what I see. I hope you stay."

"What do you see?" Mike asked.

"I know what you mean: Any city can make you feel alone and small and afraid, but when I look out here – especially on a night like tonight – I don't see an army of nobodies. I don't see the dead. I see the survivors; the ones who stayed and fought and won, and who are entitled to the spoils."

"Anyone ever tell you you're a poet?" Mike Green asked me, a smile hovering gently over his lips.

"Not lately," I answered, as the sun sank lower in the sky.

CHAPTER TWENTY-SEVEN

She answered on the fifth ring, and her voice was already thick with sleep. "This better be good..."

I was stunned for a moment. "Are you in bed?"

"Danny," Caz growled, "This had better be important."

"What are you doing in bed? You never go to bed before three A.M.. Are you sick?"

"No, I'm tired." She seemed to rouse herself, "What's up?"

"I think we've got it all wrong," I said.

"Have you been drinking?"

"No.... Yes, but just a few pints. And a bottle of wine with dinner. Oh, and a cognac after dinner."

"Good boy. But that still doesn't explain why you're calling me at this ungodly hour."

"It's just gone One O'clock, Caz."

"Has it? I thought it was later."

I checked my watch. "Well, it's not. And you need to get up, and come over here."

"Why? Because we've got it all wrong?"

"Exactly."

"Dearest, the history of humanity is a series of misconceptions and misunderstandings. If I rose from my couch every time we had it wrong, I'd rarely sleep. What, in particular, have we messed up this time."

"Dave Walker's murder," I said, and I could hear her sitting up in bed, a tiny, almost inaudible cough showing that she'd finally come fully awake.

"Go on," she said.

"We've been asking the same question that everyone has," I said.

"Which is what? Why you're calling me at One A.M.?"

"That's not late. And besides," I suddenly remembered, "I thought you were going out tonight."

"I was. I did. But now I'm home, and I'm tired; this heat's got me exhausted. So what's this question everyone's asking?"

"Well, I've just been out with Mike, and that's where the idea came to me."

I was about to launch into the detailed rationale behind my theory, when she stopped me. "You've been what?"

"Out. For dinner. With Mike. The guy from the shop a few doors up."

"Yes," she said, in the tone I liked to refer to as her Headmistress voice. It usually indicated a stiff word was approaching. "Danny, Have you spoken to Nick yet?"

"What's there to speak about? He's married. To a woman. He has a wife, Caz. What do you want me to say to him? Anything else slipped your mind?"

She sighed. "Give him a chance, Danny. Give him a chance to explain why he didn't mention it."

"I can't," I answered.

"Call him Danny. Give him the chance to explain. If nothing, you can at least make him squirm."

I sighed. Should I tell her I already had? Should I explain how the call had been stilted, confusing and – ultimately – humiliating?

No, I decided. I shouldn't. "I'll think about it," I said.

"Good." I could hear her smile from here. The Headmistress tone was dropped. "So tell me: what question is everyone asking?"

"Why anyone would kill Dave," I answered.

"And what question," she asked, "Should we all have been asking?"

"Simple," I answered, "Why did nobody try to kill Anthony Taylor?"

There was silence from the other end of the line.

"Hello?" I called. "You still there?"

"That," she finally said, "Is not funny."

"But think about it, Caz: From the moment Taylor turned up, he was antagonistic, and he was already clearly out of favour with half the people there. You've gone quiet again," I said.

"I'm thinking," Caz replied. "There were a few punches thrown at him."

"And a drink," I reminded her. "And yet – with such an obvious target in the room – someone brains poor average Dave."

"Exactly," she said. "They brained Dave. So what's this got to do with Tony Taylor?"

"What do waiters usually wear?" I asked, remembering the rows of city boys in their identikit shirts and trousers.

Caz sighed. "I don't know: White shirts? Black trousers? Dark jackets?"

"And what do mourners – at a funeral – wear?" I asked.

More silence, then: "Don't go to bed," Caz said. "I'm coming over."

CHAPTER TWENTY-EIGHT

"OK." Caz put the two mugs of coffee on the table, dolloped a slug of cognac into each, and settled herself opposite me.

"I can't believe you didn't tell me this before," I said.

"Well it didn't seem relevant," she said. "And besides, I sort of assumed you knew."

"Knew? How would I know?"

"Well, dearest, it's Tony Taylor. I thought everyone knew about Tony Taylor."

"Everyone in your world, maybe, but Caz," I swept an arm to indicate the grimy kitchen of The Marq, looking grubbier and even more Victorian in the pale blue light of early morning.

We'd sat up all night, walking through the day of Dave Walker's murder, and it hadn't taken long for Caz to admit that – when she was younger – she'd run in Anthony Taylor's circle, and that – if we were looking for reasons to kill someone – Taylor did seem to have more people with motive than poor Dave.

"He's Olivia Wright's second cousin," Caz explained, "And should have been in line for a good chunk of old Maggie's cash. But word on the street…"

"By which," I said, "I assume you mean Sloane Street."

She ignored me, "Is that he was basically disinherited some years back."

I perked up, "Why would he have been disinherited?"

"Because Tony Taylor," Caz said, with what seemed like an impolite, level of enjoyment, "Is what used – in Victorian Melodrama – to be called a thoroughly bad 'un."

"Cor guvnor, strike a light," I muttered. "Go on."

"Well," Caz sipped her coffee, pulled a face, dropped another ounce of Hennessey into the mug, sipped again, and – satisfied this time by the ratio of coffee to grape alcohol – launched into her potted history of Anthony Taylor.

"His mother died while he was still a child, and his father – the typical stiff upper lip Englishman – sent him away to school and had as little to do with him as possible. Daddy moved to L.A. as far as I can recall, and proceeded to work his way through a selection of starlets and tarts whilst somewhat quickly drinking himself to death.

"Tony, meanwhile, either fled or was expelled from almost every single school and university he attended.

"Through the whole thing, the only constant in his life was Maggie Wright. Maggie tried to take Tony under her wing, but things just went from bad to worse."

I swigged my own coffee, pulled a face of my own (almost neat coffee-infused alcohol not being my favourite beverage at five A.M.) and gestured at her to go on.

Caz sighed, as though saddened by what she was about to tell me. "He got into drugs – well, it seemed obvious that he would eventually – and there were more scrapes with the law. Which Maggie always sorted. Thing is, for all the perception of her as a gorgon, Maggie Wright had both a soft spot for Tony, and a fiercely loyal streak."

Caz sipped from the mug, considering what I'd just said. Outside, the sound of a truck rumbling slowly down the street broke the silence of the morning. The kitchen felt – for the first time in weeks – almost cool, but I knew that, once the sun came up, the heat would quickly build, until the place would be as unbearably hot as it had been since May.

"There was a girl," she said at length. "Some convent girl who'd gone into modelling – all blonde and floaty. You know the sort. And she died. Heroin. Which, the rumour mill said, had been purchased for her by Tony."

"Jesus." I swigged the brandy.

"And a restaurant – Gambera – the Italian one that had London talking for a whole year. The chef was some wunderkind, it came close to Michelin status. It should have been a marriage made in heaven: Tony loved having fun and dining out, and he had lots of very wealthy friends who loved same.

"Sadly, neither Tony nor the wunderkind had a clue about the financial aspects of running a business, and in short order they bankrupted the restaurant. The chef killed himself."

I slugged my booze wordlessly this time, then, after a silence, found the words. "What a charmer," I said, "I can see why Taylor would be written out of the will."

Caz smiled sadly and shook her head, "People don't disinherit their relatives because a silly girl overdosed, or a highly-strung chef hanged himself. Tony was around those people, and his life was a mess, but they did what they did of their own volition, Danny."

I wasn't sure I agreed with her, but I said "So why was he disinherited?"

"Because, after the failure of everything he'd put his heart into for a whole year, he started drinking heavily- he'd given up drugs after the model's death, but replaced them with booze. And then, one night, after a bottle of scotch and several gins, he ran over a cyclist.

"The girl was killed instantly. He should have gone to prison for a long time, but Maggie Wright pulled out the big guns. The girl had had no lights or viz jacket. She was basically invisible.

"The judge gave him two years. He served nine months, and when he got out, Maggie sent him off to New Zealand. I heard that he gets a monthly stipend – enough to live on, nowhere near enough to drink or drug on – and has his rent paid. But not a penny coming to him from the estate."

"So why did he come back?" I wondered.

"Maggie," Caz said simply.

"Meaning?"

"He stayed away because Maggie told him to. Because to return would have meant upsetting her, and —despite all his bravado – I think he actually cared for her. But once she was gone, there was nothing stopping him from coming home."

"And within a couple of hours of his arriving back in the country," I said, "A man dressed like him – in a white shirt, black trousers and black brogues – is bludgeoned from behind."

"You think Tony was the target, don't you?"

I nodded. "Maybe Reid was right: Dave Walker was a nobody. There was no obvious reason why anyone in the room would have a reason to kill him, but Anthony Taylor…"

"So what do we do?"

"We press Restart," I said. "We step away from the Himbos and anyone linked to Dave Walker, and we look at the people who might have had a reason for wanting to kill Anthony Taylor."

"And what about Tony?" Caz asked.

"What d'you mean?" I said, wondering when she'd gotten so matey with Taylor that she'd started referring to him as Tony.

"Well if someone intended to kill him," she said, "They failed. Which means they might try again."

"We'll need to warn him," I agreed.

Caz emptied her mug in one gulp. "I'll find out where he's staying. What are you going to do?"

"I'm going to use the one way in I have: Olivia Wrights Poison pen writer. That'll get me in to the room, and we'll see what we can find from there."

"Shouldn't we tell the police?"

"No." I was emphatic. "All we have so far is a theory. We need something more solid. Then, we can go to the police."

Caz shook her head worriedly. "Are you sure about this, Danny? I mean, would Nick want you involved in this case?"

"Nick," I informed her, "Is not the boss of me. Now, let's get the lunch service sorted, you can find out where Taylor is staying, then I'll give the Wright-Benson household a bell and tell 'em we're coming round to talk threatening letters."

CHAPTER TWENTY-NINE

As predicted, the heat built as soon as the sun rose, and by the time Ali and the ASBO twins arrived to start stocking the shelves, I was down to cargo shorts and a wife beater as a vast tray of chicken poached slowly on the hob, ready to be added to my saffron infused Greek style Filo pies.

Elaine arrived some time later than everyone else, and proceeded to noisily clink bottles and shuffle boxes of crisps around.

Caz was on the other side of the table slicing a kilo of onions into translucent slivers by hand, the job having fallen to her because we both hated mandolins having had repeated kitchen accidents with them, and because she was the only person on the planet who could sliver a kilo of onions without shedding a single tear. "Sweetheart," she'd said mysteriously, I haven't cried since 1985."

Elaine entered the kitchen, sniffed the steam from my poaching chicken, announced "My days! That smells rank," mimed gagging, and leering over at Caz, added "Mind you don't slice yer finger off your ladyship," and giggled at her own weak joke.

"Don't you have a rock to crawl under," Caz growled as she dumped another handful of sliced onions into a bowl.

"You got a guest," Elaine announced to me. "The Lesbo Queen said I should tell you to get yer arse out front pronto."

"Elaine, I don't think Ali is a Lesbian. Not that there'd be anything wrong with it if she were. And, as you're working in a Gay pub,"

"South London's Premiere Gay Pub," Caz corrected me loudly from the other side of the room.

"I'm not too keen on your language. Have you got a problem with the LGBTQ community?"

"Apart from the fact they sound like a dyslexic trying to learn his alphabet?" She snorted. "Nah. But I do have a problem with Bolshy old ladies who keep tryin' to tell me what to do while makin' me feel like shit," she snapped back.

"Maybe, if you stopped using terms like Dike-a-rella, or Lesbo Queen as though they were curses, and started behaving like Ali was a person with feelings the two of you might get along better."

"Mate," Elaine pursed her lips, her right eyebrow raised to an angle of forty-five degrees, and still managed to smirk, "I aint got much pleasure in my life lately. So the last thing I want to do is get along better with that Basic. Now: are you comin' out, or do I tell the Health Inspector that you're too busy boiling." She sniffed disgustedly, "Rats up, an' trying to fix the fuckin' world one teenager at a time?"

And she turned on her heels and was gone.

I blanched.

"Do we still have that meat mallet?" Caz asked from across the room.

"Did she," I gestured at the open door through which Elaine had just flounced, "Say Health Inspector?"

She dropped the knife. I turned the gas burners even lower, and we looked at each other across the room.

"Keep calm," Caz said. "There's absolutely nothing to worry about."

"Well," I said, "Apart from the fact that half the meat in the freezers went in there when Maggie Thatcher was in power, and that that," I gestured at the grease-encrusted fixture that hung above the hob like a fat-filled pustule. I'd been threatening to replace it for months, and, from a glance, it was clear that it wasn't so much filtering as exuding.

"All kitchens are filthy," she justified. "We'll be fine. Just stay calm."

"You've said that twice," I said, as I heard Ali's voice from the hallway.

"Just in here, Mister Tavistock," she said loudly, before erupting into the room as noisily as possible – in an attempt, I assumed, to give me warning that nemesis was on its way, and that I should probably quickly replace the extractor filter, and drag that hundredweight of dubious frozen meat out the back into a skip.

As the former would have required a HazMat suit, a gasmask and at least a days preparation; and as the latter would have needed a couple of the world's strongest men and a skip capable of taking an almost unjointed cow, neither of these tasks would have been achieved before the arrival of a diminutive, bald man wearing a pair of horn rim spectacles so large they made him look like a child playing dress-up.

I froze.

"Danny," Ali announced in her best smiley, welcoming happy voice (the one she reserved for the VAT man and the H&S inspector – well she wouldn't waste it on the punters, would she?), "This is Mister Tavistock. From The Council."

The last was said in the tone of voice that I might expect the landlady at a Resistance Bistro to introduce a visiting Gestapo officer, 'From The Nazis.'

Caz switched on her aristo smile – a facial expression meant to denote serene confidence, but which always, to me, looks like something halfway between a stroke victim and a case of mild hysteria – and – before she could ask 'Have you come far?' I leapt in, hand extended.

"Nice to meet you," I said, "I'm Danny Bird."

"I was hoping," Tavistock said in an adenoidal whine, "To meet with Mrs Carver."

"Oh." I froze again, looking over his shiny pate at Ali.

Lilly Carver was the titular Licensee of The Marq. It was she that Chopper had – decades previously – installed as Landlady. Lilly had vanished without trace back when I was still in school, and Chopper – working, one supposed, on the idea that updating the licensee to another would attract attention, and that attracting attention, particularly from 'The Council, The Rozzers or The Fucking VAT Man,' was not exactly part of his business model – had never bothered to formally replace her on the paperwork with any of the half dozen other people who had supervised the joint for him in the meantime.

Still, technically Lilly Carver was the Landlady, and her absence was likely to cause some issues here.

"Lilly – Mrs Carver, that is," I began, slowly, "Is, on holiday," I said, as Ali – mistaking my panicked glance for a request for assistance, announced, simultaneously, very loudly that our absent Publican was "In Hospital."

Tavistock, his eyes - behind lenses that had to be two inches thick – the size of salad plates, glanced from me to Ali, his gaze hovering momentarily over Caz on the other side of the room, her face a fixed mask of aristocratic semi-welcome.

"Well which is it?" He asked, his voice almost entirely nasal.

"She's," Ali started, making the sort of eyes at me that were last seen being performed by Theda Bara.

"She's in hospital. On holiday," I extemporised. "She fell down."

"A mineshaft," Ali blurted, then, realising how insane the picture she'd just painted was, reverted to the silent movie eyes.

Tavistock turned to stare at her, his glance, once again, lingering over the still silent figure of Caz, her loose white shift dress stirring lazily in the completely ineffective rotary fan we'd been attempting to cool the room with.

"A mineshaft?" He asked, sounding for all the world like an adenoidal Lady Bracknell.

"She was on a walking tour." Ali, a single bead of sweat rolling through her crew cut, across her forehead, and down her nose, attempted to explain.

"Of Death Valley," I clarified, and he turned his attention back to me.

"A walking tour of Death Valley where she fell down a mineshaft?" I didn't blame him for sounding incredulous. We should have told him she'd been beamed up by aliens; it couldn't have been any less likely.

"She's into all that," Ali said above his head, addressing the remark to me, as though we were a music hall mind reading act.

"Mad for Ghost Towns, she is," I explained.

"Loves a ghost," Ali misheard, and ran with it, much like a lemming spotting a cliff edge. "Always having séances and weejee sessions here."

At that, Tavistock bristled. "She performs joinings," he gasped, though as his voice came out of his nose at the same time he was furiously inhaling air, the gasp was more of a choke.

"No, she had to give up the welding," Ali – hysterically bounding, now, towards the metaphorical sound of crashing waves below – clarified, "For health and safety reasons."

The mention of health and Safety seemed to pull Tavistock back to the present. "I meant Spiritual Joinings," he clarified. "I myself am a believer in another plane."

"Well Lilly won't be getting on any planes for a while," Ali went for it, flinging herself off the cliff edge and free-falling towards the rocks below, "she broke both her fucking legs when she fell down that mineshaft."

"Tell me," Tavistock leaned conspiratorially in towards me, gesturing with his eyes towards the opposite side of the room where the still unmoving figure of a tall thin young(ish) woman in a white shift dress, the fabric fluttering in an almost imperceptible breeze, continued to stare at him with the sort of look that could only be described as wistfully lost, "Can you see her, or is it just me?"

"Oh, my manners," Caz exclaimed, holding out a hand, at which point Tavistock shrieked, leaped into my arms, and, realising that the gurning simpleton on the opposite side of the kitchen table was simply an onion-slicing kitchen help and not the spirit of a deceased resident of Bedlam, switched off the glimmer of humanity we'd been allowed to see, and slipped back into full Bureaucratic Bastard mode.

"We've had an anonymous call," he announced, brandishing a clipboard as Caz introduced herself, "And frankly, Lady Holloway," this last said in a tone of incredulity that suggested he found our discussion about our inadvertently potholing spiritualist landlady welder more believable than that the once-vision on the opposite side of the room had come from the peerage, "I can already see why concern might be expressed. Who," he swivelled his hugely magnified eyes back to me. "For example, who are you, and what, exactly, is your role in this," he glanced with clear disdain around the room, "Establishment?"

I introduced myself, suggested – without actually saying so – that I was a relative of Mrs Carver, and was filling in during her unfortunately extended vacation.

"What was the complaint about?" I asked, wondering whether it had been the noise, the fumes or the two corpses in the first six months of business that had brought the ire of the complainant on us.

"It was anonymous, Mr Bird," Tavistock droned, as though he were talking to a very slow person. In a coma. "If I told you what it was about, it wouldn't be anonymous."

Yes it would, I was about to say, when I remembered who I was dealing with, what was in the freezer and how quickly I could be shut down if he didn't like what he found. That done, I decided that this diminutive Maigret of the industrial kitchen could mangle the language as much as he liked; I wouldn't be the one correcting him.

"Now," he pulled himself up to his full height, which left him level with my chin, and – tilting his head back slightly – fixed me with a steely stare, "Shall we get started?"

CHAPTER THIRTY

"Lord," Caz hoiked her handbag onto her shoulder, waved farewell to my dad as his taxi pulled away towards the river, and faced the imposing Georgian fronted house in front of us. "I bet that costs a fortune to heat."

It never failed to amaze me that a titled Aristo like Caz, who could happily spend a month's salary – if she actually had a salaried job - on a pair of shoes, could, in the next moment, become an obsessive compulsive hausefrau.

"Only you," I noted, "Could think about heating a property in the middle of a heatwave." I tilted my head, shading my eyes to take in the full scale of the property. "My guess is Olivia Wright can afford a few rads left on full power. Let's just hope they're not on today."

"Are you still annoyed with me?"

"I'm not annoyed," I said, "just... confused."

"I mean, shall we start with the small fridge seemed like a perfectly safe bet," she explained, linking her arm in mine, in what I recognised instantly as a reconciliatory attempt to cheer me up.

"How was I to know that that's where you kept the dead pigeons?"

I pulled my arm free. "I don't keep pigeons – dead or otherwise. Someone planted them there."

"Ooh," she murmured, "My cousin Rupert had exactly the same thing happen to him not long ago. Only, it wasn't here, it was in Burma. And it wasn't the Health inspector, it was the local police. And," she trailed off, perhaps, finally, realising her analogy was somewhat failing, "It wasn't dead pigeons; it was ten grams of heroin. But at least," she said, brightening up, "They don't hang you for dead pigeons."

"Might as well," I muttered. "I can't prove it. Yet. But the minute I do, Elaine Falzone is gonna think the Hangman's Drop a mercy."

"You think Elaine planted them?"

I flashed back to the moment of mortification: Tavistock holding the door of one of the small fridges – usually used to store liquids – his bulk filling the hole, so that we who stood behind could see nothing of the contents of the refrigerator, or know what he was poking at with the pen he'd dramatically removed from the breast pocket of his short sleeved shirt a moment before.

"Mr Bird," he asked, at length, "Why do you have two dead pigeons on a paper plate next to an open jug of milk?"

"Pigeons?" I goggled, as he slowly slid the offending plate with the two birds – still feathered, their stony eyes staring unblinking at the ceiling.

"Pigeons," he repeated, offering the plate to me.

These were no wood pigeons destined for a game pie; they were city vermin, their necks broken, their bodies simply dumped on a paper plate, and said plate then dumped unceremoniously into my dairy fridge.

I goggled again.

"Still," Caz said, as we approached the gate of the house in Chelsea, "It could have been worse."

"Worse?" I turned to her.

"I'm not happy," Tavistock had intoned, his adenoidal voice suggesting that unhappiness was shorthand for horrified. "Not happy at all, Mister Bird."

He and I were sat facing each other at the kitchen table, the onions now slowly softening on the hob, as Caz mimed poking them with a spatula whilst eavesdropping on our conversation.

"I genuinely have no idea how those birds got there," I'd pleaded, my hands out in a beseeching pose that seemed to be having absolutely no effect whatsoever on the bureaucrat.

"The pigeons," he said, looking pointedly down at his checklist, which seemed covered in red 'X's with only a handful of blue Ticks to save me from the gallows. "Are the least of your problems. By my reckoning, Mister Bird, this establishment is in need of a change of management.

"You have venison in the freezer which has been impacted by what looks like permafrost, two dead pigeons on a paper plate in your milk fridge, ten gallon jugs of what looks like unfiltered, possibly untaxed, apple-based alcohol in your back passage, and blocked loos. Blocked, it would appear, with plaster of Paris, though why anyone would have poured plaster of Paris down your toilets is beyond me.

"And it's the toilets that bother me most, because, to be honest, if any of your customers eat the venison or the pigeons, they're likely to need them. Fast.

"I'm also unhappy," he added, gesturing across the room at a pile of bags coats and t-shirts in the corner, "With the amount of debris in the kitchen."

"Those belong to the staff," I explained.

Tavistock looked up from his clipboard, reached up to the bridge of his spectacles, and slowly removed them, before blinking myopically at me.

"I don't care if they belong to the Dalai Lama, Mr Bird; they are an obstacle, a challenge to food hygiene rules, and a trip hazard. They are, in fact, a health and safety nightmare."

"Nightmare?" Caz snorted as she pressed the buzzer mounted by the gate and advised the butler that Lady Caroline Holloway and Mister Daniel Bird had come to call on Miss Wright and Mister Benson, "It's lucky for him he didn't poke too deep into the big freezer in the cellar. I'm convinced it's got bits of Lilly Carver in it. Poor Mr Tavistock would never sleep again…"

The door opened and we were ushered into the sort of entry hall one usually only sees in the movies. The theme was Black and White, with White walls, a vast expanse of chess board tiling on the floor, a black chaise longue in the corner (cos, y'know: after walking from the cab to the house, mounting the three steps outside and knocking on the door, you're almost bound to need a lie down) and a selection of uniformly framed black and white prints.

Before us, a swooping staircase leads to the upper floors. I kept a beady eye on it, but Norma Desmond had clearly declined to make an appearance today. She was probably upstairs stuffing her chimp.

The sound of classical music drifted from somewhere deep in the house.

"This way, please," the butler said, leading us to the left and into what the magazines like to call a Gracious Drawing Room.

The space was filled with light from the vast bay fronted windows at the front of the house, and a modern designer had clearly been let loose on the place, because what would, at some point, have been a series of walls designed to separate the ground floor into different rooms had all been removed, so that the one drawing room stretched the full length of the house. The back wall – or what would once have been the back wall – was now a vast expanse of glass doors, which had been concertinaed back so that there was, effectively, no back wall, and the room just sort of bled into the garden.

A massage table had been set up towards the garden end of the room, and Olivia Wright – naked, it seemed, save for a fluffy white towel across her bum – was lying face down on it.

Kent Benson sat on an antique looking sofa, his mobile glued to his ears. "Yeah," he growled into it, "Well tell Mr Chang that the production line either reduces error rates or we're moving to the fucking Philippines. They're fucking T-shirts, Maurice. I can have 'em made anywhere, and I will have them made anywhere if Chang can't sort his fucking people out."

He spotted us, smiled, held a finger up as though to pause us, mouthed sorry, and ignored us completely for another five minutes while he berated the unfortunate Maurice.

At length, he ended the call, and rose from the sofa. "Danny," he extended a hand to me, accompanying the handshake with that backslapping thing beloved of some politicos. "Sorry about that. Business," he rolled his eyes as though we shared some common understanding; as though churning out Gazpacho in The Marq were, in some way, equivalent to running a series of sweat shops in South East Asia. "Good to see you. How are things?"

"Oh," I smiled, wondering where to start, and went with "As always, really. How are you guys doing?"

"Well," he dropped his voice, leaned in towards me, "I'm worried about Olivia. Maggie's death, the pressure of the upcoming wedding, these letters, and then the," he paused, looking for the right word, "Unpleasantness at the pub the other night. She's depressed. Very depressed. She's putting on a brave face, but I'm worried."

Olivia raised a head, "Is that Messrs Bird and Holloway?" She called, as though a half blind invalid.

"It is indeed, sweetheart," Kent filled his voice with pep and verve, and ushered us down the length of the room to where the slim bronzed figure lay, while the squat stooped shape of Jane Barton, all unibrow and crazy hennaed hair, busied herself with mixing various potions on what looked like a high tech drinks trolley.

"Danny," Olivia smiled graciously, and extended a hand to me.

As I went to shake it, Jane Barton gently, but firmly pulled it from my grip, and placed the hand back into position, palm down, on the massage table.

"Remain calm," she instructed Olivia, "And still," and she rearranged Olivia's head so that it was face down, and pointing through a hole in the table.

Lifting a phial from the trolley, Jane poured a long thing stream of oil down Olivia's spine, and commenced slowly, and with great concentration, massaging it all over the woman's back.

"This is my own mix of ylang ylang and geranium," she murmured to the back of Olivia's head. It's good for relaxing, and for uplifting. It'll help you to obtain clarity and perspective."

I felt somewhat intrusive standing by as the massage was performed, and turned to glance at Caz, who rolled her eyes and pursed her lips in a way that suggested she considered the benefits of the scented oils were being somewhat overstated.

"Shall we talk outside," Kent suggested, ushering us into a courtyard garden filled with vast terracotta pots housing scented bushes and plants.

"I've asked Goodman to bring us some iced tea," he smiled, gesturing for us to seat ourselves at a round cast iron table. "It's the little Americanisation I can't quite shake." He smiled at Caz, and seated himself. "Now, to what do we owe the pleasure of this visit?"

We wanted to talk about Anthony Taylor, and who might have been trying to kill him when they brained poor Dave Walker, but I figured we should build up to that, so I started by raising the poison pen letters.

"Ah," Kent's face darkened, "Yes. About those."

"Have there been any more?" Caz asked.

"No," he answered quickly, but I'm a little concerned that all of this attention on the negative, on the spite they spew is adding to Olivia's state of mind. She's really not been right, you know, for the past few weeks, and I wish, now, that we'd never raised the damn things with you, to be honest."

"But you did," Caz reminded him.

"And I've been doing some research," I added. "We've been trying to locate Julie Roth."

Kent laughed, and, at that precise moment, the butler appeared with a tray bearing a jug and three tall glasses.

After the iced tea was poured, the butler vanished, and Kent lifted a glass, silently toasted us, and sipped deeply from his.

I took a sip. It tasted, to me, like liquid soap. Caz, I noticed, didn't even make an attempt. The absence of anything with an ethanol base in the concoction had clearly put her off it for life.

"Julie Roth," Kent finally said. "There's a name I haven't heard in a long time."

"She was a friend of your first wife, I understand."

He snorted. "Hardly. Or, that is to say, she was a friend, but it all went very sour very quickly when Sophie invented the band. Her prototype was good, but crude, and so I took over, redesigned it, made it more functional, and user friendly, and when we launched, we had almost immediate success. But neither Sophie's prototype nor my refinements owed anything to Julie Roth.

"Still, wherever there's success, there'll always be people looking to skim a little of that success for themselves. So Julie sued."

"When she lost the case," I reminded him, "She swore vengeance."

"You think Julie killed Sophie?" Kent shook his head, "She was angry, but I don't think she was capable of something as terrible as that."

"What about writing poison pen letters?" Caz asked. "Was she capable of something like that?"

Kent considered the suggestion silently. Before he could answer, I threw out another question: "What do you think happened to your wife?"

At this, he sighed heavily. "I like to think it was an accident," he said finally. "I told the cops all along that the boat had mainly been my toy, that Sophie wasn't really a good sailor. She might have gotten into difficulties, fell overboard…" he trailed off, then, after a little more silence, during which I watched Jane Barton reach into the trolley and extract a series of towel-wrapped stones, which were deliberately placed on Olivia Wright's back – he spoke again. "Or it might have been something else.

"We were in trouble; the law suits, the vultures, the state of our finances. It might have all been just a little too much for Sophie. She'd been... down, for weeks before the event. But," he shook his head, "I still think it was an accident. But how does this get us nearer to solving the poison pen letters?"

"I'm looking for someone who would hate you enough to want to stop this marriage; to want to hurt you for some reason," I said, "And Julie Roth was an immediate standout. She blamed you both for stealing her idea; she might have a vendetta against you. Still," I sighed, "If not her, then it might be a friend of Sophie's, someone who, clearly, blames you for her death."

Kent sipped from his glass, considered the suggestion. "Sophie had friends, of course, but I can't see any of them doing something like this. Most of them started off supporting me when Sophie died, then they turned on me when the police and the press went into overdrive. By the end of the whole thing I'd been exonerated so totally that the same friends came crawling back to me to apologise. I don't see any of them sending poison pen letters today."

"Well someone wants to stop you two marrying," I said.

"Oh, beware, my lord, of jealousy," Jane Barton appeared behind us, placed a hand softly on Kent's shoulder and, with a gesture suggested that he should replace her at Olivia's side, "It is the green-eyed monster which doth mock The meat it feeds on."

As Kent moved off, Jane took his seat, and smiled at us. "Yes, she said, I know about the letters." She turned back over her shoulder, glanced at where Olivia lay dozing as Kent stroked her calves. A look of genuine fondness crossed her face. "We keep no secrets," she said.

"So who do you think is sending the letters?" I asked.

She turned her attention back to me, the almost worshipping glaze fading, "Like you say," she answered, her voice a low, slow rumble, "Someone who's jealous of their love, and who wants to ruin it."

"Do you think that what happened at the pub might be linked to this?"

"What happened at the pub?" She said. "That poor man? How could that be linked to this?"

"What do you remember of the afternoon?" I asked, avoiding actually answering her question.

Jane pursed her lips, which made the moustache on her upper lip bristle a little. "It was hot," she finally said, "and crowded. Noisy. People were coming and going. Then that cousin of Olivia's arrived, and put the cat amongst the pigeons. But, really: why would what happened there have anything to do with Olivia and Kent?"

I was about to suggest that it might have had more to do with Olivia's cousin when the lady herself – swathed in a white towelling dressing gown, and accompanied by Kent – strolled on to the patio and dropped herself into a chair.

"So," she asked, wasting no time on preamble, "have you found out who's sending those vile things yet?"

Before I could answer, Goodman reappeared, a silver salver in front of him. On it was a glass of what looked like slurry. He deposited it, wordlessly, in front of Olivia, and retired.

"This," Jane intoned in her baritone, "is wheatgrass, Psyllium husk, goji berries, chia seeds, Siberian ginseng, ginger dried placenta and purified water. It'll energise your chakras."

And clean you out like a dose of salts, I thought, as Olivia lifted the brown sludge, sipped it, made eyes like it was the nectar of the gods, and turned back to me, awaiting a response to her question.

"We're working on it," I said. "If there was nobody from Kent's first marriage who might still be around and looking to stop this marriage, the question occurs whether there's someone in your world who might not be keen on your marrying."

"My world?" Olivia seemed shocked by the thought. "Why would anyone I know want to stop us getting married?"

"Maybe one of your friends doesn't believe in Kent's innocence," I answered. "Or maybe there's another reason."

Caz spoke up. "What about James Kane?" She asked. "He and your cousin didn't seem exactly matey.

"He's the solicitor, right?" I prompted.

"Well he's more of an executor than a solicitor," Olivia stiffened. "And all that was just a silly misunderstanding. Nothing serious."

"They were strangling each other," Caz said, before adding "and why is he more an executor than solicitor?"

"It's true that Kent's marrying an heiress," Olivia said, "But I'm not as rich as people think. Well, that's to say, I don't have the money in my own hands. My parents left a sizeable amount of money in trust till my 30th birthday."

"I'm not marrying you for money," Kent insisted, pouring himself another glass of iced tea. "I'm marrying you because I love you with all my heart," he lifted her hand, and kissed her palm, his eyes never leaving hers.

Olivia smiled, and leaned in to kiss him.

Caz coughed. "So the principal's untouchable till then," she prompted, pulling the two back to the now.

"That's right," Olivia agreed. "I get the interest – which, as you can see, isn't paltry – today. And, up till now, James has been managing the funds. Once I'm married, Kent will work with him. There are so many business opportunities out there, and Kent's proven he can make fortunes. I mean, look at the Drastic Band…"

"I sensed some hostility between you two," Caz pressed, turning to Kent. "You and James not seeing eye to eye?"

Kent sighed, "The little weasel's been trying desperately to keep total control of the money, and I won't stand for him bad mouthing me around the – oh…" Kent suddenly stopped, his eyebrows knotting together in an angry look. "I see what you mean. You think he's trying to stop the wedding?"

"It's possible," I said. "Or what about Anthony Taylor?"

"Tony? Why on earth would he want to stop the wedding?" Olivia considered the idea for a moment, then shook her head. "No, Tony wouldn't have had any reason to write those letters."

This was my opportunity to get the spotlight on Taylor. "He does like stirring up antagonism," I prompted.

Olivia tilted her head to one side, considered, once again, the concept, and shook her head again, going off on what a good heart Taylor had. "Underneath it all."

"I mean," She said, "Poor Tony had the most horrendous childhood," she simpered, as though she'd been paid to do a PR piece for him. "He was a tricky teenager, and, yes, he's made some mistakes, but now he's back, people will see him for what he is, and they will learn to forgive him. They will."

The last was said with such steely determination that I decided to drop the subject.

For now.

At that point, Goodman – still resplendent in his morning suit, and not breaking a sweat, despite the fact that the patio was already feeling like a tiled sauna – appeared in the doorway to announce the arrival of Desmond Everett.

I looked at Caz, who raised an eyebrow, took the opportunity created by the diverted attention of the assembled to pour the contents of her glass of iced tea into a large bronze planter, and smiled at me.

"Saves on cab fare," she murmured, and, before I could remind her that my dad rarely accepted payment for ferrying us all over the city, Everett arrived, air kissing Jane and Kent, and hugging Olivia tightly.

When he got to Caz, the air kiss was repeated, but I got the hug.

And it was a tight hug.

And it went on a little longer than I might have accepted.

And, just as I felt sure it was about to break, he squeezed me a little tighter, brought his lips close to my ear, and whispered "I have to talk to you. In private. It's urgent."

He pulled away from me, turned back to the table, and announced he wanted to borrow me for a moment.

The announcement was greeted with complete acceptance from everyone but Caz, who raised two eyebrows and sipped from a glass now filled with clear liquid.

Everett put his arm around my shoulder, and pulled me back into the drawing room, past the massage table, and on to the grouping of antique sofas and delicate chairs gathered around a low coffee table.

He sat, and patted the cushion next to him.

"Listen," he said, "I know this is truly atrocious timing, but I'm supposed to be sorting out Kent's stag do. Last thing I'm sure you want to hear, what with the whole dead waiter situation." He mimed someone hammering a nail into a plank, and pulled a grimace.

"Indeed," I said blankly, then, apropos of nothing, "You've been friends with Kent for long?"

"Oh, good Lord, No!" He guffawed silently – actually threw his head back, displaying a total absence of noticeable fillings, and mimed the guffaw whilst no sound came from him. I dwelled on the thought that, if Posh Spice and Bertie Wooster had had a child, and then had it lobotomised, the result might have resembled Dopey Des.

At length, the conniption passed. "No," Everett intoned, "I've only known him a while. Seems like a damn good egg, mind you. I've known Olivia for – ooh – ages. That right, Livvy, old thing?" He shouted across the room.

"What right, Dessie?" Olivia asked from across the room.

"Ages," he responded, "Known each other?"

"Oh God," Olivia fanned herself with a magazine, rolled her eyes back in her head like some mystical going into a trance, and attempted to calculate how long she and the Honourable Des Everett had known each other.

I gritted my teeth and tried to decide whether – Caz and I excluded – there was a single person in the room with an I.Q. score in double digits.

"Well you met Binks at prep school, and I suppose we must have met on one of the holidays home," she finally finished. "So, what? Fifteen? Twenty years?"

"Steady on, old gel," Everett guffawed, "Giving away the age, what?"

"So you know all about the family," I prompted. "Any idea why Anthony Taylor would come back now?"

"The family?" He took me by the elbow and pulled me closer. "Things you need to know," he said.

"Olivia has had a pretty tough run of it. The whole family were a rum lot. Even Binky – best friend, you know – was a bit of a bounder. All her life she used to get terrible panic attacks. Then, she was orphaned. Her only family were the old woman or Anthony. Neither of them exactly stable, if you know what I mean. Oh, don't get me wrong: Old Maggie did what she could – ill of the dead and all that – but she was from another age."

"And Anthony?" I prompted again.

I may as well have prompted the massage table. Dope Des clearly had a topic in mind, and would let go of it only when he had completed what he set out to do.

"We all want this wedding to go off without a hitch. And that includes the stag do. Thing is: I've never done one of these things. No idea where to begin. And I'm wondering: you being a publican and all that, whether you had any ideas?"

A publican. I wondered whether Desmond had ever actually visited the twenty-first century, or experienced its marvels. "Depends how wild you want it to get," I answered.

"Wild?"

"Y'know: I mean what do you want: Shots? Strippers? Hookers? Midgets? A live sex show? A donkey?"

"Oh no. No no no no no no no." He shook his head. "None of that. Livvy would be horrified."

"Um…" I hesitated to correct Desmond, as he seemed a little confused re the attendees of a stag do, "Olivia won't be there."

"Won't be there?" His eyes searched mine, desperation growing behind them. "Of course she'll be there. Its, well, it's part of the pre-wedding celebrations."

Jesus. How did people like this survive to their thirties. "Desmond; it's called a stag do because only stags – men – go on it."

His horror increased. "Men? It's a stag do because... Oh cripes," he dropped his head into his hands.

"Desmond, why did you think it was called a stag do?"

"The horns," he moaned. "I thought we wore hats with horns on them." He gasped, as another realisation dawned, "I was only doing this cos I thought Olivia would be there. How in the name of Buggery am I supposed to do kill an evening with Benson? I don't even know the man."

"It's not just you and him," I explained, "It's you, him, and all his friends."

Desmond looked at me as if I'd just suggested he go drinking with Kent and his coterie of invisible elves. "Kent doesn't have any friends," he explained as though I were the idiot.

"Well you'll have to start making up some, then," I said. "Just people who know him, people he spends time with. They'll come. Everyone will understand that he's new to the UK and rally round."

He nodded. "Yes," he said, "you're right. It's in September. Let me have your number and I'll text you the details."

"What?" My jaw dropped. "No, I don't want to come," I tried protesting, but Desmond had already pulled out his phone, so I gave him my number, wondering how an attempt to find out more about Anthony Taylor had gone so wrong so quickly.

CHAPTER THIRTY-ONE

We were ushered directly in to James Kane's office. It was almost as though he'd been waiting for us.

It was, in fact, exactly as though he'd been waiting for us; because he had been.

"Olivia called," he confirmed, as soon as we were seated and had declined offers of tea or coffee, and awaited, silently, the delivery of his requested cup of Earl Grey. "I have to admit, she was a little vague as to the purpose of your visit, but she did instruct me to assist you in any way I could, so…" He held his hands out, palms up, as though inviting us either to bring our woes to him, or to inspect his stigmata.

The black suit had been replaced, today, by an immaculately cut cream linen suit, which only increased his resemblance to Colonel Saunders, if the Colonel had had a cut glass RP accent.

"How, pray tell, may I help you?"

I told him about the poison pen letters. My plan here was to extract any information he could give us on the letters while also attempting to ascertain if Kane might have murdered Dave Walker in a botched attempt to brain Anthony Taylor.

That was my plan, but I had no idea how I was actually going to get any of this out of him.

I needn't have worried. I've seen sieves that didn't leak as quickly as Kane.

"Oh my," he said, puffing out his cheeks. "Dear oh dear. Poison pen letters? Well I never. Oh, I knew about the fiancé's history," he said, his spoon chinking against the bone china teacup as he stirred the still steaming brew.

"I considered it my responsibility to review all of Olivia's amours. She's never been entirely worldly, you see – her nerves are rather delicate, which is understandable, when one considers the life she's had: Her parents, and then her grandmother, quite frankly, infantilised – her. The girl has suffered from panic attacks since the accident, and is, shall we say, emotionally fragile. So I Suggested to Lady Margaret that he might not be entirely," here he paused as though searching for the word, filled the gap by sipping the tea, and, when the cup was back in its saucer, finished: "ideal."

"How was that advice received?" I asked.

"Well, as far as Olivia was concerned, I was Satan. Her Ladyship, on the other hand, could see my point. But what could she do? She was already ailing, and, well, Olivia could do no wrong in her grandmother's eyes."

"And now you've gotten to know Kent?" I asked.

"Oh," James smiled, though the smile didn't quite reach his eyes. "Now I've gotten to know Mr Benson, I consider him little more than a nasty chiselling little con artist. I shall," he immediately added, "deny I said any of what's just been said, if you should ever communicate it outside of these walls. But, within these walls, I'm happy to repeat it: The man's a manipulative, scheming, conniving shit. The way he's turned Olivia against me – oh, it's subtle – on both of their parts: She's still playing nice, but won't even return my calls any more, and he's already angling for what they've both called a greater degree of involvement in the management of the estate.

"Well, I can tell you this: Until Olivia's thirtieth birthday, I have a responsibility to the Wright family estate, and he won't be getting anywhere near those funds. Neither as a husband nor as a helpmate to the executor."

"What about the money she was left by Lady Margaret?" Caz asked.

Kane shrugged. "That will, I'm afraid, has not yet been officially read. However, I drew it up, and entre nous, I fear that Lady Margaret may not have included as many safe guards as I'd hoped for. Basically, as soon as the probate is through, Olivia will be an even wealthier woman."

"And, if she was to die, all the money would go to Mr Benson?"

Kane smiled softly, and shook his head. "The money – unless Olivia has arranged a will with someone else – would go to her next of kin. And, unless she marries that little con man, he will not be her next of kin."

And someone, it seemed, wanted to ensure she never married that little con man.

"So," I asked, "Who do you think may have sent the poison pen letters?"

Kane shrugged. "God knows. It's not like she's surrounded by people who have her best interests at heart. Look at the assembly the day of her grandmother's funeral. The only people of Olivia's age were either with the staff or were the staff."

"There's Jane," Caz offered.

"The nurse?" James snorted humourlessly. "I repeat: everyone there was either with the staff or was the staff."

"They seem friendly."

"Listen," James sipped from his tea again, stared reflectively into the cup, "What I'm about to say is, for the most part, public record, so all I'm about to do is save you some time on research.

"That said, and as I have previously stated, I'm aware that certain aspects of this conversation could be construed as less than professional, and so I will not only deny most of what is being said in this room, but will sue you individually and jointly for slander and defamation if you so much as breathe any of what I am about to convey outside of this room. Understood?"

We nodded, leaning in for what – from the warning we'd just received – had to be nuclear strength gossip.

"Olivia has battled with confidence issues all her life. Even, I'm told, as a small child. She was delicate, nervy, and prone to what can only be described as emotional flights. Her parents, and her brother were – along with Lady Margaret – her world, and so when a car she was passenger in plunged off a cliff in the Algarve, killing both her parents and her older brother, her world was almost completely shattered.

Olivia was left with some facial injuries as a result of the crash. Nothing serious at all, to be frank, but she became somewhat obsessed about what she saw as horrific scarring, and so finally she went to Switzerland, where she was to have some corrective surgery.

And when she returned, she had that thing with her. She's another one who's far too involved in Olivia's life, that one. Tells her what to wear, what to think, what to eat, drink, and when to have it all flushed out of her system. I don't like it, I tell you; not one little bit. She's too controlling, and Olivia's too easy going."

I couldn't help wondering if there was anyone James would approve of in Olivia's life. It crossed my mind that, as executor of her parent's estate, he'd been, effectively, controlling her life – or at least, had the understood role of controlling her finances – for some time, and the question of how many of his opinions were formed by the fact that these other people were pulls on Olivia's attention.

"So," I tried, again: "The letters? Any idea who might be sending them?"

He sipped, again, from his tea cup, draining it this time, and, having once again replaced it in the saucer, and adjusted the cup so that the handle lay just so, fixed me with his steely blue eyes. "None whatsoever," he said, his gaze never leaving my face, "But whoever it is, I'd like to warmly shake them by the hand and share my wish that the girl will see sense before it's too late."

CHAPTER THIRTY-TWO

"Remind me," Caz muttered as the door to James Kane's office closed behind us, "To have my solicitor sign a non-disclosure agreement."

"You have a solicitor?" I asked, wondering what on earth Caz could need with legal advice.

"Sweetness, everyone has a solicitor, surely?" She looked at me as though seeing me for the first time. "I mean, who deals with, you know, the legal things in one's life?"

"What legal things? You've never been arrested, as far as I know,"

"Well, there was that time that horrific Northern woman accused me of selling counterfeit Gucci on EBay," she reminded me.

"That wasn't arrest, Caz. That was a query email from EBay asking you to prove authenticity. It was hardly hauled-out-of-your-bed-at-three-A.M. Not that you'd be in your bed at three A.M. And she wasn't Northern; she was from Potters Bar, if I recall."

"And in what direction from central London is," she shuddered at the thought of it, "Potters Bar? Anyway, Mr Ogilvie was very good and not only had EBay step down, but actually sued the lying harridan for damages. Paid for a nice new genuine Birkin for me."

"Wait: were those Guccis fake, then?" I asked.

Caz glared at me. "The very idea! I know they were entirely genuine, because I acquired them personally from the Gucci Autumn Winter shoot."

"So they weren't fake; they were pinched. I take it back, you probably do need a lawyer on call."

A cough – discrete, but distinct enough to be clearly fake, brought us back to the present, and we realised that our conversation had clearly been audible to the middle aged woman behind James Kane's reception desk.

Caz glared at the woman, and muttered something about lawyer-client confidentiality.

"I'm not sure," I said, "But think that only counts when it's your lawyer, and not when it's someone else's lawyer's receptionist."

"Ipso facto," she replied, still glaring at the now blushing woman, and speaking in tones clearly designed to be heard by the mortified receptionist, "If one word of that leaks, I shall be having another handbag at someone's expense."

She hoiked the current handbag – another gargantuan affair that could easily have accommodated an entire Spring Summer collection or a clutch of Namibian orphans, and made to swan out of the office, with me following in her wake.

Then, in the middle of the room, she stopped dead.

I collided with her, and – above my Oof, distinctly noted the chinking tones of a couple of empty gin bottles.

"Those," Caz stared at a designer coffee table in front of us, her French Manicure pointing directly at it, but her words definitely directed at the now almost cowering receptionist, "Are this month's editions."

I peered around her. On the coffee table were the expected magazines: Elle Décor, Vogue, Tatlers, Harpers Bazaar, GQ, and Yachting monthly.

Caz lifted her gaze to the Receptionist, who winced as Lady Holloway shrugged the now sliding bag back on to her shoulder, ignored the repeated chink of empty glass bottles, and stalked across the rest of the room to stand before the desk and smile – in a way that suggested the Stasi at their best – at what the sign on the desk informed us was Bridget.

"Tell me, Bridget," she asked, the voice – as it always did, when she wished to impress the easily impressed – becoming so cut glass that her lips were basically static, "Are these the usual periodicals?"

Bridget stammered, clearly having difficulty either with the diction or the word periodical.

"The magazines," I translated, wondering just what Caz was getting at, "are they the ones you usually have here?"

"Oh them? Yeah," she stammered, her smile flicking on and off as Caz continued to do her best statuesque posh bird. "Yes, I mean," she corrected, sliding into her best pronunciation. "They're the latest ones. But we change them as soon as the new issues come out."

Caz considered this. "And tell me, Bridget: what happens to the old issues when the new ones come in?"

"Happens to them?" The fear was back in her eyes. Perhaps – having heard our conversation – she was afraid that Caz was about to pinch them and put them on EBay.

"Yes," Caz clarified, "When these are no longer required. Are they disposed of in the litter, or…"

"Oh," clarity lit up her face, "No. I mean yes."

Caz raised an eyebrow. "No and yes," she said, and the three words spoke volumes about her view of poor Bridget's use of the Queen's English.

"I mean, they get chucked, mostly, in the bin. Though once or twice, Mr Kane takes 'em home for his granddaughters. Mad on fashion, them girls are."

"Ah," Caz smiled – genuinely this time, and extended a hand, "Many thanks."

Bridget, glancing at the hand, curtsied so deeply that she vanished beneath the desk, and, when she reappeared, it was to be met by Caz's steely stare, the smile gone now.

"Thank you for your help, and remember: one word about our earlier conversation and you'll be hearing from my solicitor."

And so saying, Caz's exit was completed, with me, this time, jogging to keep up with her.

"What," I demanded, as soon as we were out on the now baking street, the heat almost leaching from the walls of the buildings, "was all that about?"

Caz slid the pair of Bulgari sunglasses down her nose only far enough for me to see her roll her eyes at me, then flipped her head back haughtily, allowing the shades to snap back into place.

"Lord," she sighed, "what happened to the comprehensive education system in this country?"

"Caz," I groaned through gritted teeth, "I'm hot and tired, and I want to go home. You can remind me just how superior an intellect you have when we're somewhere air conditioned. But for now – please – what was all that about?"

"The letters," she said, pulling a lipstick from her bag, applying it in one move, and, as she dropped the lippie back into the sack, extracting an empty bottle of Tanqueray and seamlessly crossing the pavement to deposit it in a kerbside bin.

"They were made using letters cut from magazines. And Daniel, I've read enough magazines in my time to recognise which ones the letters were cut from."

"I'm guessing," I sighed, the heat finally defeating me, "they weren't cut from Exchange and Mart."

"I'm not a gambling lady," she said, though I refused for a second to believe there was a vice that she wasn't at least passingly fond of, "but I'd lay even money that every one of those letters was cut from a Harpers Bazaar."

Realisation dawned. "Like the ones that James Kane gets delivered every month."

Caz nodded. "Like the ones he supposedly takes home to his fashion mad granddaughters."

We began to walk down the street in search of a cab, the heat of the pavement actually soaking through the soles of my trainers.

"So," Caz asked, after a moment's silence, "Did you talk to him?"

Uh-oh. "Nick?" I tried to play it cool. "I tried; called him a couple of times, but couldn't get through."

"Really?" She stopped, and turned to look at me. "Only, he sent me a text to say that you'd spoken, but you'd rushed away and he was trying to get hold of you."

"He texted you? Why the hell's he texting you?"

"Because he knows I'll be able to talk to you. And – he says – because every time he calls The Marq, he gets Elaine, and can't get through. Did you tell her you didn't want to speak to him under any circumstances?"

"No. Maybe. I don't know. Caz, this isn't just a disagreement, you know. He's married. I mean, I've already had Robert to deal with. He lied to me for Christ knows how long. And now, here we go again."

"Robert," Caz stated, staring straight in my eyes, "Was a selfish unprincipled shit. What he did was shocking only, to be honest, insofar as he didn't do it earlier. And you know I never liked Robert; I could sense the wasn't right for you. But Nick, Danny. Nick is right for you."

"Once he gets rid of the wife," I answered glumly, feeling the soles of my feet roasting slowly. "Look, Caz, there's nothing that can be done. I'm definitely not about to become the other woman in this relationship. And even if I was, I'd have liked to have known that that's what I was becoming at the start."

I spotted a cab approaching from the opposite end of the street. "Anyway," I said as I hailed it, "I've got too much going on right now to deal with Nick."

"Danny, all that's important is dealing with Nick," Caz said, as the cab pulled up and I gave the driver the address of The Marq.

"No," I said, "what's important is finding out who tried to kill Anthony Taylor and ended up offing my waiter by mistake."

Caz still wasn't sold. "Why would anyone want to kill him?"

"Are you on drugs?"

"But surely there's a more obvious victim."

"Well as Hitler, Sadam and Bin Laden are all dead, I'm struggling to think of one…"

She sighed. "Right: You think this is a revenge killing, right? But most of the people in that room knew where Tony Taylor has been for the best part of the last decade. If they wanted revenge, they only had to get on a plane."

I shrugged, "Most people – even the vengeful – are lazy. And forgiving."

"Says Doctor Freud?"

"No: hear me out. I think someone hates him enough to kill him, but they don't kill him, because, well, it's not what you do is it? Get on a plane, fly to the other side of the world, hunt him down, and kill him in cold blood? So they forget about him; move on. Then one day, when they least expect it, he turns up again, looking fit and handsome and completely unrepentant. And they snap."

"So what about your clients?"

"What about them?"

"You don't think one of them might be a more likely victim?"

I made a mental note to close Caz's bar tab. "I don't think anyone could have mistaken Dave Walker for Olivia."

"No," Caz agreed, "But they could have mistaken him for Kent Benson. Like you say, one man in black trousers and a white shirt looks pretty much the same as any other.

And if we're talking about revenge, we already know that someone's trying to stop the wedding to Olivia. What if that person could see that the letters weren't working, and decided to go for more drastic action?"

"Caz," I sighed, "How did we start with the classic one victim and a room full of suspects and end up with a room full of intended victims and no idea where to begin?"

"I guess we're just clever," she smiled.

CHAPTER THIRTY-THREE

I pressed the doorbell, and had barely done so when there was a click and Anthony Taylor's voice sounded.

"Hey," it drawled, "C'mon up."

There was a buzz, and the door popped open.

Caz pushed the door open and stepped into the hallway, turning her head to me, and raising a querulous eyebrow.

"Is he expecting us?" I asked.

She shrugged, "Well, he's expecting someone."

I followed her into the lobby, all art deco fixtures and shiny parquet, and crossed to the lift. From somewhere distant, a droning air conditioner kept the lobby and – one supposed – the entire block cool in the face of the summer onslaught outside.

Caz pressed the call button. "Are you positive about this?" she asked, as though I were Daniel about to step into a wrought iron lion's den.

"He's not the poison penner," I murmured as the cage stopped with a jerk and we stepped in, "but he could be either an intended murder victim or," Caz pressed the button for floor three, "A murderer."

"A murderer?" She shot me a startled look.

"Well, if Kent was the intended victim, then the killer could have been Anthony," I reasoned.

"For what possible reason?"

"Jealousy. What?" I asked, as she directed a disdainful look at me, "He might want Olivia himself. You know what these," I stopped myself.

"These what? Poshos? Were you about to say 'You know what these Poshos are like'?" Caz gave me her most disdainful look.

The lift stopped, she flung the cage door to the left, turned to the right, stalked up to a door and pressed an almost invisible bell beside it.

The door opened almost immediately, and Anthony Taylor, wearing a pair of dark jeans, a grey t shirt that managed to look simultaneously lived in and vastly expensive, and a grin that paled as he panned over Caz's head and settled on me, filled the door.

"Well hello," he said, though the warmth in the greeting diffused markedly as he moved from Caz to me.

"Hello Anthony," Caz said. "May we come in."

Taylor looked confused, then shrugged, and stepped aside, ushering us into his apartment.

The hallway – as Spartan as I'd expected, considering he'd returned only a few days ago – lead into an opulent living room.

Here, the parquet floors were partially covered in thick rugs. Two leather chesterfields filled one wall, and a couple of matching leather armchairs filled the corners. A diptyque candle scented, I supposed, with money and arrogance, burned on a low marquetry-covered table.

To our right as we entered the room was a long low sideboard, on which a selection of framed pictures huddled.

The place was like a theme park if the theme was 30's decadence.

"Sorry it's such a mess," Taylor said, running a hand through his dark curly hair, and smiling somewhat nervously, it seemed, at both of us.

I looked round the room. Unless he'd just stuffed Dora Carrington behind the sofa, the place was immaculate.

"And we're sorry to bother you," I said, as he gestured to us to sit.

"Would you like some tea?" He asked, gesturing vaguely behind him. "I think I have tea."

"I'm OK," I said, as Caz nodded and said that she'd love a cup.

Taylor turned and left to, I supposed, head to the kitchen, at which point I turned to Caz.

"Since when do you drink tea?"

"I drink tea," she said. "Sometimes."

"Yeah, when there's a Zed in the month. What are you up to?"

"That," Caz nodded at the sideboard as she shrugged her handbag on to one of the sofas. "Check if there's any mangled copies of Tatlers in it. I'll keep him busy."

And, undoing her top button, she left the room.

I glanced at the pictures – A young couple, the woman still wearing a wedding veil; a shot of a tanned and seemingly rather drunk Anthony nuzzling into the neck of an only marginally less wasted Olivia; a picture of a blonde girl, tall and willowy, and leaning against a brick wall somewhere sunny, her gap toothed smile capped with a squint against the sunshine.

I slid open the first drawer.

Empty.

My eyes strolled along the line to a shot of a young Anthony in a school uniform standing next to a less grey version of James Kane, the latter presenting the boy with some sort of trophy, a group shot of four or five Lycra clad, mud spattered cyclists, squinting into a low wintry sun with smiles that spoke of steep gradients conquered. I wondered, fleetingly, as I slid the next drawer open, who they were.

This was the motherload. The last time I'd seen so much red ink was when I'd been round my Aunt Marlene's explaining how the electric didn't just flow through the ether.

Taylor was in trouble with Visa, Mastercard, AmEx and National Westminster Bank, though, on the plus side, Tesco had send him four quid off a ninety quid shop, though – clearly – he'd have to pay cash.

"Here we are," Taylor's voice called as he entered the room, a tray held before him.

I slammed the drawer shut, knocking over one of the framed photos, and turned around.

"What a fabulous place you have," I called in the way that only someone who's almost been caught rifling through the paperwork of a stranger can.

"It's alright," he said, placing a tray on the coffee table. "Rented, but I'll figure out something more permanent soon. Sure you won't have a cup?"

I straightened the picture that had fallen and glanced at it. A black and white portrait of Anthony Taylor and a squat man in kitchen whites, both of them standing in front of a wall of white glazed tiles, their arms crossed over their chests, their smiles seeming to suggest the future was theirs.

"Family?" I asked, apropos of nothing.

"Almost," Taylor gently lifted the picture from my grasp and, having looked at it a moment, as though seeing it for the first time, made to place it gently back on the sideboard, but stopped, and lifted it back to stare at it.

"That's Jack and me."

"Jack Everett?" Caz, who'd actually been sitting on the sofa drinking tea slammed her cup into her sofa. "I'd forgotten you knew Jack Everett."

"Yes," Taylor smiled at her, "Did you know him?"

"Barely."

"Such a talent," Taylor turned back to the framed picture, and stroked it absently. "Such a loss."

"Related to Desmond Everett?" I asked.

Caz nodded. "Jack was one of the YBC's. The young British chefs?" She watched me expectantly. "Well, you'd have heard of them if you ever read the right magazines."

Taylor smiled. "Jack and I had a restaurant: Gambera. We had a Michelin star. First ever Michelin for a Trattoria in this country. But, in the end, it wasn't enough. Neither of us had a head for business. We wanted a restaurant that our friends would want to live in, so Nick made every mouthful as perfect as he could, and I spent a fortune on PR and parties. And it worked: we were the hottest restaurant in London for a while, but, despite everything we did, the debts outstripped the income."

It seemed that Taylor still hadn't learned how to live within his means. "What happened?" I nodded at the frame, still held almost absentmindedly in Taylor's hand.

"He died," Caz announced, for my benefit. "Drowned."

Taylor put the picture down. "Have you ever heard the phrase 'Regret is a useless emotion'?" he asked. "It went down as misadventure. But it wasn't. I killed him."

"Tony!" Caz gasped.

"Oh, not literally. I let him make the kitchen he wanted, produce the food he dreamed of, and I kept the finance side from him. Which wouldn't have mattered if I'd been managing the finances; but I wasn't. The money poured out twice as fast as it came in, and by the time he found out, we were, basically, ruined. Or, he was: I had grandma, only she wouldn't cover his half of the debt."

"You can't say you pushed him," Caz insisted.

"Good as. You asked if these were family," Taylor addressed me. "I call them my sideboard of shame. Everyone here, I've fucked up in some way or another. My mother, Olivia – she never recovered when I was sent away. I was her only friend after the accident, and she forgave me again and again; only I was too busy trying to be the playboy I felt sure my dad would have wanted me to be.

"Then I met Clarissa," he gestured at the gap toothed girl. "The sweetest girl. The most beautiful soul."

He fixed me with a look of what seemed genuine sadness. "And I corrupted her. And killed her too."

"She O.D.'ed," Caz said quietly.

He nodded. "On smack I bought." He sighed "And that was – I thought – me finished. But I carried on trying to – I don't know, kill the pain? Kill myself? Instead, I killed her," he gestured at the girl in the middle of the group of cyclists.

"No excuses, no mistakes, no people are responsible for their own actions this time. I got drunk, I drove a car, and I ran her over, as she was cycling home from work."

He picked up the photo, stared at it for a long time, then said, "She was a PA in a bank. A smart girl by all accounts. Her only failure was that she was in such a rush to get home that she forgot to wear her Hi-Viz jacket. And Grandma's lawyers made the most of that.

"But it was the final straw for Grandma. So: off to Australia with me, via three months in rehab. I haven't drunk since I got on the plane."

"So why come back now?" I asked.

"Because Grandma's dead," he answered. "You didn't know her, but when Lady Margaret instructed you to leave the country and never come back, you did so. And because it's time to make amends."

"And the performance at her funeral? That was making amends?"

He considered the question momentarily and then shrugged his broad shoulders. "No. You're right. That was more entertainment. I'm willing to stand up and admit my failings. Hey: you know what? I'm willing to bet that my failings are worse than most of the people in that room.

"But the sanctimony pissed me off. Always did. Oh, Tony's the black sheep. And, by implication, the rest of them are whiter than white? Well, that aint so, my friend. But I don't really care. I'm not back to make amends to most of those people." He gestured at the sideboard. "I'm back to make amends to these people."

CHAPTER THIRTY-FOUR

"Are You OK?"

"I'm thinking," I said, summoning myself from my reverie.

"You didn't say a word all the way home." Caz gave me a worried look, and glugged half a bottle of olive oil into a huge bowl filled with chopped up pita breads, ground cumin, cinnamon and salt.

I shrugged. "That's 'cos I was thinking. Here, you're better of using your hands," I said, showing her how to mix and massage the oil and the spices together into the bread.

That done, I went back to preparing my hummus.

"What about?"

"Hmmm?"

"What were you thinking about?

"Nothing. It's silly. You don't want to know."

"No," she said, running her hands under a tap and drying them on a tea towel. "We're a partnership. Like Butch and Sundance. Laurel and Hardy. Gin and Tonic. Spill, Mister."

"He went to kiss you," I said "Anthony Taylor moved towards you. As we were leaving. The loom; you know the loom. The one where their arm comes up and they lean in. Only you sort of bristled.'

"Bristled." Caz shrugged, hoisting up the bowl of spiced pitta chips. "Is the oven hot enough yet?"

I glanced at the thermo, opened the door, and slid out the first baking sheet.

Caz tipped the bowl and the glistening spicy bread poured onto the sheet, hissing and singing, the spice mix scenting the air.

"Of course I bristled. I'm not used to people doing the loom. Especially people I hardly know."

I slid the top sheet back into the oven, pulled out the lower one and watched as the pour and hiss was repeated.

"But you do know him," I said. "You told me you used to run with Taylor's crowd when you were young."

"Er, Danny. Younger, I'm not quite geriatric yet."

"So why the bristle? An old friend moves to give you a peck on the cheek?"

"I told you. Because we haven't been old friends for ages."

"How did you escape all the lunacy," I asked, as she bustled across the kitchen to wash the bowl up, "And since when did you start washing as you go?"

"Lunacy?" Caz squirted washing up liquid into the bowl along with the stream of hot water, and almost immediately an explosion of suds filled the sink.

"Everyone Taylor touched seemed to die, go mad, bankrupt, or all three. How come you didn't?"

"Luck," she said, her back to me. "And stubbornness. I never let myself get too close to him, never gave myself entirely to the cult of Tony Taylor. So, when he disappointed me, I wasn't as heartbroken as some others were."

I took a deep breath. "Are you sleeping with him?"

She stiffened. "Sleeping with him? Why would you say that?

"Because he went to kiss you , like it was perfectly normal – this person who you say you were never really that friendly with – and because you shook your head – a tiny motion, but you definitely did, like you were warning him off, and because, since he got back, you've been acting oddly. The mysterious friend with the bad face lift, the early night that left you exhausted the next morning, like you'd been up all night."

"There's a heatwave," she said, still not turning to look at me. "Nobody's sleeping well. You're not sleeping well."

And then I knew. "Oh my God. You are. You're sleeping with him."

Caz said nothing.

"Are you out of your fucking mind?"

"No, I'm as sane as ever," she finally turned to face me. "And I'm a grown woman of," she paused, "an age old enough to have my own mind. And he's changed. Something inside has really calmed down. It's like he's finally grown up"

"I thought you didn't know him all that well? You sound like you knew him intimately before."

She hesitated, weighing up her response. "Look. Tony and I went out a few times back before he got sent away."

"What? Back when he was running over schoolgirls and bankrupting suckers? Back then?"

"He's not a monster, Danny."

I shook my head at her. "He's a one-man disaster zone, Caz. Everywhere he goes, he leaves misery."

"Oh for Christ's sake, Danny. I'm shagging him, not proposing him for the Nobel peace prize."

"And when were you going to tell me?"

"I – I wasn't. Not yet. It's a bit of fun, Danny; it'll fizzle out, and then-"

"And then I'll never need to know, is that it?

"No," she shook her head, "Listen, you've got enough going on with Nick, without me waving my happiness in front of you."

"Happiness? A minute ago, he was just a shag? Now he sounds like marriage material."

"He's a very good shag," she smiled, but I wasn't having it.

"I don't know you," I said.

Caz stood too, holding her hands out to me. "Oh, Danny, don't be so dramatic. He's moved on. I have too, and he's good for me."

"Well if he's that good for you, how come you couldn't bring yourself to tell me about him?"

"Why should I? I'm entitled to a private life?"

"You lied, Caz. You lied to me."

"Oh grow up, Daniel! It's only a lie if you intend to hurt."

I laughed bitterly. "Is that the logic they teach you at finishing school these days? You lied 'cos you were embarrassed, and you were embarrassed 'cos you know that he's a slimy piece of work. What did you think you were doing? If it's not lying, what is it?"

"How about protecting?" She snapped back. "You broke up with Nick the day after I met Anthony for the first time in almost a decade. What? You wanted me to thank you for telling me your heart was breaking, but guess what: I'm sleeping with my ex?"

"Your ex? You said you went out a few times."

"Does it matter?"

"Yes," I stepped away, headed for the door, "It does. I'm sick of being lied to. Robert, Nick, you. I thought there was more to you than that."

"More to me? Danny, I've been shallower than anyone on earth for as long as you've known me."

"No." I shook my head. "You've been good at acting shallow; at pretending you didn't care about much, that you weren't really bothered by the difference between right and wrong. But underneath, you were always honest. Inside, you always knew what was right. I don't know when you became so selfish."

"And I don't know when you became such a judgemental prig."

We stared at each other, a growing darkness seeming to fill the room.

"Are we done?" I asked, finally.

She dropped her hands – I hadn't even noticed that they'd stayed out in a silent plea. "We're done," she said.

CHAPTER THIRTY-FIVE

I spent half the night lying on top of my bed, trying to avoid thinking, let alone voicing the phrase "Why does this always happen to me?"

Instead, I tried to analyse how I felt, what it was that had hurt me so much? I mean, I'd been honest and open with each of them. Well, maybe not so much with Nick; with him, I'd been keeping our relationship at arm's length, trying not to let him get too close, in case – like Robert before him – he turned out to be a bastard.

And, instead of cheating on me with someone else, he'd been cheating with me.

But Caz was different, surely: She was supposed to be my best mate. Mates are not supposed to have secrets from each other. They're definitely not supposed to be having romantic entanglements without the other one knowing.

And then, as sleep slowly crept up on me, an idea began to form.

One which I determined to test out next morning.

It was mid-morning before I could get away from The Marq, and I spent most of the first few hours of the day giving evasive answers to Ali's questions as to Caz's whereabouts.

"I s'pose her ladyship's gone to the country seat to avoid the city 'umours" she'd sniffed when I asked her to cube up some Chorizo for the Paella I was making for the Spanish day she'd inflicted upon the staff and regulars.

"Themes is popular, Danny," Ali had announced, when she'd kicked the concept off with a Saint Patrick's Day that consisted of discounted Guinness and Jameson's, Cabbage and Bacon individual pot pies, a Corrs Tribute band who went by the moniker The Cause, and a Michael Flatley tribute act that had proceeded to put his foot through the floorboards in the snug, and punch one of the Victorian frosted glass lamp shades so hard he lacerated his fist. The whole event had been overseen by the crew cut Bar Manager dressed as a demented leprechaun – complete with orange spray died fuzz, a stick on beard, and a light-up shillelagh that played: "Danny Boy."

Some of the regulars were still receiving therapy for that night, so the thought of a Spanish Fiesta complete with Ali in Flamenco costume, my authentic(ish) Paella alongside cheap San Miguel (actually San Migel and sourced, via Yog Stopidorous, from a brewery in Rotherham) and discounted Spanish wines (which, amazingly, had come from Spain, but unsurprisingly had not been VAT registered) and all overseen by an incongruous Piñata that looked, even more incongruously, like Cheryl Cole, hadn't exactly filled anyone with joy. Then Ali had announced that the ASBO twins would be dressed as topless Matadors, and the cabaret would be a Sylvia (of "Y Viva Espana" fame) tribute act, at which point pre-bookings for what Ali was billing as the "Fiesta Di Paella" had rocketed.

She'd raised an eyebrow when I'd suggested going out, but had been mollified by my pointing out that the Paella would be done by the time I left, the Patatas Bravas, Tortilla and Gazpacho were already chilling in the fridge and would just need (apart from the soup) reheating, while the Artichoke and Serrano ham salad would just need assembling, dressing and serving.

"Besides," I said, "I'll be back long before evening, so the lunch time crowd'll make do with olives and bread.

I arrived outside Jane Barton's clinic just before lunchtime. The plaque on the wall advised Homeopathic remedies, Sports and Therapeutic Massages, Beauty treatments Body Wraps and Chakra alignment.

I'd been reminded, during the night of something that the Wright family lawyer had said. He'd had a thing for Kent, that couldn't be doubted. But he'd passed over some vague concerns about Jane Barton and her controlling nature.

I remembered that she and Olivia had been friends before Olivia had met Kent. In fact it was Jane's idea to visit Florence. "A City of Romance," Jane had supposedly called it, and that had started me thinking: Did Jane Barton have something for Olivia? And if she did, how would she handle the introduction of an interloper? How might she react if she'd taken Olivia away on a romantic weekend, only to have the object of her desire fall in love with Kent?

How would Jane feel then? Foolish? Stupid? Betrayed? Angry?

I felt all of those things now: First Nick, and now Caz.

I wanted to lock the door, open a bottle of Calvados and dive into my own private pity party.

But I didn't think Jane Barton did self-pity. She was a more solid woman, a woman of action. She'd not have drowned her sorrow, she would have done something.

Something like sending a poison pen letter.

I opened the door and stepped into a small reception room. To the left and right were low, beige sofas, with small smoked glass coffee tables before them. I glanced at the tables, and was unsurprised to see copies of Tatler and Vogue.

The same magazines that Caz said the letters had been cut from.

There was no receptionist behind the desk. I glanced at my watch. Lunchtime, I supposed, and was about to call out when I heard a low, but angry voice talking from the room behind the reception.

I stepped round the desk, and, keeping out of sight, leaned forward.

Jane Barton, her back to me, was seated at a desk. Her voice seemed less mumbled than normal, her posture straighter.

"You can't treat me like this," she said, a note of iron in her tone. She was silent a moment, listening to a voice on the other end of the phone pressed to her ear.

"Because I know," She said. "You'd like to make me the Scottish wife here, but I know the truth, and if you think…." She paused, and sighed. "No, that's not a threat. It's a promise. Two words, that's all it'll take." She listened again, and snorted humourlessly.

"You take care of me, or I'll take care of you…." She laughed this time. "Oh you can't afford to do that. Not again. You come anywhere near me, and I'll sing like a canary."

Another pause, then, "You know what I want. I want this done. I want this over with. You said you'd look after me. So keep your promises."

"Excuse me!" I turned. A young woman in a white lab coat stood on the far side of the desk, a Pret A Manger bag in her hand. "What are you doing there?"

"Ah," I smiled, extending my hand and moving back to the customer side of the desk as the receptionist took her place. "Danny Bird," I introduced myself. "Was wondering if I could have a moment with Miss Barton."

The girl raised an eyebrow, as though about to ask what I'd been doing eavesdropping at her boss' door, then, seemingly deciding that a customer was a customer, tapped, instead, at a computer before her. "She's very busy, but there might be a slot in a few days. What exactly is the issue."

"Personal," I smiled, "and I can't really wait a few days. Any chance I could see her now?"

"None, I'm afraid." She smiled, but the eyes were steely glints.

"Maybe you could mention my name," I said. "Jane knows me."

"What are you doing here?" Jane Barton appeared in the doorway to the office, an angry glare on her face, the hoarse mumble back in her voice.

"I wondered if I could have a word," I said.

"Jennie?" She glanced at the girl, who spooned a forkful of salad into her mouth, tapped at the computer again, swallowed the salad, and said "Mrs Jones in half an hour."

"You've got twenty minutes," Jane said, and beckoned me into the treatment room.

I closed the door behind me and turned to her. "Look, Jane, I won't beat around the bush," I said, "I know what's going on, and it has to stop."

Her face set in an impassive mask, and she dropped her frame into a chair by her desk, gesturing to me to sit in the other. "What's going on," she said. "I have no idea what you're talking about."

"You, and Olivia and Kent," I clarified. "I know how it feels to be betrayed," I said, realising, as I said it, that what I'd felt last night with Caz had been nothing like betrayal; rather, it had been anger at the idea of her having kept secrets from me.

Childish, I realised, feeling, already, guilty for the argument that had ensued.

"Betrayed," she laughed, "you've got no idea."

"Look," I decided to go for plain talking. "I get that you're angry. I get you want to hurt someone, but this won't work. You won't get what you want."

Jane blanched. "What are you going to do?"

"That's your choice," I answered. "I can take this back to Olivia and Kent, who will probably take it to the police." At this, a frightened squeak escaped her. "Or you can stop sending the letters, and I say nothing to anyone."

Her face flushed angrily. "Stop sending the letters?"

I nodded. "Look, Jane, Olivia loves Kent. Kent loves Olivia. It won't matter what you do, they will get married."

Jane grunted, throwing her hands up at the same time. "Listen," she said, "I don't have a clue what you're talking about, but you have ten seconds to leave my office before I call the police myself. And if you so much as breathe a word of this baseless accusation, I will sue your arse for slander. Now get out!"

CHAPTER THIRTY-SIX

Ali's "Fiesta Di Paella" went off surprisingly well. I'd had time, on the journey back from Jane's to consider whether or not I might have jumped to a conclusion about her involvement in the poison pen letters. I'd also had time to consider whether I'd been rash in arguing with Caz, and to decide that I wanted to talk to Nick; wanted to give him a chance to explain.

There was a definitely something going on with Jane Barton, though: That one-sided phone conversation had been a puzzle.

But by the time I got back, the bar was heaving, all the punters raving about the paella and the tapas dishes I'd lined up, and any thoughts I'd had of calling Caz or Nick were banished.

Ray and Dash were wearing open bolero jackets, Matadors hats, and tight shiny black speedos, into which several punters had already stuffed ten pound notes.

As I passed through the bar, I heard two of the punters debating their chances with my twin nephews.

"The one on the left. He's so cute. I definitely would."

His mate downed his bottle of San Migel, peered over his fake Ray Bans, and sighed. "Oh yes, for him, I'd bottom."

"Him?" The first one brayed like a donkey. "Girl, you'd bottom for Noddy!"

I slid behind the bar and bumped into Dash. "Here, Danny," he said, "Can we do more of these? I've nearly paid for me holiday tonight.' His brother, as I watched, bent down to pick a bottle of tonic from a shelf, and several of the punters leaned so far over the bar to catch sight of his upturned arse that I feared for the structural integrity of the place.

Ray, as he straightened up, caught my eye, and wiggled his eyebrows. "Gotta keep the punters 'appy," he laughed, as another night's accommodation hit the tip bowl on the bar.

"Right," Ali – dressed as Dona Elvira, but with her beehive wig slightly askew – shoved a pair of maracas into Ray's hand and instructed him to go shake them at the other end of the bar. "Then push the Sangria," turned to Elaine, who was making a sulky point by wearing jeans and a t-shirt with nothing remotely Spanish about them – and ordered her to get out the back with Dash and make another batch of the afore mentioned cocktail.

"I don't need 'im to 'elp," Elaine whined.

"I bet you don't," Ali snapped back, "But I want the booze in the jugs, not in you. So hop to it, princess!"

Elaine scowled, and marched off, Dash following meekly.

"Ah," Ali smirked bitterly after them, "Love's young dream. Right, we're running low on the Tortilla and the Patatas Bravas, and we're completely out of the Andalusian Pork Belly. Any chance you could whip up some more?"

"Elaine, that stuff takes hours to cook," I said, eyeing up the phone.

"So, that'll be a 'No,' then," she said. "What else you got?"

"I can do you some meatballs, some croquettes, and some Cojonudos," I said.

Ali considered the proposal. "We'll have the first two. I got no idea what the third is, so I doubt we'll sell many of them. Where you going?"

I looked back over my shoulder. "I've just got to make a quick call."

"Danny," she gestured at the crowd, "This bar exists to make money. And considering every few months you seem to kill one of the staff, I'm keen to make as much as I can and get out before it's my turn. So now would probably be a better time for the cooking and the serving than for the phoning, if you get my drift."

Was every boss, I wondered, as cowed by his staff as I was by mine? "Fine," I sighed, give me half an hour and the first lot should be good to go.

Next morning, before the sun was up, I called the number for Olivia Wright. The phone was answered by the butler doing, once again, his best Lurch impersonation.

"Please hold," he said, "I shall check if Miss Wright is available."

There was a click, and Olivia Wright came on the line. "Danny? How nice to hear from you."

"I hope it's not too early," I offered, though, quite frankly, I didn't care if it was.

"Not at all," she giggled, "I'm just off out for a sun salutation and some Ashtanga with Jane."

I had no idea what either of those was, but I suspected they didn't come in a glass or a bowl, so I simply asked her when would be convenient to call round.

"Oh, I'm off out today. I'm going to be at Monica's studios. She's got an exhibition coming up, so we said we'd take a look and help her with the arranging. You could meet us there, if you want, I'm sure she won't mind."

She gave me the address, we agreed a time, I hung up, and, as a thin sliver of light ran along the top of the roller blind in my room, got up and showered.

After showering, I called Caz, but the phone went to voice mail.

"Hi," I said, "It's me. I'm sorry about the other night. I was stupid, and childish, and I was out of order. I," I sighed, "I miss you. It's only been a day, but I miss having you around. I'm sorry. Please call me."

That done, I called Nick, and listened to the phone ring three, four, five times.

Just before the sixth ring, there was a click, and the phone was answered.

"Hello." It was a woman's voice, husky and sleepy.

She was waking up in bed next to him. I closed my eyes and saw his face, relaxed in sleep, a scattering of freckles across his nose. Then I saw her lying next to him.

His wife.

"Hello?" She said again, a little more awake this time, and with a slight accent to her voice.

I opened my mouth to speak, but nothing came.

"Who is there?" She asked, with a definite accent – and perhaps a little fear - this time. "Who is this?"

"Wrong number," I said, and hung up, my heart beating faster than I'd ever known.

I took the tube to Old Street, and walked from there to Monica Vale's studio on the edges of Shoreditch. Once, this part of the city was grubby, dirty and downright dangerous, home to the poor and the dispossessed, but today, as the sun beamed down from a sapphire blue sky, the heat bouncing back and being magnified by the office towers and the plate glass windows of the designer boutiques, it was home to yummy mummies of all descriptions, watching smilingly as their offspring devoured overpriced gelato and ran amok in what was billed as a 'Pop up fountain,' but which resembled, more, a fire hydrant that had been bust open and covered in a chicken wire sculpture of a giant flower.

I passed the mummies, the screaming kids, and the mandatory gang of hipsters, bearded, sunglassed, and sweating profusely in the ridiculously impractical tweeds that had been, back in January, decreed as 'In' this summer, and made my way to a small lane way where I found the door for Monica's studio, and rang the doorbell.

After a second ring, a deep, Germanic voice answered, I introduced myself, and, after a pause, the buzzer sounded, and I was instructed to come up to "Floor two. Not one. Two."

Such specific instructions might have tickled me if I hadn't been sweating, overheating and already feeling the effects of sunburn. As it was, I was met at the top of the stairs by a statuesque woman with a 'do' that made me wonder if, perhaps, the Khmer Rouge had gone into hairdressing. She was wearing what appeared to be a Kimono stuffed roughly into a pair of the most pleated jeans I had ever seen. If the world had ever declared a denim shortage, I suspected the repurposed fabric in this single pair might have kept the Hokkusai Denim Co. (Whose name was printed in English, French, Arabic and, I presume, Chinese, down her right leg) in raw material for several seasons.

Her hair, after the war criminal had finished hacking at it, had been dyed the sort of scarlet that my mother usually referred to as Hooker Red, and the entire effect was of a pear shaped, traumatised, time travelling Geisha. In clogs.

"I am Hildegard," she announced in the sort of bass voice that James Earl Jones built his career on. "You will walk this way." She spun around, muttering "Scheisse," as - the wooden soles of the clogs providing absolutely no grip – she lost control and her feet slid in opposite directions.

She steadied herself, glared at me, and, again, said, "You will walk this way."

She then proceeded to mince like someone who has just discovered legs or walking, along the landing, her hand flying out towards the wall several times as, I suppose, she felt her traction going and the clogs took over

At length, we came to a door, and she grasped the handle in much the same way as the unsinkable Mollie Brown might have grabbed the hand of the sailor who hauled her out of that lifeboat, shoved the door open, announced me by bellowing my name with a degree of Teutonic fury that put me in mind of a particularly pissed off Valkyrie (in clogs), and then held the door frame for balance as I squeezed by and into the huge, bright and impossibly hot space.

At the opposite end of the room, Monica Vale, Olivia and Jane Barton were seated around a table. Between them and I was a series of paintings stood on easels. They looked, at first glance, like reproductions of old masters. Then I realised, they were actually paintings of modern subjects done in the style of the masters – a teenage girl, her septum, eyebrow and tongue displaying vivid piercings, done in the style of The Mona Lisa, a Big Issue seller painted as The Laughing Cavalier, and so on.

Jane gave me a frosty glance before turning her attention from a stack of papers spread on the table before the trio and opening a small square box before her and extracting various phials of coloured liquids.

"As a vegan," Olivia was saying (and I had a flashback to a drunken version of her devouring mini roast beef Yorkshires) "I think you need more raw food in the buffet. Hello Danny. No Caz today?"

Monica Vale smiled her vacant, gap toothed smile, and went back to inspecting the images spread out before her. I realised more than ever that Caz was – to everyone – my shadow. Or was I hers? Either way, me on my own wasn't complete. And I missed her even more, as I mumbled some vague comment about her having something else to do this morning.

"What do you think?" Monica Vale asked, sweeping her arm at the images on the table. "The poster for my next exhibition. It's theme is the beauty in the mundane, the joy in the everyday."

"Alternatively," said Kent, coming up behind me, "It's about getting a load of chavs together and making them look pretty."

Monica turned to him. "My subjects were people, Kent, and were treated with dignity. They're not chavs, they're models."

"Yes," he half-heartedly acknowledged, "But surely, looking at you three gathered together, the theme should be The Blasted Heath. It's all a bit: When shall we three meet again?"

"Damn!" Jane Barton snapped as she dropped one of the phials she'd been holding up to the light. She swivelled, trying to catch it, and knocked the box over, the contents spilling out. Several of them rolled across the table and dropped to the floor.

Kent rushed over to help, and both Olivia and Monica dropped to their knees to collect the phials.

"I can handle it," Jane snapped at him, shoving his hand to one side as he reached for a phial.

Suddenly, another cry rang out, this time more panicked and Monica Vale shot to her feet, her hand gripping her throat.

"Nobody move!" She cried. "My Locket! My locket!"

"Oh Lord," Kent rolled his eyes, "What's up now?"

"My locket's missing," Monica clarified, for those who were deaf or stupid. "I had it a moment ago, I know I did."

"Well it can't have gone far," Kent said as, the last of Jane's homeopathic remedies stowed back in the box, attention shifted to the new search. "Where have you been since you arrived?"

"Here," Monica wailed, gesturing wildly at the studio, the paintings, the table, and the entire vast and almost empty space. "Just here."

"Well then, it has to be somewhere here," I said, eyeing the space, as the others split up and began checking the studio.

"The catch has been gammy for a while," Monica fretted. "I need to get it fixed, but I can't bear to part with the locket, even for a minute."

"O.K." I dropped to my knees and scanned the floor from where I stood.

The immediate realisation was that Monica's cleaner was very through: Not so much as a dust ball was visible for the entire length of the studio. Which made the glint of something metallic from beneath the cocktail cabinet standing against the wall immediately visible.

I slid my hand under the cupboard and pulled out a cheap locket on an equally cheap chain. I couldn't help flipping the locket open.

Inside was a tiny colour picture of two teenaged girls, their arms wrapped around each other as they smiled at the camera. They were both almost identical, blonde and with beaming smiles and only the gap toothed smile of one differentiating them from each other.

One of the girls was, clearly, Monica Vale. But I'd seen the other – older, but still smiling that gap toothed grin – somewhere else recently. She'd been sitting – along with a group of somewhat mismatched characters – on Anthony Taylor's sideboard.

"Is this it?" I asked, standing up and holding the item out.

Monica, spotting the item in my hand, fell on me with kisses and promises of undying gratitude, and I was finally rescued by Kent, who took me firmly to one side.

"Any news on the poison penner?" he asked, looking over his shoulder to ensure we were unheard.

"Well," I glanced over my shoulder at Jane Barton, and dropped my voice. "I think I've found a viable suspect, but I promised them that, provided the game stopped, I wouldn't disclose their identity."

He raised an eyebrow. "That wasn't, strictly speaking, the deal, was it?"

I shook my head. "No, it wasn't. But if I can stop these letters and give you – and Olivia – some peace, I figure that's got to be better than vengeance, surely."

He considered this for a moment, then shrugged. "I guess you're right," he said. "It might be best just dropped. I mean, it's upsetting for everyone, but, well, really..."

"What are you boys doing here?" Olivia came over, and Kent was, suddenly, all coy.

"Nothing, Livvy. Thought you were going shopping."

"Have you told Danny about our latest?"

"Latest?"

"They've written again."

I glanced at Kent, who sighed, and rolled his eyes.

"Look," he said, "This is getting silly. Once we start paying people to hunt this person down, we're just giving them credence. We're feeding their sense of importance."

Long words from someone who, a minute before, had been trying to get me to drop the whole investigation.

The new letter was produced, and I read it.

YOU'VE BEEN WARNED YET STILL YOU WANT TO MARRY HIM.
BENSON IS A MURDERER AND WANTS ONLY ONE THING: ££££S.
LEAVE HIM NOW BEFORE YOU BECOME VICTIM NUMBER THREE

I glanced at Jane Barton, who glared back at me as if daring me to speak.

"Number three?" I noted.

Olivia looked puzzled. "Kent? Who could victim number two be?"

"Maybe our letter writer assumes you had something to do with Dave Walker's murder," I offered.

"Ridiculous," Kent fumed.

"Ridiculous," Olivia agreed. "When the waiter was killed, Kent was with you and I in your office talking about these."

"Yes," I agreed, both gratified that Livvy had referred to my back parlour as an office, and confused as to why – if he was entirely innocent of the charges – Benson had been so keen to avoid mentioning the latest letter, or having me continue my work.

CHAPTER THIRTY-SEVEN

"Not being funny," Ali announced, as though humour and yuks were her stock in trade, "But if I wanted to be a cleaner, I'd have become one."

She held up a messenger bag. "I've cleared up the pile in the corner of the kitchen, and apart from The Duchess's stack of Lewis Vutton carrier bags, a couple of gym kits that the ASBO twins left here and never use, and my shit, this was all that was left, so I assume it's yours. Be good if you could keep the place tidier in future."

I was grateful that Ali had, without my even needing to prompt, cleared up the mess that the Health and Safety officer had kicked off about, but the bag she was proffering wasn't mine, and I was about to advise her so when a thought struck me.

"Cheers Ali," I took the proffered item, and headed towards the kitchen table, "And thanks for tidying. I'll get a few quid more into your packet this week."

"Damn straight you will," she grumbled back, "That Flamenco frock weighed a fucking ton. Royally screwed up me back. And the shoes have destroyed me bunions."

"You wore the shoes?" I asked in disbelief, and was greeted by the sort of look I imagine Dustin Hoffman gave Larry Olivier when the latter suggested he act rather than truly sweat his way through a scene in Marathon Man.

"The shoes," Ali instructed me, "are the point of the bloody outfit. You ever seen anyone do Flamenco in Flip Flops?"

I decided against pointing out that at no time had my erstwhile bar manager danced the afore mentioned dance, chose to smile gratefully (I hoped) and thank her again, and settled down to rifle through the bag.

"To be honest," Ali said as she left the room, "Much as it pains me to mention it, if you want to put a few quid for extra effort into someone's packet this week, it should probably go to the Little Madam."

"Whoa!" I looked up from the bag. "Did you just say you want me to reward Elaine?"

Ali nodded, a look on her face that suggested even she didn't believe she was doing this.

"Elaine?" I was still incredulous.

"I know," she said, "But she's been really knuckling down this morning. She's even putting the bins out. Might be a phase," she sniffed, "But if it continues, we should maybe, y'know, recognise it."

I sat open mouthed, wondering when Ali had gotten round to reading a management textbook, as she shuffled off up the hallway, already grumbling at the team ("Why are them tonics there? That's the bitter lemons' place.") Then, I turned back to the bag.

My hunch had been right. The bag contained a large paperback version of the Complete Works of Shakespeare, which had been read so many times it was dog eared, the cover bent and torn, and many of the pages bearing notes, circlings, asterisks and other marks. A flier for an upcoming show at The National was stuffed into Hamlet Act2, Scene 2, and a circle drawn around the quatrain.

Doubt that the stars are fire,

Doubt that the sun doth move his aides,

Doubt truth to be a liar,

But never doubt I love.

I put the book to one side, and poked back into the rest of the contents.

I pulled out a travel card, the photo attached bearing the requisite "Mugshot" look, and a cassette Walkman with a pair of over the head earphones that looked as though they'd been made some time in the seventies.

I pressed play and listened to a few bars of Sly and The Family Stone before I dived back into the bag, extracting, this time, a small velvet drawstring bag.

This had promise. Whatever was inside was weighty, but small, and I suppose I already knew what it would contain when I tipped it into my palm.

Even in the dim light of the kitchen, the simple gold ring glistened brightly. It was old, that much was obvious, as, even though it looked like it had recently been professionally polished, the scratches and chips of a past life were visible to the naked eye. But it was a weighty, expensive piece, and had clearly held some special meaning to Dave Walker, else why would he have been carrying it around.

I checked inside the ring itself, and found the traces of an inscription: George & Margaret 27.12.1965. Was Margaret the Maggie Wright at whose funeral Dave Walker had met his end? And if she was, who was George? And why was a waiter carrying around what looked like a wedding band with their inscription on it?

I put the ring back into the pouch, realising, as I did so, that I should probably have just delivered the entire package to the police the minute I realised it belonged to Dave, but deciding that I'd do so once I'd extracted all its secrets, and pulled out a small zippered coin purse. Inside were a twenty pound note, a ten pound note, and a couple of coins.

The final treasure, apart from a copy of the Metro from the morning of the funeral, opened at an article on a recent spate of burglaries in Islington, was the phone.

The phone that Walker had been struggling to use that morning, and on which he had had an argument with someone.

Or was it an argument? It might have been an attempt to calm down someone hysterical. Someone who was either angry with or hugely concerned by, Dave.

It was an iPhone, and a recent one by the looks of it: Compared to everything else in the bag, it was in pristine condition, with not a scratch or a mark on it. I opened the phone, and went straight to the last number dialled.

It had been dialled at 2100 the night before his death, and, I discovered on hitting 'Redial,' had been to a Pizza Hut.

Next, I went to the last call received, and saw a mobile number to which no contact name had been added. I checked the log on the phone, and found the same number popping up - either as calls received or made - several times a day, for as far back as the phone had been in use.

I hit redial, and listened as the iPhone dialled through, the other end rang, and rang, and rang, and, after six rings, went to voicemail.

Only, the voicemail was an electronic voice which did little more than tell me that the person at the number I had dialled could not answer right now, and invited me to leave a message so that they could get back to me later...

I hesitated. Did I really want to let whoever was at the end of this line know that I had the phone, that I had something which connected them - however tenuously - with Dave Walker? Had I not already done so by ringing them: I mean, they'd see the missed call number and know that someone had called on Walker's phone?

In the end, the machine at the other end made up my mind for me by timing out, saying Thank You in that disconcerting electronic voice, and terminating the connection as abruptly and definitively as Dave Walker had been terminated.

The second most frequently called number had a name next to it. I hesitated a moment, then pushed dial.

CHAPTER THIRTY-EIGHT

The phone rang three times before it was answered by a man, a note of caution and confusion in his voice.

"Hi," I said in response to his confused hello. "Is Liza there?"

There was a moment of silence, then the sound of a cigarette being slowly inhaled, held, exhaled, and a throaty chuckle came down the line.

"Oh, child, Liza hasn't been at this number since Thatcher was in power. Now suppose you tell me what you're doing with my sister's phone?"

Suddenly, one of Naimee Campbell's comments about Dave Walker having a sister – a sister who neither of the ASBO twins had been able to locate – made sense. Dave's sister was the camp kind, and this man on the end of the line was her.

I ran through the story of why I had the bag, and Liza was silent for much of it.

At the end of my story, Liza dragged, again, on the cigarette, held the smoke, exhaled, and, at length, spoke: "Davina could be a total pain in the arse. You got that, I suppose? No idea that this wasn't the 1890's anymore; a total inability to deal with the fact that everything is half-arsed these days?"

I acknowledged the behavioural ticks.

"But you know what? That was just her. There was never – absolutely never – any malice in it. If anything, she was just the most simple, childlike creature around. She could be a pain in the arse, but she didn't deserve to end like this."

I agreed totally with the comment. "Listen, Liza," I said.

"Oh, love, Liza's a name I haven't used for years. I've been Sue Narmee, Virginia LeThrush and – let me think – oh, yes, Phyllis à Glass since then. Nowadays, I'm Mangelina Jolly, but you should probably call me Lionel till we get to know each other. Then I'll let you know what you can call me."

On the table before me, my mobile vibrated and lit up with an incoming text. I glanced at it, and saw that the text was from an unknown number.

"Well, Lionel, I think we should probably meet. When would be good for you?"

He named a time next day, gave me his address, and we rang off.

I picked up my mobile, and opened the text.

So ashamed, it read. You were right. I can't go on. Tell Kent and Olivia I'm sorry. It was signed with a single initial – J – and, as I looked at the text, a shiver ran up my spine.

This was not good.

I shoved Dave's stuff back into his bag, hid it in a cupboard, called Caz, and, having gotten through, once again, to voice mail, left a message before I slipped my phone into the pocket of my cargo shorts, and headed out of the pub, ignoring Ali's requests re the dinner service, ran up the street to Mike Green's place, and shoved my head through the door.

The builders had built an impressive oak and granite counter at the other end of the space, and were in the process of adding more paraphernalia. None of them could tell me where Mike was, so I decided I'd have to deal with this without either him or Caz.

In the taxi en route, I called Nick, got through to his voicemail, and told him what was happening.

I could imagine him advising caution, and in fact instructing me to turn the taxi round, head back to The Marq and await his return call.

Well, he was a police man. What else would he say? Smash the door in, dude; and fill your boots? I wasn't of course, about to turn the taxi round, partly because the text had been sent to me, and partly because, as, in my head, he was telling me not to go to Jane Barton's clinic, I was pulling up outside it.

CHAPTER THIRTY-NINE

The plate outside the clinic gave the opening hours as 0900 – 1700 Monday to Friday. My watch showed a quarter past seven, so I knew that the front door should not have been unlocked.

But it was.

I knew, further, that I should not have pushed the door open and stepped into the reception room, but that's exactly what I did.

The reception was – as it had been the first time I'd been here – empty, and – again, just as before – a voice was coming from the treatment room.

I called out, but no answer came. The connecting door, this time, was firmly closed, so I stepped up, knocked on it, and, getting no answer, turned the handle slowly, and pushed the door open.

The voice I'd heard was suddenly clearer, and was a local news reader discussing the fact that police had made an arrest as a result of the ongoing investigation into a series of burglaries in North London.

On the desk to the left of the room was a half empty bottle of Jim Beam, a single glass beside it, and to the right was the massage table, the trolley beside it laid out with oils and potions.

The news ended, and the radio switched to a weather forecaster whose voice told of their boredom at the fact that, for the twenty-fifth day running, they could predict nothing but record high temperatures, no rain, no fog sleet or hail. Not even a thunderstorm. Just more of the same.

"Enjoy the heatwave, folks" he said, with no obvious pleasure in his voice. "I know I shall."

The chair from behind the desk – a standard wheeled swivel affair - was lying overturned in the middle of the floor.

And above it, hanging from a length of bright orange nylon washing line, was Jane Barton. One look at her – at the glassily bulging eyes, and the dark face, frozen in a look of anguish and shock – told me all that I needed to know, and, as if to confirm my diagnosis, the news ended, and the DJ on ClassikHits, his voice full of a bouncing smiling sunniness that merely added to the surreality of the scene before me, thanked the weather man, and announced that "Up next is a classic from Jean-Jacques and the boys: The Stranglers, with Hanging around!"

CHAPTER FORTY

"Well, at least you're talking to Nick again," Caz announced, slamming a triple G&T down in front of me, and waving the bottle at Mike Greene. "Sure I can't tempt you?"

"No thanks," Mike said, "I've a lot to do later. So what happened next?" He prompted me.

"The police came," I answered him, "And took a statement from me. And that, sadly," I addressed Caz, "Was the only time I talked to Nick. It was hardly a gushing reunion."

"It's a start," she answered. "Better than the studied silence you've both been practicing these past few days. "How did he seem?"

"I dunno," I shrugged, "Like someone who was taking a statement from a barman who'd just discovered a massage therapist hanging from the roof of her own treatment room. Y'know: chatty."

Caz turned from the freezer in the corner, chunks of ice in her fist. She threw half of them into her glass, crossed to me, dropped the rest into mine, topped my gin back to the brim, and poured herself a new gin with a splash of tonic. That done, she sat, and shook her head at me.

"Firstly, you are a landlord, not a barman, secondly, Jane was a New Age Jacqueline of all trades, not just a masseuse, and thirdly, Nick's known you long enough to know that asking you to stay away from a crime scene is like asking Kim Kardashian to step away from the cellphone, and expecting you not to poke around a mystery is like expecting her not to post a selfie every ten minutes. You're talking again, and that can only be good."

"So are we," I said, and she waved the fact aside as thought that were always a foregone conclusion.

"So what are you going to do tonight?" Mike asked. "You want to come out for a drink? Get over all this?"

I glanced at what had to be half a litre of gin in a glass before me, and shook my head. "Thanks for the offer, Mike." I closed my eyes, saw Jane's feet – one still wearing a Birkenstock, the other showing toenails painted a surprising canary yellow, which contrasted ghoulishly with the purple toes - recalled thinking She's taller than I remembered, and shivered.

"It's thrown me a bit."

And the sound of Jane's voice You come anywhere near me, and I'll sing like a canary, rang around my head. She wouldn't be singing now. Or ever.

Despite the heat, I shivered. This was no suicide. Someone had shut her up.

Caz threw a concerned glance at me, and said "D'you want me to stop over."

I smiled bravely – I hoped bravely, though I knew she'd see through me – and waved the offer aside. "To be honest, I think I'm gonna get my dad to pick me up. Might stay over at my parents for a couple of days. And Caz, about the other night."

"You're an old fashioned boy, Mr Bird," she said, swigging from her glass, "Which is one of the things I love most about you. But we're not all that old fashioned; or that principled. So next time you want to get all Mother Superior on me: Don't, and we'll be fine. Agreed?"

I held the glass up in toast. "Agreed."

"So," she asked, having swigged from hers, "Now that you and PC69 are talking again, when are you going to discuss the whole, y'know Mrs PC69 situation?"

"Now who's getting all Mother Superior?" I asked.

"The difference," she answered, looking to Mike Green for backup, "Is that you, my dear sweet, old fashioned little gay, need mother superioring. Now, call him. Agreed?"

I shrugged assent, and toasted the two. "Thanks for coming round," I said.

"Hey," Mike smiled back, "That's what friends do."

"And besides," Caz said, "When I saw the Standard review of last night's Fiasco Di Paella, I knew I had to rescue you before that bar manager of yours has claimed my crown as the best PR woman in London."

Mike's jaw dropped. "The Standard reviewed you?"

"I know," I grinned at him, and recited from memory: "Five Stars, a proper old fashioned boozer with surreal humour, efficient (and cute) staff, happy patrons and tapas to die for. Tapas to die for," I repeated, smiling at Caz. "That's my food, that is."

Mike shook his head. "How long have you had this talent? You know," he clarified to my puzzled look: "The ability to fall into a vat of shit and still smell of roses."

"Since he met me," Caz replied, tilting her head as though awaiting the pop of flash bulbs, "And that's not the smell of roses, dear boy: That's Chanel."

CHAPTER FORTY-ONE

It was the smell that roused me.

I was dreaming of Jane Barton and Dave Walker when I smelled burning.

The burning wouldn't have registered a moment earlier, when Jane Barton, her face still lividly bulging, and Dave Walker, gore still oozing down the back of his shirt, had been sat in straight backed chairs, silent, unmoving, and staring at me in an accusatory way, as though saying: Come on, then. Sort it out. But the scent hit my nostrils as the dream morphed into something else; something that vanished almost as soon as the scent registered.

And I woke up.

Silence. In my room, at least. Beyond my room, out past the cracked-open window and the fluttering curtains, was a distant police siren, wailing into the night, the constant low hum of the city, and the sounds of a struggle, a strangled cry, and of glass bottles being kicked around.

And then, above it all, there was the smell of burning.

A smell that seemed too close for comfort. And, accompanying it, there was the sound of crackling, as of wood splitting.

Underneath me.

I threw the sheets off me, and dashed across the bedroom to the landing.

Out here, the smell was stronger, and I could see smoke. Not the thick billowing kind, but enough to tell me that the pub was on fire.

I took the stairs two or three at a time, more throwing myself down them than running, and, at the bottom of the stairs, I stopped dead.

The entire back door was aflame.

I looked behind me, down the hallway to the bar, which seemed dark and still. The fire, for now, seemed localised, but it was already spreading, the flames reaching up to the ceiling , and outwards to scorch the walls on either side of the door.

Behind me, lined up against the wall, were three newly delivered beer barrels, and above them, fixed to the wall, was the phone. I dialled 999, and told the operator what was happening. They told me the fire brigade was on the way, and advised me to leave the pub via the front door and under no circumstances to tackle the blaze.

I hung up, and eyed the silent bar behind me.

I could be out of here in a minute, but that fire was spreading. And fire is unpredictable. How long would it take the fire brigade to get here? Ten minutes? Twenty?

In five, it would have caught the ceiling or the wallpaper, and would spread down the hall. I had to put this fire out, or at least stop it from spreading. But how?

As I was watching, waiting for the ceiling to catch fire, the flames caught the doormat just inside the door, and that, rather than the ceiling or walls, suddenly burst into flame, adding another incendiary layer to the conflagration.

I ran to the bar, grabbing the ice bucket, knowing that the contents of an ice bucket would be unlikely to quench this blaze, but feeling I needed to try something. I needn't have bothered: Ali had efficiently emptied every ice bucket after closing. Likewise, most of the shelves were emptied, waiting to be restocked the next morning.

I ran back to the hallway, where now the doormat was blazing away, threatening the carpet around it.

I loved Ancient History at school, and particularly the Ancient Romans, and I remembered that, when a fire broke out in Ancient Rome, because everything was so closely packed together, so wooden, and so dry, it was almost certain that the whole city would go up, if you didn't create a fire break.

And sometimes, whole houses or blocks of houses would be simply torn down so that the fire could not catch them, and the spread could be limited.

What I needed, right now, was a fire break. I needed something to move this fire away from the door that was, by now, cracking and splintering,, tiny flickers of black ash floating down the hallway towards me.

Which was when I realised that I was choking on smoke.

I ran back, again, to the bar, still desperately grasping for a way to move this fire away.

When it hit me.

Or, rather, I stumbled over it.

In the dark, and the smoke, I walked into one of the barrels, stubbing my toe so badly that the pain had colour and light.

When I'd finished suggesting the heavy metal barrel had Oedipal tastes, I realised that it might actually be my way to break the flames.

I was a weedy kid at school, not one of those ones who was always sick, or who was always picked on, but just one of those who wasn't very sporty, and would be second division material for the bullies.

Then puberty hit, and it was obvious that I wasn't, shall we say, as other boys. Suddenly, the bullying stepped up a notch, and almost every day I was either handing over my lunch money to one bully or having (and losing) a fight with another (usually because I'd already given my lunch money away to the first one, and thus the second had – as a matter of honour – to beat me up, since what was the point of being a bully if the money was already gone; beating me up became, at that point, almost a consolation prize).

So my brother Paddy, who was a year above me in school, finally had a word with me, and took me to the local boxing gym.

"I don't like sports," I'd whined. "And I don't like boxing."

"Yeah? Well I don't like being the laughing stock of the school cos my pansy brother would rather get his head kicked in than throw a punch, so you can shut the fuck up and start fighting, or I'll pop round when Whistler Moore's finished pulping you and have a go myself.

"Listen," he put his arm around my shoulder, "You're my brother, and always will be. And I love you, no matter what happens. Cos you're a good kid, Dan; but," he said, adopting the world weary tone that only a brother 18 months older than you can, "the world is full of fuckers who make Whistler Moore look like a Balla-fuckin-rina. And if you don't learn to fight them, you'll be unhappy for a lot of your life, and frightened for the rest of it.

"So: You wanna learn to box?"

"I'm gonna tell mum you said 'Fuck,'" I smirked back.

"Yeah?" He grinned, playfully twisting my arm behind my back, "Well you'd better do that after you've learned to fight me off, cos if you dob me in, I'll beat the living shit out of you!"

So, that summer, I learned to box, at Flatface MacKenzies 'Boxing Gymnasium' off the Old Kent Road, and within a week of my return to school, I'd been suspended for punching Whistler Moore so hard I broke his nose.

My mother was mortified, the other school bullies were mollified, and Paddy gave me all his comics and sweets for a week, though whether that was because he was proud of me, or because he was afraid I'd tell my mum of his part in my disgrace was – and remains – a mystery.

Flatface MacKenzie had a pretty Spartan setup in what was basically a disused warehouse, but one of the exercises he particularly liked was designed to build shoulder strength, leg stamina, and to work the lower back. It basically consisted of lifting a bag of cement, and throwing it as hard as you possibly could – whilst still retaining your balance – across the room.

Or, at least, it started as a bag of cement, but it ended, as I remembered now, by lifting a beer barrel, and hurling it.

I judged that the door had to be structurally compromised by now, and figured that, if I hit it just right, it should smash outwards, taking (hopefully) the majority of the flames with it.

Of course, there was always the risk that there might be some sort of blowback that would throw the flames back into the hall, and possibly right into my face.

But it was a chance I'd have to take.

I planted my feet firmly on the carpeted floor, lifted the first barrel overhead, tilted backwards slightly, remembering that the power here came from the shoulders throwing the barrel, rather than from trying to swing it back (which would more than likely make me lose control and throw my back out to boot), but it had been ages since I'd done anything like this, and I wasn't sure if it would work.

It didn't. The barrel arced through the air, hit the door, with the distinct sound of splintering wood, and bounced back into the hall, drawing with it a shower of sparks that scattered across the carpet and threatened to ignite.

Undeterred, I lifted the second barrel, steadied myself, felt my legs complain at the weight, took a deep breath, flexed by shoulders, and hurled the thing, full force, at the dead centre of the door.

The impact was loud and solid, and the door – already fatally compromised by the fire – flew off what was left of its hinges and into the alleyway outside.

At that exact moment, the first barrel made a strange sighing noise, which quickly became a hissing, and then there was an explosive bang as the valve, damaged, no doubt, by the impact and the heat, opened, showering 60 pints of beer up and outwards, the impact making the barrel spin so that it became a sprinkler system dousing the remaining flames in IPA, the beer caramelising as it turned to steam, so that, by the time the fire brigade arrived to put out the still flaming door in the back alley, the first man on the scene sniffed the air in the hallway and said "Phew! Smells like a brewery in 'ere!"

CHAPTER FORTY-TWO

"Here. For the shock." Caz handed me what looked suspiciously like a champagne cocktail. "What? I put two spoonsful of sugar in it." She toasted me, and downed half of hers in one slug, before sliding another cocktail towards Ali, who sat, more miserable than normal (if that was even possible) beside me at the kitchen table.

"Who'd want to burn this dump down?" Ali asked, sniffing suspiciously at the glass, before sipping, raising an appreciative eyebrow, and sipping again, "I mean, it's Chopper's pub. Whoever did this was signing their own death warrant when he finds them."

"If he finds bothers looking for them," I said, swigging from the flute before me.

"Oh, he'll look for them," Ali stated, "And when he finds them," she drew her finger across her throat in the style of a Hollywood Mafiosi.

"Right," Dash came into the kitchen, "That geezer's finished with the door. It aint pretty, but it'll hold up if anyone tries to get in."

"Cheers, Dash," I said, "She in yet?"

Dash looked sheepish. "Not yet, but the tubes are a mess."

"She?" Caz asked.

I sighed. "That's what I meant about if Chopper looks for the burner," I said, glancing at Ali. "I heard a female voice last night, in the middle of all the chaos. A sort of squawk. It was Elaine."

Ali's face dropped. "You think Elaine torched the pub? Why would she do that?"

"Well, she's hardly been a fan – of me, or of the place – this past few weeks."

"But she'd perked up," Ali protested. "She even put the rubbish out."

"'Ere, mate," a stranger's voice echoed from the hallway, and Dash turned aside as the door fitter entered, a litre of Vodka in his hand, "You throwin' the stuff away these days?" He asked, jokingly, "Only, if you don't want this, can I take it off your hands?"

Ali leapt to her feet, swiping the Smirnoff from his grip. "Where'd you get that?" She demanded.

He shrugged, seemingly unconcerned that the trophy wasn't his anymore. "Was in an open bin bag out the back. I was movin' them round to tidy up, and it fell out."

Ali looked at me. "She was putting the bins out."

"Walker was right," I said: "she was shorting punters on doubles. Till she'd shorted enough to cover a bottle, then, when she swiped it, your stock control wouldn't show it up."

Ali's eyes glinted the way, I suspect, those of a mongoose do when faced with a Cobra whose been masquerading as Trainee Barmaid of the Year. "The mardy little tart!" She hissed. "I'll fucking string her up!"

"This aint right," Dash protested, "She was settling in."

"Oh grow up, you dappy twat," Ali turned on him, "She was playing you as much as she was playing me."

"No," Dash – the picture of young love desperately seeking reciprocation – protested. "If she was swiping vodka, then fair enough: I get it. It's part of her nature. But why's it still here? I mean, if she came round to get her booze, why torch the pub?"

"He's right," I agreed. "And, having torched the place, why leave her bottle behind?"

"Maybe she only meant to light a small fire," Dash offered.

"What? Just half burn the fucking joint down?" Ali snapped back.

"It might have got out of hand, and then she didn't know what to do."

"I got a suggestion," Ali drained her champagne flute and accepted a refill from Caz. "She cudda called the Fucking fire brigade. Or done a Joan of Arc an' flung her worthless arse on the flames." Her cheeks flamed, though whether from the fizz or the fact that she'd been betrayed by the girl who, only the night before, she'd been asking me to reward, was hard to tell.

"I never thought I'd say this," Caz replied, "but she's got a point." She toasted Ali, who, confused by what seemed to be an entente between her and Lady Muck, finally, and with an air of suspicion toasted her back.

"So how do we find out what happened?" Dash asked. ""How do we find out where she is?"

"There's only one thing for it," Caz offered: "call her. Or her parents. Find out why she's not turned up for work this morning."

I had a better idea.

The phone only rang twice before Chopper picked it up. "Danny," he sounded almost avuncular, this man who – the Sunday papers would have us believe – once disposed of a rival gangster by having him crushed alive inside a Vauxhall Viva at a scrap deposit in Dagenham.

"Great to hear from you. How's my little princess doing?"

"Um," I looked across the table where Ali, Dash and Caz– the latter quietly mixing another batch of Champagne cocktails – stared back at me. "Elaine's, um…"

Elaine's what? Gone berserk with petrol and rags? Not quite over her juvenile alcoholic phase? So fucking deranged she makes you look like a Benedictine monk?

"She's fine," I said. "Doing fine."

"Oh, so you've heard from her, then," he asked.

"Heard from her?" Shit. Was I not supposed to have heard from her?

"Listen," he carried on, as though he'd not even been expecting an answer. "Wanted to thank you for arranging this training course. When she called last night and said she'd be away a few days, I'll admit I was a bit iffy." He chuckled;

the sound of a man imagining how long it'd take for a Nissan Micra to be pulverised with me inside it.

"Funny really, innit, the idea of me being worried. I mean, if you believed the papers I'm Genghis Khan crossed with Al Capone. But Lainey means the world to me. Rest of the family's not up to much, but that little girl... You know what she is?"

Psychotic, I wanted to say, but instead, I kept silent, figuring he hadn't quite finished his monologue.

"She's a fighter," he answered his obviously rhetorical question. "Doesn't soften up easy. So, when she said she was going to learn cookery with that Lady Caroline, I was well chuffed."

"She's gone to learn cookery with Lady Caroline?" I said, and watched as the aforementioned member of the gentry sprayed a half glass of Veuve Cliquot and Courvoisier across the kitchen table.

"Bit of class that Lady Holloway," Chopper said. "Just proud that she's passing her cordon bleu skills on to Elaine. I was so pleased when Lainey called an' said she was going to spend the weekend at Holloway Manor. I knew you lot would be a good influence on her."

Considering Chopper's previous idea of a good influence had been getting his deranged granddaughter extra maths tuition from a man known as Frankie "Fishmonger" Harris (so called due to his skill with a filleting knife, allegedly) I was not exactly flattered by the faith Chopper had placed in Caz and I.

The truth was that Elaine was a delinquent, one so far out of control that even her dear old granddad – the most feared thug in South London – couldn't handle her. He'd not so much placed her in our care as dumped her in our unpaid crèche. And now she'd attempted to burn the joint to the ground and gone on the lamb.

"Well, when she's back," the befuddled gangster almost cooed, "Tell 'er from me that I'll be expecting Chicken Chasseur, an' all that Cordon Bleu stuff for breakfast."

Cordon Bleu? Caz thought that anything beyond heating up a tin of soup was a skill innately in the working classes, but if Chopper and his snobbery were giving me a break, I was going to jump at it. "Absolutely, Mr F. Got to go…"

I ended the call and looked up at three faces in differing states of horror.

"She's missing, aint she?" Dash asked.

"Chopper thinks we're looking after her, don't he?" Ali said, the not so subtle suggestion that whatever happened to her while we were 'Looking after her,' would be entirely our fault.

Caz, meanwhile, having gathered the gist of the conversation, merely said the phrase "Cookery classes," in the tone that a vicar might say Anal Gangbang, "I have neither the desire nor the inclination to ever engage in such practices."

"Well Elaine told him she was going to cookery classes at Holloway Hall."

"Firstly, sweetheart, there is no Holloway hall. There is Beaumont. And secondly, Elaine Falzone would not be caught dead in a dusty draughty pile like the house. Even if she were invited. Which she most certainly wouldn't be. What the hell is going on?"

"I don't know," I admitted.

"Well you'd better figure it out," Ali snapped, "And fast. Cos if you don't figure out where she's got to, and get her back, Chopper'll make being burned alive in your own pub look like a pleasant way to spend an evening."

As she spoke, my phone rang. I glanced at it, and saw an unknown number. Thank God, I sighed. She's calling to apologise. Dash is right: it was a prank that got out of hand, all's forgiven, and no need to ever mention this again.

I snatched the device up, hitting answer, and talking even before the thing was to my ear.

"Elaine, where on earth have you been?"

But it wasn't Elaine at the other end of the line. It was a very drunken Desmond Everett. I glanced at the clock on the wall, saw that it said 10.15a.m., and allowed myself a brief moment of being shocked that anyone could be so shitfaced this early. Then, I observed my best friend opening another Veuve, while my bar manager fetched clean glasses and my nephew swigged Courvoisier straight from the bottle in an attempt to drown his broken heart, and thought Glass Houses, Danny.

Everett was wittering on. "... Not right. Not right at all, you see. Couldn't have been that way. Not at all. I mean, you see what I mean, surely?"

"Listen, Desmond," I interrupted him. "Bit of a crisis at this end. Any chance I could call you back?"

He paused in his rambling. "Crisis? Yes, of course, but..." and he was off again rambling. "S'pose I should do the right thing. Was just so sad. So sad. But you're right. Thank you."

I had no idea what he was going on about, but I needed rid of him fast, so I let him hang up, and turned back to the team.

"Booze down, folks. We've work to do. Ali, open up shop. Dash, get your brother in here: I've got some research you boys need to do."

"What are you two doing?" Ali asked, gesturing suspiciously at Caz and I.

"We, while the twins here complete their research, are going to go visit an old queen. And hopefully, get some answers."

CHAPTER FORTY-THREE

The apartment door was opened before I'd even stepped out of the lift.

A tall, middle-aged man, the silver in his buzz cut head sparkling in the sunshine behind him, stood smiling in the doorway. He was wearing a button down shirt, so dazzlingly white that the glare almost obscured the Polo logo on the breast, and a pair of pale blue jeans so tight that, at first glance, it seemed he was bare legged and suffering from terrible circulation.

"You must be Danny," he beamed, extending his hand. "And friend." The smile dimmed as he caught sight of Caz behind me.

"Lady Holloway," Caz bypassed me, and introduced herself, taking the offered hand and shaking it vigorously. "How kind of you to see us."

Lionel, predictably, was a pushover for a posh bird, and, any trace of frostiness vanished, he ushered us into his flat, introducing himself to Lady H as "Lionel Stamp, your Grace," and informing her that it was, "A pleasure to have you here," as though he were the director of an old folks home, and she were about to open the Jeremy Clarkson ward for the Terminally Nasty.

The interior of Stamp's flat, considering it was nine stories up a Hammersmith Tower block, and had necessitated a ride in a lift which seemed to have been scented with Yankee candles in smells of cabbage and old urine, was breathtaking.

Here, the scent of Jo Malone lime and basil filled the air, the long hallway was plastered with old theatre posters framed in black ash and aligned with military precision, and the floor under our feet was polished oak.

"Would you mind," our host said, gesturing at our shoes, and I realised that he was already barefoot, and sporting toenails painted a vibrant scarlet.

For a moment, I had a flashback to Jane Barton, but I pushed that down, and slipped off my shoes, before following Caz and her new best friend down the hall and into a living room that was even more jaw dropping than the hallway.

Here, three sides of the room were vast windows, beyond which the city – a heavy heat haze hanging over it like an unexpected gas bill – lay, seemingly consumed by the inertia of the day.

An air conditioning unit hummed quietly in the corner, it's issue barely rippling the leaves on the plants dotted around the space.

The floor was, again, polished wood, which co-ordinated with the plants, the huge leather sofa and armchair, and the chunky coffee table to create the air of a gentlemen's' club in a conservatory in the sky.

"My," Caz sighed, seemingly genuinely, "What an amazing apartment."

"Oh, d'you like it?" Lionel beamed, "Well, I have had a few years to get it right. Can I get you both anything to drink? Tea? Coffee? A Gin and Tonic?"

Caz smiled beatifically at him, "Why Mister Stamp, I'd marry you for that."

Stamp smiled, winked at me, pointed out that Caz was, "Not really my type, dear; I like 'em a little butcher," and left the room to fix our drinks.

"I don't know what you're grinning at," Caz said, without even looking at me. "He said a little butcher. And you, sweetheart, are about as butch as this divine cashmere throw."

She fingered the impressive item, and threw herself down on the sofa. "Why can't you have more friends like Mr Stamp? He seems lovely."

"Yes," I said. "So genuine, and honest and not at all bitchy. Like some of my friends. I really should take your advice more often."

"You're not still going on about Tony, are you? He's an old friend, and I didn't tell you because you were having your, difficulties with Nick."

"No, I am not still going on about Tony. And difficulties is something of an understatement, wouldn't you say?"

Caz sighed. "It's the Irish in you, of course. They don't so much carry a grudge as wear it like," she swept the throw around her shoulders, and stood to her feet to inspect the look in the gilt framed mirror that filled most of the wall opposite, "A divine purple pashmina of resentment and barely suppressed fury. Sweetheart, the fact he's married shouldn't bother you. It's the twenty first century, you know. People have been jumping married men for ages now."

"Ooh," Stamp re-entered the room before I could pass comment, set his tray of drinks down on the sideboard under the mirror, and, handing tall, frosty, glasses to us, nodded appreciatively at Caz, "Very Sophia Loren," he murmured cryptically, "And I fully agree with the married man comment."

He turned his attention to me, "Jump him, love. I don't know who he is, or what the issue is, but take it from me: a man in your bed – married, or otherwise – is better than empty space. Look at you: You're young and gorgeous. You should be throwing it round like a bishop with a censer. But you didn't come here for romantic advice, did you?" He gestured at the sofa, picked up his own gin, and settled himself into the chair. "What can I do for you?"

"We were hoping you could tell us a little more than we already know about Dave Walker," I said.

"Ah." He nodded, his smile dimming momentarily, "Davina. How do you describe your soul mate?"

"I'm sorry," I said, "I hadn't realised you were a couple."

Lionel shrieked, his horror dissolving quickly into cackling laughter. "A couple? Jesus, love, I was never deranged enough to go there, and – to be honest – never damaged enough for Davina to be interested in me. Do you like marijuana?"

The question took me completely by surprise, and I stammered my response "I get giggly and chatty, and, um, not really a fan."

"What he means," Caz explained to our host, "Is he can't take more than a drag before he turns into a very bad Carol Channing impersonation. Lightweight." This last aimed directly at me.

"And what about you, Lady Holloway?"

"Oh, Mr Stamp, one simply adores anything that removes one from the ennui of modern life. Don't you?"

"I do," he acceded, as I tried to suppress the voice of Harry Champion in my head performing I'm ennui the Eighth I am, I am…

We relocated, via a kitchen decked out in state of the art utilities that I could only dream of, to the balcony, where Lionel sparked up a spliff, dragged deeply, handed it to Caz, and, after another sip of his gin, turned to me.

"Davina – David – and I were sisters from the moment we met each other at Central. We were studying," he announced, his voice morphing into a perfect impersonation of John Gielgud, "The theatre, dear boy. Well, I was," he said, his voice changing back. "All I ever wanted to be was in the business – didn't care whether I was acting, lighting, costume, or ushering – and believe me, I've done all of them, and a few others in my time. But Davina – who I've known since before Cher had her second nose – wanted only to be an Actor with a capital 'A.' For her, it was Othello and Peer Gynt; nothing else was acceptable.

"Problem was that Dave wasn't a great Actor. He wasn't terrible, just dull. With a capital Duh. Pedestrian. Utterly without life. And always – even when trying to tell a gag – so fucking serious looking. Like he'd just spotted something nasty, or knew exactly what you were up to, and was disgusted at the thought.

"He wasn't so much a Method actor as a Methodist actor. Oh, he tried: Audition after audition after audition. He even – for a while - changed his name. Well, everyone was doing it at Drama School, and it carried on for a while afterwards. You'd bump into a Sally in the street, and she'd have become a Sophie overnight; or a Frank would become a Franceso, and be going about talking like he came from Turino 'stead of Tottenham. For a while there Dave was Daniel Walken. You know: Like Christopher? Still couldn't so much as carry a spear convincingly.

"I even got her a few stints with me. I was already getting a name on the drag circuit as Alice Klaar, so we got Davina dragged up and shoved her out there as Carola DeBells.

"Well," he accepted the joint back from Caz, dragged deeply, held the smoke a moment, and, exhaling via his nose, carried on, "You can probably imagine what a complete fucking shambles that was. Frankly, if she'd gone on as Maggie Thatcher at a miner's convention, it couldn't have gone flatter. Top up, Ange," he giggled, nodding at Caz's empty glass, and taking it – and his own- back into the kitchen.

"So," his voice carried out to us, accompanied by the clink of ice and the hiss of tonic water, "He sort of drifted into what he liked to call 'Service,' which I used to wind him up by suggesting had the ring of Rent about it – albeit a rent boy who could do Hamlet rather than hand relief. But it really meant a stint as a butler for hire, a waiter, front of house at some posh Italian restaurant; you name it. And, of course, all that was money in the bank – more money that he'd ever earned on the stage."

Lionel floated out to us, handed Caz her drink, and stared out over his balcony towards a crack in the buildings through which the river rolled indolently along.

"Then Mark – his boyfriend – got sick. If you know what I mean. Davina dropped everything and stayed at the hospital day and night. I remember saying to him, at one point: 'Sweetheart, Mark's the one who's supposed to look skeletal.'"

He sighed, sipped his drink, and turned back to us. "But Mark got better; well, not better exactly, but he got over whatever it was that had been trying to kill him that time, and Davina found some marks on the back of his hand. Absolutely freaked out. Convinced it was Kaposi's sarcoma, and he had days to live.

"Turned out they were liver spots. Silly queen was right as rain, but Mark got sick and better like a see-saw for a couple of years, and Davina insisted on being there all the time, like her presence could stave off the worst. Then," Stamp took a long pull on the joint, handing it back to Caz, "Mark did die. No warning. Right as rain one night, and had a massive coronary on the 155 to Clapham.

"Davina was destroyed. By the time she'd got her life back together again, she knew it was over re the acting. But that was fine, 'cos, as much as she loved the acting, she'd twigged re her abilities – or lack thereof. Plus, there was always the waiting."

"So do you have any idea," I got to the point of our visit, "Why anyone would want to kill him?"

Lionel giggled, "Oh love, everyone who ever spent more than ten minutes getting dressed down cos they'd disappointed him would be a suspect, to be honest. But no," he shook his head, "He had no real enemies. Except himself; he was his own worst enemy, especially where men were concerned."

Caz perked up. "Unsuitable men?"

"Lady H," I muttered, "Is our expert in unsuitable men."

Caz smiled at me the way Mary Scott might have smiled at Liz One, and, pausing only to mutter "Glasshouses, dear," turned back to Stamp. "Were there any unsuitable men in the picture lately?"

"Well," Lionel leaned in conspiratorially, "She was always one to keep things close to her chest, if you know what I mean."

We both nodded that yes, we did know what he meant, and Caz gestured to him to continue.

"To be honest, he'd had no luck with men since Mark, but lately he'd been totally loved up. Someone he'd met on the internet. Younger, I think – though he'd have been unlikely to meet older on the internet. I mean: Alzheimer's and the internet hardly go hand in hand do they? Dave had a couple of gins here a few weeks ago, and opened up a bit.

"Turns out the other half was madly in love, and Dave felt the same way. Despite the age gap, which – the way Dave carried on – was centuries. So I says 'Do it, then; tell him how you feel,' and Dave – as was his wont – went all coy. Said he was afraid to make a move in case the sparrow flew. Shame he didn't do it. Assuming he didn't."

"Why wouldn't he?"

"Well… I got the sense there were some… issues."

"What sort of issues?"

"Oh, my child, with Davina, it could be anything: Closeted. Confused. Certifiably insane. He once courted (for several months) a man who turned out to be on the lamb from Roehampton. I told him, the minute Gerald started kicking off about MI5 being shored up in the loft, and the fact that the cockroaches were packed with C5, that there was something off there. They lived in a ground floor flat, to begin with, and Gerald – well, she was hardly James Bond, if you know what I mean.

He paused, as though remembering the story of Gerald's demise, then said, "Wouldn't have surprised me if this one was married."

"Married?"

"Oh, poor Davina had history. She never met a married ,man she couldn't understand."

I looked at Caz, who smiled beatifically, offered the joint to Lionel – who waved it aside – and, placing it into the ashtray on a small table beside her, asked Lionel. "So was this one married?"

"Search me, dear, "he said. "This one was mysterious. Like Gerald, only without the Spies. Or the exploding roaches."

CHAPTER FORTY-FOUR

I clicked "End Call," and turned to Caz.

"What?"

"I'm not sure," I said, as my dad slowed the cab to take a corner. "Could be nothing."

"You've got that look that says you think it might be something."

"Desmond Everett," I said.

Caz sighed. "What's Dopey Des been up to now?"

I slid the cab window back down, the breeze rushing in as we hit the Hammersmith Flyover and picked up speed, the petrol fumes and pollution mixing with my dad's Acqua di Gio to make the scent of summer in London.

"He's not," I said, "answering his phone."

"Dearest, I doubt he knows how to. Dopey Des is one of those boys for whom nannies were invented. And why does his inability to answer calls bother you?"

"He called earlier," I said, filling her in, quickly, on his call.

"Ah, the drunken, rambling call from a posh boy. Have you met my family? It's what one does when one has a trust fund and absolutely nothing to do on a warm afternoon: get wasted and call randomly. Well, that or invest in internet start-ups. So, he was upset by Rasputin's death?"

"Caz!"

"What? Oh Danny," she shook her head at me as though I were a charming but clearly incurable idiot, "the woman was an afghan hound. In miniature, hunched up, pot-bellied form, but still: there is absolutely no reason for anyone to have a plaitable beard. They sell stuff in Boots," this last word pronounced as though it were one which had never, previously, passed her lips, "For God's sake. No," Caz shook her head definitively, "looking that – for the want of a better word – rough these days isn't unfortunate; it's deliberate."

"But she's dead," I protested.

"So's Evita Peron, but I bet she still looks better than Jumpy Jane at her liveliest. I swear, the woman twitched like a frog on a hotplate; I've seen Tourette's sufferers with calmer body language. And stop giving me that look, Mother Theresa: You know as well as I do that the whole twitchy hairy mystic thing went out of style with the Maharishi. And he only got into style because he had the Beatles. Jane, meanwhile, had poor Olivia, whose confidence is so low she needed a friend with more facial hair than her grandfather to feel good about herself. So what are you going to do about that?" She nodded at my phone.

"I dunno. He sounded genuinely upset."

"Lemme get this straight," my dad announced from the front seat of the cab as traffic slowed to a complete standstill on the Cromwell road, "You've got a mate who called you a bit worse for wear, and clearly upset. And now you can't get hold of him?"

I nodded, as Caz rolled her eyes and said "If he's anything like my brother, he'll already be en route to Marrakesh for the weekend, or ensconced in Boujis with a blonde who manages to be simultaneously too cheap and too good for him."

"Yeah, well," my Dad sighed, "he could be doin' that." He manoeuvred the cab into another lane, shot daggers at a car attempting – even at five miles an hour - to cut him up, and looked in the rear view mirror at us, "But you sound bothered by this, Dan."

"Well," I searched for the words, "he just sounded," I searched for the words, finally settling on "despairing."

"So?" My dad glanced back in the mirror, "What d'you want to do?"

"I want to check up on him," I finally said, "Only I don't know where he lives."

Caz heaved a sigh so heavy I was convinced her lungs had deflated. "You boys. You're so soft. We women don't get all this touchy feely over drunk dialling, you know," and she pulled her phone from her bag, shot me a warning look, dialled, and, as the phone was answered at the other end, smiled, licked lipstick from her teeth, and launched into "Hello big boy."

I doubted she was talking to Desmond Everett, as the last time he'd been referred to as a Big Boy had probably been by his Nanny, and had almost definitely been before puberty.

"Yes," she paused, her smile widening momentarily, and actually sighed. "I had a good time too. Very good."

And that's when I realised she was calling Anthony Taylor.

She giggled. "Yes, well, that's very kind of you, but," she caught my eye, straightened up, and attempted to run a hand nonchalantly through her hair. Which, as the hair was held in place with enough lacquer to finish off a pack of polar bears, merely resulted in her trying to turn a phone conversation to the point whilst attempting to extricate her perfectly manicured nails from her coiffe without ripping her own locks out. "I'm," she grunted as her hand flew free, a long strand of blonde hair – with surprisingly dark roots – attached, "Trying to get hold of Dopey Des. I don't suppose you have his address, do you? Oh, you do? Smashing. And its..? Really? Earls Court? Thank you lovely. Oh yes, I shall definitely thank you in person. Soon as…" She giggled, thanked him again and, ignoring my disapproving glare, chatted some more, before finally hanging up, and turning to my dad.

"Awfully sorry, Mr B, but if you boys are determined to check in on Dopey Des, you'll need to turn around."

CHAPTER FORTY-FIVE

"See, I told you: Marrakesh." Caz looked pityingly at me as I banged once again on the door of Desmond Everett's mews flat.

"Desmond," I squatted down, shouting through the letter box, "Are you in there? It's Danny. I'd like to talk."

Behind me, on the opposite side of the courtyard, a door opened, and someone stepped out.

"I've called the police," a woman said in tones that would have made the Duchess of Devonshire sound like Eliza Doolittle, pre Prof Higgins, "And they're on the way!"

I stood and turned around. "I'm not sure there's any need for that, Mrs-" I held my hand out, and the lady in question – ninety if she was a day, and wearing, even in this heat, a tweed skirt and a voluminous pink silk blouse that seemed to be formed from the jowls that hung pendulously from her jaw and neck like some sort of fleshy dinosaur – actually shrunk from me.

"It's miss," she said, "and this is a quiet mews. We won't be having with scenes like this. Shouting. Squatting."

You wanna come round my neighbourhood, love, is what I wanted to say. Instead, I smiled in, I hoped, my little-lost-boy best, and tried again. "I'm so sorry for the noise, miss. My name is Danny – Daniel Bird. We're just trying to get hold of my friend Dope – um, Mister Everett."

"Well he's clearly not in, is he?" She snapped back, her jowls quivering like an angry turkey.

Behind me, Caz sniggered. "Told you: Marrakesh."

The old dear's hand suddenly plunged into the folds of her blouse, and pulled out a pair of spectacles attached to a thin gold chain. She put the specs on and squinted at me.

"I know what you look like," she announced in tones so cut glass they were positively Waterford, "and if I see you around here again, I'll have the law on you!"

"We're wasting our time," Caz said. "C'mon; let's go."

Lady Bracknell's scarier granny glanced over my shoulder, and stiffened. "Holloway!" She barked, and, behind me, Caz gasped. "What on earth are you wearing? A lady should never show so much flesh. Get over here this instant!"

"Shit," Caz muttered, pushing past me, a beaming but, I could tell, uncertain smile plastered on her mug. "Miss Hastings! How are you? It's been... Ooh, how long has it been?"

"Not long enough, Holloway. I said you'd end in the gutter, and," at this she glanced pointedly over her glasses at me, " I was, quite clearly, correct. Shouting. Squatting. Peering through people's letter boxes. Your father will be informed. Oh yes, have no doubt of that, Holloway. I shall telephone him this instant."

"Oh, Jesus," Caz sighed, turning her face towards me, and muttering out of the corner of her mouth, "I knew this was a stupid idea. It's my governess. She's barking mad, and deaf as a post. Dopey Des could have been singing Nessun Dorma all day and she'd know nothing."

"She, Lady Caroline, has had a hugely expensive and extremely efficacious hearing aid fitted. And insanity, if I recall, runs in your family, not mine. Now stand here," Miss Hastings jabbed a finger so bony it was almost skeletal at a point well within what should have been her personal space, and scowled at a now clearly blushing Caz. "And explain yourself girl."

"Um," Caz – all traces of sophistication vanished, shuffled over to the spot indicated, and, head hung, stood like a naughty schoolgirl.

"Speak up, girl! She was always difficult," Hastings, her view of me clearly in the ascendant now that she had Caz to pick on, addressed me, before turning her hectoring tones back to a cringing Caz. "What are you doing here, and what is your interest in Mister Everett?"

Caz mumbled something.

"I said I've a hearing aid, gel, not a bally radar. Speak up!" And I swear, if the old dear had had a ruler, she'd have rapped Caz over the knuckles with it.

"Desmond – Mr Everett, that is – called my friend earlier, and seemed very – um – upset," Caz stammered.

"Upset?" She waved the word aside. "Man's an idiot." We were in agreement on one thing, then. "Always mooning about, lost in his own world. No backbone," Hastings decided, "That's what's wrong with young people these days. No character. It's all need and deserve, and no sense of duty. Don't even make their own beds, half of them," she finished, as though this were clear evidence of the collapse of society, and that hordes of bed making Visigoths were likely to sweep up The Kings Road any day now.

"What was he upset about?" She addressed this to me, waving Caz, momentarily, to one side.

"I'm not sure," I said, adding, before she could accuse me of being obtuse, "I think he might have been drinking."

She tsked at this. "Yes, he was no stranger to the grape. Much," she turned her attention back to Caz, "Like you, if I recall. Thirteen," this addressed to me, "And squiffy as an actress. Disgraceful behaviour." The watery blue eyes swivelled back to me "And so – on the basis of a drunken call – you've come round here, disturbing the peace and squatting in the mews."

This was the third time she'd referred to squatting as though I had been discovered attempting to take a shit in the street. I was unsure how else I was supposed to shout through Desmond's letterbox without getting my lips level with it; but then, I supposed, Miss Hastings would have preferred me not to be shouting through anyones letterbox.

"Well, you see, a friend," I hesitated to refer to Jane Barton as a friend of Des's. The two had mixed in the same circles. And yet, her death seemed to have hit him hard. Why, I wondered? "A friend of Mr Everett died recently."

"Hanged herself," Caz offered, receiving, for her efforts, a witheringly dismissive glance.

"Yes and Mister Everett seemed to have been hit rather badly by the event."

"Obviously," Hastings murmured thoughtfully. "One doesn't come into close proximity with tragedy without being touched by it." Here, she glanced rather pointedly at Caz, and stiffened. "So you've come to check that your friend is well."

"Safe," I said, realising, as I did, that that was what had been gnawing at me since receiving Des's call: People were dying, and a sense of danger was building. I suspected Des was not entirely well in any sense of the word, but I was more concerned that he was in some sort of danger.

"Safe." Miss Hastings considered the word.

"Have you seen him?" Caz interjected. "Mister Everett?"

Hastings shook her head. "I've been away with Lady Carmichael – she sends her love, by the way. Wonders what ever became of you and Bunty. You seemed, she said, to have had so much in common."

Caz blushed, but said nothing.

"I've just arrived back," Miss Hastings continued, so I wouldn't have seen him since," she rolled her eyes as though counting backwards, "Thursday."

"What about the other residents?" I asked, gesturing at the other four front doors in the mews.

Miss Hastings snorted, "Two Russians, a Singaporean, and a Banker who got divorced last year, and hasn't been in the flat since then. I'm afraid, Mister Bird, that Mister Everett and I are the residents of this mews."

I sighed, defeated again, and Miss Hastings cast a steely glance over both Caz and me, before seeming to make a decision.

"Wait here," she said, and stepped back into her flat, reappearing a moment later with a small coin purse. She fiddled arthritically through it, and extracted a small key.

"I will accompany you both, for the express purpose of confirming whether Mister Everett is in his flat or not. That," she fixed us each with her stare, "shall be the limit of our incursion into the gentleman's home. Are we understood?

Caz and I nodded, and the three of us set off across the courtyard.

CHAPTER FORTY-SIX

We stepped into the flat, Miss Hastings leading the way, and calling "Mister Everett! It's Miss Hastings, from number three! I have Lady Holloway and Mister Bird with me! Mister Everett? Are you there?"

She paused, listening, and then turned to us. "I think that settles it, don't you?"

I glanced to my left where a small shelf served as a hall table. On it were a wireless router, and a bowl. In the bowl were a set of keys and an oyster card.

"Can we take a look?" I pleaded. "Just to make sure he's not unwell."

The last word received a raised eyebrow; enough for me to sense she understood exactly what I meant by Unwell.

"Bedroom and ensuite," she said, gesturing to the door on our left, "Guest room," this to the door on our right, "And living / diner," she nodded ahead.

Caz knocked on the bedroom door, calling his name, and, getting no answer, opened the door and stepped inside, the two of us following her.

The bed was unmade, supporting Miss Hastings's assertion, a discarded pile of clothes – jeans, a shirt a pair of Calvin's and a single black sock visible – lay in the corner, in front of a small walnut wardrobe.

The bedside tables housed, on the right, a radio alarm clock, the time glowing in the half-light let in by the closed shutters on the window, and, on the left, a single walnut photo frame with a picture of a crowd of teenagers, including a young Des, all dolled up in tuxedos and cocktail frocks.

On the wall opposite the bed, a widescreen TV sat, a red light indicating that it was on standby.

I dropped to my knees, and peered under the bed. A suitcase, surrounded by dust balls, and the other black sock. Nothing else.

The bathroom was tidy, only a can of shaving foam – the lid lying beside it – and a Gillette razor sitting beside the sink. Miss Holloway, unable to help herself, picked up the lid and clicked it back into place on the can.

"This seems intrusive," she murmured. "Perhaps we should go."

"Please," I said once more, "Let's just check the rest of the rooms. I'm really not comfortable with this."

"The gentleman is clearly out at work," Miss Hastings announced, though her voice held somewhat less conviction than it had earlier in our conversation.

"Miss Hastings," Caz said, "Desmond doesn't have a job. He has a trust fund. And, whilst I'm also not entirely sure that there is anything wrong here, Mister Bird has, let's say, a talent for knowing when things aren't quite right. Please, let's just check the rest of the flat."

Hastings sighed, and stepped aside. "As you wish," she said, gesturing at us to lead on.

The living room bore all the traces of someone having simply popped into the next room. The TV here was also on standby, but the Sky box was still flashing, indicating that something was playing on it, and had simply been put on Pause. A magazine was open on the coffee table, the TV and DVD remotes next to it, and the Sky remote was sitting on the arm of a large green upholstered sofa.

In the kitchen/diner, Miss Hastings Tsked again as she inspected the sink, where several dirty dishes and a small pot still crusted with the leftovers of a tin of beans sat, spattered by the dregs of what looked like tea.

I leaned forward, peering into the sink.

"What on earth," Miss Hastings demanded "Are you doing?"

"What," I gestured at the sink, as I picked up a tea towel and began opening cupboards with it, "Would you say that is?"

"Unwashed dishes," she responded definitively. "as I said: No pride. No character."

"No Fairy Liquid," Caz added.

"And no teacups," I finished.

"I beg your pardon?" Miss Hastings demanded, as they both looked at me as though I had suddenly started speaking gibberish.

"In the sink," I said, as I opened a cupboard and found what I'd been looking for, "Someone has thrown the remains of a cup of tea. Or two. You can clearly see it – that beige milky liquid in the plate. There's even some of it in the pot."

They both peered into the sink. "Indeed," Miss Hastings said. "And this is of interest how, exactly?"

"Because there's no teacups," I said. "Why would someone make a cup of tea, drink half of it, throw the rest down the drain, and then rinse up their teacup?"

Miss Hastings glared at me. "Because that, Mister Bird, is the correct order of things. One doesn't simply leave dirty cups and – Oh!" She paused, eyeing the detritus in the sink, "I see what you mean."

"Look," I gestured at the cupboard, "Cups and mugs, all standing on their bases. Except," I added, indicating a pair of white, silver rimmed coffee mugs, "For these two, which have been dried and replaced in here upside down."

Caz glanced back into the sink, observed the two mugs, and bit her lower lip. "This doesn't seem right, does it?"

I shook my head. "Desmond was clearly of the school of 'fill the sink till you've run out of plates or cups.' My guess is he had a visitor. One who didn't want their presence registered. One who pitched the remains of the tea Des had made for them both into the sink, rinsed and replaced the cups, and let themselves out."

"But if they did that themselves," Miss Hastings replied, "It would suggest that Mister Everett was," she searched for the word, "incapacitated when they left."

It was my turn to nod, and say, "Indeed."

"Well, where is he, then?" Caz asked, turning around the kitchen.

We trekked back across the living room, and entered the guest room.

Here, boxes were piled in the corner, piles of old DVDs sat atop a pine dresser, and a bed, stripped of bedlinen, sulked in the corner. The shutters were completely closed, casting the room in twilight.

We searched fruitlessly under the bed, and were on our way to the guest bathroom when something chimed in the back of my head.

"Wait," I said, and the two women froze on the spot, looking expectantly at me. "The rug," I said, turning and heading back to the living room, Caz and Miss Hastings following, until we all stopped, colliding into one another, in the doorway.

"What are we looking at?" Caz whispered, then added, "And why am I whispering."

Miss Hastings shushed her loudly, and looked expectantly at me.

The coffee table sat on a large Persian rug – all reds and oranges and moth eaten enough to suggest it had come from whatever country pile Dopey Des had been raised in. And, on top of the rug, a designer coffee table – all angular and metallic, and totally at odds with both the rug the sofa and the rest of the room – sat testament, I suspected, to the fact that Desmond was one of those people with more money than style or taste.

"Look at the Sky remote," I whispered. "It's on the arm of the sofa, within easy reach. Look at the kitchen sink: Dishes waiting to be done. Now, look at the coffee table. What's on it?"

The ladies recited the contents of the table: "A magazine. A couple of remote controls."

"A bowl of pot pourri," the last from Miss Hastings in a tone that suggested her view of Pot Pourri wasn't far removed from her view of crystal meth.

"Now look where the coffee table is," I said. "It's on the other side of the room, nowhere near the sofa. Everything on it is well out of reach. Why would Desmond – a man who clearly had a lazy streak – put his coffee table out of reach of the place he sat?"

We stepped into the room.

"He wouldn't," Caz said.

"He didn't," I answered, going to one end of the table, and indicating that she should help me lift it.

The table to one side, I kneeled down, and rolled the rug back, and heard Miss Hastings's "Oh, the poor boy."

The carpet beneath the rug was stained almost black with blood that hadn't entirely dried, so copious was the amount. It glistened dully in the sunlight filtering into the room through the half-closed white shutters, and, as another idea formed in my head, I stood, and, without saying a word, walked back into the bedroom, kicking aside the pile of clothes and, with the tea towel from the kitchen, tugging gently at the door of the wardrobe.

The door moved slowly, then flew open as the corpse of The Hon Desmond Everett, his face whiter than bones, pitched out of its place of concealment amongst the bedding from the guest bedroom, and landed, half-in and half-out of the wardrobe, his arm flung outwards as though pleading for my help.

And in his hand, half visible, the chain dangling loosely around his wrist, was a small gold locket. One I'd seen before.

"Miss Hastings," I called over my shoulder. "were you telling the truth earlier when you said you'd called the police?"

"Young man," Miss Hastings responded, reaching the bedroom doorway behind me, and stopping dead, "I always tell the truth."

And, as if on cue, we heard the sound of a car pulling up in the mews outside.

CHAPTER FORTY-SEVEN

It was late that night by the time Caz and I got back to The Marq, and Ali was just chasing out the last of the stragglers with cries of "You might not have homes to go to, folks, but we have, so thanks for your company, but it's time to head off into the night now. Thank you."

She paused, and, seeing that there were still one or two who hadn't started moving towards the door, bellowed even louder: "I'll be turning the lights on full strength in five minutes, so unless you want that number opposite you to see what you really look like in bright light, I'd get moving, boys!"

A chorus of outraged squawks ensued, and the rest of the sparse clientele supped furiously up and started heading towards the door.

"Oh look," Ali announced to the ASBO twins, "The wanderers return. Thanks very much for leaving us to run this place tonight without so much as a bowl of Velo-tee to hand out for dinner service."

"Don't start, Ali," I answered, hauling my tired arse onto a bar stool as Caz walked directly behind the bar and, having filled two glasses with ice, waved one at Ali and the twins, received affirmative nods, and pulled out three more glasses.

Ali ran round my side of the bar, growled "Move it, Maureen" at a tall skinny gentleman who'd been half passed out at the opposite end of the bar, manhandled him out of the pub, and locked the door.

"What's happened?" She asked, as Caz slid a half pint of gin, barely touched by tonic water, my way.

And I told them.

Afterwards, the only sound was the jukebox tinnilly trilling some old Stock Aitken Waterman masterpiece in the corner.

"Fuck," Dash said, at length.

"Quite," Caz said.

"So have they arrested this artist?" Ali asked.

"Well, she's probably being brought in for questioning," I said, "But I doubt they'll charge her."

"Why the fuck not?" Ali demanded.

"Because," I sighed, "she'll have an alibi, or there'll be insufficient to no DNA evidence, but mostly because she didn't do it. She's innocent."

Ali snorted. "Like innocence ever stopped them charging anyone."

"True, that," Caz deadpanned, toying with the slice of lime from her gin. "So, what makes you so sure she didn't do it?"

"The very thing meant to make us think she did do it: The locket. Monica Vale has a locket with a dodgy clasp. It keeps falling off her, but it's so important to her that she knows, immediately, if it's dropped off. So, do you really want me to believe that she could skewer Desmond Everett, watch him bleed to death, go into the bedroom, strip the bed, wrap him up, drag him into the wardrobe, rearrange the furniture in the living room, and – at no point – fail to notice that the locket was missing?"

"Adrenaline?" Caz offered. "I mean: she has just stabbed a man to death. Clearly reason was not top of the agenda."

I shrugged. "You might be right. But you know what this looks like to me?"

From somewhere in the back of my mind, a bell began to toll. An idea was forming.

"We're waiting," Ali said, jolting me out of my reverie.

"It looks," I said, "like gilding the lily. Like someone who decided that killing Desmond Everett wasn't enough: They had to hide the body, delay discovery, then – when it was discovered – ensure that suspicion was pointed at Monica Vale."

"But why would anyone want to do that?" Caz asked.

I sighed, "Because whoever did this has a taste for drama and no idea of when to stop."

Ali looked at Caz. "He's doin' that thing again, isn't he?"

"Least he's not playing the violin and smoking crack," Caz responded, and then had to clarify the point to a bemused Ali, who clearly thought I'd taken up both activities, though which one – the drugs or the noise from a novice violinist – was most upsetting to her was unclear.

"Ray," I said, changing the subject, "Did you get anywhere with that bit of business I asked you to run?"

Ray, wordlessly, dipped down under the bar, dug around in his messenger bag, and, standing again, slid a sheet of paper across the bar. "Pretty much what you suggested," he finally said. "sorry."

I smiled sadly, slugged my gin, and slid off the stool. "Par for the course, mate. Well, no time like the present, I suppose."

"Where you goin'?" Ali asked as I headed towards the door.

"Just got to see a man about an inferno," I said, as Caz reached for her handbag. "No," I held a hand up, "Give me a few minutes, OK?" I asked, glancing at Ray, who nodded. "I just want a few minutes alone. Pop over in a bit. Just in case."

Ray glanced wordlessly at Dash, who lifted a bottle of wine from the bar and held it out to me. "Just in case," he said, miming clubbing someone.

I took the bottle, and nodded thanks at Ray.

The four looked wordlessly at each other. In the background, the jukebox continued to play tinny pop music. I let myself out into the street, the heat – even at this hour – bouncing off the walls, and crossed the road.

CHAPTER FORTY-EIGHT

There was no sign of life at Mike Green's shop, but I banged on the door again. "Mike? Hey, Mike? You in there?"

Eventually, a thin crack of light appeared through the plate glass window, and I heard movement from within. I banged again. "It's Danny."

There was a scratching sound, and then the sound of a lock being undone, a chain released, and the door cracked open.

"Danny." Mike appeared at the crack, his face in half-light, his whole body seemingly pressed against the door. "What's up?"

I smiled, in what I hoped was a friendly way. "You living in here now?" I asked.

"Just," he glanced back over his shoulder, "Catching up. On some paperwork. Busy, y'know."

"Yeah." I nodded. "I can imagine. Everything OK?"

"Busy," he said again, his voice a monotone.

I held up the bottle of wine. "But you've got time for a drink, surely. With me?"

There was a moment of silence, as though he were debating the prospect, then the door opened, and he stepped back. "Sure," he was breezy again, his usual self, "Come in the back; it's less dusty there."

He turned and began walking through the darkened shop. I stepped in, and pushed the door closed behind me, but used my thumb to flick the latch, so that the lock didn't engage.

He put no lights on, so the shop was in almost full darkness, but even still, I could see them lined up against the walls. I drew no attention to the tables and chairs, and followed him through to the office at the back, where his deceit could no longer be hidden.

We were standing in a kitchen, with a gas hob, shiny stainless steel work tops, cupboards for ingredients, and two huge fridges.

I smiled, as though surprised. "Hey," I said, "nice kitchen."

He turned towards me, and my smile faltered.

Mike Green – smiley positive, excited Mike Green, who had left a grim life behind in the North to come south and open his dream 'menswear' shop – looked dreadful.

His skin was ashen, his eyes dull, puffy and encircled by rings so red that he looked like he'd been crying for days. His skin was ashen, and his hands were visibly shaking.

"I'm," he faltered, plastered on a smile that barely registered as one, and never even approached reaching his eyes, "I'm thinking I might not open the clothes shop. Might do something with food. I mean, the kitchen's here, so, y'know…" he faltered, then, seeming to steel himself, smiled, nodded at the bottle in my hand, "Glasses?"

I shook myself out of my reverie. "Yeah," I smiled, unscrewing the cap on the bottle of wine, and, after he pulled from one of the cupboards two pristine red wine glasses, poured an inch or so of Shiraz into each. "Santé," I toasted him, and sipped from my glass.

He looked at his, as though trying to make sense of a universe that had gone out of control. "I… clothes, y'know. Not really my thing."

"No." I nodded. "Not your," I paused, as though searching for the right word. "Not your passion," I finally finished. "Right?"

"Yeah." He brightened, swirled the glass, lifted it, inspecting the ruby red liquid, as vivid as blood, swirling in the glass, held the lip to his nose, inhaled, his eyes closing, and sipped slowly. "That's good," he announced.

"Ali's got a good supplier. So what is?"

He paused, confused, as though trying to get his thoughts together. "Is?"

"Your passion," I pressed. "You told me that you'd always dreamed of owning a menswear shop. If that's not what you always dreamed of, what is?"

"A restaurant," he finally said, his eyes not meeting mine. "I always wanted a restaurant. Not a huge mega place, just something more like a café bar that does great food. Somewhere the locals can enjoy everything from a great bacon sandwich to a bowl of Chicken Chasseur."

"And that's what this is gonna be?" I gestured over his shoulder, back into the shop. "I saw the tables. The chairs. I sort of guessed when I saw the coffee machine going in. I mean, it made sense, the idea of a menswear shop that offered espresso. Nice USP. But I never saw any clothes rails, any hangers, anything beyond a state of the art Gaggia. Then, today, I had a friend of mine check with the council. All those builders, there had to be a planning application. This shop is zoned as retail catering. You've applied for a liquor licence too."

He smiled sadly. "You got me. I reccied the area, saw that they were badly in need of something decent, food wise. I mean, there was the pub, but really: greasy pasties, and sweaty ploughman's. How much of a threat could a grim Victorian boozer be? I should have gone in for lunch."

"So you leased the place, started work on the refurb, then discovered the pub was doing decent business with food."

He sighed, smiled sadly again, sipped his wine, and nodded. "It was one of the electricians. Went in every day for lunch. Had the gazpacho. Raved about it for days. Got me," he paused, sipped again, "concerned."

"So you started trying to sabotage the kitchen," I said, remembering fagash in Olivia Wrights punchbowl, a dead pigeon in the fridge, and an anonymous call to the health inspectors.

"It was business," he said flatly.

"It was sabotage," I answered, equally flatly. "And it wasn't necessary, Mike. It's a pub. The food isn't that great."

He laughed. "Yes. Yes, Danny, it is that great. And it's got attention. The Standard, the likes of Monica Vale, the buzz around it all. It's everything I didn't want it to be. And it's going to get better."

"It's a pub, Mike. I spend half my time running around town trying to sort out my car crash of a life. The food is a side-line, and everyone knows that. This," I gestured behind me, "This will be a proper restaurant. It'll be everything The Marq isn't, and we could have lifted each other up."

"Yeah, well," he smiled, and this time the smile nearly reached his eyes, before they teared up, "I'm not sure I want to continue. I'm thinking of going back up north. Not sure I have the fight left in me, to be honest."

"Mate," I stepped over to him, felt him stiffen as I hugged him, "It didn't have to be a fight."

At this, he finally laughed, but it was a sound laced with bitterness. "Yes it did, Danny. I lied. About a lot of it."

"I figured," I said.

"I grew up in care. I grew up in houses where you took what you wanted, or you had everything you had taken away from you. I went to families that either wanted me for the money I'd bring in, or just wanted some perfect son. I got used to putting on the act – I don't care, or I care deeply; whichever they wanted. But it still didn't work.

"One way or another, I was always back at the homes. But I had a plan. I had a dream, and I was good at saying and doing what needed to be done to get where I needed to be. I got the money together for this – Jesus, the things I needed to do to get the money for this." He shuddered, and emptied the Shiraz. I refilled his glass, three inches deep this time.

"Then you realised The Marq was – what? Competition?"

"Like I say, Danny, it's take, or have everything you've ever wanted taken from you. I like you, you know. I really like you."

"And yet," I said, my wine untouched, "When everything failed – the sabotage; the call to the council – when you'd reached desperation levels, you nearly burned me to death."

He choked. "What?"

"The fire last night. Someone shoved burning rags through the back door. We thought it was an attack on The Marq. But this wasn't someone who wanted to burn the pub down. If that's what they wanted they'd have started the fire in the bar – they'd have set fire to the front door."

He shook his head, his lips moving. But no sound came from them. Behind him, I saw the shop door open silently.

I shook my head. "This wasn't an attack on the pub. The pub's at the front. This was an attack on the kitchen."

Ray, Dash, Ali and Caz appeared in the doorway. So much for catlike tread, I thought.

Mike's voice cracked. "You weren't supposed to be there," he whispered. "You said, that day, that you were going to go home and stay with your parents."

I nodded. "I know. I know, Mike. It got late, I was tired. I decided to stay. But you thought you'd be torching an empty building, destroying the kitchen. Even if the bar was able to open, the food element would be over."

"It just," he whispered, unable to look me in the eye, "sort of spiralled."

I nodded. "Where is she, Mike?"

He suddenly became aware of the mob standing in the doorway, and started, knocking over the glass, and, amongst squawks and general noise, grabbing for a tea towel and dabbing at the spilled wine.

"Mike." I reached a hand out, and stopped his dabbing. "You're a dreamer. You're not a killer, and you're not a kidnapper. You were setting the fire, she was tip toeing around the alley trying to find the vodka she'd hidden earlier. She stumbled over you, and you had to shut her up. Where is she?"

"It just," he whispered, his eyes – crazed now, like an animal caught in a trap, looking desperately for an escape, looked into mine, darted away, seeing me, not seeing me, knowing that all was lost, "It just spiralled."

"Oh Jesus, Mike, please tell me you didn't do anything stupid."

He laughed, finally. "Stupid? The most stupid fucking thing I ever did was come here and try to restart my life. Like I get to restart."

"Mike," I tried again, holding a hand up to restrain Dash, who'd made a move forwards, "where is she?"

"There." His eyes darted to a cupboard on the opposite side of the room.

I crossed the room, pulled on the door handle, and realised the door was locked. "Key," I demanded, and he dug into his pocket, and slid a key across the worktop.

I opened the door, and peered into the darkness.

A flight of stairs lead down to a cellar. A dim bulb came on when I flicked the switch, and – with Ray and Dash grabbing an almost flaccid Mike Green, we – en masse – descended the stairs.

What followed wasn't pretty.

We found Elaine – seemingly healthy – tied to a straight back chair that had obviously been intended, originally, for the restaurant. Two linen napkins, knotted together, had been used to form a gag. Her eyes – as red and puffy as Mike's - blazed with fury, and, in seeing us, she went into convulsions in an attempt to tear her bindings free.

I shushed her, went behind and, along with Ali, began untiring her.

As soon as the knot on her left wrist loosened, she tore her hand free, ripped the gag from her mouth, and commenced hurling abuse at a now openly weeping Mike Green,

"You are so fucking dead, you fucking psycho."

"Shush, Elaine," I said, struggling with the next knot.

"Shush?" She twisted in her chair, her fury transferring to me. "Did you just fucking shush me? You're fucking dead an' all, you fucking nonce."

"Really?" I stepped back, gesturing to Ali to do the same.

"You let this fucking lunatic lose in my Nannu's pub. I'm gonna see you skinned alive and fed to the fucking pigs, you fucking loser. An' as for you," she turned her eyes back on Mike Green. "He'll cut your fucking bollocks off an' feed them to you first, you cunt."

I shook my head. "Where'd you learn such language, young lady?"

"Language? Language? Her face was close to apoplexy, all purple sweaty snotty rage, constrained only by the fact that she'd realised that, since Ali and I had stepped back from the multiple knots on top of knots that we'd been untying, no amount of furious tugging at the ropes had actually moved her so much as an inch closer to being released. "Get me out of this fucking chair!" She suddenly screeched, her demand aimed generally into the room.

Dash moved to release her, and I warned him off with a glance.

"Elaine, the only reason you're here, in this chair," I said, but she interrupted me.

"Is 'cos I caught that fucking maniac trying to torch the fucking pub, you arsehole," she shrieked, "so get me out of this fucking chair now, or I'm gonna make it even worse for you when I get out."

"Worse than feeding me to the pigs?" I asked.

She paused, forced herself to step away from the fury, and switched on the sweetness – or the nearest approximation of it she could make while wishing unspeakable acts upon my person. "Look, I was goin' back to the pub to check on something."

"Really?"

"Yeah. I – um – I thought I'd left the gas on."

"In the kitchen?"

"Yeah." She brightened. "I thought I'd let the gas on."

"He found the vodka," Ali said flatly, and we watched as Elaine's face paled, the sweetness faded, and she was left with a wordless 'Oh' on her lips.

"Look," she said, "I pinched a bottle of Voddie. So what? You think my grand pa's going to look poorly on that when this freak tried to burn you to death and kidnapped me?"

"You called your Grandfather up – sometime before you vanished – and told him you were going on a residential cookery course with Caz here." I gestured at Caz, who slunk into the shadows, as though even the suggestion she'd ever be anywhere near a residential cookery course had caused the ground to open up and swallow her.

"Says who?" Elaine demanded.

"Says Chopper himself," I answered. "Or is he a lying nonce too?"

Elaine choked on her fury, and finally said, "Some friends and me were goin' away for a couple of days. To a party."

"Ah," I nodded, "The vodka."

"Yeah, well, it was teenage high jinks," she said. "Gramp's'll get that, He won't do nothing to me," she sneered, directing her most venomous glare at a now almost gibbering Mike Green, and reserving a little leftover fury for me. "Unlike you two."

"No," I said, "I suspect he'll more likely vanish Mike here, and possibly crack a couple of my ribs. Only, he won't find out, Elaine."

"He what?" Her lips moved wordlessly, her puzzlement growing deeper and deeper, until she finally laughed out loud. "Oh, you're a fucking treasure, you are. Now get me out of this fucking chair, or so help me, I'll help him dig your fucking grave myself."

"You poured plaster down the toilets. You pinched a bottle of vodka. You even told Mike, here, when to best enact his little acts of sabotage. I know, cos I caught you on the phone, and you got all defensive."

"I what?" Her eyes blazed at Green. "You Fuck," she spat, before looking back at me. "What's wrong with him? Is he out of his fucking mind?"

"Nice try," I said, "But the subject won't be changed, Elaine: I don't know when you met Mike – probably one of the first days he popped in for a pint - but I'm willing to bet it was you who told him about the Memorial lunch, and got him thinking about what would happen to his business plans if we had a big society success.

"And on top of it all, you were about to flit off on a two day Bender with Christ knows who, after he explicitly told you to keep your mouth shut, your nose clean, and your hands out of the till. I doubt you'll get vanished, Elaine, but I suspect that there's only so much that even a doting grandfather can take. And if there's one wrong word from you, then I shall ensure that Chopper finds out the whole story."

"I stopped," Elaine whimpered, nodding at Mike Green. "at first, I was really fed up. I got dumped here. Punished. I didn't want to be here, and not one of you liked me."

"I did," Dash said quietly, so quietly that Elaine seemed not even to hear him.

"You all treated me like shit, like you didn't want me round, and I was stupid and useless. Then he said he hated the whole place too, and asked if I wanted to help him fuck with you all. But after a while, I started to like it here." She half smiled in Dash's direction. "Ali started showing me how to do stuff. Dash was looking out for me if I messed up. Even you weren't as fucking miserable as you were at the start. So I told him I didn't want to do it no more."

"Jesus, Elaine. You're a pain in the arse, but once you put your mind to it, you get things done. You just," I shrugged, "Were putting your mind to the sort of things that your Nannu would not look very kindly on.

"And if he sent you to us as punishment for your last little escapade, think what he'll do to you this time, if I have a word."

"You wouldn't dare."

"Try me."

Once again, she returned to tugging at her bindings, the chair rocking backwards and forwards as she yanked.

I stepped forward, squatted down by the chair, and put a hand up. "Stop," I said, and, as she calmed, I looked her in the eye. "Mistakes, Elaine. Everyone makes them. Doesn't mean they have to have their lives destroyed by them," and, as the rocking finally slowed, I untied the rest of the ropes.

The instant she was free, she flew at Mike Green, punching him full force in the face, resulting in a shrieking and now profusely bleeding Green collapsing to the floor as his diminutive blonde assailant wound up for another attack, yelled, "That's for tying me up you fucking loon," and collapsed in tears onto Dash, who stood, shocked, for a moment, before enclosing her in his arms, and hugging her tightly.

I looked around me at the darkened cellar, as Ali and Ray helped Mike Green to his feet, then I said, "Mike: I'd suggest you go upstairs, collect what you can, and go away. Now. Before Elaine – or I – change our minds and make that call."

Ray and Ali walked with Mike.

"Dash, can you take Elaine back to The Marq. Get her some tea – sweet. No fucking booze – she's sixteen – and keep her company. We'll be over in a bit, and get this sorted."

Dash, his arms still around Elaine, nodded seriously, and the two slowly made their way up the stairs.

"So when did you become so Zen," Caz asked quietly from the shadows.

"I dunno," I smiled, "maybe when a friend of mine taught me to be less judgemental. Mistakes were made."

"Doesn't mean they have to destroy people's lives," she echoed my earlier comment.

"I know," I nodded. "I'll make the call."

"Tonight?"

I nodded. "Just as soon as we've sorted this mess."

CHAPTER FORTY-NINE

I lifted the beer bottle, looking at the myriad droplets condensed on it, and pressed the cool glass to my forehead, closing my eyes as the events of the past few days replayed in my mind.

The kitchen was empty, the whole pub silent.

Mike Green had been seen into a mini cab, what little he could grab of his dreams stuffed into a couple of suitcases, and had last been seen heading North, towards Saint Pancras.

Elaine had been mollified, then coached on the story she was to feed Chopper if asked about her experiences at Holloway Hall. To ensure she'd have some homework to feed him, I'd shown her how to cook an omelette.

"An omelette?" She snapped. "I was supposed to be at a Fucking Cordon Bleu school. And you want me to make him an omelette?"

"Call it a soufflé," I answered, "And let him think you're just not very good. Oh, and Elaine, get some new friends. The ones you had – you know: the ones you were going to party with? None of them even looked for you when you didn't show. They didn't call your dear old Gramps to ask where you were. They didn't call here to find out if we'd seen you. If it wasn't for Dash and Ray, we'd all have assumed you were just at home sulking. Mates should be there for you. Just saying."

And off she'd gone into the night, accompanied by Ali who, for once, she was not abusing, leaving the ASBO twins, Caz and I.

And, after giving Ray a request to do a little more research for me, and thanking Dash for taking care of Elaine, I'd mimed a wide yawn, and wished them all goodnight.

"You're going to call?" Caz had prompted, and I'd nodded, promising that, yes, just as I'd given Mike Green a second chance, I would call Nick and allow him to explain and make good.

And that's exactly what I'd done, calling his mobile number, waiting as it had rung three, four, five times, and, as I was just about to hang up, hearing the pickup, and a female voice, sleepily, saying "Hello?"

I froze.

"Hello?" She said again, a little more awake now, an edge – perhaps, it seemed, of fear – present in her voice.

"Hi," I coughed to clear my voice, started again: "Hi. Is Nick there?"

There was a pause, the sound of rustling, as, I suppose, she sat up in bed, then: "No," she said. "He's at work. On nights. He forgot his mobile. Left it behind by mistake."

"Oh." I wanted to hang up, to end the call then, and not have to humiliate myself or – and I knew how egotistical this sounded – hurt her. But I didn't. "You must be his wife," I heard myself saying.

"Mmm," she murmured, almost noncommittally. "And you must be Danny. Hello. It's nice to finally talk to you."

"You know who I am?" I asked, my heart racing as I tried to figure out what she could possibly know, what he could have told her, and how I could get away from this call without making things worse for us all.

"Your number," there was a pause as, I presume, she checked the display on the phone, "is..." and she recited my number back to me, "Right?"

I agreed that, yes, that was my number, and she said, "I'll call you back," and hung up.

I didn't wait long – maybe a minute, maybe less. Long enough for me to walk to the fridge, pull out, and open a bottle of beer, lug from it, return to the table, and pick the phone up.

At which point, it rang, it's shrill tone making me jump. I hit answer, noticing, as I did, that she was calling me back from a land line, and held the phone to my ear.

"Danny?" She was fully awake now, her voice still retaining something of the smokiness.

"Hi. I - I'm sorry: I don't know your name."

"It's Arianne," she said.

Of course it is. Nora, or Rita would be too prosaic. Instead, I get Arianne.

"There's so much," I said, "That I don't know about you."

"Yes," she sighed, "I expect there is. But I know everything about you."

Everything?

She cleared her throat. "I know, for example, that you are the man my husband is in love with," she said. "And that's really all I need to know."

"I don't understand," I said, "I know nothing about you."

She laughed. "You are, I think, shocked. But yes, I understand. Nick. He tries, always, to do the right thing. To make everyone happy, and in doing so, things…"

"Spiral," I said.

There was a silence, then, when next she spoke, I could hear the smile in her face. "Yes," she said, "They spiral. All because he tries, always, to do the right thing. I love him for that."

I was silent.

"You are confused," she said. "I try to be clear, but sometimes my English – and also, I think, my – how do you say – approach – is that the right word? – confuses more than it clears. You English are so restrained, so contained, I think. You are used to subtlety, to things not being the way they seem. And then you, if I remember, are half Irish. Nick tells me this, and I remember some books I had, back," she faltered, "before. And I remember: The Irish, always, are obsessed with words, with saying and writing, and never really making the point. And so, I think, you, Danny, perhaps, are swamped by text and subtext, and truth is drowned somewhere in there.

"But with me, there is so little time for subtext. And that, sometimes, confuses."

Jesus, I thought, your English is better than Ali's. Did Nick marry a professor of English Lit?

Aloud, I agreed that, yes, I was very confused, wondered to myself if she was actually trying to sound like a female Yoda, and she laughed again, somewhere between a smoky chuckle and a sad recognition of the futility of trying to make sense of the motivations of this honourable man we both loved, then said, "Well I, perhaps, should explain some things."

And she explained.

CHAPTER FIFTY

The phone was picked up on the first ring, and he gave the name of the station, his rank, and his name, and just hearing Nick's voice made my heart flutter.

Yes, I know: I am a thirty-something homosexual male in a city filled with life and vibrancy and danger. I have my own successful business and a decent amount of both friends and self-respect, and yet – I can not deny it – my heart fluttered, like it used to when I was terrified on the first day of school or the last day of a relationship.

It wasn't like some timpani of doom, or anything; it was more like my heart – and, eventually, my whole body – was just vibrating.

"Hey Nick," I said, and had to clear my throat and try again. "How are you?"

"Danny. Please don't hang up. We need to talk. I need to explain."

"Nick, I called you," I said, and he stopped.

"Oh. Yeah, that's right. You did." He was silent a moment. "I've been calling, but I either get voicemail, or Ali tells me she'll leave a message."

"She's been leaving them," I said. "But I haven't been calling back."

He was silent.

"Wanna know why?"

"Look, Danny-"

"Shut up. Shut up and listen. I'll tell you why: Cos I was afraid. Afraid of what I'd hear if I called you back. Afraid of what you'd say. Afraid that I'd say I Love You again, and you'd say I'm very fond of you. And then I spoke to someone this evening, and they told me a story, and I wanted to call and tell you the story."

He was silent for a moment, then, I assume, realising he didn't have his mobile with him, he said, simply, "Arianne."

"It's a story about a woman who doesn't remember anything until she woke up, as a young girl, in a cold bare room in a city somewhere, alone.

"Who wishes she didn't remember all the things that were done to her – who still struggles to believe that even the things she did were things that were, ultimately, done to her. For years. Who doesn't even know her own name, only the name that was done to her."

"I should have told you," he said.

I swallowed. I needed to get this out, needed him to know I understood. "Until one day the man who owned her – she still thinks of him as her owner, though she knows this is wrong, knows he had no ownership over her; that the very concept of ownership over someone is impossible – the man who owned her was murdered. Violently, and in a way that brought the police into her bare room.

"And she remembers how the local police – some immured to this scene they had seen so many time before, some corrupt enough to be part of the mechanism that created the scene – wanted to just move her on – to the streets, to the side, to whichever man would own her next.

"Until one of the policemen – a foreigner – began to ask questions, and realised – as she had at eight or nine – that there were no answers, only the blankness of walls, looks, sky."

"I couldn't," he choked, started to cry at the other end of the line, in what I assumed was a darkened office. "I just couldn't."

"It's alright," I said. "If it was you, Nick, if you were that foreign copper only there on an exchange scheme, you would have had problems. If it was you, the local plod would have told you to mind your own business, knowing that you'd be going home soon, and could hardly take the evidence with you. I mean: she had no papers, and could hardly travel with you.

"It's not like you were married or anything. If you were married, she'd be allowed to come into the UK with you."

He sighed heavily. "I should have told you," he said.

"Yes," I said. "If you – a serving police officer – had married someone for the purposes of transporting them across borders and into the European Union, doing something that was illegal, and could cost you your career, I would expect you to advise me, on a job phone that could be listened to at any moment.

"Because, of course, to do otherwise: to evade avoid or attempt to not discuss the issue on a work phone, would be wrong."

"I tried to talk to you," he said.

"And I kept avoiding you," I answered.

"But I had four months, only I didn't say so at first."

"And the more you didn't say anything," I said, "The more it.."

"Spiralled," he said, "Out of my control."

"How come doing the right thing," I sighed, tilting the beer bottle to the ceiling, draining, it, wanting another, and another, but knowing I had work to do, "Gives us so many chances to fuck things up?"

"And I did," he said, "Fuck things up. And I shouldn't have. 'Cos I love you, and you should never have been put here."

"But here is where we are. So: the question is, what next? And, for the purposes of the tape," I announced in my best stage FBI voice, "And of anyone who might listen to this in the future, I love you too, mate, even though you're a happily married police officer with a wife who's going through UK immigration procedures. But I'm also someone with some theoretical questions to ask you about some recent murders."

"I thought," he said. "We'd agreed you wouldn't get involved in any more murders."

"Theoretical," I reminded him, and heard his snort of derision.

"Go on," he said.

"Jane Barton."

He went quiet, and I could hear his fingers tapping on a keyboard.

At length: "Suicide," he responded.

"They say. I want the reports."

"She was hung."

"Hanged," I corrected, conscious that he'd chosen the unspecific in his description: Not She hanged herself, but something that told me that Nick was thinking the same way I was.

"Pictures are hung, Nick, and sometimes men, but you'd know all about that. People are hanged."

"Anything in particular?" He said, ignoring my double entendre.

I paused. "Toxicology. Take a look at the bloods. She didn't kill herself. And while you're at it," I said, abandoning any attempt to sustain the theoretical bullshit, "Get someone to take a look at Desmond Everett's place."

"We looking for anything in particular?"

I told him.

"That's not going to be easy to find."

"It's in a suitcase under the bed," I said, more certain than I wanted to be.

"This wouldn't have anything to do with a dead waiter, would it?"

"Everything. Can you get me the reports?"

"Will you talk to me if I do?"

"I'm talking to you now, aren't I?"

"And will you forgive me?"

"For being honourable and – as your wife says – for being English? I think we can work on that."

"I'll call you back," Nick said, and hung up.

CHAPTER FIFTY-ONE

He didn't take long.

I'd enough time to walk to the bin, drop the empty bottle into it, pass by the fridge and pick up another, switch on the radio, open the beer, turn on my laptop, and listen to a verse a chorus and three lines of the second verse of something on a station that still played three minute pop songs before he rang back, and I picked up.

"Hanged," he said, as I heard the crash of an espresso machine behind him. "But unlikely to have hanged herself. Post mortem shows a massive dose of a Benzodiazepine drug in her system. Coroner reckons there was enough to create a dissociative state. She'd have been awake, but unable to move or speak."

"Or stand on a stool and put a rope over a beam."

"Exactly."

I was silent.

"I'm so sorry Danny. Arianna was a situation that I should have dealt with better."

"Arianna," I said, "Is a woman not a situation. And if what I've heard tonight is accurate, your only fault was in trying to keep everyone happy. And in lying to me, of course." I tapped at the keyboard, "But there'll be time to deal with that later. Anything about the other thing?"

"The Everett place? I've asked a car to go round, but it'll be an hour or so."

I was silent.

"What does all this mean, Danny?"

"It means," I said, "I think I know who murdered Dave Walker, Jane Barton and Desmond Everett. Call me back when they check under the bed."

CHAPTER FIFTY-TWO

"He looks familiar," James Kane said as an even more muscle bound than usual Darryl O'Carroll dispensed a quinoa and kale cup and faded into the distance.

Monica Vale's vision of Working Class Life presented as High Art – but not in a patronising way – was coming to life, tonight, in a stucco ceilinged ballroom in St James'. The walls were corniced, plastered, and hung, alternatively, with nineteenth century light fittings, and with Ms Vale's actually quite good paintings of pub brawls in Wetherspoons, done in the style of The Battle of The Golden Spurs by De Keyser, A queue outside JD Sports represented a la Lowry, and a startling mammoth still life of a KFC Family Bucket that might have been painted by Van Gough if he'd taken a break from them sunflowers.

Kane crunched his mouthful of leaves and rambled off as Caz sidled up to me.

"Aren't you offended," she asked, "by all this?"

"All this?" I grabbed a canape made to look like a miniature doner kebab with an eye-drops worth of chilli sauce on it, and shoved the thing, whole, into my mouth, wishing, as the waiter vanished into the distance, that I'd grabbed two.

"Y'know: The co-opting of your culture for the entertainment of a wealthy upper class that spends most of its time mocking, if not openly abusing the poor and working class."

"Caz, I've read the catalogue too. And," I shrugged, "the pictures are nice, the audience are, well, people, which means some of them will get what Monica Vale is trying (I think) to get across, and others will just go Ooh, look at the funny proles, so my offence, or acceptance, is somewhat pointless, really, isn't it."

"You're nervous," she said, snagging two glasses of champagne from a tray, realising, from my outstretched hand that I assumed one of them was for me, handing me a glass, calling the waiter back, and grabbing another one for herself. "You always get pedantic when you're nervous." She necked half of the first glass and pulled the sort of face you normally get on someone who's swigged vinegar instead of vin de France. "Prosecco," she spat.

"When did Prosecco even become a thing? Cheap nasty stuff, and people are falling over themselves for it. I blame the working class palate. And Jamie Bloody Oliver."

"Sweetheart, you blamed Jamie Oliver for the rise of Isis."

"Well all the money we spend on Pomegranates must be going somewhere," she mused, sipping her Prosecco and, seemingly, deciding it was safe to drink if done slowly. "So: what time is show time?"

"About," I necked my perfectly acceptable prosecco, as the last of the gallery curators completed their speeches "Now," I said, and moved towards the dais in the corner.

"Excuse me," I said, as a couple of security guards moved to block me mounting the dais, "I just have something to say," and before they could stop me, a certain Detective constable of my acquaintance stepped forward, flashed his badge, and muttered something to the men.

At the same time, the bulky figure of DI Reid waddled up behind me, displaying his total lack of understanding of the concept of personal space, and he growled right into my ear "You're only getting this chance 'cos you did so well with the Day case, Bird. But if you fuck this up for me, you'll be sorry."

Fuck this up for you? Jesus, I was the one who was about to stand up there and dish out the most convoluted explanation for a murder ever.

I stepped onto the dais, and tapped the microphone.

Nothing.

I waved at the security guards and the sound engineer at the opposite end of the room, who had already started packing up, and tapped the mike again.

Again, nothing, but I'd gained the attention of half the room, who were gawping at me as though I were some part of the artwork. Perhaps they though Chav Barman Waving His Arms about. Mixed media: Skin, Bones and Topman Blazer was a performance piece. Whatever, they were quietening, their attention directed my way.

Which, of course, caused the attention of the rest of the room to be directed my way, and a series of Shussshes, Quiets, and – above it all – the sound of Caz demanding Haven't you got anything a bit more French by way of Fizz – echoed around the room.

Monica Vale looked up from a conversation with a man possessing the most outrageous handlebar moustache I'd ever seen, and frowned.

Not far from her, James Kane nodded at Freddie Rosetti, and the two men stopped talking.

Anthony Taylor, Olivia Wright, and Kent Benson paused in their discussion, and all stared at the stage, clearly puzzled to see me trying to attract the attention of a roomful of people who'd been stuffed full of prosecco and party food, and were now debating how quickly they could skip this joint and get a taxi into Soho.

I watched as Monica Vale slowly made her way through the throng, her fixed smile clearly showing a degree of concern that this – now she thought about it – uninvited prole was about to ruin her big opening.

She passed Lionel Hook – who, doubtless, in his alter ego as Mangelina Jolly would have made great comedic use of the phrase ruin her big opening - and who was now in deep conversation with Naimee Campbell, as she and her trio of Himbos, all in the process of doling out mini kebabs, pork pies made with meat from acorn fed wild boars and fish n chip flavoured foam in miniature beer glasses, all paused and looked my way.

Fucking Poirot never has this trouble, I thought, as Vale reached me, and held my arm in a surprisingly vice like grip.

She's stronger than she looks, I thought, as she dragged me to one side.

"What the hell are you doing here?" She demanded tersely.

"Trying to help you out," I answered. "You're on bail while the police try to figure out how your locket ended up in Desmond Everett's cold dead hand."

Her grip loosened. "What do you know about that? I was told they'd be discrete until after all this."

"Wait: You got hauled in for murder, and they agreed to keep it quiet? Jesus, every time I get dragged in, there's a local gangster waiting for me when they let me out." One rule for the rest of us, I inwardly sighed, wondering if I'd ever thought, as a happy-go-lucky teenager, that the adult me would be more surprised by social inequality than the fact that I'd just uttered the phrase every time I get dragged in for murder.

I mean, the idea of getting hauled in once would scare most people; but here I was just acknowledging it as an occupational hazard in running The Marq.

I needed, I decided at that point, to consider new career options.

"I won't have my night ruined by the likes of you," Vale said, confirming Caz's opinion that the likes of me were being co-opted to make the career of this middle class poseur.

"I found the body," I snapped back. "I saw the locket. I know you're innocent. And, if you'll let go of me, and get the fucking sound back on, I can tell you who the real killer is."

"Tell the police," she snarled. "This is their job."

"But you're an artist," I smiled back. "And this – the unmasking of a dangerous killer at the opening night of your exhibition – would be great publicity."

She instantly released me, the truth of my statement reflecting in her eyes, and waved at the sound guy to reconnect the mike.

"Besides," I muttered to myself, "The police like the story, but they prefer, y'know, evidence. And I aint got too much of that…"

CHAPTER FIFTY-THREE

"Hello everybody," I called, and winced as a shriek of feedback echoed around the room.

Caz, at the far end of the gallery, strolled over to the A/V guy, slipped a laptop out of her capacious handbag, handed it to him, and ordered him to connect it. As he did so, her eyes dipped back into the bag, and a look of pleasant surprise crossed her face. She dipped back into the Gladstone and withdrew a mini bottle of what – even at this distance I could see - held Veuve Cliquot champagne, and she carefully opened the bottle, snagged a straw from a discarded glass, popped it in, and settled back, looking, for all the world, like a modern Madame Desfarges in Stella McCartney.

"I'm sorry to interrupt your evening," I said, "But I have a short presentation to make to you all, and I hope it will help make sense of some recent events.

"Not long ago," I said, as a close up black and white picture of Dave Walker – a much younger, Dave Walker, wearing what appeared to be an Elizabethan ruff collar – appeared behind me, "a man named Dave Walker was murdered."

The screen behind me – if the presentation was working correctly – would now be showing a photo of the inside of the loo at The Marq, after Dave's body had been removed, but before the blood had been cleared up. I glanced behind me. The picture was there.

I glanced back to a now silent room. All eyes were, suddenly on me, as though the import of what was going on had finally sunk in.

"He was a waiter, but he was also a friend, a lover, a fan of order and correct behaviour, and – in his younger days – an actor."

The picture shifted, this time showing the full shot that the close up of Walker had been cropped from. This was a troupe of drama students in full Elizabethan drag for a play. And right in the middle, standing before a cauldron, was Dave Walker. A trio of women – a tall, statuesque brunette, a shorter, plainer blonde, and a tiny slip of a girl with a gap toothed smile and an ill-fitting wig – stood around him, the taller one with her arm around Dave's shoulders.

Lionel Hook – who had provided the picture from his personal collection, stood at the other end of the line-up, looking uncomfortable in hose and a starched ruff. His eyes, looking, now, on this artefact of a past life, teared up, and he wiped his eyes, and blew his nose into a puce coloured handkerchief.

"But a motive for his murder seemed, shall we say lacking. He'd been followed from behind and beaten, his head smashed in by his attacker, in a frenzied assault. He was followed from behind," I repeated, "So did his killer, perhaps, think he was someone else?

"The day in question was as hot as hell, and the event at which he was murdered was a funeral luncheon, so all of the men – the guests, as well as the waiting staff – were wearing black trousers, white shirts and black ties.

"Perhaps someone thought they were murdering a more likely suspect."

I noticed that Nick and Reid, along with Caz Dash and Ray, had discretely gathered together the principal suspects, that Naimee and Lionel, Filip Troy and the even more bulked up figure of Darryl O'Carroll had been added to the group, and that all had been surreptitiously shepherded through the crowd so that they were now gathered at the base of the dais.

"But who could the intended victim have been?" I clicked the clicker I'd discovered at the base of the lectern, and was gratified that, instead of plunging the room into darkness, I managed to change the picture on the screen.

Ray had done a great job with the presentation. This slide had a collage of pictures of Anthony Taylor, Kent Benson James Kane and Desmond Everett.

"There were other men present that day, but there were three who were the subject of animosity prior to the killing, and one who would afterwards be murdered. Anthony: You – by your own admission – have ruined lives." Taylor looked sheepish, but nodded his agreement to the statement. "You've been, as they say, a bad 'un. I'm told you're rehabilitated, trying to make amends for your past sins, but perhaps someone decided that revenge – rather than forgiveness – was due.

"In the room that day, were Monica Vane, whose sister you accidentally killed, Desmond Everett, whose brother committed suicide when a business venture you were managing failed, and James Kane. Neither you nor James had any great love for each other."

Anthony nodded in agreement, while James opened his mouth, as though to protest.

To shut him up, I moved on to other possible victims.

"Kent: Your business ventures have resulted in law suits and accusations that your fortune – your first fortune – was made when your wife at the time stole another woman's invention. The same wife who, ultimately, went missing. You were accused of murdering her. Many of her friends never forgave you, even though the police, eventually, had to drop the case and admit there was no evidence she'd ever been murdered. Again, did a misplaced attempt at revenge play a part in the killing?

"James: You're holding the purse strings over Olivia Wright's fortune. With you out of the way, Olivia, Kent, and maybe even Anthony, might have hoped they'd gain access to the fortune that you were keeping from them."

"Preposterous!" Kane barked. "It's a legal structure. If I died, someone else in my firm would become executor."

"Besides," Kent announced, "Both Olivia and I were with you when this waiter was killed."

"Indeed you were," I admitted, clicking the switch, and changing the picture to a shot of one of the poison pen letters.

"You were discussing a spate of poison pen letters you'd been receiving. Somewhat oddly, as Olivia said that you'd been strongly resisting saying anything to anyone about them, wanting to avoid bringing the police in, and yet, suddenly, out of the blue, you wanted to discuss them with me."

"Well, Lady Caroline did such a great job of praising you," Olivia said, smiling at Caz, who smiled back hiccupped gently, and sipped her champagne through her straw.

"Yes," I said, "But it did seem odd that you'd choose that exact moment – right in the middle of a funeral – to grab me and discuss this topic. You hadn't received any letters recently, and – for all you knew – the writer had stopped."

I clicked back to the picture of the four men. "There was a fourth man there that day. Desmond Everett. A genial, somewhat simple soul. A school friend of Olivia's late brother, who everyone present seemed to like – or, at least, tolerate. And yet, despite no animosity being openly directed at him, Desmond Everett," I clicked, the screen changed to a blow-up of a pic of Dopey Des torn from the society pages of one of the papers, "Was stabbed to death three days ago.

"Odd that the three men who should have been murder victims on the day are still alive; that the killer – who seems to have made a mistake when they killed Dave Walker – didn't try again; that none of you three," I gestured at the men, "Has had an attempt on your life, and yet Desmond Everett is dead."

"Maybe his killing was unconnected," Filip, the perm tanned massage therapist member of the Himbo club spoke up, then blushed deeply when all eyes turned on him. "I mean, what's the connection?"

"Good point," I said. "Why would anyone want to kill Dopey Des. He wasn't entirely mature, and not entirely smart either. So what possible threat could he present to anyone?"

"Maybe he killed himself," Troy – seemingly ignorant of the fact that, having stabbed himself, Des would have had to move the rug, drag the coffee table across the room, wrap himself up in a duvet, and climb into the wardrobe. The groan that went round the room showed that nobody else had overlooked these facts, and the thespian went back to inspecting his eyebrows in a small compact.

"I heard it was a burglary gone wrong," Kent said.

"Could be," I answered, shrugging, "Except that nothing of value appeared to have been stolen from his flat. The TVs, the DVD players, a very expensive Bose sound system were all still in situ. And, we believe, he'd had tea with his killer before he was attacked.

"What sort of burglar has tea with their victim before killing them? And, having killed them, what sort of burglar then walks off without searching the house and stealing everything of value?"

"That doesn't make sense," Naimee Campbell – looking like a larger, female, more orange version of Filip, said.

"It couldn't have been a burglary," Monica said.

"It wasn't," I said, "and in their haste to hide the body and get away from the scene, the killer forgot to search the place. And that was where they made their biggest mistake.

"That, and the fact that – rather than leaving the body as it was – they overdressed the set. By planting evidence designed to direct suspicion at Miss Vane here."

There was a collective gasp around the room, and a murmur of interest as even those who'd decided this was going on too long suddenly perked up.

"My locket," Monica said.

"A locket that had a broken clasp; one that had slipped off you previously, and that the killer, when next the locket fell from you, decided would be the perfect diversionary device.

"Except that, rather than diverting suspicion from them, it directed suspicion. Initially at you, but ultimately at the fact that the killer had to be someone who had not only a connection between you and Desmond Everett, but the opportunity to be in close proximity to you, when the locket came undone."

I could see Naimee and the Himbos noticeably relax. They figured they were off the hook.

They couldn't have known what was coming next.

CHAPTER FIFTY-FOUR

Caz has, previously voiced the opinion that I am an attention whore, and as if to affirm her assertion, I drew everyone's attention back to me. "We've diverted from the question we were considering," I said. "Namely: Why would anyone want to kill Desmond Everett?" I clicked the lectern, and the picture behind me changed to one that Nick had provided: an old battered suitcase, sitting in the middle of a luxurious Persian carpet.

"I noticed this when I discovered Desmond Everett. He was a pretty untidy person: the sink was full of dishes, the spare bedroom was jammed with junk he had no current use for, and yet his bedroom was pretty tidy. It had only what he felt he needed to have beside him."

Click and the picture changed to one of the framed photo on his bed side. It was Des, Olivia Wright, and a bunch of bright young things, all younger and happier, and dressed as though for a ball.

"It had the picture of the woman he loved."

Olivia cried out "He was my friend. We were never lovers!"

"He loved you from afar, Olivia. A classic schoolboy crush. Always trying to summon up the courage to say how he felt, to ask you if you felt the same way. Always afraid that asking you if you felt that way would result in you saying No, and in him losing the little of you that he had."

I glanced at Nick as I said this, satisfied, to be honest, that he seemed to be blushing as deeply as I was.

"And then you met Kent, and, after a whirlwind romance, you got engaged."

"But Des was happy for me," Olivia said, as Kent put his arm around her. "He was happy for both of us."

"This," Kent finally said, anger visible on his face, "is going too far. Do you actually have any idea who killed Des, or are you just enjoying games with Powerpoint?"

I pressed the clicker. The same suitcase, only this time it was open, and displaying the piles of magazines, the torn out letters clearly visible, the scissors and glue still in a little plastic bag on top of them.

"Des was your anonymous letter sender," I said simply. "It was Des who couldn't stand to see Olivia marrying you, Kent. Not because of your past as – how did he describe it? – a wife-killer, but because he couldn't bear to see anyone marrying Olivia."

"But Jane Barton was responsible for the poison pen letters," James Kane said, "She admitted to that in her suicide note."

"I know," I said, in mock surprise. "And imagine how confusing that must have been to dear old Dopey Des, who knew she couldn't have been the poison penner. I mean: If she wasn't consumed by guilt at my unmasking of her activities – and she couldn't have been, if he'd been the guilty party – why on earth would she have killed herself?"

"Desmond Everett tried to call me on the night he was killed. He was drunk and upset and confused, and I had a crisis on my hands and didn't pay attention to him. That is something which I will be guilty about till the day I die. Because if I'd listened to him – if I'd heard what he was saying – this whole chain of tragedies would have made sense, and I would have – might have – been able to save his life.

"Because, you see, Desmond Everett was calling me to confess. To admit that he had been writing the letters all along. And if he was the writer, then Jane's suicide – so easily written off as the actions of a possessive, controlling woman who had acted out of a combination of shame at having been exposed, and of anger at losing her grip on the young, wealthy woman who she'd attached herself to – made less sense. It would attract attention to the act, and to the woman herself.

"But I didn't listen, so Desmond, needing to confess, needing someone to talk to, rang the next number on his phone, and spoke – without even knowing it – to the person who had murdered Jane Barton. And sealed his fate."

"So why would anyone murder Jane?" Olivia asked.

"Because – as I overheard her say some days previously – Jane knew something. Something that she was threatening to disclose. Something that would destroy everything for the person who decided to silence her. My mistaken exposure of her as the poison pen letter writer just gave the murderer another diversionary tactic to make the murder look like a suicide."

"You sure you're not the killer?" James Kane sniggered, and received a venomous glare from both Caz and Monica Vale.

"I've been set up for murdering Des," Monica said. "I don't think this is a time for jokes, James."

"Sorry," Kane, suitably admonished, looked sheepishly at Monica, and both looked back at me.

"Olivia," I said, "Where did you first meet Jane?"

"At a clinic," Olivia answered, "In Switzerland. After my parents," she swallowed, "after they died, I was unwell. I spent a lot of time in and out of various clinics for the next few years."

"I appreciate this may be painful," I said, "But could you tell us your injuries?"

Olivia blushed.

"What the hell does any of this have to do with a bunch of random murders in London years later?" Kent demanded, wrapping a protective arm around her.

"Everything," I said, my voice gravelly. I cleared my throat. "Olivia – can you?"

She took a deep breath. "I was suffering from what was called Survivors guilt. Severe depression. An inability to accept that it hadn't been my fault that I had survived while they had died."

She looked at me, tears in her eyes. "Go on," I prompted.

"I also had a fractured pelvis, a broken arm, a broken nose, and severe lacerations on my face, and some minor burns on my left shoulder and back."

"So the clinic where you met dealt in psychological as well as physical trauma," I clarified, and she nodded, "And Jane Barton – the woman who became your nurse therapist on your release, who became your friend and confidante – when you met, she was not, as some have assumed, a nurse working in this clinic, was she?"

"God, no," Olivia smiled, "Why would I end up best friends with some agency nurse? Jane was a patient."

"You had plastic surgery there, didn't you?" I asked. "I mean, a broken nose, severe lacerations, some burns; it would have had to be surgery."

Olivia nodded. "Yes, it wasn't for vanity, I just had to have my face, basically, repaired."

"And what about Jane? Why was she in the clinic? Was her presence, do you think, for vanity?"

"Jane was there for a facelift. She'd always been overly conscious of her looks."

"She said," I interrupted. "I mean, you had never met her before this clinic, right? So your knowledge of her past, or of her reasons for wanting cosmetic surgery in a Swiss clinic could only ever be based on what Jane told you, right?"

Olivia nodded. "That's true, but…"

"And the surgery – Jane's surgery – was it a success?"

"I guess," Olivia said, confusion evident in her voice.

"Yet Jane – who I and others have referred to as Plain Jane - was a hunched, hairy, somewhat oddly shaped woman who seemed, almost, to have passed plain and approached outright ugly."

"How dare you!" Olivia's eyes blazed. "My friend had a beautiful heart. She was a beautiful soul."

"Maybe," I said, "But the surgeons in this – one assumes – hugely expensive Swiss Cosmetic Surgery clinic still left her with a permanent five o clock shadow, a monobrow, something approaching a hunchback, and a shuffle that made her move like Richard The Third.

"Which is odd, isn't it? Especially since I heard her quoting Shakespeare at you once. Something about the green-eyed monster which doth mock the meat it feeds on. That, I think, was Othello. And when I overheard her threatening someone on the phone, she used the phrase I won't play the Scottish Wife which seemed – even then – unusual phrasing.

"Until I realised that the Scottish Wife referred to Lady Macbeth, and that the only people who ever referred to Macbeth as The Scottish Play, and to Lady M as The Scottish Wife, were actors. So, had Jane ever been an actor?"

Olivia Wright shook her head, "She was a trained aroma therapist, Reiki master, masseuse, and homeopath."

"Yet she could afford an expensive Swiss clinic."

"She said she'd come into some money," Olivia whispered, her confusion over the facts becoming evident.

"And spent it on plastic surgery that left her with a monobrow, a five o clock shadow, and a hunch," I said, clicking again, and changing the picture back to the bunch of drama students gathered, proudly, around the cauldron.

I clicked again, and the picture slowly zoomed in on the faces of Dave Walker and the tall beautiful brunette standing next to him, and, as the crowd watched, Ray's magic sketched a unibrow onto the brunette, shaded and broadened her jaw, darkened her hair, and drew the fringe down over her forehead and eyes.

Another gasp went around the room, though, as half the assembled had obviously never met Jane Barton, I couldn't tell whether the gasp was at the sudden revelation that the tall gorgeous brunette of Dave's drama student days had, for some reason, changed herself into the hunched hairy friend of Olivia Wright of recent years, or whether they were just shocked at the use of such basic photoshopping skills in the presence of the crème de la crème of the art world.

Whichever, those people who had known Jane Barton understood the point of the reveal.

"Jane knew this waiter?" Monica said, puzzlement plain in her voice.

I nodded. "Jane Barton knew this waiter. Whose name was David Walker, but who – in an earlier life – had been Daniel Walken. You know: Like Christopher Walken? Dave's friend Lionel," I gestured at Hook, who, with a wave of his hand acknowledged the attention of the crowd, and then turned his attention – and theirs – back to me "said something interesting to me. He said that everyone was doing it at Drama School – changing their name. You'd bump into a Frank in the street, and he'd have become Francesco, or a Sally who'd become a Sophie."

"Your wife was an actress, wasn't she, Kent?" I asked.

"What's that got to do with anything," the American looked up from his phone, paused in his texting, and growled.

"Well, she was Sophie Bourne when you met her. But I noticed that her parents were John and Elsie Barton, so I guess she'd changed her name as well."

"I guess," he sneered, "But I never asked."

"Really?" I said, my disbelief open. "But, when she vanished, didn't you look into every aspect of her life, trying to find out what had happened?"

"You know I did," he said, edging away from Olivia towards the dais.

"And you knew your wife well?"

"Listen, dude, unless you want a law suit slapped on your scrawny ass, this shit ends now," he snarled at me, from the edge of the dais.

"And yet," I said, "Just now, you failed to recognise her."

I clicked the button, and the picture changed to a close up of the tall brunette, clicked again, and a still from a Drastic

Band commercial, showing the same statuesque brunette – a little older, and wearing a bright pink leotard, but unmistakably the same woman, appeared alongside it.

"I," he paused, "I wasn't looking at this bullshit," he answered, "I've got a business to run."

"No," I agreed, "You were texting. You were texting, which means you couldn't possibly have seen the picture. Just as, on the day that Dave Walker was killed, you were sitting in a room with Olivia and I discussing a series of poison pen letters – letters which you had previously attempted to wave away.

"You couldn't have killed Dave, because, as he was being killed, you were engaging me to investigate their source. Only, you made several attempts, starting almost the next day, to persuade me to drop the investigation. It was almost as though you didn't want me to investigate; as though the discussion on the day in question had been little more than a diversion, an attempt, perhaps, to set up an alibi for yourself."

"Why the hell would I need an alibi?" He demanded.

"Well you wouldn't," I admitted, "But your wife might."

"This is ridiculous!" Olivia laughed. "Surely Kent would have recognised his wife if she'd been sitting under his nose all this time."

I smiled sadly, noticing how Nick had appeared at Kent Benson's side and prevented him from moving by placing a firm grip on his elbow. "It worked like this," I finally said, and the room seemed to lean forward.

CHAPTER FIFTY-FIVE

"Kent and Sophie Benson make a fortune from a bit of fitness kit that takes the world by storm. They live the high life until the lawsuits arrive, and fairly quickly, the money begins to run out.

"Then one of them realises that there's an insurance policy on each of them. If either of them was to die, the survivor would receive a huge pay out. So the plan for one of them to fake their death is formed.

"They need a reason for the courts to formally declare the missing partner as dead. At that point, the insurance will pay out, the missing partner just has to stay missing a few years, and then the two can meet somewhere and skip off into the sunset with most of the pay-out intact.

"I'm guessing it was Sophie who put herself forward to 'die.' She was an actress, could more easily vanish, and the police and public would be more likely to believe that Kent had murdered her and – in their haste to build a case – declare her dead so he could be charged with murder.

"Meanwhile, Sophie needs to not only vanish, but alter her appearance. There was, Lionel Hook told us, an epidemic of Method acting amongst their class at drama school, and I'm guessing that Sophie Bourne was not the sort of actress who just puts on a wig and a funny accent. She went to the opposite end of the spectrum, making herself so plain and so hunched that she barely resembled the missing woman.

"I remember thinking, when I found her body, that she looked taller than I remembered. I realised, of course, that that was because she'd spent a lot of time hunched and swathed in shapeless clothes, all to make her look shorter and fatter than she actually was.

"And then the plot begins to spiral. I've heard that word a lot the last few days: The best laid plans, things done for the right reasons, mistakes that lead to bigger mistakes until the end state is worse than it ever needed to be.

"Sophie – calling herself, now, Jane Barton, meets and befriends a shy English Heiress who's in the same clinic as herself. This girl has always avoided crowds and cameras, and lives with her aged grandmother in a big old house in the middle of nowhere.

"You couldn't, really, imagine a better hideout, if you were a woman who was supposed to be dead.

"But gradually, of course, another plan started to form in Jane's mind. The insurance pay-out was a decent chunk of change. But Olivia Wright, after the death of her parents, and on the death of her grandmother, would – provided she lived long enough for her trust fund to pay out – be worth hundreds of millions.

"Hundreds of millions." I repeated the phrase, watching as Olivia Wright, her face changing to a look of horror, turned to stare at Kent Benson.

"Livvy, sweetheart," Kent beseeched her, as he attempted to push back through the crowd to her side. Nick held him where he was, and Olivia Wright turned her face back to me.

"Please go on," she said, her voice barely a whisper.

"Jane arranged for you to meet Kent – it was a trip that Jane had suggested, a way to cheer herself up after – she claimed – a failed romance. And, on that trip, you meet Kent, who already knows exactly what to say to you, how to behave, how to win your heart. Because, of course, he's been prepped by Jane Barton, the only friend you have. The friend to whom you've disclosed your deepest desires.

"You said that Kent was almost too good to be true."

"And he was," she finished for me, as James Kane put his arm around her.

"So the stage was set," I said, as Caz finished the Veuve, rattled the bottle to confirm it was empty, placed it on a discarded tray, and, dipping into her handbag, retrieved another miniature champagne, miming her surprise and pleasure at me, opened it, inserted the straw, and consumed sipping whilst her eyes scanned the crowd.

"Kent would woo Olivia, Jane would stay by her side as confidante to make sure the plan stayed on track, the two would marry, and, at some point in the future, Olivia would have a tragic and fatal accident.

"Except Maggie Wright smelled a rat. She wasn't keen on the American with the dubious past, and communicated as much to her family solicitor. But before she could act on her suspicions, Maggie Wright died."

"It was pneumonia." James Kane said, "The doctor agreed."

I nodded. "Perhaps it was. Or perhaps, if we were to exhume her, we'd discover some poison – something that might, say, be used in tiny amounts by a homeopathic nurse, but which could be distilled down and fed to an old, frail, and already sickly old woman to speed her exit.

"Either way, Maggie Wright dies, and the only obstruction to stage two of their plan is out of the way. The engagement is announced, and the funeral is held.

"If Maggie Wright hadn't been a Southwark girl made good, the funeral and the wake might have been held at the big old house, away from everyone and anyone, and three people would not be dead, but the clock would be ticking on Olivia Wright's life.

"My guess, Kent, is that you assumed that, even if you were accused of murdering Olivia, you'd be able to pull the same thing you'd pulled previously – setting up a perfect alibi that drew just enough attention to yourself, but ultimately proved that you couldn't have committed the murder, while Jane – who few people would be looking at – would actually perform the deed.

"Hence her Lady Macbeth comment. She was willing manage you, willing to take action where necessary, willing to endure what must have been painful surgery, and years of constant method acting for you.

"What she was not willing to endure was you having a change of heart. She wasn't prepared for you actually falling for Olivia Wright. Or, perhaps, for you realising that, if you married Olivia, you'd be able to live in luxury for the rest of your life without killing her: You'd be her husband; you'd control the funds. No need to kill a wife who – once you'd cut the ties with James Kane, Des Everett and any of her other protectors – would be entirely at your mercy.

"I doubt that Dave Walker would have ever recognised Jane, but when he wheeled the punchbowl out, she recognised him, and his fate was sealed. There was a scream, someone dropped a glass, and at the same moment, Anthony Taylor walked into the pub, so everyone thought those events – the shocked scream, the smashed glass – were connected to his arrival, but they weren't.

"They were Jane, recognising him, and suddenly realising that if he recognised her, both games would be up.

"So, Jane called you, pretended to be one of your business contacts, filled you in, and advised you – a repeating pattern here - to get an alibi while she dealt with this situation. She nosed around the kitchen, found a weapon, followed Dave to the loo, and – for her own sake, but maybe mostly for yours – committed murder.

"Then, later, she realised you were having, if not second thoughts, at least considerations that would make changes to the plan. Changes that she didn't like. The plan was for Olivia to die, and for you and Jane to skip off into the sunset, not for her to remain in costume forever as you enjoyed a happy and financially enjoyable marriage to Olivia.

"She still loved you, Kent. I saw her looking at you and Olivia once, assumed her doe-eyed admiration was for her friend. But, of course, it wasn't. It was for you, the man she loved, the man she'd gone through hell for. And she decided to fight for you.

"Well," Kent announced to the whole room, "This is a hell of a story, but I'm not seeing any proof."

"You killed Jane Barton," I said, "because she'd ceased to be of use to you, and because you wanted to change the plans. And because hell hath no fury like a woman scorned, and the scorning of Jane Barton was likely to destroy not only your current plan, but your whole life.

"Thing is, Kent, once you decided to cut Jane out of the plan, and to silence her permanently, the mess – which had started spiralling the moment Davie Walker wheeled the punchbowl in – went into overdrive.

"So you pinched a load of Olivia's tranquillisers, ground them up, went to visit Jane Barton, doped her, and – when she was semi-conscious – hanged her. Then you sent me a text from her phone, scattered the set dressing that would suggest she'd been overcome by remorse at my exposing her as the poison penner, and waited for me to discover the corpse."

"Prove it," he sneered, and I pushed the button one last time.

On screen, a long and rather boring list of data appeared, accompanied, in the top right hand of the screen, by a dark smudge, and in the bottom right corner of the screen, by a screenprint from my phone of the text that I had received from 'Jane'.

The police had provided the smudge, which didn't really prove a lot, but were still awaiting the data that Ray had, unofficially, acquired for me earlier that day.

Nick, spotting the screen of data, mouthed "What the Fuck?" then, realising my bluff, turned his attention back to restraining Kent.

"Your fingerprint," I said, "Lifted from the handle of the cupboard in Desmond Everett's flat. You washed up the cups, tried to make it look like he hadn't had a visitor. I'm guessing you were super careful not to leave any prints, but you slipped when you closed the door."

It was a partial print, and not of much use, really, but I was hoping that Kent would not be au fait with these things – I certainly hadn't been till Nick had explained it to me, but it didn't really matter, as Kent – as I'd expected – had a response ready for me.

"So I've been to Everett's apartment? He was a friend of my fiancée. The guy was my best man, for Christ's sake. Of course I was there."

"When were you last there?" I asked.

"I don't know," he laughed nervously. "Week's ago. Months."

"So not in, say, the past week."

"Absolutely not!" Kent insisted.

"But you were there the day he died," I said, gesturing at the computer printout that took up most of the screen, "Just like you were at Jane's when she died."

"The day she died," he shrugged, "Maybe. And who says I was anywhere?"

"When she died," I answered, "Gesturing back to the screen. This is a data dump from your mobile provider. It triangulates your phone with various points, at various times. That's what says you were anywhere, Kent. And that's also what, by pure coincidence, shows your phone located in Desmond Everett's flat the day he died, and in Jane Barton's flat at exactly the same time someone was using her phone to text me."

I was bluffing, somewhat, but it worked as I'd hoped.

"You little Limey Bastard," Kent snarled, snatching his arm free from Nick and reaching into his pocket.

"I wouldn't" Caz said, her voice laced with menace, and Kent's eyes widened in surprise, his hand freezing. "Stick 'em up," Caz ordered, her attempt at Chicago gangster coming across more like Maggie Smith playing Bonnie Parker.

Kent put his hands up, his shoulders drooping in resignation, and sighed. "OK," he said, "I'll come quietly."

Nick and Reid appeared, took hold of Kent, cuffed him, and lead him away, disclosing that what Caz had been poking into his back had been, rather than a Smith and Wesson, a miniature bottle of Veuve Cliquot.

The widow, I felt, would have been proud.

"Baby," Kent stopped by Olivia, "this is all a mistake."

Olivia stared into his face, took a deep breath, as Tony Taylor put an arm around her waist, set her face into a look that I'd last seen carved in marble at the National Gallery, and said "I'm afraid, Kent, that I shall have to break our engagement."

CHAPTER FIFTY-SIX

"Mum's just gone out," he said, standing in the doorway, looking paler, thinner and, somehow, smaller than I remembered him looking last time we'd met.

"I know," I answered. "I've been waiting for her to leave."

Jonas Campbell shook his head in confusion. "But why?" he started, and I stopped him by lifting the bag at my side.

"Cos I have something for you," I said, and he stepped to one side.

I stepped into the hallway, closed the door, and followed him into the kitchen.

"I don't understand," he finally said, and I smiled.

"Neither did I," I admitted, "At first. And neither, I suspect would many people. How old are you, Jonas?"

"Twenty," he said shyly, his red rimmed eyes never leaving the bag that I'd placed on the worktop, his fingers curling and uncurling as though the longing to touch the bag was barely containable.

"And Dave Walker was..?"

"The kindest, sweetest, most honourable man I ever met." Jonas answered, tearing his eyes from the bag and staring into mine. "What's that got to do with anything?"

"There was quite an age gap," I said, "between you and him."

He froze, his mouth open, his eyes flicking from the bag to me, then, at last, he said: "So you know?"

"That you were lovers?" I answered. "Yes. But why it was a secret is something I'm puzzled by."

"People would never understand," Jonas sighed, "They see a younger man with an older one, and the jeers start. They think there must be something funny going on. How could I possibly love him? How could he possibly see me as anything other than a young bit of trade."

"And did you?" I asked. "Did you love him?"

His eyes filled with tears, he reached out, finally, and grabbed hold of Dave Walker's shoulder bag as the tears spilled down his cheeks, and finally, a sob, a sound like a dying animal might make, exploded from somewhere deep within him, and, still holding the bag, he collapsed to the floor, his arms curling around the cheap canvas and plastic relic as he tried – and failed – to stop the pain issuing from him in choked sobs and screams.

I watched him for a moment, then dropped to the floor and put my arms around him, shushing him quietly, as he rocked slowly backwards and forwards, the grief bursting from him in noises that moved from cavernous echoing sobs to, finally, guttural choking barks.

"How did you know?" He asked, at length. "Nobody knows. Nobody. We couldn't tell anyone. He was afraid they'd laugh at him. Afraid that I'd hate him for ruining his life.

"I couldn't have borne that. I didn't want anyone to ever hurt him. My mum – she would have fired him. I didn't care: I told him so, but he wouldn't let me tell anyone, he was so afraid that it would ruin everything, and so nobody could know. And now – since it happened – I haven't even been able to cry. I can't face letting my mum know, now. It's all ruined. How did you find out?"

"Heinz." I nodded towards the corner where the kitten – clearly more house broken now, and allowed out of its crèche in the kitchen cupboards watched us silently, as though trying to understand these two humans, sat on the floor with a cheap bag between them and a desperate sadness hanging over them.

"While your mum was on holiday," I said, as Jonas wiped snot and tears away with the back of his hand, "I'm guessing Dave stayed here with you."

"We could be safe," he smiled ruefully, "playing like we lived together. He made dinner. I ironed shirts. We watched TV," he swallowed a sob, "It was," this time the sob burst forth, another fusillade of tears washing down his cheek, "Perfect."

"You fed the cat," I added, "And Dave got scratched. I saw the scratches on his wrist." I held off mentioning that I'd seen the scratches when I'd discovered the body: That was an image this young man didn't need in his mind.

"That's how I knew. I found out that he was happy, that he had someone in his life who made him happy, but that it was, as they say, complicated, and I wondered, at first, if those complications had lead to his death. Then I remembered the phone – the one he'd struggled to use. The one that had, it seemed, been a gift to him by someone who understood technology, who didn't see him as an old geezer, and I figured the two – cat scratches and technology – lead only one place. Plus, there was the cufflink.

"Dave had mislaid a cufflink. When I came here, I made a cup of tea for your mum, and – looking for teaspoons – I opened the drawer over there. And – although it took me a while to realise it – I saw the missing link."

Jonas sobbed again, but managed to pull himself together and struggled, still holding the bag closely, to his feet.

I followed. "When I realised that Dave's murder was the result of the stupidity and panic of people involved in a plot Dave couldn't even have been aware of, I was happy.

"He was happy when he died," I said, "he was in love, and that love was reciprocated. And that makes me happy, Jonas, cos we do so many stupid, and sick and wrong things for love. We tell lies to the very people we love, so as not to hurt them.

"We feel guilty about the things we do, and we let that guilt build a wall between us and the very people we love.

We let our own pride – our own fear of losing the ones we love – turn us into judgemental prigs, and we chase them away before they can hurt us. But none of that happened with you and Dave. You loved him, and he loved you till the end."

The end made me recall the moment, that morning, that Caz had informed me that her romance with Anthony Taylor was over.

Tony, it seemed, had become closer than ever with Olivia Wright.

"I thought," I'd said, "That you two were – y'know – an item."

Caz had smiled. "I am the daughter of a penniless Duke," she'd observed, "And either Gamble or Tristran will inherit what little money is left when Pops dies, so: No money, no prospects, and of an age when one really should have been married off. Would you – if you were the dashing Anthony Taylor – see me as marriage material?"

"But you're brilliant," I said, "funny. Gorgeous. You wear a hat better than anyone I've ever known."

"You're quite right: Olivia doesn't have the neck for a hat," Caz said, as she commenced chopping the carrots I'd peeled and put before her.

"Even more pointedly," I said, "Aren't they cousins?"

"Second," she sighed.

"Still a bit weird."

"Oh sweetheart, if second cousins marrying each other was off the menu, the aristocracy would have been speaking Turkish by about 1920. Let's just comfort ourselves that Anthony is, at least, smart enough to stop her putting all her money into an Albanian Botox mine…"

I smiled at Jonas. "There's a lot to be said for love. Whatever it looks like," I said, wondering what my boyfriend's wife looked like, hoping she was plain and dull, but suspecting she wasn't, "And wherever it leads us."

Jonas sighed deeply, ran a hand over his face. "What am I gonna do?" He asked me, as though I had answers.

From my pocket, I pulled the one thing I'd removed from Dave's bag before giving it to the boy. "He wanted you to have this, but he'd been afraid to give it to you."

Jonas took the bag, emptied it into his palm, and stared at the ring, slim, gold and pure.

He looked up at me, and repeated his last question.

"What am I gonna do?"

"I don't know," I said. "I truly don't. I don't even know what I'm going to do, Jonas."

I patted him on the shoulder, thought better of that, and gave him a hug, which he reciprocated, holding on to me like a drowning man holding on to a life buoy until – as though remembering he'd had swimming lessons – he finally let me go, and I bent to scratch the kitten's head as it purred curiously.

"Here's what I do know," I said: "The more we sit around waiting; the longer we spend afraid of taking action, the more we end up losing control.

"There's a lot to be said for living. Just doing it. Putting things off – delaying asking that question; telling that person you love them; being yourself, telling the world you're in love – it's all such a waste of time. And we have so little of that to begin with."

And, waving one last time at the kitten, I smiled at Jonas Campbell, who still stared in wonder at the ring now placed on his finger, and let myself out.

THE END

Acknowledgements

Book two. You might think I'd be finished saying thank you, but I'll never be done pointing out how fabulous people are, and how glad I am that they are part of my life.

So:

David / Dad / Ray / Anne-Marie / Sue / Steve / Hannah / Toby / Lilly / Luke I couldn't live without you. Thanks for Love, laughs, and reality.
Veronica / Tony / Jason / Karen / Pat / Liz / Lee / And all the Fulham Massive: I wouldn't be here without you. And neither, come to think of it, would half the punters in The Marq. Thank you for Love, support, and a place to stay.

Lauren Milne Henderson. Advice. Contacts. Prosecco. And a personal introduction to Lady Caroline, whose opening words: "Would you mind holding my asparagus, darling, only it's bleaching the Vuitton," left me speechless.

Justine Solomons / Julie Vince / Norma Curtis Writing as a business is hard. Having people who know this, and who still love the whole affair makes it so much less scary. Having them forgive you when you misspell their name first time out is another reason to love them.

Martin Walker. For Camel Love, The One About The Bank, and for reminding me that I'm worth the effort.

Kelly / Mark / Matthew Sheehan: Thanks for sunshine, smiles, cuddles, waves, pools, the Pacific Ocean, the Coromandel, beauty, barbecues, brilliant sunshine and Boggarch. Love you.

Warren and Carl. The BDC. Always there for me, and always ready to remind me that – whilst I may be a fucking genius – it's my fucking round.

Torsten Lambrecht & Jens Boje: I promised you gays and cats, and I delivered. You owe me dinner.

Claudette Rich, for helping me find the passion.

John Barbour, for his insights into Nick's behaviour.

David Bowie & Prince: Alive when I started, and dead when I finished. Your voices, your art, your brilliance, informed me, my world, and all the characters in it. Thank you for helping make me what I am.

Chris McVeigh. Mister Fahrenheit. Thank you for your honesty, passion, and integrity, and for reminding me to keep mine. I know you'll probably get the lawyers on to me for saying this, but: You're OK, and we're better for having you around. Love ya, Big Guy!

Printed in Great Britain
by Amazon